I0713106

KINGMAKER

THE FIRST SEAL OF
THE KRYPTEIA CONSPIRACY

MICHAEL KOOGLER, JED QUINN, & JAREN RILEY

KINGMAKER

THE FIRST SEAL OF THE KRYPTEIA CONSPIRACY

BY MICHAEL KOOGLER, JED QUINN, & JAREN RILEY

Copyright © 2015 Michael Koogler, Jed Quinn, & Jaren Riley

This is a work of fiction. Names, characters, businesses, places, events and incidents are either the products of the author's imagination or used in a fictitious manner. Any resemblance to actual persons, living or dead, or actual events is purely coincidental.

All rights reserved, including the right to reproduce this book or portions thereof in any form whatsoever.

ISBN: **978-1-943519-02-6**

Book editing by Elizabeth Humphrey
Bookworm Editing, Littleton, Colorado USA

Book cover art, packaging and design by
Kreative Storm Press, Coralville, Iowa USA

Author Information at:

www.michaelkoogler.net
www.jedquinn.com

*Dedicated to Experience
and everything she has taught us.*

NOTE FROM THE AUTHORS

In the summer of 2001, the three of us sat down to write a book together. Michael wanted to pen an end-times epic, Jed hoped to write about a complex and terrifying conspiracy theory, and Jaren wanted to follow a hero's arc all the way from beginning to end. We decided to merge all three into a collaborative work of apocalyptic fiction that we hoped would be unlike anything else on the bookshelves today.

We spent the next ten years crafting Hade's Gambit, the first book in the Krypteia Conspiracy, and finally released it in July of 2012. As the reviews came in, we were thrilled to read that people thought our book was "fast-paced," "intense," full of "unexpected twists and turns," and that "the characters were great, and Hade was one of my all-time favorite villains."

The knock we repeatedly got, however, was that at a quarter of a million words and 854 printed pages, it was a definite commitment to pick up and begin reading. Combined with those small parts of a book an author never feels like he or she got quite right the first time, we made the decision to work through another round of intense edits and then re-release what had been one large book into two much more manageable volumes. Kingmaker, the book you hold in your hands now, comprises the first half of the original Hade's Gambit. The second book, Risen, will encompass the other half. The Rise of Cain will soon get the same treatment, and after that, three more volumes are planned to finish Hade's story and The Seven Seals of Krypteia.

If you've read Hade's Gambit before, we welcome you to our improved vision of the Krypteia Conspiracy. If you are new to our series, we promise you a whirlwind story that will take you places you never thought possible. And as always, we thank you for joining us on our journey. We hope you enjoy.

"And when he had opened the second seal,
I heard the second beast say, 'Come and see.'

And there went out another horse that was red:
and power was given to him that sat thereon
to take peace from the earth and that they should
kill one another: and there was given unto him
a great sword..."

Revelation 6: 3-4

PROLOGUE

Lower Antelope Canyon, Navajo Nation, Arizona: To most everyone else, the old medicine man meant nothing. To the old man, however, everyone else meant everything. It showed in his sand paintings; scenes and symbols woven together as if by magic, with not a single grain of brightly colored sand out of place. No one knew how long he had been creating his masterpieces, but he had never stopped what he was doing; never wavered in his daily routine. Each morning before anyone in the tiny settlement began stirring, he wandered thoughtfully through the barren hills and valleys of the Arizona reservation. He took solace in his walks, often thinking back to times when the world was a purer place.

While the old man's daily trek was physically demanding, it gave him the time to visualize the picture he would create when he returned to his modest hogan. Once there, he would gather his battered jars and bags of sand and crouch in the dirt, the colored grains trickling carefully through his fingers until a mesmerizing representation of the Navajo origin story, or an equally intricate geometric pattern, emerged. Some days the local children would congregate to watch; other days, tourists passing through on their way to photograph the slot canyons would stop to observe him work. Most days, though, he painted in solitude.

In some aspects, today was no different from the countless other days that had passed in this forsaken country. By the time the sun had risen above the eastern horizon, he had already settled into his customary place, piles and jars of sand colored by ochre, gypsum, charcoal, cornmeal, and powdered flower petals waiting to be turned into scenes of unimaginable beauty. But as he knelt at the eastern edge of the circle and began to paint in the traditional sunwise direction, it became clear this day's painting was different. The hues were darker, the order disturbed, the time-honored patterns absent. It was unlike any scene he had created before. It was of the gathering storm.

But that was not the only difference. Had anyone else witnessed the old man's final creation, something else would have become significant as well. The old man began singing as he painted; a remarkable act, as he had never before uttered a single word to anyone. To everyone in the village, he had always been a mute.

Until now.

Until he began painting for the last time.

He painted frenetically as the sun rapidly warmed the desert air, his wrinkled and sun-browned hands guiding the streaming sand as quickly as the visions came to his mind. Chanting softly to himself in an ancient tongue not heard in nearly two thousand years, the picture began to emerge, coming to life from the scattered swathes of colors. When he finished, the old man rocked back on his heels and his craggy voice fell silent, his deep-set eyes roaming over the final story of mankind laid out before him. To the untrained eye, the images were easily explainable by anyone with even a rudimentary knowledge of Indian lore. To those few with a deeper knowledge, they signified much, much more.

The picture was dark, a hazy gray land covered by storm clouds of black and purple and surrounded by jagged mountains on both sides. On the left side of the dry painting loomed a monstrous shadow, a black-robed robed figure towering over snow-capped peaks that rose in perpetual gloom. The larger figure was surrounded by numerous smaller figures of darkness, scattered about the scene from one end to the other. On the far end of the image, and in stark contrast to the black figure and its minions, a small halo of white appeared to hang suspended in the air. Within the glowing sphere, one could faintly make out three individual points of light, solitary figures in an overwhelming sea of darkness. Yet even that little sphere of purity was tainted, for upon closer inspection, one could see tiny flecks of black, as if dark sand had somehow found its way into the white during the creation of the painting. Whether by accident or design, only the old man knew.

The implication of the picture was painfully obvious—a facing off of two sides in an epic conflict. Darkness besieged the light, an approaching storm in which the single bastion of safety was already small and overwhelmed. It was a storm thousands of years in the making. It was the beginning of the end.

For several long minutes the old man stared at the finished image, contemplating the uncertainty of the future. And then, casting a final look at the last sand painting he would ever create, he began to ceremoniously destroy it, carefully sweeping away the images in reverse order of their creation. He knew dire consequences could befall him, and the three he was charged with protecting, if he neglected this important task. Finally finished, with the sound of creaking joints and popping bones, he rose slowly, tucked an ancient-looking wooden tube into the waistband of his tattered denim jeans, threw a ragged, brown cloth bag over one shoulder and slowly walked out of his hogan. The old man looked across the barren landscape at the setting sun and, in deep thought, he began his journey north out of the village, never to return.

High above him on a southern bluff, a solitary figure stood in the shadows of a shallow cave entrance. Protected from the desert sun, dark eyes watched the old man depart the haven he had known for years. Clothed all in black, a heavy trench coat rustled in the hot desert breeze, but the figure remained motionless, oblivious to the heat. Only his lips moved as he softly recited a verse he had recited countless times before. "And when he had opened the second seal, I heard the second beast say, 'Come and see.'" The figure smiled, showing perfectly white teeth. "Come and see, old man. Come and see."

CHAPTER 1

Salt Lake City, Utah: Midnight on the campus of the University of Utah knows two seasons. From November to March, the lawns and trees hibernate beneath a thick blanket of snow. As the months pass, students carve paths across the snowy blanket with their boots, snowshoes, skis, sleds, and snowboards. The resultant pattern rivals an Amish quilt both in imagination and in complexity. At midnight, the temperature dives below freezing, the moon rises, and millions of snow crystals reflect its soft glow.

In March, it takes only one day for the snow to melt and the landscape to emerge like a butterfly from its cocoon. Daytime temperatures vary from brisk to scorching, but midnight is the great equalizer. The clouds of a cool day insulate the land at night and keep it warm, whereas the oven-like heat of August succumbs to the cooling touch of a clear midnight sky. In this way, midnight on this campus knows only two seasons; the pristine slopes in the winter, and the pleasant coolness of endless summer nights.

On one such summer night, Gideon Mombera Sumbawanga and Chris Matthews walked along the sidewalk between the university's field house and football stadium. They were a pair in perfect contrast: one young man all of seven feet tall walking with a friend who would never reach six. Gideon was in prime physical shape, an Adonis in every sense of the word, and Chris freely admitted he enjoyed Double Whoppers with extra cheese more than he should. As they walked, Gideon's long strides carried him forward effortlessly and Chris had to almost jog to keep pace.

Usually Gideon walked the path alone after practice, but tonight had been a special night, so Chris had tagged along with him. Gideon had just worked out in front of a final scout from a long line of talent scouts he had performed for over the past year. He wasn't exactly sure why he had even agreed to this particular showcasing of his considerable skills; it wasn't as if he had anything left to prove. Most of those with knowledge of the basketball world considered him the next Michael Jordan or LeBron James. Gideon, however, simply wanted to be himself, to set and live by his own standards and perhaps elevate himself above the icons of his sport.

As they made their way back to the dorms, Gideon untwisted the lid from a bottle of water, drained its contents in one long drink, and tossed the empty into a garbage can from twenty feet away. His friend couldn't have been more pleased.

"Benjamins, man!" Chris said loudly, oblivious to the outside world. "The next time you suit up, you'll be playing for cash!" Chris laughed again, enjoying the idea some people in this world got paid a ridiculous sum of money to play basketball, and Gideon would soon be joining their ranks. "Welcome to 'The Life!'"

"The Life," as they always referred to the future, had been Gideon's dream since he was a small boy in Africa. Now, as he walked with Chris, he realized the life he had dreamt of lay only days away. Bars would fill with fans on game days to watch him, men would follow Gamecasts on their phones in church on Sundays, young men would revere him and women would flock to him. And now, with all his dreams about to come true, he could finally move on from his distant past in Tanzania. It had been a long time since he dwelt on the memories of his loving father and his supportive sister. With the world finally at his feet, Gideon wasn't about to give his past any more thought then he had to. "The Life" was finally within reach and his life was now about what lay before him and not what was behind.

The two young men descended into a tunnel along the path that ran beneath the road and led to the stadium parking lot. A single lamp lit the tunnel's entire length, casting an orange glow on the concrete walls. Chris' laughter and its reverberating echo in the confining space snapped Gideon out of his brief reminiscence about his past and he smiled as he reminded himself of the paychecks to come. As they approached the midpoint of the tunnel, the predictable echo of their conversation and footfalls was interrupted by the sound of someone politely clearing his throat. The tunnel had been empty when they entered, of that they were sure. Looking toward the source of the sound, Gideon realized that they were no longer alone as the shape of a man, backlit by the orange light, stood in front of them, blocking their way.

The silhouette showed a frame as tall as Gideon's, but this man easily outweighed Gideon by more than a hundred pounds. The man's back faced the lamp but the reflection from the walls did not lighten his features. Sunglasses veiled his eyes and a ragged beard hid the rest of his face. Black covered him from head to toe—from his motorcycle boots, leather pants, and tee-shirt, to the leather trench coat that was thrown casually over one shoulder. Oddly, the light appeared to avoid touching him; none reflected from his glasses, nor did it reflect from his skin or clothing. And from what Gideon could see, the man's face was well-tanned and criss-crossed with faint scars, ancient wounds from what could have only been a hard lived life.

Then Gideon saw his arms. They were corded with muscle and covered with tattoos—obscure symbols and unsettling images—that gave every indication they covered his entire body, with the exception of his face and his hands. At that moment, as Gideon was transfixed on those odd, out-of-place hands, the man shifted slightly and light glimmered from his fingernails—clipped, cleaned, and well taken care of. They stood out completely from the rest of his visage.

Gideon, still relishing the idea of being on top of the world, decided the best course of action was to ignore the stranger and walk by him through the tunnel. The man had other ideas. As Gideon and Chris came closer, the stranger took a deliberate step sideways so he was now standing directly in their path.

"I'm sorry to bother you," he said in a surprisingly pleasant voice, "but I have a friend in dire need of something and I was wondering if you could help?" Before they could respond, he went on, his voice deep and soothing, almost hypnotic. "It really is only a small thing," he said warmly.

Gideon was still somewhat taken aback by the man's sudden appearance, but he had grown weary of people asking him to sign on to causes. Chris, always there to keep his African friend out of trouble, shifted between the two. "Listen, man," Chris spoke up bravely, daring to step closer, "my friend and I have nothing you could want. We don't deal or do anything illegal, if that's what you're after. All we want is to get back to our dorm."

At this point, the man lost all hint of civility. "First of all, Chris," he said quietly, his voice venomous, "I have no desire to speak to you. I've come to speak with Gideon, son of the one they call Mwalimu, the teacher," he added, turning once more and looking the tall youth in the eyes. "Secondly," he went on, "you are gravely mistaken. You do have something my friend needs. So I ask you again, Gideon Mombera Sumbawanga, will you help?" He finished with a perfectly wicked smile that showed brilliantly white teeth that were as out of place on him as his manicured nails.

Gideon stood immobile, completely confused by what appeared to be the ranting of a lunatic. He wanted to run, but found his legs wouldn't move. Terror threatened to rise up and engulf him, but he fought back the fear and stood his ground. "I don't know what your deal is," he finally said, regaining some of his poise, "but who are you?

How do you know so much about me?"

"I have many names, Gideon," the stranger answered easily, his voice suddenly pleasant once again. "The one I go by most often these days is Hade. As to your second question, I know more about you than perhaps even you know about yourself."

"What…" began Gideon.

The stranger held up a hand, quickly silencing him as he explained. "I can tell you every teacher you have ever had in school. Can you do that, Gideon?" He did not wait for an answer. "Let me pick one at random," Hade stated in the tone of a professor explaining a complex equation to his class. "Do you remember Mrs. Makambako, who had a precious little baby girl and missed the last three weeks of classes before you took your exam at the end of Form Four? She was replaced by a young Mr. Joseph Mpanda."

If Gideon was shocked before, now he was completely dumbfounded and he stared incredulously at the strange man.

Hade continued with a flourish, obviously enjoying himself. "I can tell you that your father's favorite kind of soup is tomato, your uncle's favorite Elvis record is Blue Hawaii, and your sister's favorite colors—in order—are purple, pink, blue, and green. I can also tell you the names of every girlfriend you had in Montana, including Sheri and Denise." Hade threw an exaggerated wink at Gideon as he went on. "I can tell you how you broke your right arm as a baby when you fell out of your crib and how you hate the taste of lemons, yet love the taste of limes." At this, the pleasantness once again left his voice and he leaned forward and whispered dangerously. "I can also tell you how you're going to die tonight from a genetic defect and how your friend Chris is not going to live long enough to regret walking home with you." He finished, his voice dark and ominous. "Are you convinced yet that I know what I'm talking about?"

"Sir," Gideon began, his voice almost pleading. "I'll give you whatever you want if you'll just leave us alone."

Without answering Gideon's plea, Hade slowly turned around and for the first time focused all his attention on Chris. "I'm afraid I don't need you for the rest of this, Chris." He smiled, his teeth gleaming in the pale light of the tunnel. "Don't worry—this won't hurt at all."

As terrified as he had ever been, Chris made a last, desperate break for freedom. But before his first step hit the ground, the dark man put a forearm to Chris' face with inhuman speed and power. The wet crunch of breaking bone reverberated through the tunnel as the blow shattered the young man's skull and severed the underlying arteries with the bone shards. Chris' body was slammed against the tunnel wall, before he crumpled to the ground. He was dead in an instant, his eyes open and staring up into nothing.

The blood drained from Gideon's face as Hade turned his attention back to him. "Such a crap-shoot, isn't it?" Hade rumbled. "Genes, I mean."

Gideon shook his head, desperately trying to come to grips with what had just happened to his friend. "I… I don't know what you mean…"

Hade went on, his tone hardening. "But of course you do, Gideon, and I imagine if the basketball scouts knew about it, you would already be an afterthought, don't you think?"

With those words, a familiar feeling of constriction clinched Gideon's heart. Breathing became more laborious and sweat erupted from every pore. He bent over and pulled a clenched fist to his chest. The muscles in his neck heaved with each breath, trying to lift the ribs and inspire life-giving breath.

"You're playing the odds, Gideon, hoping no one will find out about your heart condition; hoping nothing will ever trigger it. Oh, it's certainly true that there are ways to shift the odds in your favor and I'm sure you've done everything you can to do so. But I would say your case differs slightly from the norm." He paused and smiled as he leaned closer. "You see, Gideon, your problem this evening is that we stacked the deck a little. The term used today in educated circles is Idiopathic Hypertrophic Subaortic Stenosis, or IHSS. In other words, you have a gene that causes the central wall in your heart to thicken. These thick, non-distensible walls cause a backflow of blood into the lungs that leads to shortness of breath, chest pain, and even fainting spells. To compensate for this failure, the chamber, which feeds blood into the affected chamber, dilates. Are you with me so far?" he asked, grinning wickedly. "I'm dumbing this down a bit for your benefit."

"Please…stop," Gideon pleaded breathlessly, but Hade simply ignored him.

"As I was saying, the dilated chamber stretches the underlying electrical conduction system of the heart, leading to abnormal heart rhythms. Electrical pulses from that dilated chamber try to drive your heart at an unsustainable high pace. Now, to prevent this from driving your heart too fast, there is a built-in circuit breaker called the AV node. Unfortunately for you, you have built-in circuits that actually bypass the AV node and allow the heart to beat too fast. These bypasses are significant only when the AV node blocks impulses which then hit the bypass tract at just the right time…and then?" He smiled, leaning closer to Gideon once more. "Your heart becomes a runaway train and sudden cardiac death results. All you need to accomplish this wonderful medical marvel is one parent with a dominant trait for IHSS and then, just for good measure, both parents with a gene for the bypass tract. Mix well, bake at ninety-eight degrees for nine months, and voila."

"How…how do you…" Gideon couldn't secure enough air to

finish his question.

"How do I know about you?" Hade finished the young man's question. "I'm not one to brag, but I've given your case special attention. And I think it'd be easier to show you, rather than explain it."

Hade extended his hand, placing it flat against Gideon's chest. It was almost as if an electric current seized him as his body went rigid. The charge receded and suddenly, from Hade's touch, there flowed a strange and penetrating warmth. Like a blanket, it spread to cover Gideon until he felt his consciousness begin to blur. Glare from the orange lamp caught his attention and he turned to look at it. As he stared, the lamp deepened its orange hue and its borders rippled and transformed into the perfectly circular outline of a setting sun.

Dust blew across the horizon that was now before Gideon, and he felt his knees begin to buckle. Quickly, he shut his eyes to clear the hallucination and after a few moments, he noticed the sound and sensation of wind whipping from his left to right. An oven-like heat baked him and the wind brought no relief. Fear gripped him and prevented him from opening his eyes; but then, in the recesses of his mind, something whispered to him to look and see. Obeying the silent command, he did so and quickly recognized the small settlement just outside of Ujiji where his mother had been born and raised. Somehow, he was back in Africa.

In disbelief, he slowly began to walk down the empty path that led through the tiny village until he came to his mother's house. The house had been damaged by bandits and rebuilt when his mother was but a small child, but here, in his vision, it appeared as if new. Noise from the house startled him and he strained his ears to listen, the sounds taking on the form and rhythm of whispered speech, trying to calm the screams of a crying baby. As Gideon quietly approached the house, the voices became more distinct. They belonged to men, and they sounded agitated.

As he neared the dwelling, a voice erupted from within. "Idiots!" Something in a corner of Gideon's mind recognized the voice and he recoiled instantly, pain grabbing at his chest.

The voice continued, muffled rage permeating its message, "The child stays here. I didn't drag her across half the globe to waste her. Let me remind you she is the crux of this task. Destroy what you will of this hut and take what you want, but the girl is to remain unharmed. Any damage to her, even one cut or bruise, and you can all expect to die in the most agonizing way imaginable. Am I clear?" There were murmurs of agreement before the voice finished. "Good. Now see to it."

Gideon remained with his back pressed against the east wall of his mother's home. His mind raced, trying to decipher the meaning of what he was experiencing. As his thoughts accelerated beyond reason, he suddenly felt a crushing blow that knocked him to the ground and sent pieces of the wall showering down all around and on top of him. The child inside the house cried out with the terrified desperation that only a newborn could express. Frantic and confused, Gideon wished with all his might to be anywhere else but here.

As if in answer to his unspoken plea, the baby's cry dimmed to a constant drone, and when Gideon slowly looked up, he again saw the orange lamp and heard its unwavering humming. The vision was gone and the scene surrounding the lamp had returned to the university tunnel. The heavy hand of the man still pressed against his chest, pinning him to the wall. The man's fingers seemed to grip his chest, as if attempting to push through Gideon's sternum and grasp his laboring heart.

"It's a shame you aren't strong enough to witness the rest of your mother's story, but someday the world will recognize the greatness of that day," Hade said quietly. "You see, Darwin was right to a point about the randomness of natural selection, but what he didn't understand is that over centuries you can create something new, something special, if you have the time and the patience."

Gideon could only shake his head in desperation, his mind awash in terror, his heart laboring to continue beating.

"Fortunately, I had plenty of both," Hade continued with a smile. "You see, my dear boy, there has been nothing natural in your selection. We made you. We made your mother, your mother's mother, and a number of generations before that. You are perfect in every way—the perfect soldier, the perfect carrier, the *pièce de résistance*. Why, we have even engineered you right down to the perfect way to kill you."

Hade smiled wickedly and leaned even closer, his hand moving up Gideon's chest to his neck. His fingers walked along well-defined muscles, searching until they finally came to rest at the side of Gideon's Adam's apple, where the carotid pulse could be felt. Then, he began to push.

"Just relax," he said in a voice so quiet and breathy that part of Gideon's brain wondered if it was coming from the same person. "This will be perfect—not a scratch on you." He pressed harder. "The time has come, Gideon, to give your life for the good of another; for the good of humanity. I know it doesn't seem like it right now, but trust me, you are going to be every bit the hero you thought you were going to be."

Gideon stood helpless and paralyzed in the man's grasp, fighting for breath, feeling the blood drain from his face as the realization of what was happening came to him. Consciousness began to blur as Gideon's thoughts became disjointed; memories of his recent vision collided with thoughts of home and his father. Thoughts of his father triggered memories of all the things he had taught Gideon about life:

the importance of virtue, selflessness, and prayer. And for the first time in years, Gideon offered a silent prayer to whoever might be listening. He prayed for assistance, for someone to save him, for lightning to strike the force of nature that clutched at his neck, for salvation.

Glare from the orange lamp caught his attention. As he stared, the lamp deepened its orange hue and its borders rippled and transformed once again into the outline of the setting sun. His thoughts swirled and he saw his father standing before him. The sight startled him, but the clarity of this vision made him question if it was really just a hallucination or whether his father had indeed come to him in his final minutes. His father's face furrowed in concern and Gideon could see his mouth move, but could hear no sound. The form of his father began walking slowly toward him, extending his hand to assist his son. He stopped abruptly and, looking deeply into his son's eyes, his face took on an expression of understanding that his son was in dire peril. But he could do nothing. Gideon was dying.

"You're too late," Hade whispered, looking directly at the vision of Gideon's father, seemingly able to see him as clearly as Gideon could. "He's mine now."

Every visible muscle in his father's body and face locked in a stance of defiance, but he was powerless to save his son. The older Sumbawanga's eyes shifted to where the form of the shadow man stood beside his son, holding him pinned against the stone wall of the tunnel. Eyes scanning side-to-side, up then down, he studied the figure. Then he stood motionless until at last, his son's heart slowed to a stop and the vision faded to blackness.

Smiling, Hade turned back to look at the lifeless form that had been Gideon Sumbawanga. "Pity it had to end this way," he finally said with a contented sigh, letting Gideon's body slide down the wall into a sitting position. "But some things just must be, Gideon, and who are we to try to stop the inevitable? It doesn't always work out how we want it to, though, does it?" At that point in the one-sided conversation, he shifted from a pensive to a rather animated state. He crouched down and stared into Gideon's dead eyes. "But what an opportunity for you, dear boy," he continued with a nasty smile. "You're the last one, so the saddles are finally filled. You wanted fame and, by hell or high water, fame is what you're going to get. Welcome to 'The Life', Gideon, my boy."

With that, he began whistling an old Johnny Cash tune as he reached into his coat and pulled out a small black case. Opening it up, he pulled out a stainless steel surgical scalpel and briefly held it up to admire. The surgeon's knife gleamed in the dim light and Hade went to work.

CHAPTER 2

The Vatican: Deep within the bowels of the Vatican, a simple oil lamp burned as Father Michael Dalacourt studied the ancient Latin text before him. He had purposefully unplugged the electric light in the room and lit the lamp because he felt it connected him more closely with those who, over the past thousand years, had spent their days in this room. He loved the smell of the burning oil and believed it cleared his mind, which helped bring him closer to his God. He was still a young man, particularly for one who was already a Father in the service of the church's most holy head, but God had placed him here for a reason and, tonight of all nights, he believed that reason was becoming much clearer to him.

"I don't know what you wish to find," spoke a second man who was seated in a plush, red velvet chair across the table from the young priest. Impeccably dressed in the robes of the church, with aging yet sharply distinguished features, the stare coming from his cold eyes toward his young protégé indicated, as much as the ice in his voice, how futile this endeavor was.

"To be honest, I really don't know," replied Dalacourt tiredly, his face still turned toward the old text, his weary eyes scanning the Latin as quickly as he dared, lest he miss something important. "I only know something doesn't feel right. In truth, this whole occurrence feels almost vile. Perhaps that is what disturbs me so."

"'Thy dead men shall live, together with my dead body shall they arise. Awake and sing, ye that dwell in the dust: for thy dew is as the dew of the herbs, and the earth shall cast out the dead,'" Archbishop Francis De Solei quoted importantly, a smile never leaving his patrician face. "Isaiah 27:19, Michael. 'Vile' would hardly be a word I'd use to describe such a miracle. Indeed, if it's enlightenment you seek, look no further than that scripture."

"Forgive me, Your Excellency, for I don't wish to be disrespectful," the younger priest replied quietly, this time looking up at his mentor, a man he owed so much to. "But I hardly think that particular scripture applies to what we have experienced."

"'For, behold, the Lord cometh out of his place to punish the inhabitants of the earth for their iniquity: the earth also shall disclose her blood and shall no more cover her stain,'" De Solei quoted again, never wavering. "Isaiah 27:21. I pray you open your eyes, my son, and see what is truly happening before it grows too late. We are indeed witness to a wonderful miracle, one of many that I foresee being visited upon us in the coming days. The dead have risen here in this holy house of the Lord, Father Michael. Can you deny that?"

The young priest bowed his head. "No, Your Excellency," he said quietly and truthfully. "That I cannot dispute."

"Nor should you," continued De Solei knowingly. "We are witness to a miracle from God and to deny that which you know to be true is not only dangerous, it's blatantly blasphemous. The raising of the dead can mean only one thing—the end has truly come and the great and wondrous day of the Lord is at hand."

"I'm familiar with the prophecy," Dalacourt said, shaking his head and wondering how he could convince the older man something was still very wrong. In the end, he could only say, "I'm just not convinced Father Oliveira rising from the dead is a signal heralding the ushering in of a new dispensation." He fell quiet, realizing he had just crossed a line he had told himself earlier he would not cross.

"And since when has recognizing the truth for what it is been deemed presumptuous?" De Solei replied in an almost condescending tone, his eyebrows rising ever so slightly as his patience began to wane. "Perhaps if you allowed a bit more light into this room you might be able to see more clearly what lies before you. Does not Revelation 20:13 state 'I saw the dead, small and great, stand before God; and the books were opened: and another book was opened, which is the book of life: and the dead were judged out of those things which were written in the books, according to their works'?" He leaned back in his chair and crossed his arms, his features smug. "The dead are risen and the Day of Judgment is finally at hand. Surely you must see that."

"Have you looked at him?" Dalacourt suddenly shouted, slamming a hand down on the musty tome as his frustration boiled over unbidden. "Have you spoken with him? Have you even tried? Even if all that you believe is true and this is indeed a blessed miracle, then why do you keep him locked up, hidden away from the eyes of the world? If he has indeed risen, then should not such a miracle be shown to the people?"

For several long moments the elder priest was silent, his face a mask of stone. His eyes glittered with anger and, when he finally spoke, there was no denying his rage, although his voice remained calm. "I am disheartened at your outburst, Michael," he said icily, emphasizing the young priest's name and purposefully omitting his title in the rebuke. "I thought I had tutored you better in your manners. However, of more concern to me right now is your lack of faith. God has wrought a miracle before your very eyes and you disbelieve it because you do not understand it. We are not to know all of God's ways and, when we do not understand Him, we are commanded to take His works on faith. Perhaps our Beloved Father Oliveira has issues that we are as yet unaware of and his current condition is part of God's punishment."

"You cannot believe…"

Francis De Solei held up a hand to silence his young charge and save him from crossing yet another line. "I believe what I know to be true because I am a man of God. You are supposedly a man of God as well, Michael, yet you blaspheme Him with your search for an answer that is already before your eyes."

Father Michael Dalacourt lowered his head, slowly breathing in and out to calm himself. "I beg forgiveness, Your Excellency," he finally said quietly, knowing he had overstepped his bounds. "I'm merely confused," he finished meekly.

De Solei stood up, his sharp features tight. "I may absolve you in time, Michael," he said, reaching across the table and placing a hand on the younger man's shoulder, more in a condescending way than a forgiving one, "but God may not be so forgiving." He held out his hand for the young priest. Dalacourt leaned over and kissed his ring and bowed his head. The archbishop then turned around and walked toward the door, his rich robes rustling across the stone floor. He paused at the door for a moment and turned back to look at his protégé. "Wherefore I say unto you, all manner of sin and blasphemy shall be forgiven unto men: but the blasphemy against the Holy Ghost shall not be forgiven unto men'."

"Matthew 12:31," Dalacourt answered softly, accepting the rebuke, his eyes still downcast. De Solei simply nodded once and then turned and walked out of the room, leaving the young priest alone with his troubled soul.

Michael Dalacourt sat motionless in the room for some time after his mentor left, a thousand thoughts running through his mind. Was Francis De Solei right about him? Had he indeed blasphemed the Holy Ghost by disbelieving what De Solei claimed was an obvious miracle and portent of a glorious future? His extensive knowledge of the church both past and present gave him no answers, and so his mind turned to the one way he knew he could discern whether De Solei was correct or not. The answer wasn't in the ancient Latin text laid out before him, nor would he find it in any of the other tomes the Vatican kept within its deepest vaults. The answer he sought lay in the man who had once been Father Francisco Nunez de Oliveira and perhaps was again, at least according to Archbishop Francis De Solei.

Inwardly, he shivered as he played over the events of two days past. Father Oliveira had been a fellow priest visiting the Vatican from his parish in Mineas Gerais deep within the Brazilian rain forest. He had been at the Vatican less than a week before he had suddenly fallen ill. The sickness struck so quickly, the man was dead before a doctor could arrive. Solemnly grieving for their fallen brother, they put the body in a cold room deep within the subterranean catacombs of the Vatican to await preparation for burial. The next day, when the mortician arrived to prepare the body for internment, he had found Father Oliveira curled up in the fetal position in a corner of the room, his hands battered and his fingers torn and bloody from beating on the inside of the locked cold room door. The dead Father was now very much alive, or so it seemed, and therein lay the apparent miracle.

Of those few brethren who were made aware of the incredible occurrence, there was much debate and Dalacourt took some measure of personal satisfaction in knowing he wasn't the only one having doubts about the significance of the events. Archbishop De Solei, however, had immediately and unequivocally pronounced it a miracle, one in which the ramifications should be carefully considered before making a formal declaration to the public. With the backing of His Eminence, De Solei swore everyone involved to absolute secrecy and politely insisted the terrified mortician remain a guest within the Vatican until the church could prepare the world fully for what was to come. The literal Second Coming of the Savior was finally upon them.

With a sigh of resignation, Father Dalacourt gingerly closed the ancient tome and looked toward the door. He had been expressly forbidden to do what he was about to do, but a part of him was thinking that if he had truly blasphemed the Holy Ghost then his soul was already damned and therefore he had nothing else to lose. It was a pronounced struggle within—the desire for truth versus his loyalty to Archbishop De Solei.

It was a loyalty that ran to his very core.

Michael Dalacourt had begun his life growing up poor in Greensboro, North Carolina to, as he used to call them, tongue speakin', Bible-thumpin' Baptists. His idyllic childhood came to a tragic end one day when a DC-9 his parents were on, skidded out of control on an icy runway and crashed on takeoff from the Piedmont Triad International Airport. Twelve passengers and one crew member were killed in the resulting flash fire that consumed the rear half of the plane. His parents were among the dead, so badly burned that it took weeks to positively identify them.

The real tragedy was that his parents never should have been on that plane—the idea of affording a vacation getaway was a rather absurd one to a family who lived quite satisfactorily on generic canned goods and with a mother who knew how to cook with whatever she had. Yet somehow, they had won an obscure Winn Dixie grocery store contest and were to be whisked away for a three-day getaway to a picturesque winter cabin in Vail, Colorado.

Fate, it would turn out, had other plans and just like that, Michael Dalacourt's life had been turned upside down. At eight years old, the young boy was suddenly orphaned. The state of North Carolina located his only surviving relative, a step-aunt in Boston, Massachusetts. It did not matter that young Michael did not know the woman and, in fact, had never even heard his mother or father speak of her. Before he knew it, he was on a plane to Boston to be turned over to and raised by his Aunt Helen.

Aunt Helen was a staunch Catholic and she immediately set forth to "drive the devil" from him. Michael found himself enrolled in a Catholic school almost from the moment he stepped off the plane. His days were spent studying history, math, and church doctrine and his evenings and weekends were spent studying the scriptures with Aunt Helen when not attending mass. Playtime was non-existent.

Most children in his place would have found the routine and the challenging expectations maddening, but for the young boy who had suffered the tragedy of losing his parents, he felt strangely at peace. His aunt was kind to him, if demanding. She took care of him, fed him and clothed him, and made him feel like he was a part of her life. He also found that he had a particular penchant for the history of the church and quickly became a favorite of the nuns who taught at the school. A year later, Michael Dalacourt had settled well into his new life. He loved and missed his parents dearly, but he had grown to love his aunt, as well. Even better, she had grown to love him, too, and he was finally happy again.

Unfortunately, fate once again had other plans.

Even today, Michael Dalacourt remembered the knock that came at the door one afternoon as he was studying after school. Two police officers, accompanied by Sister Mercer, the acting headmistress of his school, had come to break the tragic news to him. Aunt Helen was dead, shot to death outside of the First National Bank of Boston in a failed robbery attempt.

Once again, Michael Dalacourt had lost his family. With no more living relatives, he was now a ward of the state, but Sister Mercer tucked him into a small room at the convent before the sun had set that day. And there he remained, growing up under the tutelage of the sisters who taught his classes and Father Dunkirk, the long-time retired priest who oversaw the school itself.

Father Xavier Dunkirk was a huge man by any standard and took a special interest in the young boy's upbringing. He was a hard taskmaster, sometimes even to the point of cruelness, but he was forward-thinking and he drove Michael Dalacourt to be more than he thought possible.

The retired priest died on the eve of Michael Dalacourt's twelfth birthday, but by then the young man's life had been laid out clearly before him. He had thrown himself into his studies and learned as much as he could of the church, her history, and what God expected of His children. There had to be a reason for everything he had experienced in his short life and he was driven as never before to discover it.

At the age of sixteen, Michael was fluent in Russian, German, Italian, Spanish, and, of course, Latin, and was thoroughly knowledgeable about the Bible, including all Catholic teachings, traditions, and doctrines. At nineteen, he enrolled in seminary and spent nearly eight years there as both a student and then an instructor of Latin.

He eventually caught the attention of the Vatican and one Francis De Solei, a powerful archbishop in the church, who had him appointed to the Vatican, one of the youngest to receive such an honor. De Solei had made no secret of the fact that the young man would perhaps one day make a fine Camerlengo, and his tutelage was heavily steeped in the finances of the church.

Today, all of that seemed distant. With a sigh of resignation, Father Dalacourt straightened and ran a hand nervously through his sandy hair. Convinced that this was the only way, he walked from the room, his destination set.

The desire for truth had won out over loyalty.

Soon enough he found himself deep within the catacombs and standing outside the heavy oaken door that kept Father Oliveira hidden from the eyes of the world. This part of the Vatican was rarely used, and it was with no small amount of trepidation that he reached up and slowly slid back the wooden window grate. After pausing for a moment to steel his quaking nerves, he peered inside. The room was dark. Father Oliveira had broken the single dim light bulb not more than ten minutes after he had first been incarcerated there two days ago.

"Father?" Dalacourt questioned quietly, his eyes scanning the darkness of the room beyond, trying to find the old Brazilian priest. There was a small shuffling sound from across the room, but he could see nothing past the dim square of light cast on the floor from the open panel. "Father," he repeated a little more urgently. "I wish to speak with you."

There was no answer.

"Father Oliveira," he said again, his eyes straining for any type of movement from within. "Please, I beg of you to speak to me. Tell me, why have you come back and what message do you bring?"

A hollow voice, gravelly and difficult to understand, answered from the darkness. "*E deu o mar os mortos que nele havia, e a morte e o inferno deram os mortos que neles havia, e foram julgados cada um segundo as suas obras…*" It trailed off in an indecipherable slur that sounded almost like a hiss.

Father Michael Dalacourt stood frozen in front of the door. He didn't speak Portuguese fluently, but he knew Latin well enough to pick up the similar words. "Revelation 20:13," he whispered to himself, shaking his head in disbelief. "You really have come back. But why?"

As Dalacourt stood awash in a sea of thought, the mangled hand of Francesco de Oliveira thrust out through the open window grate, fingers grasping Dalacourt's throat. Moments later, blackness took him and Dalacourt remembered nothing more.

CHAPTER 3

Tel Aviv, Israel: Relaxing in shorts and a tank top to deal with the still-oppressive heat of the night, Rebekkah Kassem kicked up her long legs and propped her bare feet on the nearby coffee table as she adjusted the laptop to look into the camera. "I can't move to the States right now, Lex," she replied to her online friend's question.

"Why not?" Alexis Kennedy pressed while seated in her own living room half a world away, connected with her Israeli friend by Skype.

"Not the right time," Rebekkah replied. "Soon, though."

"It's just that I worry about you. Israel is not exactly safe these days."

"That's the price I pay for living in the 'Holy' Land."

"For a while, I thought things were getting better there," Alexis said, twirling her hair.

Rebekkah tapped the screen irritably. "You need to stop that, Lex. Bad for your hair."

"Yeah, I know."

"Back to the point, though, you're right," said the Israeli. "It's gotten bad this past year. It feels even worse than normal."

"I don't know how you can stay out there," Alexis replied, reaching for her hair again, but tapping her own screen instead. "See, I do have some willpower."

Rebekkah smiled. "One of these days I'm going to have to get out there and visit."

"That would be incredible! I can't even imagine what a blast we would have together!"

"Trust me, I wouldn't miss it for the world, Lex," was her reply. "You have no idea."

"At least for a week or two. It would be nice to actually see you in the flesh."

"We Skype all the time, Lex," Rebekkah countered.

"That's not the same and you know it," Alexis said. "I can't very well tote around my laptop if I want to go shopping with you."

"Well, be patient. I'll get there soon enough. I've been in Israel since I was nine and I suppose I'd like to go back to the States some day. I do kind of miss it."

"Well, my door is always open. You can come and stay with me and my family for as long as you want," Alexis said. "By the way, Owen says hi."

"Right back at him," Rebekkah answered with a wink. "How's that going, anyway? Are the birds still chirping?"

"I guess so, but I'm just not sure he can hear them yet. How's that for an answer?"

"I suppose I'll take what I can get."

With that, Alexis abruptly changed the subject. "So how's the fight going?"

"What fight?"

"IDF."

"No worries," Rebekkah answered, her mouth turning up in a smirk. "It's not really a fight anymore anyway."

"Are they giving up?"

"Don't know. Don't care," was the reply. "The Israeli Defense Forces know they can't have me. Dual citizenship has its perks."

"I'm just glad you don't have to get mixed up in the insanity over there."

Rebekkah shrugged indifferently, clearly not concerned. "You can't live here without getting mixed up in the insanity. It's the Holy Land, remember?"

"Better to live away from it," Alexis countered.

"I'm a lot safer than you think."

"Famous last words."

Rebekkah sat straight up, her head cocked to one side as if she was listening to something. "Hey, Lex," she said softly. "Hang on a sec."

Without waiting for a reply, the young Israeli set her laptop on the couch and quickly stood. Soundlessly, she walked to the single window in her small room and cautiously pulled back the heavy curtain to peer out into the night. While the world was wrapped up in worrying about the political insanity that was transpiring in her homeland, as well as in the neighboring Arab countries, far more dark and sinister events were largely going on unnoticed. Like the one that was happening in the street under her window at that very moment.

She had heard the first pleading scream while she was cyber-chatting. Now, from her darkened window, she watched the attack take place through the jaded eyes of someone who has seen countless incidents of indescribable suffering—someone who knew when to mind her own business.

Three floors below, the victim in the street was a young man, probably not much older than she was. He was dressed in jogging clothes now spattered with blood. There were two would-be murderers, big men who knew what they were doing. While one of them pinned the struggling man's arms and pressed them painfully into the pavement, the other straddled his chest, fingers reaching for the young man's neck. The doomed victim managed one more strangled scream in the night before the killer's powerful hands clamped around his throat.

From her window, Rebekkah watched as the man died, his eyes rolling back in his head and his body going limp. Without a word, the men released their hold on the corpse and stood up. The girl didn't flinch when one of the murderers looked up at her, cold and vacant eyes glittering in the pale glow of the streetlights. She returned his gaze unafraid. A moment later, the killer forgot about her and the two men placed the dead man's arms around their shoulders, positioning the body so it was between them. Slowly, they shambled down the street, openly supporting what those who hadn't witnessed the murder would likely assume to be their drunken friend.

Rebekkah Kassem looked across the street and noticed hers was one of the few windows open. Perhaps that was the worst sign of all when no one even bothered to take notice of a murder. She shook her head at the madness of it all.

Letting the curtain fall back into place, she walked back to the sofa, pausing to look briefly into the mirror that was hanging on the wall. She was a very pretty woman with dark skin and deep, penetrating eyes. Her cheekbones were high and pronounced and her long black hair was pulled back into a tight French braid. She gave her image a quick once over, pursed her lips, then frowned at what she saw. A large cockroach slipped out from behind the mirror and skittered along the top edge of the frame. She watched it turn itself perfectly and latch onto the wall, never breaking stride, and head straight for the window. It paused near where she had been standing, then slipped behind the curtain and disappeared. With a shrug, she turned to sit back down in front of her computer.

"I'm back," she said, placing the laptop across her legs.

"Everything okay?"

"Some poor guy just got murdered out in the street," Rebekkah answered with a frown, her eyes straying to the window again.

"Are you serious?"

The Israeli woman nodded. "Wouldn't be the first time I've seen it," she added.

"What'd you do?"

"What would you want me to do, Lex?" she answered, sounding somewhat exasperated. "Remember, it's different here than your life in the States."

"You at least called the police, right?"

"It wouldn't do any good, Lex," Rebekkah answered, a frown on her face. "People get murdered here all the time when the suicide bombers set themselves off. One man getting strangled in the street these days isn't going to do a whole lot to get the authorities riled up."

"That's insane!"

"Like I said earlier, you learn to live with it."

"I just can't imagine what it would be like to see someone killed," Alexis said sadly.

"You might want to prepare yourself, Lex. We're never as safe as we pretend."

"Why would you say that?"

"Because I read the Bible, just as I know you do," Rebekkah said. "Things are crazy all over the world and it spreads every day."

"Well, it's not so bad here, yet."

"It will be someday. And when it does, you never know when it's going to be you who has to pull the trigger."

"Oh, that's cheerful," Alexis said glumly, fighting and failing against the urge to nervously twirl her hair again.

Rebekkah laughed. "You're hopeless, you know that?"

"Yeah, well what are you going to do?" On the other side of the world, Alexis stretched and then looked back to the camera. "I'm going to sign off. I've got to get some supper and it's probably way past your bedtime."

"It would be if I ever slept, Lex. I'll catch you online again in a few days."

"Sounds good. Just be careful," Alexis finished.

Rebekkah Kassem nodded and smiled, then shut down the Skype chat. For a moment, she wondered how Alexis would fare in the same situation she was in. Could she to handle the depression, the disease, and the death? Rebekkah wasn't optimistic about her friend's chances.

She dismissed the thought as she sauntered back to the window. The night was still young—there was no telling who else she might see murdered under the full moon over Tel Aviv.

CHAPTER 4

Ferguson Canyon, Utah: Rushing water gushed over countless rocks on its race westward and down the narrow channel of Ferguson Canyon. In some stretches, the rocks slapped the water into such frenzy that a mist filled the canyon and one had to shout to be heard over the tumult. In others, the water washed against the canyon face and in one such spot, the water actually swept under the granite wall for a short distance due to a section of the rock that protruded from the wall as it ascended thirty feet. At that point, the face came to a small ledge, above which the cliff rose straight up. The forest canopy within the canyon limited visibility of the rock face above one hundred feet and kept the canyon cool even on the hottest days.

The canyon dissociated its visitor from any sense of being in the real world. Its walls ran parallel and as little as one hundred-fifty feet apart in some stretches, combining with the canopy to completely seal off the heavens themselves. This shield against the universe also implied a freedom from the laws of the universe, and no visitor here would express surprise if the animals suddenly spoke or if gravity released its hold. Here in Ferguson Canyon, there were two ways to escape the real world: hike or climb.

Owen DiConte preferred to climb.

Seven feet below the point at which the canopy met the canyon edge, an inch-wide nub of granite protruded from the cliff wall. On it stood Owen, his left hand clutching the wall above, right hand in the chalk bag, and one foot pressed against the wall for balance. His left shoulder and forearm ached with the familiar burn of holding one position for too long, but Owen continued to hold steady as he berated himself for his mistake. The next step in the sequence of this ascent required a tall reach with the right hand, but a tall reach required a mobile right leg. Unfortunately, Owen's right leg occupied the small granite nub and was therefore quite immobile for the moment, while the hold gripped by his left hand was level with his left hip and provided absolutely no leverage to lift himself any higher.

In other words, he was stuck, burning energy by holding his position and wasting more by stepping out of sequence. He had planned out the entire ascent for weeks, closing his eyes and reviewing the path in his mind as he sat through his classes or while trying to fall asleep at night. Climbing solo gave Owen a heightened sense of challenge. It invigorated him and made him feel like he had conquered the mountain on his own terms. Yet, after all that preparation, he had abandoned his plan when he saw what looked like an easier hold.

He closed his eyes and took several deep calming breaths. He would have to be sharp and focused to reason his way out this one. Knowing the limitations of his body were close to being reached, he pressed his chest against the rock face and felt his balance to see if he would stay against the face without the use of his hands. He released some of the tension in his left shoulder, then his forearm. So far, his balance held and his right foot felt solid on the small nub. He silently said a short prayer, telling God he was sorry for bothering him again and promising for the fifth time that summer that he would stop climbing without a rope if God would just help him out of this one last jam.

Then he released his handhold, keeping chest, hands, and face pressed to the cool rock. With his right leg slightly bent, he inched his upper body to the right until his left hip and shoulder stood above his right foot and he was in perfect balance. Then his right leg pushed to a standing position, his toes on the nub lifting his entire body, and his left hand reached blindly for the next hold. As much as he hated his situation, part of him thrived on the rush of blood throughout his body. At times like these, he felt an awareness of exactly where every body part stood in relation to the others and in relation to the rock, the trees, and the cosmos.

His fingers reached high and penetrated the leafy canopy, warmed by sunlight. They felt the rough edge of the hold as he tugged with all his might and then threw his right hand above the canopy to search for its next hold. He lifted again and his head suddenly broke out of the tops of the trees like a diver surfacing for air.

In a moment, the crux of the climb was over. A plateau welcomed the climber and pointed west toward the setting sun. Owen threw his leg up over the edge of the stone table and levered himself up to lay on the warm granite. He said a prayer of thanks, offered an apology for asking for help so often, and smiled at his most recent episode of poor judgment. Part of him wondered if he would ever learn, while another part hoped he never would.

He loved to climb because it pitted him against the unconquerable power of the mountain, but he never seemed to win unless he prayed, so he supposed it wasn't all that fair to say he defeated the mountain alone. Many times, he would lay and wonder why God chose to help him when, after all, it was his own poor judgment that put him in those predicaments in the first place. All the same, he appreciated the help and smiled as he pictured God shaking his head in exasperation at some of the things Owen did. It was easy to think about God in these mountains. Here, he felt close to the heavens when everything else stood below.

After a while, Owen roused himself from his thoughts, looked west, and walked toward the mouth of the canyon to watch the sun set. Ferguson Canyon itself opened westward to overlook the Salt Lake Valley, which rested between two mountain ranges like the calm lull between two giant waves in the ocean. Each range, the Wasatch on the east and the Oquirrhs on the west, ran from the southern horizon to the northern. The Point, a peninsula plateau jutting westward out of the Wasatch Range, bound the southern view. A similar point extended west from the northern Wasatch where the capitol building of Salt Lake City could be seen.

Upon reaching the mouth of the canyon, Owen seated himself on a grassy slope overlooking it all. A breeze brought more warm air from the south and he let his body relax. The valley was recovering from a wet winter and the river this year was higher than usual. Because of that, there was green grass to sit on—a rarity—and Owen took great pleasure in it. The locals called these the Everlasting Hills. While such grandiose things tend to make people feel small, these mountains did not. They stood strong and watched over the valley like sentinels, whispering of peace and security to the citizens within their walls. At that moment, the bottom curve of the sun touched the peaks of the Oquirrhs and the mountains connected to the heavens.

The setting sun cast a shadow that marched down the slopes of the Oquirrhs. Far below, lights from homes began to dot the valley as the stars above dotted the sky. Slowly, the shadow ascended the Wasatch and reached out to Owen. As he had many times before, he waited in anticipation of the coolness the shadow would bring, a welcome relief from the dry heat and an end to a good day.

Yet, when the shadow finally shrouded his feet, Owen was immediately startled from his thoughts. The shadow bit with an unexpected heat. Sunset usually spread its cooling blanket over the valley as if to tuck it in for the night. Tonight it felt as if something hot and sticky were being poured over him, and it left his mind ill at ease. The usual friendly whisperings in the rustle of grass and leaves were gone, their faint sighs disconcerting and almost hostile. Only when another breeze stirred—cool this time—did Owen finally move. On a normal evening, he would sit and watch the valley until he felt like joining the world of man again. Tonight, he hurried toward his car. He could feel deep within him that something was very, very wrong.

He tossed his climbing gear into the back seat and used the twenty minutes it took to drive home from the canyon to empty his mind and rid himself of the uneasiness he had felt earlier. The road leading away from the canyon boasted some of the most beautiful and expensive homes in the valley. They fed his imagination of affording such a home one day, and that thought put him in good spirits once again. His mind wandered. Dreams of amazing inventions, superhuman abilities, and saving the damsel in distress seemed so close to reality for him that many times he believed all he lacked was the opportunity to perform such feats. He had no fear of sharing his dreams with others, either. They would laugh them off or laugh at Owen for being so boyish at his age. Every time this occurred, he would simply smile and enjoy their laughter. He believed so much in his ability to accomplish anything that he was oblivious to the doubt of others.

He was deep within his thoughts when a corner of his mind caught the words of an announcer on the radio. In that moment, his whole life turned upside down.

"...Chris Matthews was found dead on the university campus this morning," the announcer continued. "Preliminary reports indicate foul play and suggest he was in the company of star basketball player, Gideon Sumbawanga, at the time of his death. Authorities have been unable to locate Mr. Sumbawanga and are concerned for his safety. University of Utah campus police have been quick to point out he's not a suspect at this time."

Owen hurriedly turned the radio to a news station. It didn't take long to find what he was looking for. "Matthews and university star basketball player, Gideon Sumbawanga, were last seen leaving the campus gymnasium late in the evening and authorities are asking anyone with any information on the events of last night or the whereabouts of Gideon Sumbawanga to please contact them immediately."

Panic rose within him as Owen changed the station several more times and heard the same story again and again. This couldn't be happening, not to Gideon! Gideon seemed so untouchable and on top of life. There had to be some mistake. They said he was missing, not dead, but what had happened? Where was he? And what about poor Chris? Chris was dead!

Owen's mind couldn't keep up with his heart and with a cry of frustration and anguish, he pulled his car off the road, narrowly missing sending it over the edge and into a deep ravine. He felt trapped and couldn't seem to draw a breath. Opening the door, he stumbled out and fell to his knees. Overwhelmed by the horrible news that one of his best friends was missing and another dead, Owen broke down. He knelt and cried silently.

After some time had passed and he had begun to process his grief, the thought came to him that if they hadn't found Gideon's body, that meant his friend might still be out there somewhere. And if that were the case, then he was wasting precious time kneeling here and feeling sorry for himself. With a supreme effort, he fought back his emotions and picked himself up off the ground. His purpose was singular. He had a friend to find and he wasn't going to stop until he found him.

CHAPTER 5

Tsarskoe Selo, Russia: It was a cool, spring afternoon and Petr Zhugravinsky was sitting alone at his mahogany dining room table, wondering how he was going to tell his family he was leaving them forever. He had invited his father Lavrenti, his two grandfathers Vladimir and Mikhail, his two brothers Nikolai and Sergei, and five of his cousins to his Roman-style apartment in the small villa of Tsarskoe Selo just outside of St. Petersburg. He had always loved this city and he imagined it held the same allure for him as it had for the descendants of the Empress Catherine Alekseyevna, who received the land from Peter the Great in 1710.

It had become the site where tsars like Nicholas and Alexander, and empresses such as Catherine and Elizabeth, had come for the summer months to relax away from the eyes of the world. It was the Russian rulers' Mount Olympus, where they could live as gods on Earth. This was where decisions had been made that allowed Petr's country to rise from a second tier nation to one of the most powerful empires the world had ever known. And yet, this town was more than just a living memorial to the greatness that had been tsarist Russia. It was a "town of muses," where painters, architects, and, perhaps most importantly for Petr, poets came to make a better future. The muses had touched Petr here as well. It was in this city he had first felt the urgings to become something more than what his heritage held for him.

Swirling a glass of Smirnoff vodka, he waited for his family to arrive. Most of them would come from their traditional homes in St. Petersburg and arrive early, but his brother Nikolai, who was trying to move the family quickly up the Russian mafia hierarchy, had relocated to a more suitable neighborhood and would certainly show up last. The two brothers had been through a great deal together and they shared a deep bond that was rare even with brothers, and yet it was Nikolai who Petr was running from the most.

Nikolai was a savage beast at heart, capable of bringing the family an immense amount of glory and wealth or destroying everyone associated with it. He was a risk taker in the extreme, the perfect embodiment of the "New Russian," who lived life on the edge in an effort to get rich quick and stay powerful forever. And because of his almost tangible fear of turning into a monster like Nikolai, Petr had begun to distance himself from the family business.

It was well known within the family that he wanted a different sort of life than the one offered by his inherited relationships. He was extremely bright—everyone agreed with this—and he had unlimited potential. The family believed if they gave him enough time to come to his senses, someday he would become one of the most powerful men in St. Petersburg—perhaps all of Russia. Even Petr himself understood he was perfectly situated and possessed all the right tools to rise to greatness.

Those were the hopes of his father and most of his family who could see past their own ambitions. They wanted Petr as he was, only without his conscience, for it was his conscience that kept him from fully joining the family. The Zhugravinsky family was one of the leading mafia families in St. Petersburg, which made them deceitful, shallow, treacherous and, when necessary, brutally murderous. Petr possessed all of those traits, but he felt he couldn't have been more different from his family. He often tried to envision himself as a poet, a traveler, and a deep thinker, but he was painfully aware none of those terms had ever been used to describe a Zhugravinsky before.

Petr would later recall that he had been correct about that evening. Nikolai had indeed been the last one to arrive and he did so quite drunk. His father and grandfathers, along with his younger brother Sergei, had not consumed any alcohol.

They had good reason to abstain. For the past week, they had been wondering what kind of announcement could be so important that Petr would call them all together like this. While there was a certain measure of danger in this type of gathering for a family such as theirs, their true preoccupation had been the fear that Petr was going to leave them. To their dismay, their fears would be wholly confirmed.

With his family finally gathered around the table, Petr opened his arms wide and shouted, *"Tovarish,"* the Russian word for comrade. It was an inside joke for the family, which had never been strong supporters of communism and had welcomed capitalism and the opportunities associated with it. Petr's family, which usually would have laughed out loud and had a few toasts to the "Party" after the prompt had been given, let out a few, uncomfortable half-laughs and waited for Petr to continue. They weren't going to make this easy for him.

"Thank you for coming tonight," he began, his deep voice betraying a hint of sadness and uncertainty. "I'm sure you are all wondering why I've asked for this meeting, so let's not beat around the bush. I've decided to take a break from the family business."

Immediately, several voices were raised, but Petr held up a hand to silence them. "Please, let me finish and then I'll listen to you speak your peace." His family fell silent as he continued, "As you're aware, I'm planning on graduating next week from the University of St. Petersburg with a double major in Literature and English."

His younger brother, Sergei, interrupted with a round of applause and an energetic congratulation. Petr allowed himself a small grin in Sergei's direction, who of all his relatives, was closest in disposition to him, and then went on with the bombshell. "I've also decided to accept an offer to continue my education in the United States."

"America!" roared Nikolai as he stood up and violently slammed a hand down on the table. "Are you mad, Petr?" he shouted bitterly. "You have an obligation to this family!"

"Kolya," interrupted another voice and Nikolai immediately went silent as his father slowly stood, a scowl on his deeply lined face. He had used Nikolai's childhood nickname, which those closest to him were still allowed to use, but only with caution. Lavrenti, however, had no such compunctions about reminding his son that to him, he was still a boy. "We appreciate your devotion to this family," he went on slowly, "and we're as aware of Petr's obligations as you are. But, Petr has earned the right to speak and we're obliged to listen."

The eldest Zhugravinsky son went red with rage at the scolding and fixed Petr with a look of murderous fury, but he fell silent and collapsed back into his seat, saying nothing more.

Petr nodded his head slightly at his father, who had also once again seated himself, and continued. "I shall be going to the United States to continue my schooling at the University of Utah. It's a great school, one of the best, and I've received a full scholarship to attend. It's my wish you'll let me go with your blessings."

"Go then," Nikolai spat as he rose to his feet, fire in his eyes. "I no longer know who you are. The Petr I once knew would have stood by me to the ends of the world, not flee when it's convenient. A true brother would never leave, not for all the rubles in the world. This family will find out what the rest of us are made of." He cast a glance at each of his cousins and a final glare at Petr, before turning and stalking out of the room.

Lavrenti Zhugravinsky closed his eyes and sighed deeply as he settled back into his chair. After a few moments, he opened them and looked directly at his middle son. "You see what you bring upon this family, Petr? Discord and anger, and for what? A chance to play school boy in America? I'm sorry, but I don't understand where this childish fantasy comes from."

Petr started to reply, but Sergei's cell phone cut him off. His younger brother spoke quietly into it and then excused himself and walked out of the room and onto the deck overlooking the palace.

Lavrenti took the silence to drive home his earlier point. "You've had your chance to speak, Petr, and whatever decision you make, we will honor it, however unpleasant it is for us to do so. But, now it's my turn and you shall listen to the words of your father, as any son should."

Petr nodded solemnly. He loved and revered his father, even if he didn't always agree with him.

"I'm growing weary," the older Zhugravinsky went on. "When your grandfather turned the family business over to me, he did so knowing all the major decisions were mine to make. Right or wrong, I was in charge. My plans were to do the same with you, but now you're leaving and I'm forced to continue on without you. It is most unfortunate to have sons as I do."

"What of Nikolai or Sergei?" Petr offered.

Lavrenti smiled and scoffed. "You would have Nikolai lead this family? He's as loyal as anyone, but he has no patience for what it takes to actually run the business. And Sergei is much too young and inexperienced. I'm afraid that without you, he'll follow the path Nikolai sets for him."

The youngest of the Zhugravinsky sons came back into the room, pocketing his phone. "Papa, I'm sorry to interrupt, but we have a small problem," he said nervously.

"What is it?"

"In light of Petr's news, maybe it's better we took care of this without him."

"No, no, Sergei, tell us what you know," Lavrenti said loudly. "If anything, perhaps Petr will help us solve this problem before he leaves us." By the look on his face, the old man knew Petr wasn't going to help much, but he also knew he had to give his son a final chance. If he had known what Sergei was about to say, however, he never would have let Petr hear it.

"Okay, Papa," Sergei sighed, "you know best. Remember that problem with the Petrov family in the meat packing district? Well, Nikolai decided to take care of three facets of that problem, if you understand me. They're all distant relations, so we shouldn't be too worried about direct retribution, but this could get out of hand."

Lavrenti Zhugravinsky stiffened, but he kept his rising anger in check. "Go on, Sergei."

The youngest son cleared his throat and continued. "It appears Nikolai felt it would send the right message to the right people that they shouldn't try to start working the district," he faltered at that, knowing he was failing in his attempt to somehow exonerate his elder brother. Murder was, after all, a family affair, which held repercussions for everyone and therefore everyone had to agree to it. Unfortunately, this wasn't the first time Nikolai had acted on his own—but judging by the look on the face of his father, it might very well be the last.

"Who called you, Sergei?" Vladimir Zhugravinsky pressed, speaking for the first time that evening, having kept any emotion at Petr's announcement carefully hidden.

The young man swallowed thickly and looked at his grandfather. "It was Sasha," he said, referring to one of their men who was well-known for his loyalty to the head of the family. "Nikolai had him and Josef meet the Petrovs out by the docks to send the message."

"And the problem?"

"It seems while they were cleaning up, someone stole the bodies."

"Stole the bodies?" Lavrenti asked skeptically. "How can someone walk in and snatch a couple of bodies out from under their noses?"

"That's just it, Papa," Sergei continued with a helpless shrug. "They're gone and our boys have no idea what happened to them. With any luck, they'll find whoever took them and take care of it quickly. We definitely don't want any loose ends out there."

"No, we don't," agreed Lavrenti. "See to it this problem is taken care of. And Sergei?"

"Yes, Papa?"

"Find Nikolai and let him know how disappointed we all will be if this isn't resolved fully."

"Yes, Papa," agreed Sergei, before turning to look at his brother. Nothing needed to be said between them—the look on his face was enough. A moment later, he was gone, the door slamming behind him.

At last, it was Lavrenti who spoke again. "Such is our legacy, my son," he said gravely as he swept his arm through the air to indicate all that was about them.

"Which is why I can't be a part of it," Petr answered, his expression grim.

"It was on you we had pinned our hopes for change," the older man went on. "Nikolai has too much of the old world in him. For him, killing is always the answer, and I'm afraid it will always be so."

"Sergei could lead this family," Petr tried to reason again.

"Were he ready for that task, he would have stopped Nikolai from doing what he has just done. No, Petr, Sergei is no more ready to take over the reins of this family than Nikolai is. You have long been the only one we could count on."

"And I say again, Father, that is a path I can't follow," Petr replied, unwilling to give in.

"Then you will do what you must," his father said finally with a resigned sigh. "I ask but one favor of you before you leave."

"Anything," Petr responded, meaning it.

"Go after your brothers. They will need you to fix this problem. Perhaps they can learn from your final example."

Petr sat silently for a lengthy moment, took one last sip of vodka, and smiled. "Of course, Papa."

"Thank you," Lavrenti said as he stood up. "Call me when everything is taken care of."

Without another word, Petr's father, as well as the rest of the family, filed out of the apartment and out into the night. Thirty minutes later, Petr was being driven toward the meat packing district by his personal driver, silently swearing to himself all the way. After twenty minutes, the car turned a corner and came to a stop behind another of the family vehicles. Nikolai and Vanya were standing near the car, engaged in a hurried and hushed conversation. Of Sergei, Petr could see no sign. Fastening an icy countenance on his face, Petr opened the door and stepped out of the car. As much as he detested it, this was where he was at his best.

CHAPTER 6

Ujiji, Tanzania: David Livingston Sumbawanga sat in the shade on a gnarled, worn chair made out of a long-dead mango tree, relieved to finally be out of the heat. Leaning forward, he closed his eyes and rested his forehead against the smooth wood of an intricately carved walking stick made from the very same tree. He had just returned from the local cemetery, and needed time to think over a pressing matter. While he was not a politician or a civil servant, and thus he did not have any real authority in his village, his education and place within his society gave him a perceived authority that most elected officials in the region lacked. As such, he had been asked to help investigate a string of grave robbing throughout the region.

Seemingly random bodies had been dug up out of recent graves and had vanished. So far, fourteen bodies were gone. Things would have been simple if the corpses had been either wholly Christian or wholly Muslim, because then half of the population could have been cut out as suspects and there would have been at least a possible motive—the desecration of the body of a perceived "enemy" by extremists from either group. The problem with that theory was that seven of the bodies had been Christian and seven Muslim. What was worse was that rumors were beginning to spread that one of the men who had died in the village six weeks ago had been seen alive in Kasulu, a town almost thirty miles away. This wasn't the only report of the dead walking among the living in the world, but when something like this happens so close to home, it is cause for panic indeed and people did just that.

For some reason, David Sumbawanga had always been called upon to help in difficult times, but he had always been happy to do what he could. This would be no exception. He had been born in 1946, which was the seventy-fifth anniversary of when the American, Henry Stanley, had wandered into the village of Ujiji and found an emaciated Englishman he presumed to be David Livingston. Supposedly, the two met under a mango tree, just down the road from David Sumbawanga's own house. In fact, there was a descendent of that very same tree with a plaque commemorating the event. While in the grand scheme of things, the encounter was not one of the most important events in recorded history, it provided Ujiji with a reputation and a history, as well as giving it an opportunity to claim a small piece of the tourist pie. David's parents found themselves caught up in the moment of the anniversary and named their third son after the explorer and missionary, thus linking his fate with the elder Livingston forever.

David loved to read and soon became known throughout the region for his intellect. He grew strong and left as soon as he was able to attend the university in Uganda, eventually making his family proud when he graduated with honors and a biology degree. He managed to return home just long enough to get married to a wonderful girl who bore him a son they named Gideon Mombera—Mombera meaning, "he loves adventure" in Swahili.

Things were beginning to settle down when David received a prestigious scholarship to study abroad in Belgium, and so he left his small family behind for two years while he obtained his master's degree in conservation. He found out after he had already flown out of Dar es Salam that his wife was pregnant with their second child. He laughed eight months later when he learned that his wife, who now went by the title "Mama Gideon"—as all mothers in the region went by the name "Mama" and their first born son's name—had named his newborn daughter Chuike, which means "she brings peace in time of trouble." Obviously, his wife was sending him a message that she missed him very much and was anxious for him to return.

The next year flew by and it was on the morning of his graduation that terrible news arrived. There had been an accident. His beloved wife had been hit by a Dhala Dhala bus and had died at the scene. She had managed to push Gideon out of the way and had used her body to shield Chuike from the brunt of the hit, thus saving both her children's lives by sacrificing her own. Devastated, David returned home to arrange for the funeral and then do the best he could raising their children himself. Out of necessity, he soon found himself helping his two older brothers with their fishery, his previous wanderlust forgotten in some lost and dusty corner of his mind. The business prospered, allowing him to give his children almost anything they could want. He was also able to continue his work on conservation locally and, although it was not all over the world as he had originally hoped, he was more than willing to do his part to improve his tiny corner of the planet.

He worked ceaselessly to bring money, resources, and people to help preserve Lake Tanganyika and, in the process, create a network of friends and contacts throughout the world. Through his successful fisheries and impressive work with conservationism, David eventually became a well-recognized and important figure throughout the Kigoma district. He was called "Mwalimu," which meant "teacher," but denoted much more than that. While he would never deny he wished every day that his wife were still with him, everything else in his life was nearly perfect and he had little reason to complain. There were, of course, many offers to remarry, and while he never explicitly decided to remain a widower, he never felt very comfortable with the idea of remarriage. He was relatively wealthy, he was well-respected, and he had two healthy children. He had gotten to the point where he felt like he did not need anything or anyone else in his life to feel fulfilled and happy.

His daughter, who truly was a blessing to him, had a great deal of her mother in her and thus was happy to be wherever family was. She was a hard worker and always had a smile on her face. While he was pleased she was getting married next summer, he was also concerned about how he would continue without her. He knew he could do so more easily if his adventurous son had not left and, as he often did, he thought of the day his son had departed for the United States. He had been happy for his son, as all of Gideon's long fought for dreams were coming to fruition.

"I'll make you proud, Father. I'll work hard. This is what's best for me," Gideon had said.

"You have always made me proud, Son," David had replied with a smile as well as tears. "Remember what you've been taught. Know that even the unseen will protect you and help in your times of need." As he had watched his son get on the railroad car that would take him to the airport in Dar es Salem, David offered a prayer in his heart that would be repeated several times a day until the two would be reunited.

With a tired sigh, David closed his eyes, the musty heat of the mid-day forcing him to relent to its intensity. He leaned back in his chair, when he felt a tugging on his soul, as if something deep within was pulling at him. His inner vision began to swirl, twist, and shift until finally, all was still again. Alarmed, he opened his eyes.

He stood in a dark tunnel, an orange light casting an eerie glow upon all within. His son, Gideon, was nearby, just out of reach, pinned against the wall by a giant of a man. To the side lay a body. David stepped toward Gideon, his hand held out before him to help. But he drew no closer to his son. Something kept them apart.

Gideon was dying. David could see that Gideon's consciousness was beginning to fade, held paralyzed in the grip of the monster. "I'm here!" David shouted, but it mattered not. He knew he was not actually in the tunnel with his son, as much as he knew that what he was witnessing was all to terrifyingly real.

"You're too late," the dark spirit whispered, looking directly at him. "He's mine now."

Every visible muscle in David's body and face locked in a stance of defiance, but he was powerless to save his son. The older Sumbawanga's eyes shifted to where the form of the shadow man stood beside his son, holding him pinned against the stone wall of the tunnel. Eyes scanning side-to-side, up then down, he studied the figure. Then he stood motionless until at last, his son's heart slowed to a stop and the vision faded to blackness.

David Livingston Sumbawanga blinked and found himself suddenly back in front of his yellow stucco house, seated in his gnarled, old mango-wood chair. He could not explain what he had witnessed, but he knew it was no mere vision. Gideon had been in dire peril. Worse, he was likely dead. No reasoning in the world could explain to him why that was. But he would find out. He would discover what had become of his son. He would discover who the shadow man was. The answers were held in America.

He was on a plane that night.

CHAPTER 7

Sao Paulo, Brazil: Located on the corner of Dr. Chucri Zaidan and Roque Petroni Jr. Avenues, the Blue Tree Towers Morumbi Convention Center Hotel was just one block away from the Brazilian offices of Legio Incorporated and thus a suitable site for the award ceremony. On this night, the auditorium was filled to its five hundred-fifty person capacity with dignitaries and other important individuals. While many of them were powerful and influential leaders of Brazil, none of them matched the charisma, authority, and power of the two men standing behind the long, white table in the front of the convention room. Though dwarfed by the gigantic windows opening up to show the skyline of Sao Paulo, the two were the kind of men Horatio Alger would have been exceedingly proud of.

The man on the left was Jose Maria Wilson Nunes da Silva dos Santos. Born into an extremely impoverished family on the outskirts of Recife, Brazil, he had grown up with more appellations than prospects. As he got older, he learned firsthand that life for Brazilian men of the Northeast typically centered around fútbol—or soccer—alcohol, and women, and usually in that order. For those lucky, talented few who could master the *joga bonito*, or the "beautiful game," a whole world of opportunity opened up. *Futebol* was the one and only chance most young men in Brazil had to make a name for themselves.

While there were those who became internationally known, the most famous of the famous being Pele, the Brazilian night sky was filled with lesser stars who still shone brightly in their own country. Wilson, as he was known to the world during the 1970 World Cup where he was a surprise contributor on Pele's last championship run, was just such a star. He used his fame on the pitch to help him enter the business world and, by the mid-eighties, he had quietly become one of the richest men in Brazil. And yet, for all of his wealth and ambition, he still enjoyed maintaining the image of a poor boy who did well enough with what he had been given. Wilson was all about his image, and ensuring he could strike a chord with the populace was important for him because he had ambitions to someday run for president.

For that reason, and really that reason alone, he stood behind the long, white table with another self-made man, Vittorio Emanuele Legio, better known to the world as Victor Emmanuel Legio. At that moment, Wilson was presenting Legio with an engraved plaque in recognition of the man's work in protecting Brazil's environment. He had recently purchased sixty thousand acres of prime Amazon forest bordering the Parque Nacional do Pico de Neblina to be set aside for research and for natural habitat for the thousands of species unique to the area. It was a wise move on Legio's part—not only did it appear as if he was concerned about the environment, but it also gave him a large amount of land where few people would bother checking up on how concerned he actually was. While Legio planned on leaving most of the prized region alone, he also wanted that specific part of the forest due to the various plants found only under its mysterious canopy. Those plants provided excellent possibilities in aiding the incredibly lucrative business of cancer research, and he knew the person who cured cancer would go down in history as one of the greatest humans to ever walk the earth. That person would also die the richest man on the planet. Since Legio was currently only the seventh richest man in the world, he was always looking for ways to bump himself up the chart.

It hadn't always been that way for Victor Legio. Like Wilson, he came from an extremely humble background. But unlike Wilson, he had no desire to use that past for future gain. In fact, if he could have completely wiped out his heritage, he would have. It disgusted him to think of where he came from. He was born the grandson of poor Italian immigrants who had come to America from the small village of Scurelle in the northern province of Trentino. His father, Oreste, was the first one born in America in a small town in Wyoming named Rock Springs. Eventually, Oreste met a young Italian girl named Rosa and they settled in Ogden, Utah.

They had three children—two girls and a son they named Vittorio Emanuele, after the great King of Sardinia who had united Italy. The family never had a lot of money, but they were nowhere near as impoverished as Wilson's family had been. With their economic status came opportunities for Victor, and he aggressively seized them. He quickly began to impress his teachers with his analytical skills and found himself in advanced courses. Eventually, he outgrew his high school and, by the time he was sixteen, he was attending Weber State full time. He graduated there at the age of nineteen and moved on to UCLA, where he had a Ph.D. by the age of twenty-two. While there, he began tinkering around with computers and, by the age of twenty-five, he had not only found his destiny, but had already made his first million in the computer industry. By thirty, he was one of the five hundred richest men in the world and, by the age of thirty-eight, he had cracked the top ten. He was Victor Emmanuel Legio, named for a self-made king and nearly a self-made king himself.

Unlike Wilson today, Legio had no desire for political office. He was quite happy to pull strings from behind the stage and thus made few attempts to cull public favor—unless a situation like today's award ceremony came up. As Legio stood at the platform, accepting the award from the former Brazilian soccer star, he had to laugh at the moment. He had no illusions about the purchase of a large part of the rain forest being for the good of society, and even after exploiting it, he had no illusions about anything other than his own personal gain. Looking over at Wilson, he knew that the former athlete had no desire to be standing here basking in the glorious sham of the award, either.

Indeed, Wilson could not have cared less about the Amazon; it was a natural resource to be used for the betterment of Brazil, just as the Americans had plundered their own natural resources to become the world's dominant country. That this *gallego* was buying it now did not worry him in the least. When he was president, he would just expropriate it right back. It was all part of his plan.

When the ceremony ended, Wilson kissed his wife goodnight—it had been the first time he had seen her in nearly a month—and hopped into his limousine to get to the airport. Legio, drained from the long day, just wanted to go back to his rented penthouse suite on the twenty-fifth floor of the Renaissance Sao Paulo Hotel and fall asleep, preferably before the imminent rainfall arrived. He had to wake up at four to catch a flight for a summit meeting in Paris on importing U.S. technology into the European Union.

He slumped into the back of his darkened limousine, his eyelids already heavy. The lights were off to give him a head start on his slumber. A roll of thunder sounded overhead and a slow chill crawled along his neck as a sudden realization dawned on him—he wasn't alone.

"Hello?" There was no answer. He slowly placed his hand on the door's armrest and keyed the intercom to speak with his driver. "Driver," he said, his voice tight, "turn the lights on please." His driver did not reply. "Did you hear me?" he snapped. After a few more seconds of silence, Legio leaned forward, his hands fumbling in the darkness for the little seat drawer that held an old .45 snub-nose. Gathering all the courage he could muster, he began to talk to whoever must be hiding in the shadows. "Do you have any idea whose limousine this is?" he spoke to the darkness. "Tell me who you are so I know what name to have engraved on your tombstone!" His fingers closed around the pistol and he swung it up in front of him, pointing it blindly toward the other side of the compartment.

For what seemed like an eternity, there was nothing, and then a soft chuckle came from the recesses of the other side of the car even as an almost rotten, earthy smell filled the interior. Reflexively, Legio squeezed the trigger and was rewarded only with the click of an empty chamber. Half a dozen similar clicks later, Legio let the gun drop to the seat beside him.

"Are you quite done yet, dear boy?" the intruder's voice spoke, sounding amused. After another moment of silence, the light finally flickered on and there, sitting across from Victor Legio, was a very large man dressed in black, with a matted beard and dark sunglasses. His fingernails were manicured and his voice, when he began to speak, sounded nothing like what one would have expected.

"Hello again, Victor," the man said with a grin. "To answer your question, I know exactly who this limousine belongs to, as do you. It's mine. Now, as to engraving my name on a tombstone? I'd like to see something on it about being a hunter, a conqueror, a brother, a ferryman—actually, I'm not sure you could find a tombstone big enough to include everything you would need to. Still, I imagine my demise is a long way off, so there's no hurry. Yours, on the other hand, is much closer," he said with a knowing wink as he leaned forward. "By the way, the next time you try to kill me, you might try loading your gun."

Victor Legio sat in hateful silence, staring at the man who was both his antagonist and the main reason he was where he was today.

With a laugh, the man continued, "You never have been very good with firearms, have you, Victor? A trained marksman would have been able to feel the weight of the gun and know it had no bullets. Still, even with six bullets at this close range, I doubt you would have seriously harmed me. I'm guessing you would have missed with at least four, if not five, of your shots. Of course, none of that really matters now, but I must say, isn't it rather bad form to try to murder your mentor?" Hade finished with a chuckle as he produced a long cigar from under his coat and proceeded to bite off the tip.

Of all the people in the world Victor hated—and that list was rather long—this man was the most despised of all. He hated everything about him: his smell, his bad biker appearance, the tone of his voice, and the fact he somehow managed to appear from nowhere and blend into the darkness as if he weren't really there at all.

Victor shouted with fury. "Mentor?! You are no such thing to me, Hade!" He was so virulent that spit flew across the limo as he spoke. "Now get out of my car this instant! You have no right to be here. I owe you nothing!"

If Hade was listening to Legio's rant, he gave no indication. Instead, he pulled another cigar from within the folds of his black trench coat and held it out to the enraged businessman. When Legio, breathing heavily, made no move, Hade simply shrugged and slipped the cigar back into his coat before pulling out a cheap Bic lighter. He lit his cigar, took a long puff, and then fixed his gaze on the old businessman. "Now, Victor," he began casually, "enough of the theatrics. Here you are, all rich and educated and acting like you're a prince and I'm just a lowly pauper. I tell you, it's as if you've forgotten your roots." He sat back and took another drag on his cigar before exhaling the stream of acrid smoke.

Legio could only sputter. "Out." He was already losing some of his forcefulness as his mind began to ponder why Hade had decided to pay him a visit now after so long. Unfortunately, none of the answers he could come up with even came close to offering consolation.

It was obvious Hade had been having fun with the billionaire, but at this point, his demeanor changed abruptly. He leaned forward in the spacious compartment and his voice turned to ice. "I'll admit that I'm slightly offended by your tone, Victor," he said quietly. "Who's been there by your side, through the good times and bad, helping you when you needed it most? Who kept you out of jail when you were just starting out? Who helped convince the Senate not to pass the law that would have broken your company up? And I haven't asked for much in return, now have I? Considering your net worth and everything you have today, I've actually gotten very little in return for my investment." Hade reached out and patted Legio on the knee. His tone changed once again to the point where he almost sounded jovial. "What do you have to say for yourself, Victor my boy? Can't we all just get along?"

Victor's resolve disappeared. He was a man known throughout the business world as one of the sharpest and shrewdest dealmakers ever. Yet in the presence of this monstrous man, his considerable abilities had been reduced to shambles. "I'm still, I mean, what I want… I don't know what I want. Sure, we can get along. But, what… how did you get into my limo, anyway?"

"You're kind of all over the place there, Vic," Hade pointed out with a condescending shake of his head as he leaned back and threw an arm over the backrest of the seat. "But I can tell you that you're asking the wrong questions. The question you really need to be asking is this, 'What can I do to help you out, sir, before you grow impatient with me and break my neck?'"

"I'm sorry," Legio said quietly. "It's been so long. I thought I had finished everything you wanted from me a long time ago. Of course, I'm still willing to do what's needed," he continued, falling into business mode. "But right now is such a bad time. I've got Paris tomorrow—it's a make or break deal, you know. If you could give me a week or two, I'll help with whatever I can. I give you my word."

Hade stared at Victor Legio for several moments, before breaking into a grin and laughing. "You know, Vic," he chuckled, leaning forward and patting him on the knee again, "I don't think you're hearing me right. I don't think you realize just how much I know about the Victor Emmanuel Legio of today. Add that to what I know about the Victor Emmanuel Legio of the past and you could be the first man in the world to be looking at a four-digit prison sentence." Hade paused to let his words sink in before continuing. "Putting that aside, I feel I should remind you there is nowhere on this earth you could go that I couldn't find you. Now, do you really want to spend the last few days of your life looking over your shoulder waiting for me to kill you?"

Victor, his heart fluttering at the realization Hade could, and probably would, kill him, gave a very slight nod of his head.

"Atta boy," Hade smiled and sat back again. "I'm glad to see we understand each other. It's so important these days, don't you agree?"

Legio said nothing and only stared.

Hade ignored the look. "Now, let's talk business. Today just so happens to be your lucky day, *amigo*. I don't need anything specific other than for you to simply remember that your debt to me is nowhere near paid. I'll give you your precious few weeks, perhaps even a month or more. Go to Paris and tie things up there as planned and then get back to the office."

"And do what?" Legio asked, terrified of the answer.

"I think you already know the answer to that," Hade replied with a grin. "The time has come for you to make sure your business is lined up, in order, and easily run from the shadows. I need it all together in one nice big package with your name written legibly on the card. You can decide if you want to gift wrap it or not, but don't bother with the bow. It's not my style. But it has to be done and it has to be done within the next few weeks. Do you have any questions?"

"Yes," Legio managed to gather up the courage to ask. "Why now?"

"Why now?" Hade repeated, looking bemused.

Legio pressed ahead. "I haven't seen you in seven years and you pop in today, in Brazil nonetheless, and expect me to have everything put together and easily controllable within a few weeks time. It's ludicrous and you know it. I could lose everything trying to do what you ask." Even as Legio finished, he realized it wouldn't matter. Hade always got what he wanted and no amount of persuasion or manipulation on his part would sway the big man.

Hade's voice softened, becoming almost sympathetic. "Oh, I know, I know. You think you can take control of things and people and turn them to your advantage because it's something you do every day. Isn't that right, Victor?"

Legio tried to look away, but Hade's look had him locked up tight.

"What you need to remember, Vic, is that I'm not 'things' and I'm certainly not 'people.' I'm your benefactor, your patron. You might even say I'm your guardian angel. And tonight I've come to let you know the wild ride of Victor Emmanuel Legio is about to end." He smiled and threw his head back, puffing gently on his cigar and blowing the smoke upward so it hung over them like a noxious cloud. "You've been extremely fortunate to have a friend like me in your life, Victor. In the end, if you just do what I say, you might live to tell the tale."

Legio's shoulders slumped down in defeat and his eyes glazed over as if he had finally understood something he had been trying to avoid for a lifetime. He had little doubt as to what his fate would be. He knew that his life was forfeit whenever Hade decided that time had come and the man's sudden appearance today meant that time was fast approaching. "Obviously, from where I stand, things don't look very promising," he said quietly, but with a voice that was steady.

"No, I'd say not," Hade agreed.

"Well, I've lived my life believing any deal can be improved," he went on. "Suppose I do exactly what you want?"

"I would expect nothing less, Victor," Hade replied with a smirk, truly enjoying the banter.

"But what can I do to keep you from killing me afterward? There has to be something you want that would enable me to stay alive."

Hade puffed on his cigar, digesting what the businessman was saying. He knew how good Legio was in the business world and he knew Legio would move heaven and earth to work a deal to save his own skin. Of course, Legio's life was already forfeit, that much was certain. Hade had big plans for Legio when the time came—he had, after all, created him for just such a purpose. But Victor didn't need to know that just yet. A Victor Legio who thought he might live beyond the next few weeks would be a more effective Victor Legio. He smiled widely. "Just be a good boy, Victor," he finally said. "Certainly, your luck has run out for the moment, but that doesn't mean it's completely over for you." The big man switched gears and waved his cigar at Legio as if trying to emphasis a point.

"My good friend Syrus, the Roman poet, once wrote, '*Fortuna vitrea est; tum cum splendet frangitur.*' Fortune is glass; just when it gleams brightest, it shatters. Remember that, Victor, and please, for all of our sakes, be a good boy." Hade took another puff, then waved his hand in a dismissive gesture. "Now, get out of my car." Hade's voice, which had been rather quiet and unassuming during the latter part of the conversation, shifted on the last sentence. It was hard, solid, and it was quietly so forceful that there was no questioning the demand.

Victor Legio, realizing the car was stopped, opened the latch slowly. He gave Hade one last, long look that mixed both hatred and a deep resolve to change the future Hade seemed to have planned for him, before stepping out of the car and into the pouring rain. He shut the door behind him without a word, already beginning to feel the rain soaking through his tuxedo, and watched as the limousine drove off into the deepening night.

For the first time in years, Victor wondered why it even mattered anymore. He immediately stopped himself cold. As long as he was still breathing, it did matter. Stiffening his resolve and holding his hands over his eyes to shield his vision, he noticed a taxi off in the distance and began to walk toward it. Legio allowed himself to smile as the cab pulled to a stop in front of him. Victor Legio was still alive and, right now, that made him a very dangerous man.

CHAPTER 8

30,000 feet over the United States: Father Michael Dalacourt found himself in both the enviable and unenviable position of flying around the world in a 767 while enmeshed in what he felt was the greatest theological occurrence since the resurrection of Jesus Christ some two millennia past. It was enviable because he had time to ponder what was happening and hopefully come to some relevant and important conclusions. It was unenviable simply because his journey removed him far from where decisions were being made and he felt it was a punishment for a sin he hadn't committed. He'd been afforded a great amount of time to think over the unsettling events of the past few days and, as the miles flew by underneath him, he found himself wondering if he'd been wrong about the whole morbid and terrifying episode deep beneath the Vatican.

In hindsight, he supposed he could consider himself lucky Archbishop Francis De Solei had secretly followed him on his ill-thought out errand to see the recently risen Father Oliveira. The Brazilian priest might have indeed been resurrected, but somehow he had gone stark raving mad during the process. Dalacourt winced as he touched the bandage around his neck that protected the healing furrows in his flesh where the dead man's hands had torn at him.

De Solei had proven to be his savior at that moment, pulling him away from the murderous grasp of Father Oliveira. Dalacourt couldn't shake the nagging suspicion that his mentor knew more than he let on, despite his heroics, and therein lay the challenge for the young priest. Part of him abhorred the thought that his advisor might be misleading him, and the other part couldn't be convinced otherwise.

Despite the near tragedy in the catacombs of the Vatican, De Solei still believed Father Oliveira's condition was attributed to something horrendous Oliveira had perpetrated in his life and had yet to be absolved of by God. Dalacourt felt there was something else at work and it was precisely because of his skepticism of the Archbishop's thoughts on the matter, that he was now somewhere high above the United States—penance for his perceived missteps with his mentor.

After the unfortunate incident in the catacombs, De Solei had called him to his office as he was rising for early mass. Upon arriving, Father Dalacourt had walked across the room, knelt on his left knee and kissed the archbishop's ring.

"I bid you a good morning, Father Michael," De Solei said cheerfully. It was almost too jovial and Dalacourt was immediately on his guard. "I trust you slept well?"

Dalacourt lied and nodded his head in the affirmative as he took a seat across from the archbishop's mahogany desk.

"Excellent," De Solei went on with a smile. "We have much to discuss."

"My penance," Dalacourt stated meekly.

De Solei continued to smile. "Let's say I'm certain it will be an interesting morning for you." He slid a file folder across his desk and indicated Dalacourt should take it.

"What's this?"

"A plane ticket," answered De Solei evenly. "There's also a bus ticket, as well as formal instructions regarding protocol. All other expenses will be covered by the church as they arise."

"I don't understand," Dalacourt said with growing dread. "Am I being dismissed?"

"On the contrary, Michael," the archbishop replied. "You're being given an assignment."

"An assignment?" he repeated incredulously. This wasn't at all what he'd expected.

"Indeed. I have decided that, with your desire to discover the truth about what happened with Father Oliveira, you might be given a chance to exercise your sleuthing skills and investigate something seemingly related to what has happened to our dearly departed and now risen Father."

"I still don't understand."

"Allow me to explain then," De Solei answered almost smugly. "I've received a report that several graves in a small town in the United States have been opened. This comes directly to me from Father Thomas Sparrel, who leads St. Michael's Catholic Church in the town of Belle Plaine, Iowa." He paused for dramatic effect. "It would seem these desecrated graves are missing their bodies."

"Grave robbers?"

"I think not," De Solei replied quickly. "I know you are thinking that six missing bodies in Iowa is nothing spectacular, but you must trust me when I tell you this was no ordinary grave robbing. The graves were excavated with precision and the manner of their extraction suggests someone might have had a hand in helping release these individuals." De Solei again paused for effect with his last statement.

"But," Dalacourt struggled, "they're dead."

"Apparently not," replied the archbishop. "I have reports that one individual was seen alive as he walked along a road a full week after he was supposedly buried."

"So you're saying the opened graves mean these people have risen from the dead? How?"

De Solei smiled again. "That is for you to find out, my impetuous young charge," he finally answered.

"But why choose me, Your Excellency? After what I did, why are you asking me to go? Are you not afraid I might discover something that might prove my suspicions are founded and accurate?"

"On the contrary, Michael," De Solei answered easily, "I am sending you because I think you will indeed find the truth you seek and that the truth is exactly what I have been telling you it is."

Michael Dalacourt was silent as he tried to absorb it all. He was aware the archbishop was staring at him, waiting for him to speak. When he finally did, it was to ask, "Where did you say it was again?"

"Belle Plaine, Iowa," De Solei answered, smiling warmly. "You'll be joining Father Thomas Sparrel from St. Michael's. He's expecting you."

That had been two long days ago and Father Michael Dalacourt had used the time since then to think about what was happening. He had to admit De Solei might indeed be right, that the dead might actually be rising and that prophecy was coming to pass. But he still couldn't shake the feeling there was something more going on.

Much more.

CHAPTER 9

Tsarskoe Selo, Russia: Petr Zhugravinsky walked down the sidewalk, his head down and his hands in his pockets. He was as angry at himself as he was with his family. He was due to leave for America and yet here he was—right after he had told his family he was leaving—back at the docks to help his brother, Nikolai, at the behest of his grandfather, Lavrenti.

Muttering to himself and aware there may well be unwelcome eyes on him, he walked past his brother and his cousin, pointedly ignoring them. He knew without seeing that after a few moments, they were following him while continuing their conversation as if nothing was amiss.

Petr continued along the sidewalk that ran the length of the refrigerated warehouse and then turned into an alley that ran between the warehouse and a block of rundown apartments and small shops. He had taken two steps when a powerful arm snaked around this throat and caught him off guard.

"You betrayed us!" the voice of his older brother hissed, tightening his grip.

Unable to breath, Petr didn't panic; instead, he felt his brother's weight pressing forward on him and calmly stepped backward, turned his hip into his attacker, and threw him over his shoulder. It was a simple judo throw, but Nikolai hadn't been expecting it.

Nikolai crashed to the greasy pavement and quickly jumped to his feet, his hand going into his coat. But Petr was faster, his Glock 9 already out and pointed at his brother's head.

"I didn't come here to fight you, Nikolai!" Petr snapped angrily, his voice low so as not to attract the attention of any unwanted ears. "I came to help you!"

"I don't want your help, Petr," Nikolai replied, his voice shaking with fury. "I don't need your help!"

"Nikolai," Vanya cautioned, trying to diffuse the bitter tension between the two brothers, "let him speak."

Nikolai glared at his cousin but said nothing as he wrestled with the violent anger inside him.

Hoping to give Nikolai a few moments to settle down, Vanya turned to Petr, his own voice hardening. "Why are you here, Petr?" he demanded.

"I'm here because you screwed up!" Petr whispered heatedly, slipping his gun back underneath his coat and then jabbing a finger toward Nikolai. "If you aren't careful, you'll both find yourselves in a box."

"We can take care of this ourselves," Vanya continued, but Petr cut him off.

"Don't be ridiculous," he snapped, looking back and forth between the two as if they were children in need of a scolding. "You pursued an unsanctioned kill on three distant relations of our chief competitor and then lost the bodies! You have brought a war to our doorsteps!"

"You don't know that," Nikolai rebutted, but his voice was strained.

"I do know that!" Petr seethed and tapped the side of his head to illustrate his next point. "I know because I pay attention. I've dealt with Dmitri Petrov several times, brother. Mark my words, he'll retaliate."

"It would cause a war," Vanya interjected, trying to sound convincing, but failing. "No one wants a war."

Petr turned his angry gaze on his cousin. "Are you certain of that, Vanya?" he asked. "If Petrov was content to remain away from our holdings, he would never have sent three of his family, distant or not, into our territory."

"A trap then?" Vanya asked, his voice low as the shock of what Petr was telling them began to register.

"A trap," Petr answered in the affirmative.

"This is crazy talk," Nikolai spoke up, trying gamely to defend his actions. "Petrov would not dare go against us."

"He will if he can muster support for what he will claim is retaliation for killing members of his family. Petrov is no Zhugravinsky, but that doesn't mean he's not a formidable foe." Petr stopped and looked around, as if just remembering something. "Where are Sasha and Josef?" he asked, his voice suddenly concerned.

Vanya shrugged and Nikolai began looking around. "They were supposed to be here," he began, but was cut short by the sound of a nearby gunshot, somewhere in the building housing the apartments and shops.

As one, all three Zhugravinsky men had their weapons out and were moving silently toward the rear of the alley, looking for a less obvious entry into the building than through the front door. Vanya was the first one there, pulling open a door and briefly peering inside. The hall beyond was dark and he pulled his head back out of any potential line of fire.

"The shots came from inside, somewhere toward the back," he said quietly as the brothers quickly joined him and flanked each side of the battered metal door.

Before either could reply, there were three more gunshots in rapid succession. At that point, the brothers were moving. They were not untrained when it came to gun violence and their coordinated movement into and down the hallway spoke to years of working together. As Vanya followed them, he could not help but wonder how powerful the Zhugravinsky family would be with Petr at its head and

Nikolai as its chief enforcer.

Moving silently down the gloomy hall, the trio reached an even darker stairwell. Without a word, Petr motioned upward. Nikolai took the lead, cat-walking up the stairs, his gun at the ready. Petr and Vanya followed and they had reached the second floor when they heard voices.

The voices were low—angry and threatening. They were also very close. Nikolai was ready to step out into the hall, but Petr quickly grabbed him by the shoulder. When his brother turned angry eyes on him, Petr merely pointed upward. There, set into the corner of the hall, was an angled mirror. It was filthy, cracked, and in bad shape, but it provided a good view down the hallway. Similarly, anyone in the hall would have a good view of the stairwell, too.

Two things were in their favor: the stairwell they were hiding in was dark; and the man standing in the hall with a gun wasn't looking at the mirror, but rather through an open doorway into an apartment where the angry voices were emanating from. A voice rose in anger, followed by the sound of something heavy smacking flesh. Nikolai stepped around the corner, gun raised. The man in the hall had only a moment to face the newcomers before the eldest Zhugravinsky put a bullet in his head, sending the man flying backward, dead before he hit the floor. More shouts followed and another man stepped into the hallway. He, too, was dead before he could fully register what was happening.

"Vanya, the hallway!" Nikolai shouted, stepping in front of the doorway, his gun leveled. Two more shots and a third man in the room fell dead as Vanya dashed off down the hallway to secure it against any others who might be lurking.

Nikolai stepped into the apartment, gun raised, looking for others and intending to finish it as quickly as possible. He never saw the barrel of a gun flash out of the darkness from a side bathroom, pressing against his head for only a moment. The tell-tale boom of the .45 echoed in the hall and Nikolai fell forward. But the bullet only smashed into the ceiling as Petr, who had been following his brother, had lashed out with own hand, slamming the gun upward so his brother was spared a gruesome and instant death.

Petr followed the deflecting blow and grabbed the extended arm before it could readjust its aim on Nikolai. Holding the arm, he spun forward, letting his momentum pull the triggerman out of the bathroom and slam him into the facing wall. Before the man could recover, Petr closed and drove a knee deep into the man's gut. With a grunt, the gunman pitched forward and Petr deftly plucked the weapon out of his grasp as he fell. The young Russian snapped a kick into the man's face for good measure, rendering him semi-conscious and a definite non-threat.

He trained the gun on the incapacitated would-be killer and Nikolai jumped to his feet. Without bothering to thank his brother, he stepped into the room to survey what had happened. It was a tiny two-room apartment, horribly filthy, with a single flickering bulb hanging from a ceiling that showed more wood than plaster. A dull, green threadbare couch was set against one wall with a broken coffee table lying in splinters before it.

On the floor before them Sasha and Josef lay dead—Sasha with a bullet hole above his right eye that was still trickling blood and Josef with his white shirt soaked with blood, three bullets having turned his chest into hamburger. It was Josef's falling body that had reduced the coffee table to splinters. Sergei lay slumped on the floor as well, his hands bound behind his back and blood running from a deep gash on the side of his head where he had obviously been pistol-whipped. Nikolai knelt down to check on his brother and, seeing him stir and hearing him moan in pain, breathed a sigh of relief. A moment later, he had cut Sergei's bonds and helped him up into a sitting position on the dirty couch.

With a growl of anger, he turned back to the lone survivor who was leaning up against the wall under his own gun, which Petr held at his head. Nikolai glared at his brother, refusing to recognize he had saved his life. Instead, he said coldly, "You are a Zhugravinsky, Petr. Now you may prove it by killing this Petrov garbage."

The brothers locked gazes for a moment, before Petr lowered the weapon. With a deft move, he flipped it around in his hand and then held it out to Nikolai. "The threat is ended," he responded, refusing to allow himself to be baited. "A better message would be sent by allowing him to live, Nikolai."

Nikolai calmly took the gun from Petr and turned it back on the defenseless man. With his eyes still locked with his brother's he lowered the weapon and pulled the trigger over and over again, emptying the gun's bullets into the torso of the man. He never once broke his hateful stare with his brother. "My message is better," he said quietly with as much venom as Petr had ever heard before.

At that moment, Vanya stepped into the room, his gun drawn.

Still staring at Petr, Nikolai continued to speak quietly. "See to Sergei, Vanya," he ordered, dropping the empty gun onto the bloody corpse of the man he had just killed. To his brother, he finished. "You are no longer needed here, Petr," he said icily, brushing past him and into the hall.

For the longest time, Petr simply stood silently, listening to his brother's fading footsteps.

Vanya, supporting a groggy Sergei, stopped momentarily with the youngest Zhugravinsky brother leaning heavily against him. He laid a hand on Petr's shoulder. "He's still your brother, Petr," he said softly.

"Don't judge him too harshly."

"That's not my brother, Vanya," he replied, his eyes scanning the carnage of the room. "That's a monster."

"You could bring him back," Vanya countered, a slight tremor of hope in his voice. "He wasn't always like this."

Petr didn't answer. Instead, he bent down and picked up the gun Nikolai had discarded. Without a word, he pulled out a handkerchief and carefully wiped the gun clean of prints, before pressing it back into the hand of the dead man. Straightening, he looked at Vanya. "Take care of Sergei," he said quietly.

"You won't stay? Even after this?"

"Especially after this," he corrected. "This is not my life, Vanya."

"But it is your family," Vanya scolded. "You would walk out on them even with what Petrov has done here?"

"Nikolai started this war, but he is right about one thing," Petr said quietly. "Dmitri Petrov will get his message."

He walked past his cousin and moved slowly back up the hall. Killing was not unknown to him. He had done it before when there was no other choice. But this? He had seen the demon within his brother. It was the same demon that dwelt within him, one that he carefully controlled. But he also knew that control would always be a struggle and he had to put himself as far away from this life as possible. No, there was nothing for him here. Whatever would be, would be. But Petr Zhugravinsky would no longer be a part of it.

CHAPTER 10

Salt Lake City, Utah: Owen DiConte sat on one of the hard wooden chairs in the Salt Lake City Police Department waiting room, his head in his hands as weariness threatened to drag him down into much-needed sleep. He had been there for two hours, flanked by his equally tired friends, waiting for word from David Sumbawanga, who was still meeting with detectives.

It had been four days since David's son, Gideon, had disappeared. The three friends had spent a good portion of those four days looking for their missing friend in Salt Lake City and the surrounding valley where they thought he might be, hoping they might catch a miracle. Despite everything they hoped, though, they knew it wasn't likely he would be found by a few college friends out looking for him.

Of the three friends who were now waiting in the police station, Owen had been closest to Gideon and felt the loss most sharply. But Luke Jorbo and Clint Reed had known Gideon well enough to call him their friend and it hadn't been easy on them, either. Owen had known Luke since elementary school, and the two had been nearly inseparable all their lives. But as the young men grew older, Luke had begun to dwell more and more on the deeper meanings of life. Since he returned from doing missionary work in Uruguay, he talked more about God and eternity. Old passions such as soccer and the mountains still held a place in his heart, but he was a changed man. At six-foot-three, with a square jaw, deep brown hair and green eyes, it was easy to understand why Luke rarely spent weekend evenings at home reorganizing his closets.

Clint Reed, while not as physically gifted as Luke, could still hold his own in most sporting activities. He preferred to focus on the concrete and sequential aspects of life, which had always consisted of an overall blueprint: finish college, start a business, get married, have kids, live happily ever after. For him, the most important part was to have as much fun within that blueprint as possible. When it came to esoteric conversations, he steered it toward concrete thinking, changed the subject, or turned on the television. He had met Owen and Luke their freshman year at Bingham High School in South Jordan, a suburb of Salt Lake City, and had quickly bonded with both of them. While he wasn't the dreamers Luke or Owen were, his friends broadened his horizons while he managed to ground them just enough. It was a happy medium all the way around.

There was a fourth member of their group who wasn't with them at the police station. Chad Anderson had been absent from the ongoing drama, as he wasn't due back until next week from Great Britain where he'd been studying abroad. When news reached him about Gideon's disappearance, he'd tried to get a flight back immediately, but the thousand dollar switching fee had been too prohibitive.

Chad had met Owen and Luke in the fourth grade when his family relocated from North Carolina. Though not quite as tall as the other three, he was the fireplug who always made life interesting. Rambunctious and energetic, he fancied himself a Blake Edwards' *Pink Panther* Cato-like figure, someone who kept everyone constantly vigilant by surprising them when they least expected it. He was also the brains behind their yearly road trip to San Diego—a trip that was supposed to be coming up very soon. Reality, on the other hand, was close to preventing that trip from taking place this year, and all of them keenly felt it.

Gideon's disappearance was that reality. Up until a short time ago, the prevailing questions had been, "Where is he and what happened to him?" The authorities had not even ruled out Gideon being Chris' murderer, either, and that had been enough to make Owen's blood boil.

It had been four long and torturous days and, while more and more people had resigned themselves to the sad fact Gideon was probably gone for good, his father had arrived from Africa the day before, fully convinced he could find his son. The elder Sumbawanga had stated he wouldn't leave the country until his son had been found, and his fervent love for his only son had affected Owen deeply. Owen had begun this search out of desperation to find his friend. Later, he would realize he was doing it as much for his friend's father, as anyone else.

At first, the official school of thought was it had been a kidnapping. Gideon was projected to be worth millions in the very near future—surely someone had gotten antsy and nabbed him before the big payout, hoping to cash in. Most everyone still believed it was just a matter of time until a ransom call was made and Gideon would be returned unharmed.

Unfortunately, just an hour earlier, the police department had released new information that moved Gideon from being a possible kidnap victim to being a likely murder victim. The new information was soul-crushing.

The door to the conference room opened up and all three young men quickly raised their heads. David Sumbawanga, looking every bit like a man who had not slept for four days, emerged with one of the detectives who had been working Gideon's case. He wearily shook hands with the official, thanking him, and turned to face the three young men. The look on his face said it all.

"They're giving up," Owen snapped loudly, standing up. David quickly raised his hands in the air to soothe the situation, but Owen was faster and stepped toward the detective . "You're giving up, aren't you?" Owen accused him angrily.

The official, an older man with short graying hair and distinguished features, gave Owen a truly apologetic look, before answering. "Look, Son," he explained as patiently as he could. "I know this is your friend we're talking about. But you need to face facts. We're probably looking for a body now."

"Then look!" he challenged, clearly unwilling to back down.

"We will, Mr. DiConte," the detective answered almost helplessly. "We just have to scale back the search for now, at least until we run across something concrete that will give us a clearer idea of what happened."

"It's been four days, not four years," Owen snapped. "Why scale back a search that is only four days old?"

The detective sighed and shook his head. "Look. You've heard the report, right?"

Owen had. They all had. The new information the police had revealed just a short time ago was the presence of blood at the crime scene—a lot of blood. It had been pooled on the ground near Chris' body and had been splattered on the concrete walls and ceiling of the tunnel. Preliminary DNA tests came back showing that the blood was a familial match to the elder Sumbawanga. The police had then held a news conference about the findings and pointed out that, with the amount of blood found at the crime scene, it was impossible for the young man to be alive; Gideon's body had probably lost its entire volume of blood.

"I'm sorry," the detective went on tiredly, "but we've got a rash of disappearances now that take precedence—the governor himself lost two nephews last night, right here in Salt Lake City. We have more Amber Alerts than ever before. We don't know what's going on and we simply don't have the manpower to devote to a single missing person's case right now."

Owen started to reply, but David rested a hand on his shoulder from behind. "It's all right, Owen," the elder Sumbawanga said softly. "The detective is correct."

The detective gave the older man a grateful look and a nod, then quickly hurried away, disappearing into the bustle of the police station that was inordinately busy.

Owen watched him go, then turned to Gideon's father. "So what happens now?" he asked, fighting to keep his frustration under control.

David sat down heavily on one of the wooden chairs. David was the kind of man who caused people's eyes to light up when he entered a room, and Owen had been drawn to him the first time he saw him walking up the steps into the police station some forty-eight hours before. It was easy to see where his son had acquired his intensity and drive.

Today, he was but a shell of that man. He was exhausted and his voice was the quiet whisper of a man who had lost everything. "There is little more we can do, Owen," David answered quietly.

Owen slumped back into his own chair. "So, it's over?"

"The police will continue their investigation in a smaller fashion," David replied tiredly, placing a hand on his forehead as he fought the fatigue himself. "But there's little more you and your friends can do, Owen. It's a murder investigation now."

Owen's anger quickly flared, which was a rare occurrence, but he caught himself just as quickly. Speaking as calmly as he could, Owen said, "I know the valley and can keep looking without getting in anyone's way. Gideon was my friend. He'd do the same if it were any of us."

"And I am his father," David interjected softly, patting him on the shoulder again. "You were a fine friend to my son, Owen, and I am forever grateful. He spoke of you many times in his emails to me. My son wasn't a selfish person, Owen. He wouldn't want you to forget about school, about family, or about other friends. He wouldn't wish for you to lose yourself in this."

"But, he was my friend," Owen started to protest, then shut his eyes tightly as the grief threatened to rise up and overwhelm him.

"I know," David said, his own voice trailing off. He took a moment to gather himself and when he spoke, his voice was slightly stronger as he stood up. "Come, my new young friends. There are still things for us to discuss and I'd prefer to do so while breathing fresh air."

The three followed the elder Sumbawanga out of the police station. They stopped on the steps and waited as David looked up in the sky. It was a bright afternoon, the sun warm but not yet hot. "Your country is indeed beautiful," he said, looking at the nearby mountains that cut their shapes in the skyline. "I can see why my son so loved it here." Turning to look at Owen, he went on. "He had wonderful friends, too, and I'm certain that was no small thing that kept him here."

"Gideon was great," Owen sniffed, looking at his feet. "I just can't believe he's gone."

David walked down the stairs, the three boys trailing him. "None of us are ever truly gone," he said thoughtfully as he walked. "Our loved ones will always be in our hearts, should we choose to let them remain there." He cleared his throat. It was obvious he was attempting to keep his own spirits up, but his grief was still powerfully evident.

"So what will you do?" Luke asked the older man as they walked.

"If I answer truthfully, I believe you might think of me as a hypocrite," David answered with a sad smile.

"You haven't given up searching for him, have you," Owen said knowingly.

"Would you believe I had a vision of my son last night?" He paused and looked at them expectantly. "In it, I was reunited with him."

"You found him?" Owen asked.

David shrugged. "I'm not certain if I found him or he found me," he replied thoughtfully. "It was a strange dream and it left me with more questions than answers."

"So you'll keep looking then?" Clint asked softly.

"There are things I must know," David answered plainly. "It wasn't a pleasant dream and it wasn't the first I've had about him."

"It's happened before?" Luke asked.

"I had a vision on the day Gideon disappeared," he answered. "In it, I saw my son, but he was cast in the deepest of shadows. He wasn't alone."

He stopped on the street corner and turned to face the trio. When he spoke again, his voice was quiet and resigned. "Words cannot express my feelings of gratitude for all of the sacrifices you've made for me and my son. I'm truly grateful for everything you did, but today your toil must come to an end. The police will still search, of course, but it's time you returned to your lives."

"And you?" Owen asked.

David offered a sad smile, then turned and began walking down the street again, the three young college men falling into step with him once more. "In light of the new information the police have shared and the doubts they have that Gideon is still alive, we will hold a memorial service for my son," he replied, his voice cracking just slightly. "Gideon's life was touched by many people. It's only right to provide closure for anyone who wishes it."

For the longest time, Owen was silent. Every emotion ran through his mind and in the end, only one remained—acceptance. "It's odd," he finally said, his voice cracking. "Over the last few days, the same thought has been floating around in my head. I keep remembering the scripture that talks about leaving the ninety-nine for the one."

"You speak of the 'parable of the sheep'," David said quietly. "It's in the book of Luke."

Clint nodded his head as they walked. "That verse never meant for you to leave the ninety-nine forever, Owen. What if a pack of wolves was attacking your sheep and you noticed one was missing? Would you leave all ninety-nine to be slaughtered while you rescued the one? Absolutely not," he answered the question himself. "You've gone after the one, but you have others back at home who need you. What about your family? What about school? What about Alexis?" Clint paused for dramatic effect and then continued before Owen could protest. "If you're not there for them, what will happen? How many will you lose when you have looked so long and hard and still not found the one?"

David smiled. "He speaks the truth, Owen," he said softly. "And unfortunately, the wolf seems to have already claimed my son, so you would likely be searching in vain."

"I know," Owen finally admitted with a sad sigh. "But how do I let this go?"

"Go home and kiss your parents," Luke spoke up. "Tell them you love them, then get some sleep."

"You were a special friend to my son, Owen," David said and turned to face them once more. "Now if you'll pardon me, I'll take my leave here," he went on. "I desire some time to walk and think. The service will be in two days at the Valley View Memorial Park. I have already made arrangements. Will you come?"

They all nodded in the affirmative. "Absolutely, sir," Luke answered for them.

David Sumbawanga smiled sadly. "I had originally envisioned a vigil as we prayed for my son's return. Now I'm afraid it must be a final good-bye. I'll be grateful for your attendance," he said. "May God bless all of you."

The elder Sumbawanga turned slowly and walked down the street, Owen and his friends watching him go. "It's really over," Owen finally said softly.

"I just hope Mr. Sumbawanga finds peace somewhere in all of this," Clint added somberly.

"You know," Owen said. "If I don't get some sleep, I'm going to pass out."

"Yeah," muttered Clint. "I'm with you on that."

"Before we head home, what do you guys think about San Diego this year?" Luke asked, steering the conversation to their long-planned upcoming West Coast road trip. "Chad will be home in a few days. Do you think it's right to still go?"

"I think we should," Clint answered after a thoughtful pause. "We have to go on with our lives. Gideon wouldn't be happy if we cancelled because of him."

"My uncle said we could use his cabin at Fishlake again for some trout fishing in the mountains," Luke added. "I think that would be a good way to clear our heads and recharge our batteries."

"I agree," Owen said. "A night on the lake, a stop in Vegas for some golf and then on to San Diego for a few days of volleyball on the beach are exactly what I need right now."

"Absolutely," Clint nodded.

"Okay," Luke agreed. "I'll Skype with Chad tonight and let him know we're on."

They exchanged good-byes and went their separate ways. As Owen walked toward his car, he considered their loss and what they were all going through. As sharply as they felt the grief as Gideon's friends, he couldn't imagine what David Sumbawanga was going through as a father. Owen shook his head sadly and a tear rolled down his cheek. It was difficult, to be sure. But as his mother had always drilled into his head, despite the trials one must face in life, the sun will always rise the next morning. Things had to get better. He certainly couldn't conceive how it could get any worse.

He had never been more wrong in his life.

CHAPTER 11

Park City, Utah: Windy Covington walked the streets of downtown Park City, Utah, with no particular destination in mind. She was free for the moment with nothing to do and nowhere to go, giving her plenty of time to think.

At five-foot-eight, tanned and fit, with dark brown hair falling well past her shoulders in curls and deep blue eyes, she walked with the confidence of a woman who had been told her entire life that she was beautiful. Dressed in a ridiculously short skirt, an incredibly tight, low-cut red blouse, and her favorite tall, black "hooker" boots, she could be taken for a young college co-ed—or something else. But Windy Covington wasn't interested in any of the looks she was receiving today. She was so calloused and jaded to the effect she had on others that she was nearly blind to it. Underneath her cool demeanor, Windy was anything but just another girl. Her outfit today was chosen out of pure spite for those whose necks would twist to get a better look.

Only twenty-seven, Windy was already filled with the wisdom of decades, and it was that wisdom, and a dark host of experiences, that made her who she was. She hated herself—she hated what she represented and hated what had become of her life. As if to mock her self-hatred, her cell phone began to ring with R.E.M.'s *"It's the End of the World As We Know It"*, interrupting her quiet contemplation and she winced at what it meant. She hated her cell phone, a black and orange Samsung Smartphone that was as much a ball and chain as it was a reminder of when her life had been painfully wrenched onto a road she could never hope to leave. Normally, she wouldn't have hesitated to answer it, but holding it through the lyrics "Six o'clock – TV hour. Don't get caught in foreign towers" gave her a few more precious moments to hate the person calling her.

Before R.E.M. could go any further—she was well acquainted with the severe punishment she would receive if she allowed too much time to pass before she answered—she thumbed the green answer icon and put the phone to her ear.

"Hello, Master," she said, her voice dripping with sarcasm, "how can I be of service to you today?" Whatever hold the man had on her and her life, he could never take away her hatred of him. Sometimes she considered just making him mad enough to kill her outright and free her from her miserable life, but the logical part of her mind reminded her that he had the will and the ability to make her death rather prolonged and agonizing. Despite her own internal strength, she knew she wasn't prepared for that journey, so she took her shots where she knew she could with no repercussions—or at least small enough punishments she could abide them.

"Well, well, aren't we in a good mood today," the voice on the other end answered. "To what do I owe this unbounded happiness? Surely, it isn't anything I've done?"

"It's always something you've done, Master," she replied, skating the edge of an insult.

"Always so full of joy and happiness," he replied, his sarcasm matching her own.

"I've had a great teacher," she countered spitefully and then quickly changed the path of the conversation. Over the years, she had learned just how far she could push him and she had just about reached today's limit. "I assume you have a job for me?" she questioned, her voice turning carefully neutral.

"Not only happy and joyful, but perceptive, too," the man went on, always the one to get the last dig in. "But you are correct, Windy. I do have a job for you."

"When do I start?"

"Very soon," he replied. "You'll need to be in position in two days, so you won't have a lot of prep time. But the upside is that it's a local."

"A local?" she repeated with a hint of concern. That was a first. In the past, her jobs always took her out of state and sometimes even out of the country. To be given a mark here at home wasn't only odd, it was downright unsettling.

"Yes, a local college student," the voice on the other end repeated. "This is actually the very job I've been preparing you for all of these years."

"I find that hard to believe, sir," she dared to say. "I've seduced some of the top minds in the world at your behest. What can some local yokel have over the men I've set up for you in the past?"

"Let's just say you are on a need-to-know basis, Windy," he answered, his voice betraying no hint of anger. "And at the moment, you don't need to know."

"I understand," she replied. "Who's the mark?"

"Slow down a bit, my dear," he said. "I need you to understand this one is special."

Weren't they all? She remained silent, though, wisely refusing to give voice to her thoughts.

"I need you to be in top form for this one, Windy," he continued. "I absolutely need the best from you."

"I've always only given my best, sir," she answered flatly like a good soldier. "This will be no different."

"Good, good," came the reply. "The target is a no-name, Windy, no one newsworthy at any rate. I want him to fall in love with you."

"That shouldn't be difficult," she said, knowing it would be similar to the many others she had worked to the same end. "What approach do you want?"

"The high road," he answered.

"Come again?" she asked after a moment's hesitation.

"This one is different, Windy. He's a good one. He has high standards and ideals, whatever you want to call it. But he's also rather naïve."

"Naïve?" she said, beginning to understand his orders. "Okay, I've done that before. Tougher nut to crack, but I won't have any problems."

"Yes, but you need to be as high road as possible. There is also another girl involved with him. I want you to set up something special between the three of you."

"A love triangle?"

"Precisely," he answered wickedly. "Get him to fall in love with you and begin to question his feelings for this other girl. The messier it gets, the harder they both will fall."

"Am I to understand she's also a mark?" Windy asked carefully. It was rare, but not unheard of, for him to give her targets who she would normally be uncomfortable with. She had no issues whatsoever with seducing men and setting them up for whatever her handler had planned for them. It was a different task altogether when she was asked to set up another female, and it always left her feeling anxious and depressed.

"No, she's to be left alone," he answered.

"I understand, sir. It will be like Moscow."

Three years ago, Windy had been sent to Moscow with the orders to set up a love triangle between herself and the patriarch of a major Russian mob family and his mistress. For three months, she had done just that. Shortly after she had been extracted, the mistress killed the man and ignited a firestorm that eventually took down the whole family and paved the way for a new family to step into the role of leading Russian Mafioso families.

"Yes, you did absolutely fantastic in Moscow," the man said fondly. "The Zhugravinsky family still sits atop the heap, too, right where I want them to be. It was indeed one of your best jobs for me and confirmed to me you could handle what I need from you today. So yes, same scenario, significantly higher stakes."

"Yes, sir," she agreed, wrinkling her forehead in disgust at his praise. Any time her caller praised her, she felt dirty. But she was extremely careful not to let her feelings be known.

"I'm going to send you his dossier," he went on. "Look it over and learn about him. You'll be attending a memorial service for a friend of his in two days."

"Yes, sir."

"You might want to change your clothes, too," he said slyly. "Showing up in that little red number and the hooker boots you're wearing right now isn't exactly 'the high road'."

"Yes, sir," she answered quietly as ice crawled along her spine. She barely kept in check the desire to begin looking around wildly for some sight of her antagonist, but he'd made comments like that in the past and she knew from experience the punishment for attempting to locate him was severe.

"And Windy?" the voice questioned, taking on a final dangerous tone. "I'll broker no failure on this one. Do we understand each other?"

"Perfectly, sir," she answered tonelessly.

Without another word, he hung up. Windy held her phone motionless for the five seconds it took for it to chime with the information her handler sent to her. When the file arrived, she glanced at the name briefly before opening it up.

Owen DiConte.

CHAPTER 12

Belle Plaine, Iowa: The Greyhound bus rolled to a stop in front of a quaint little downtown restaurant called the Lincoln Café, and Father Michael Dalacourt rose from his seat. He hadn't been overly pleased when told he would take a bus for part of his journey, but De Solei had assured him it was appropriate and he didn't feel he was in any position to argue with his mentor. The archbishop was sending his protégé on a fact-finding mission, not a press junket, and thus coming into town by bus would offer the best way of remaining under the radar. Plus, De Solei had said somewhat smugly, in today's difficult economy they should willingly agree to do whatever it took to save the church a little bit of money. Besides, it might be a wonderful opportunity for him to listen to the common people discussing the current plight of the world.

Unfortunately for that idea, Dalacourt turned out to be one of only five people on the bus, and the hour-long trip from Cedar Rapids to Belle Plaine lent him nothing in the way of conversation with the other four passengers, who all seemed to be wrapped up in their own little world. It had been a silent journey and, with a resigned sigh, he let the others disembark first before finally stepping off the bus and onto the curb. He walked leisurely around to the side of the bus and collected his bag before looking up and taking in his surroundings.

It was a charming little town—most locals normally referred to it affectionately as "small town, Iowa". The café the bus had pulled to a stop in front of was closed, and it was only one of a couple dozen businesses on a two-block one-way main street. It was afternoon and, while there were a few cars parked along the street, there was no one else about except for one man who was hurrying down the sidewalk toward him. Judging by the white collar the man wore, the young priest knew who it had to be.

"Father Dalacourt?" the approaching man asked tentatively, extending a meaty hand in greeting.

"That would be me," he responded with a smile, accepting the handshake. "You must be Father Sparrel of St. Michael's."

"That's right," the man replied, darting a quick glance over his shoulder as if he was afraid someone might be following him.

Dalacourt quickly sized up the priest in front of him. He already knew Father Sparrel was the presiding pastor of the tiny town's only Catholic Church and it was his letter that had prompted De Solei to send Dalacourt to meet with him. Sparrel was a short and somewhat overweight man in his fifties, but he had a kindly face and Dalacourt thought him to be warm and pleasant despite his apparent nervousness. "I understand life has gotten somewhat exciting in your little town here, Father," he said reassuringly, hoping to put the anxious man at ease.

"You might say that," Sparrel answered with a thin smile. "But I must confess I don't feel any joy or excitement about what is happening."

"I understand the sentiment completely," Dalacourt nodded, thinking back on his own often-troubled thoughts concerning what was happening in the world today.

"Well, Father," said the older priest quickly, clearing his throat and looking around again. "I imagine you must be tired. I have already procured a room for you across the street at the Herring Hotel. It's not the fanciest place in the world, but it's all we have in town and will at least afford you some degree of privacy."

"Actually, if you don't mind, I'd much rather get started on the investigation," Dalacourt stopped him. "I'm quite rested and there's still light. Perhaps you can take me out to the cemetery and we can discuss matters along the way."

Father Sparrel hesitated momentarily before shrugging his shoulders. "As you wish, Father. St. Michael's is just up the block and I have a car parked there. The trip out to the cemetery will be short."

"That would suit me fine. I find small towns invigorating," Dalacourt replied with a smile, breathing deeply. "They give one a sense of openness."

Sparrel led him across the street and up the block to the church, where a beat-up Lincoln Continental—obviously elegant in its day—sat waiting in the small church parking lot. They got into the car and Dalacourt listened as Sparrel explained the details of what had recently happened. Six graves had been opened in the cemetery over a week ago, holes carefully dug down to the coffins, the caskets then unsealed and opened. The bodies were missing with no trace of them left in their final resting places.

At first, it had been a shock to Father Sparrel, who had officiated at the funeral of four of those people three days after they had been killed in an automobile accident on a nearby highway. It had been a major heartbreak in a town of less than two thousand residents, and the entire community had been affected. But the bigger shock came when someone called the police station two weeks ago and reported they had seen one of the supposedly dead men walking along County Road 131, heading toward Blairstown. The reports could not be substantiated and no trace of the man was found, but it was enough for Father Sparrel to rush a letter off to the Vatican, outlining the strange events.

Sparrel turned the car into the tiny lane that led to the wrought iron gate of Oak Hill Cemetery and immediately stopped. He switched the car off and sat in silence long enough for Dalacourt to read the plain-looking white sign near the gate that warned visitors not to dig up pots or plants.

After a few moments, Dalacourt broke the quiet. "You seem nervous, Father," he said gently. "Is there anything you would like to talk about?"

At that, the priest turned to squarely face the Vatican visitor. "Tell me honestly, Father," he finally said. "What does all this mean? You have been sent by the Pope himself, so you must know something of what is happening here."

Dalacourt offered him a smile. "Actually, I've been sent by Archbishop De Solei, but I assure you he's acting in accordance with the wishes of His Holiness. As far as what's happening in Belle Plaine, all I can say is that's the reason I'm here," he replied plainly. "I would be remiss to say there's nothing going on because we both know that would be a lie. I'm just praying God will open our eyes and let us see this for what it really is, instead of perhaps what someone wants us to think." His last comment was directed as much at himself as it was to Father Sparrel, and again he felt the same cold uneasiness that had been with him for days.

"This is more than simple grave-robbing," Sparrel said flatly. "This is something entirely different."

Dalacourt nodded, pushing his own doubts away for the moment. "I agree with you," he replied. "The missing or the risen dead is more than a little disquieting."

"You have seen this before." It was more of an accusation than a question, and Father Sparrel looked suspiciously at the Vatican's emissary.

Dalacourt smiled warmly and replied with as little confrontation as he could. "You are far more observant than you let on, Father Sparrel," he said. "Forgive me for not being forthright with you from the start. It goes against my own instructions to even say this much to you, but yes,

I've seen this before."

Sparrel allowed himself a momentary look of triumph and then leaned back in his seat and sighed. "So what is the church afraid of?" he asked abruptly, apparently not at all worried about how he came across.

For a moment, the young priest froze, taken aback by the abrupt question. A number of thoughts ran through his mind, and the darker recesses of his brain once again whispered of the possibilities of a grand conspiracy, urging him to be upfront with the older priest. However, not yet ready to fully rebel against his mentor and his explicit instructions, he straightened himself and returned Sparrel's gaze. "Of that, I'm not yet at liberty to say, Father," he answered stiffly. "I suspect you're already considering some of the possibilities and ramifications of having the dead rise and apparently walk away, if we're to believe the reports. Let me assure you, the same questions are being asked at all levels of the church, but let me also point out something else. If this is all truly prophecy coming to pass—and it very well might be—then what does this mean for the rest of the world? Are we in the final days? Is God prepared to pour out his wrath upon the wicked? Before we begin preaching such a thing to the masses, let's be absolutely assured this is indeed what we're dealing with. The consequences of spreading such a message and turning out to be wrong would be catastrophic."

Sparrel looked hard at Dalacourt again, before turning away with a sigh. "As you wish, Father," he said tiredly. "It's obvious to me this is no small matter for the church and I apologize for seeming brash. We have gone through a lot here and I am on edge."

Dalacourt waved him off, attempting to ease the man's deep concerns. "No need to apologize," he said quietly. "For what it is worth, I understand your concerns quite clearly and I share them."

Sparrel offered a weak smile. "I only hope you discover what's going on, Father. This town is already on pins and needles and you know how rumors can be in a town this size."

"I can only imagine," Dalacourt replied with a knowing nod.

Sparrel sighed again and gripped the steering wheel. "Well," he said, turning the conversation to matters at hand, "do you intend to spend a lot of time out here today?"

"Enough that you should go back to town and attend to your duties. It's not far and I can walk back to the hotel after I'm through."

"I'm sorry, Father Dalacourt," Sparrel replied stubbornly, "but I simply cannot allow that. You're here at my request, and as a representative of the church's most holy head. I will return to collect you when you are finished. I insist."

"Very well, then," Dalacourt acquiesced with a sigh, knowing this was an argument he couldn't win. "Give me two hours. I have much to consider." He got out of the car, bid farewell to the priest, and shut the door. Dalacourt watched Father Sparrel pull away before he turned to the task at hand.

He wasn't sure why he'd come to the cemetery first, since he might discover more information from speaking with others in town, but something felt right about being here. Perhaps being out here would afford him the greatest opportunity to silence his own doubts. He started into the cemetery, hoping it would be that easy. He passed under an iron arch and glanced at a stone mausoleum dated 1892, before walking toward a pair of very old white marble tombstones, each with a small flag stuck into the ground nearby. He paused to kneel by the markers for a few moments and knew by the bronze medallions next to each that these individuals who lay resting were military men. The writing on the other side of the tombstones confirmed his thoughts—one was a navy man who had died in World War II and the other was in the infantry and had died on May 1st, 1918, during the

First World War.

Dalacourt bowed his head and offered a silent prayer of tribute to those who had died in wars before and those who had yet to die in the wars ahead, before rising and looking up the hill at the rows of tombstones. Flowers, likely from the last Memorial Day placement, still dotted the grounds and a soft June breeze blew through the trees, giving him a sense of peace he hadn't felt in a long while.

He began walking up the hill, his eyes searching from side to side, but in the end, it wasn't difficult to find the opened graves. Each had a large mound of dirt beside it as well as yellow police tape cordoning off the violated plot. Stopping at the first one under a large family stone with the name Coburn, he stepped over the tape and knelt down at the edge of the hole. He was surprised at how neatly the task had been accomplished. The casket lid had been taken out of the grave and was leaning against a mound of dirt. Peering into the pit, he saw a sheet of heavy clear plastic draped over the open casket and coffin, protecting it from the elements until the authorities could figure out what course of action they needed to take. Standing up, he again surveyed the cemetery.

That was when he saw the old man.

He took a hesitant step toward him. The man was seated on a nearby stone bench, his back up against a tree and his arms folded in front of him. The priest could tell the man was ancient, with sun-browned skin and long, silver-white hair. He wore ragged Levi's and a tattered flannel shirt; a sweat-stained cowboy hat rested on his knees. His worn sandals were propped up beside him and his eyes were closed. He appeared to be sleeping. Dalacourt was stunned he hadn't seen him until just now. He paused, not wanting to startle him, but the stranger spoke almost immediately.

"You're a long way from home, Father Dalacourt," the man said quietly, his eyes still closed as if he were napping. His voice was deep and commanding, but ancient at the same time.

Dalacourt stared in utter amazement. "How would you know that?" he asked guardedly. "And how is it you know who I am? Did the Vatican send you?"

The stranger opened his eyes and fixed them on the priest. He stared long and hard before finally smiling and replying warmly, "I heard about you from Father Sparrel."

Dalacourt felt himself relax. He hadn't been prepared to meet anyone in the cemetery and was even less prepared for such a cryptic opening, but the old man's answer was plausible enough. "May I inquire your name?" he asked, walking up to the man and extending a hand.

The stranger took it and pulled himself slowly to his feet, wincing as he did so. "Call me John," he said as he brushed off the brim of his battered hat and placed it back on his head.

"Are you a local here, then, John?" Dalacourt asked.

"No, I'm not," John admitted, his deeply lined face wrinkling with a smile. "I've come a long way already and I've still got a long way to go."

"And where would that be?"

"Oh, here and there," John answered nonchalantly with a wave of his hand. "Been here in Belle Plaine for a couple of weeks now. Happened to be around for the excitement, too, so to speak."

"It's not every day bodies turn up missing from a cemetery in such large numbers," Dalacourt nodded, "particularly in a tiny town like this."

"Oh, you'd be surprised, Father," John said knowingly as he kicked his sandals flat and slipped his wrinkled feet into them one at a time. "These are strange times we're living in—stranger than most people might think. But you probably already know that."

Dalacourt looked at the man curiously, his eyes narrowing. There was something about the stranger that tugged at him, something almost familiar. "What brought you up here to the cemetery, John?" he asked, trying to get more information, hoping to work some recognition loose within his mind.

"It's peaceful," John replied easily. "And it's a great place to think." He turned from Dalacourt and began walking down the hill at a leisurely pace, heading toward the gate and the road beyond.

Dalacourt watched him for a few moments and then hurried after him. "Wait a moment," he called out. "Where are you going?"

"This way," John said plainly, pointing straight ahead as he walked.

The young priest stopped and watched the man curiously. Something within him was telling him John was important—or at least knew something of the happenings of late.

Before John reached the gate, he stopped, turned, and looked at the Vatican emissary.

"With eight deaths in just the last few weeks here," John said, indicating the cemetery with a wave of his arm, "that's really something for a town this small, eh?" Then without waiting for an answer, he turned and walked through the gates and up the road, heading into town.

Dalacourt watched him go, utterly mystified. The old man's words were cryptic, but his presence was a strange comfort, as if the priest wasn't alone anymore. He couldn't even begin to explain it. For far too long in his life he had felt singled out, alone in his thoughts and duties as a priest studying in the Vatican, and that feeling had intensified recently due to his own rebellious feelings. Now, here was someone who had popped into his life for all of five minutes and Dalacourt suddenly felt more sure of himself than ever before.

What was more important, though, was John's last statement as he had walked away. The significance of the remark wasn't lost on Dalacourt and he began his search again, going quickly from headstone to headstone. By the time Father Sparrel returned to pick him up Dalacourt was waiting, his work complete and his mind racing. The answers, he felt, were now tangibly close.

"Did you discover what you needed to know?" Sparrel asked as Dalacourt slid into the passenger seat and shut his door.

"Father Sparrel," he said, ignoring the initial question. "Tell me about those who died recently."

Sparrel looked at him quizzically before answering. "There's not much to tell really," he finally said as he pulled the car out of the lane and back onto the road. "The four softball players were all younger gentlemen in their mid-twenties. Two of them were brothers—one worked at the sale barn and the other got married about a year ago and has a small farm north of town up near Irving. One of the others tended bar at the Oasis Tavern in town, and the fourth helped coach football and baseball at the high school. That's really pretty much all I can tell you, Father, other than they were good men."

"How did they die?"

"It was a freak accident," answered Sparrel with a sigh. "They were apparently run off the road on Highway 212 just south of town on their way back home from Marengo. They went down an embankment and their car flipped and ended up in the Iowa River. All four of them drowned—couldn't get out of the car. It was tragic."

"I'd have to agree," Dalacourt said softly. "Did the coroner say anything about why they weren't able to escape the car?"

"He didn't know for sure," answered Sparrel sadly. "Funny thing is, if they hadn't ended up in the river, they probably would have all been fine. There wasn't any real damage to the car and no serious injuries that would have kept them from getting out. He thought they probably were either in shock or unconscious and they drowned before they could try to escape."

"So what about the two who died in the fire?" Dalacourt asked, changing the subject. Some of the information De Solei had supplied to him earlier had indicated that a total of eight people had recently died in the small town. A house fire had claimed two of them – a father and a son. "Were their bodies destroyed by the burns they suffered?"

"Actually, their bodies were in pretty good shape and their funerals were open casket. They died from smoke inhalation, plain and simple," Sparrel answered. "They were trapped in the basement and couldn't get out of the house when it caught fire. In the end, the fire burned down everything, but the basement was pretty much untouched. The firefighters got them out of the house alive, but both died on the way to the hospital. It was heartbreaking."

Dalacourt closed his eyes and sighed.

"This is a small town," Father Sparrel continued sadly, his eyes on the road. "When someone dies, the whole town grieves. When six people die, it's too much."

"I cannot fathom how difficult this has been for you," the young priest responded compassionately and he paused before asking his next question. "But that wasn't all, was it?"

Sparrel turned and looked at him quizzically. "What do you mean?"

"Two others died recently, too," Dalacourt said, thinking about the other two new graves he had found in the cemetery, both untouched.

"Oh, you mean Anna Hedge and old Claude Jacobi," Sparrel said with another sigh. "Not unexpected, but no less saddening. And what's even more sad is, with the other six deaths, those two are pretty much overlooked."

"How old were they?" Dalacourt asked gently.

"Anna was in her eighties," Sparrel answered. "Claude was ninety-seven. Both were residents of the Belle Plaine Nursing and Rehab Center."

"Father," Dalacourt begin, trying to phrase his question correctly, hoping not to upset the man further. "Do you wonder why Anna's and Claude's bodies weren't dug up and taken, too, especially since they died about the same time as everyone else?"

"It's difficult enough to try and cope with the deaths and subsequent disappearance of six bodies," he answered almost angrily. "I'm sorry I haven't taken the time to consider why the criminals left two bodies and took six."

"Believe me, I understand," Dalacourt said quietly, reaching over and patting the man on the shoulder. "We'll speak no more of it."

They drove the rest of the way in silence and Father Sparrel dropped the priest off in front of the hotel, a run-down three-story structure that showed signs of new construction. Dalacourt collected his bag from the back seat and entered the building, going directly to his assigned room to try and make sense of his thoughts. It was small and cramped—enough space for a bed, a desk and a television stand, and nothing else. He dropped down immediately onto his bed and pondered things for the better part of an hour before his world was turned inside out.

CHAPTER 13

Salt Lake City, Utah: Owen had never attended a memorial before. Until now, he had counted himself among the lucky few who had never had to bid someone close a permanent farewell. He had always expected his first funeral to be one of his older relatives, not that of a friend. If anyone was to die young, it should have been him and not someone like Gideon, who had the world at his feet. Owen had survived a few near misses over the years and death seemed imminent on several of his adventures. But he had never really given it much thought. Now, someone he knew and cared deeply for was dead and it no longer seemed as trivial.

Owen looked toward the Wasatch Mountains. The aged sentinels wore a blanket of pale-green this time of year. Above the tree line rose gray, granite peaks. Many times throughout his life, Owen could have sworn the mountains had reflected his own feelings. When life was good, the mountains projected a sense of vivaciousness; when calm, they whispered of peace; when difficult, it was easy to see the jagged rocks as dangerous. But today, they appeared oddly oblivious to the goings-on. To Owen, they stood erect and immovable, as tense as soldiers on watch.

Lowering his gaze from the mountains, Owen looked to his two friends walking alongside him. They, too, looked toward the mountain range. One of them, Luke, finally turned his head away from the mountains toward Owen and Clint and spoke. "They look strange today," he remarked quietly, concern touching his voice. "They seem…on edge," he finished, his brow furrowing in thought.

Clint steered the conversation back to the moment, keeping his eyes on the peaks as he spoke. "This will be a good resting place for Gideon," he added somberly. "Until the end of the world, maybe even after, these mountains will stand tall and strong, just like Gideon."

"Then this will truly serve as a permanent place of rest for him," Owen concluded somberly. The thought ate at him, but he didn't have time to focus on it for too long, as they soon arrived at their destination.

The Valley View Memorial Cemetery spanned several peaceful acres inside the city limits. As the three young men approached the chapel, Owen wondered what this event would be like. Having never been to a memorial before, concern over proper etiquette interrupted his attempt to focus on the true purpose of the meeting. Was he supposed to outwardly express his grief and mourn with those who mourn? Or was he supposed to lift the mourners' spirits? Should he just steel his face from emotion and put on a tough front? Growing up in Utah, he had often heard people say funerals or memorials here were notorious for their lack of grief. People rarely wore black to a memorial and it was perfectly acceptable if no one cried at all. Why cry about someone going to heaven? To that, Owen would have to concede the point.

And yet, this doctrine failed to completely settle his heart during this, his first real encounter with death. Owen might have finally let go of his friend, but he still missed him. Perhaps he was being a bit selfish, but Owen felt as if something had died within him when Gideon had disappeared. Whether Gideon had known it or not, he motivated others to focus and work harder toward their own dreams. Now it felt to Owen as if Gideon's dream had died and, if Gideon's dream could die, perhaps his could, too.

Mentally resurfacing from the ocean of his thoughts, Owen noticed he had reached the yard surrounding the chapel. He also looked around and saw he was the only one there wearing a black suit. It was his only suit, but he felt mortified by how out of place he must seem. He looked to his friends and asked, "I'm wearing black. Is that too morbid?"

"I think you've exaggerated the happy Utah funeral," Luke laughed softly, trying to break the tension. Looking at the ground, he continued. "Black is more than appropriate on a sad day like this. You mourn as you need to."

The three young men continued their trek in silence as they topped the last green hill before the chapel, which they realized lay under siege by the media. Several vans lined the streets outside the building, each with a satellite on its roof and cables that spilled from its doors. Men and women scurried to and fro, jockeying for the best position to film the people entering the ceremony. Some stood on the sidewalk, silently daring any competing crew to wander onto their turf. Tripods with screens littered the lawns, along with reporters holding microphones and rehearsing scripts. On occasion, the reporters would spot a mourner of importance and descend on him or her like vultures to the fresh kill. While the young men had realized their friend was special, they hadn't realized just how newsworthy his demise had become.

Walking the last few steps toward the chapel, the men each tensed up and hoped nobody would notice them. *Just leave us alone and let us remember our friend*, they thought collectively. Each of them walked deliberately toward the front door, staring at their own feet intensely enough to burn holes in their shoes. Thankfully, the members of the media paid them no mind.

A large man in a black suit stood at the doorway, keeping the media out. Not a single wrinkle disturbed the dark brown skin of his face. It looked like carved and polished stone. In contrast to his face, his suit bore many wrinkles where his massive muscles threatened to erupt from beneath the fabric. His gaze locked on the approaching young men. Stepping aside, the man welcomed them with a voice as resonant and low as a cello. Owen, for his part, was just thankful to see someone else at the memorial dressed in black.

Passing through the chapel doors, they relaxed in unison. The tension in Owen's shoulders relented, his jaw loosened, and he unclenched his fists. He continued to walk ahead. At first glance, the pews in the chapel were quickly filling to capacity; a dull murmur of lowered voices surrounded them. All of the friends common to Gideon and Owen sat in the middle pews. Behind them sat Gideon's teammates. Owen knew most of them. All of them gave the three young men forced smiles and quick nods.

"Looks like we're sitting here," Clint had stopped just inside the chapel doors and nodded toward the last bench, which was one of the few that still had places to sit.

The three of them seated themselves and Owen quickly cast his gaze forward. Gideon's father, David, sat in the front of the chapel in the first pew. In the year Owen had gotten to know Gideon, he had shown Owen only one picture from his past. That picture revealed nothing of the place where he had lived, only the blue sky and his father's smiling face—a face Owen had come to respect over the past several days. As David Sumbawanga finally stood and climbed the three stairs to the pulpit, the low drone in the chapel silenced. With his hands clasped behind his back, he addressed the crowd.

"I welcome you on behalf of my son and your friend, Gideon Sumbawanga." His voice transmitted a sense of peace and reassurance. To look at him, one couldn't help but compare him to an ancient tree. His skin, creased with age, resembled aged bark. The thinness of his limbs gave the impression of leafless branches, but he stood as firm as a tree whose roots held strong. There was no denying the strength that lay within him.

As he spoke, talking about his son in happier times, Owen cast his eyes over the congregation. Among the attendees, Gideon's old college coach from Montana sat in the third row, closing his eyes so tightly his eyelids were a stark white and nodding so enthusiastically that his whole body rocked. He had practically adopted Gideon and Owen knew he must have felt a suffering akin to Gideon's real father.

Behind the coach sat rows of athletes, coaches, and professors who knew both Gideon and Chris—whose own memorial would take place in two days. The professors had rallied behind Gideon as the poster boy for student athletes. Whenever possible, they had used Gideon as the perfect example of an athlete pursuing his degree during the orientation meetings for the incoming athletes. Owen had always supposed Gideon's dedication to his studies derived from an inner desire to be a complete man. Now, after having met David, Owen decided any young man with a father like that would strive to be great at everything.

Finally, his eyes arrived at the pew just ahead. Five persons to his right, a young woman caught his attention. All heads to her left and right nodded with the lullaby of David's voice, while her own rested motionless on a swanlike neck. Dark brown hair wrapped behind her head into a bun, with several short wisps of hair straying downward. It was all held in place by a vertical black pin pointing downward along her neck to a black silk dress. Her gaze, oriented slightly to her left toward the exit, gifted Owen with a view of her profile. It was just enough for him to notice her luminous blue eyes. Owen had only seen blue like that one other time in a picture of a glacier some thirty-five meters thick, but just thin enough to transmit light, where the layers of transparent whiteness had refracted the light into a blue, crystalline glow.

Owen openly stared at the girl, David's words fading into the background of his mind. Almost immediately, he felt stabs of guilt from looking at her that way. He noticed her turn slowly in his direction. Immediately his heart pounded and catapulted adrenaline-laden blood throughout his body. Reflexively he bowed his head and fixed his eyes on his hands. With the adrenaline still rushing, he silently berated himself for staring so long she had almost caught him looking.

Eternal minutes passed. Owen counted to a hundred three times, each time telling himself that at one hundred she would have turned her head back to the front and couldn't possibly be looking in his direction. A fourth time he made the same promise. By the count of fifty, he began to notice an interruption in the rhythmical oration. The interruption came from the mourners. Owen lifted his eyes and saw a change overcoming the people surrounding him. One by one, several members removed handkerchiefs or tissues, lowered their head, and let the tears flow. Some cried audibly, some silently. Many appeared comfortable with their show of grief, while others stifled it and sat perfectly erect, their eyes on David as they hardened their facial features against the perception of weakness that a show of tears would become.

It was then David's final words penetrated Owen. "In the end, Gideon courageously followed his dreams. He aspired to unite his dreams with reality. Those dreams arose from the heart of a wide-eyed, adventurous boy—thus the source of our devotion to him. We love him because we hope to be like him. The purest and deepest longings of our hearts plead with us with every beat from the time of our childhood." His hand rose to his chest as he continued. "They tell us, 'Follow your dreams, follow your dreams.'

"To truly honor Gideon, I challenge each of us to emulate him. By honoring him in this way, we shall live fuller lives and perhaps inspire others as Gideon inspired us." He finished and rested his aged hands on the podium. The grain of the podium's wood blended with the contour lines of David's skin. As if David also noticed the blend, he took a long, silent look at the podium. Then, placing his hands behind his back, he lowered his head and descended the stairs.

A lake of tears threatened to erupt from Owen. The constricting pain in his throat returned. Owen clenched his jaw and suppressed his emotions. *I'm glad you're in a good place*, he thought, wondering if Gideon could hear him. *But I miss you, man.*

As he tried to keep the tears in, he noticed for the first time an open door to his left, and saw, directly through the opening, his friend Alexis, sitting in the chapel's foyer. He looked away from her quickly, for some reason not wanting her to see him cry.

Alexis Kennedy missed Owen's quick glance, which was peculiar seeing as she had been staring at him for most of the oration. Having arrived late, Alexis hadn't been disappointed to be relegated to the foyer as she felt uncomfortable attending the memorial of someone she hadn't known very well. While she'd been surprised and pleased at the strength and intensity of David Sumbawanga's words, and she was sad for the loss of his son, she'd truly come to the memorial in a show of support for Owen.

Owen and Alexis had met the year before in a chemistry class attended by three hundred students, almost all of whom wanted to be doctors, dentists, veterinarians, or scientists. Among that sea of aspiring professionals, nerds, over-achievers, and class clowns, they had found each other in the back row. They both preferred the back row, but for entirely different reasons. Alexis preferred it because professors noticed more when people participated from the back. Owen preferred it because he had a habit of falling asleep in class.

One fortuitous day, Owen nodded off in the middle of a lecture as he normally did, and dreams of playing volleyball filled his head. In this particular dream, his setter gave him the most beautiful set in recorded history. As he jumped to hit it, he realized this spike would seal the gold medal for the U.S.A., so he struck the ball with everything he had. In moments like those, when the mind loses itself so blissfully in its imaginings, it sometimes fails to disconnect fully from the living body, and Owen's entire body jerked as if spiking the ball.

His arm slammed the desk, sending his papers and pen flying through the air. Sitting next to him, Alexis witnessed the whole thing and harnessed every ounce of strength she possessed to keep herself from bursting out laughing. Looking at Owen, she recognized that look of confusion most people exhibit when waking from a particularly deep sleep. Then she saw Owen's face change, his eyes focus, and a broad smile light up his face. Ignoring the irritated glances from most of the rest of the class, as well as the professor, he looked at Alexis with a wink and said simply, "We won the gold."

"What?" Alexis' nose wrinkled and her eyes narrowed in question as she bent to help him pick up his things.

"In my dream," he explained in a happy whisper as if it should be the most logical thing in the world. "I spiked the ball that won the gold medal."

Though he never knew it, Owen had captured part of Alexis' heart by sharing his dream with her that day. She felt drawn to the college student who could still dream like a young boy. From that point on, they would always sit together in the back of the class. Alexis gave herself the mission of trying to keep Owen awake every day in class and, to his own credit, Owen tried hard to stay awake so Alexis could pay attention to the lecture instead of to him. On her way to the memorial today, Alexis had tried to convince herself she was going in order to keep Owen awake during the eulogy. He needed her, after all.

Alexis knew he thought of her as his college buddy, the girl who once brought sour candy to class in an attempt to keep him awake. She also realized if she didn't want to get hurt, she couldn't hope for more. Over time, others had tried to convince Alexis otherwise. Her girlfriends claimed to see sparks flying between the two when they spent time together. They even went so far as to say Owen had come close to asking her out several times. Thrilling chills surged through Alexis every time she heard such comments, but so much time had passed without such an event that she had begun to lose hope.

A brief urge to play with her hair emerged again, only to be quenched by the movement of people who had been finally released from David's entrancing speech. As everyone began to leave the chapel and make their way outside, Alexis tried to find someone she knew to walk with. Owen and his friends had disappeared quickly outside and so, after a few minutes of milling around without finding anyone else, Alexis decided she might as well walk by herself.

As she walked, she kept an eye out for Owen, hoping to find him so she could let him know how sorry she was for his loss. She wanted to be strong for him, so he could cry if he wanted and wouldn't feel the need to console her. She smiled for the first time all day at the thought that perhaps it wouldn't be so bad if he consoled her. In fact, she thought to herself, it might not be that bad at all.

The service was followed immediately by those awkward moments where no one knew exactly what to do or say. Eventually a line formed of people who wanted to say one last good-bye to Gideon and one more, "I'm sorry for your loss," to David. As people made it through the line, they broke up as if on cue into small groups.

A voice sounded softly behind Owen. "From laughing to deep in thought at the drop of a hat; now that's a complicated man." The musical voice and laugh that followed were unfamiliar to Owen, so he ignored them, but the voice continued. "Chris told me all about you, Owen, but he never hinted you were complicated." The laugh came again.

Owen turned around and noticed her—the same beauty that had captured his attention in the memorial chapel. With her blue eyes looking at him and the most inviting smile imaginable, she stood in front of him. Excitement washed over him and he tried to look without staring, thrilled that she had initiated the conversation herself. At least he was sure she had said his name. Owen tried his best smile, a smile he hoped made him look confident. He held his hands behind his back, which he always considered a relaxed look, but also one of self-control. "Hi, I'm Owen," he said and immediately regretted it. No points for creativity, he thought sheepishly.

The attractive young woman laughed again as if she knew exactly how Owen wished to present himself and also knew he was failing miserably. "I know who you are, as evidenced by the fact I called you by name," she went on as she extended her right hand with a warm smile. "I'm Windy, a good friend of Chris'."

Owen grasped her extended hand. Goose bumps immediately covered his arm as he felt the soft skin of her slender hand in his. "Sorry, what was your name again?"

"Windy, as in the cool wind blowing across your body on a hot, summer evening." She paused, noticed her words had had the desired effect of completely dumbfounding him, and continued. "I'm sorry if I bothered you, but I don't know anyone else here and was feeling a little out of place. When I saw you standing here, looking as lost as I felt, well, I thought I'd solve both our problems." As she talked, her gaze dropped to her black satin shoes and her feet shifted so she now stood with her legs crossed.

If Owen believed what his psychology professors had taught him, he would say she was lying or at least not telling him the whole truth.

Then her feet resumed their original position, but her eyes looked even more intently to the ground. "Okay, I suppose that's not the whole truth," she admitted as if she had read his thoughts. "To be honest, I've seen you playing volleyball with Gideon a couple of times in the past. I asked Chris if he knew you and he said he did and you were a really nice guy." Finally, she raised her eyes to meet Owen's again and that disarming smile reappeared.

All of this was too unbelievable. The gorgeous woman standing in front of him had actually been asking about him and this had stunned him. The clever words that stood just beyond his reach before, now stood on the other side of the world. Thankfully, Windy saved him from himself.

Her eyebrows rose slightly and her tone became more serious, "I'm sorry for the loss of your friend, Owen," she said softly. "Chris was my only real friend. He stuck with me when nobody else would and now I'm left with no one to turn to." She paused and looked hard at the ground. "I'm sorry," she said quietly. "That must sound so selfish. The world has lost two kind young men and I'm feeling sorry for myself."

This revelation sent stabs of shame through Owen. This poor girl was mourning the loss of her only friend and Owen was pondering how he looked to her. She needed more than his clever words here, but silence ensued as he continued to struggle with his vocal chords. Windy looked expectantly to Owen and he replaced his confident smile with a sincere one. Caught between shame and the desire to say something helpful, he said nothing.

The silence stretched.

Windy inhaled deeply. "Well, it was nice to have finally met you, Owen," she said, her voice one of someone who was trying to salvage a tiny bit of dignity in a conversation gone horribly wrong. She stepped to the side and started away. Watching her leave with her shoulders held gracefully back, desperation squeezed Owen with a suffocating grip. Each beat of his heart pleaded, *Say something! Say anything!*

"Maybe the best way to honor him would be to help others as he helped you," he finally stammered. The pounding of his heart quickened, ecstatic he had heeded its plea, and Owen felt relieved to discover he could indeed speak. But most of all, he was thankful the woman stopped. Perhaps he had said the right thing. She turned her head. Encouraged, Owen humbly offered more. "You thought your feelings toward Chris were selfish. Well then, turn them into something selfless. Help someone lonely, like he helped you."

Her gaze sharpened and stripped him of his confidence and he decided he had better stop talking before he ruined what appeared to be an acceptable offering to that point. After a brief moment, Owen noticed tears building in Windy's eyes. To his surprise, she steeled her features, blinked her eyes rapidly, and collected herself.

Her smile returned and chased away any remnant of tears. "So you're as smart as he said, too. Thank you for your insight and understanding. I'll bet people like you never need pep talks like this," she said softly. Then, without another word, she turned and walked away.

Owen's heart wished to follow her, but something caused him to hesitate. Part of his indecision was his attraction to her mixed with a genuine concern, but that wasn't all. In five minutes, she'd managed to strike him dumb with her beauty and evoke heartfelt advice from him. She coaxed from Owen the desire to protect her, but at the same time made him feel vulnerable. His heart slowed and the dialogue of the groups around him penetrated his consciousness. He saw Luke and Clint returning from their conversation with David and with a sigh, moved to join them.

As Windy walked away, she hoped her anxiety hadn't shown. Reviewing her encounter with Owen, she cringed. Her decision to leave had come from panic, something she still felt occasionally when she was losing control of a mark or a situation. Failure in this case could cost her life, or worse.

As she slipped through the crowd of mourners, she examined the previous conversation to discover how Owen had reversed the situation and placed her at his mercy. He was handsome, but that wasn't it. She had dealt with handsome men on more than a few occasions. It was his silence, she quickly concluded. His silence was powerful. From within the cocoon of that silence, he had bored through her with his deep brown eyes. Without a look of overt suspicion, he sifted her statements for truth and saw the lies. That silence forced her to admit to some of the lies and the intense scrutiny made her story sound flawed. She feared he would detect too many

The sincerity with which Owen had spoken penetrated her aching heart, threatening to thaw some of the ice that had formed around it over the years. He genuinely wished to help her. At that point, her eyes, dry from exhausting her store of tears years earlier, found a new source. She wanted to slap him for that, but even more, she wanted to condemn him to a fiery pit for the last statement he had evoked from her. That wasn't part of the script. All she had heard about Owen's charisma proved to be true. Another first.

The strains of R.E.M.'s infuriating song started up in her purse, surprising her and quickly bringing her back to reality. Windy's muscles tensed, her nerves prickled, and her sultry sway turned to a hurried walk. She had to answer the phone immediately, but she couldn't do it here, not without having first ordered her thoughts on her encounter with Owen. When she couldn't bear the stress any longer, she slid her finger across the screen and spoke in measured tones: "I can't speak now. Call me in twenty minutes." The phone quickly went dead and she felt a pit of terror open up within her as she shoved it back into her purse.

Dread from knowing the future consequences of what she had just done began to suffocate her. She saw a bus pulling up to a stop across the street and without looking to see its destination, she waved to the driver to catch his attention. The bus slowed and she quickly crossed the street to board it, safe for the moment. She knew, though, that safety would be fleeting.

From a distance, Alexis caught sight of the young woman getting on the bus. She shook her head. *Can't even go to a memorial without taking a business call*, she thought. If there was one thing about Salt Lake City Alexis knew, it was the town was full of people just waiting for their chance to make it big in the world of business.

Alexis consciously forced her mind back to the memorial. Approaching the group surrounding David, she recognized Owen's friends Luke and Clint. Both of them were conversing at length with David concerning the nature of God and the afterlife. Looking around, she realized there were still other groups waiting for their opportunity to speak with David and her chance of even offering her condolences was next to nothing. She also realized that, despite all her efforts on this day to support him, Owen hadn't noticed her. She drifted toward the exit but turned and looked one last time at the group surrounding Gideon's father. Frowning, she left the memorial and headed to her apartment.

Owen looked up in time to see Alexis departing and mentally kicked himself for not going over to her earlier. He could have, had he not bumped into Windy. But by the time she had left, it was his moment to talk with David and now Alexis was gone. If only he had the nerve to tell her how he really felt about her, she might say she felt the same way. His friends had continuously told him it was better to find out for sure than to kill himself worrying. Of course, that was easier said than done. Besides, how could he tell her he had eyes only for her when he had become so quickly awe-struck by Windy? No, he decided, he had a bit more growing up to do before he was ready to risk actual feelings on Alexis.

Fortunately, his mind was removed from the impossibilities of love when Clint grabbed his shoulder. "Come on, dreamer," his friend said. "Let's get going."

"What's wrong?" Luke added, noticing Owen's saddened expression.

"Nothing," Owen said and forced a smile. "Just thinking about Gideon." It was a lie, which made him feel worse, but he wasn't about to bring up his conflicting emotions for Alexis.

Clint smiled. "We all miss him, Owen. But I don't think Gideon would want us to starve, and I'm famished. Let's go get a bite to eat."

"Is food all you ever think about?" Owen asked, and this time the smile wasn't forced.

"When I'm not thinking about girls? Yeah," Clint said with a mischievous grin.

Owen sighed and shook his head, but it was a sigh of relief as he let the pain of the past week fade slightly. He was truly glad to have his friends with him. He draped his arms across the shoulders of Luke and Clint as they walked out to Clint's car, sparing one last glance up at the mountains. The jagged peaks standing sentinel over Gideon's spirit were still silent and foreboding. With a slight chill, he realized he would never again see those mountains quite the same.

CHAPTER 14

Salt Lake City, Utah: Petr stood alone in his small apartment bathroom, looking at himself in the vanity mirror. He still could not get over how different he looked without his goatee. In a world of power relationships, a young man needed to appear older than his actual days and his facial hair had accomplished much for him in that regard. But after days of deliberations, Petr had resigned himself to the fact that he needed to shave it off to make a break with his past. He was now regretting it. "I look like I'm fifteen again," he grumbled.

As his coal-black eyes reflected back to him in the mirrored surface, he wondered if he had chosen wisely in all of this. Was it truly the best decision he could have made? Or was he the greatest fool of all time? To throw away money and power was one thing, but to do so while throwing away one's family was perhaps too much. *Time will tell if I chose correctly*, he thought to himself.

He combed through his jet-black hair one last time and walked into his living room. He still couldn't get over how small the room was. He had never lived anywhere so tiny, so dirty, and so dark. It was only one step up from a hovel and not a very big step at that. He reminded himself as he put on his shoes that he should never have agreed to live in university housing. They had been persistent, though, explaining how it was in his best interest to live close to campus and that as an international student he was required to live in the dorms his first year.

It had seemed like a weak argument at the time, but he didn't have the desire to fight the university over it and perhaps lose his spot in the program. So he had stuck it out, believing the housing department's words that he would save a fair amount of money by living in purgatory. Of course, he might still have gotten a different living assignment if he had known what he didn't spend on rent he would make up for on bug killer to get rid of all of his uninvited houseguests, and electric fans to cool himself in the absence of an air conditioner.

With a sigh of acceptance, Petr slung his new, green backpack over his shoulder and tried not to slam to door as he left. He walked the short distance from his room to Morrill Hall where his class would be held, arriving a few minutes early in order to make a good impression. His algebra class had already met at eight that morning, which made for a horrible six-week's schedule of classes at eight a.m. and six p.m. His morning class had been interesting, but mostly because he was one of only two students in the room. The other was a forty-five-year-old truck driver who hadn't actually signed up yet because, as the man claimed, the computer had said it was full. Technically, that made Petr the only student. It came as no surprise that class let out after five minutes so the professor could find out what had happened to the rest of his students.

As Petr walked into the relatively small room that evening where his English class would be held, he noticed it looked like a repeat of the morning. Once again, there was only one other student in the room. This time, however, it wasn't an older truck driver, but a younger female student. Petr could only shake his head and wonder again if he had made the right decision. After sitting down, getting his paper and pencil out and looking one last time at his schedule to make sure he was in the right room, he glanced up at the young woman sitting a few rows in front of him and wondered if perhaps he should say something to her. The instant this thought entered his head, his hands started sweating and his heart kicked up a pace or two, which was odd in that he had never experienced that kind of a sensation with any other girl. Perhaps it was simply that she was an American and therefore a relative unknown aspect of this strange new country. With that thought firmly entrenched, he calmed himself and spoke.

"Strange, isn't it?" he said, leading with a question he hoped would prompt an answer. He'd never talked to an American girl before and noticed his voice had slightly wavered. Worse, his hands were still clammy, and the girl hadn't even turned around to look at him. Perhaps she hadn't heard him or maybe she was simply ignoring him, so he cleared his throat a bit and somehow managed to repeat his statement. This time, she turned her head toward him, but still didn't look directly at him. She answered Petr's question with one of her own.

"What's strange?" She seemed somewhat preoccupied, giving Petr an unclear signal as to whether she was uninterested in him in particular or just had something else on her mind.

The first thing that struck Petr was how beautiful she was. She was of slight build with a fair complexion and medium length sandy-blonde hair.

"Strange we're the only ones here," he said, hoping he wasn't sounding foolish.

She was still looking in his direction, but hadn't made eye contact. "I suppose so," she replied, her voice sounding impatient. "Personally, I'm not very happy to be in this class at all. I found out just last week that an AP English class I took back in high school no longer counts for college credit, so here I am, retaking the course so I can get into med school. It's so ridiculous."

To Petr, she looked as if she was either going to start crying or heave a chair through a window, neither of which had been the response he had been hoping for.

"Med school, eh?" he finally said. "That's really great. I know several doctors back home." He paused and tried to think where to take the conversation, but drew a complete blank and fell silent.

"I do wonder where everyone else is at, including our teacher," she went on. "This is the right room, though, isn't it?"

Now she was looking directly at him. She didn't show any signs of becoming either impressed or disgusted with him, so he responded carefully. "Yes, I think it is. The same thing happened to me this morning. I'm in an algebra class at eight and it was just me, the teacher, and some truck driver who wasn't even signed up for the course."

"You're in that class?" She asked, a little more animated now. "Wow, what a coincidence! I have to take that one, too, for the same reason I'm in here," she finished, wrinkling her nose in distaste. "How lame is that?"

"That's great to hear," Petr began, but caught himself quickly.

"Yeah, well, I wasn't there this morning because I was at a gathering with a few friends," she said with a sad smile. "So it's just the two of us then?"

Petr couldn't believe his luck. The first American girl he had met here in the States had turned out to be not only beautiful, but in both of his classes. Perhaps he would rethink his sinking appraisal of America. "Yeah," he answered, smiling. "But at least there was a teacher in that class. I don't know where this one is."

She spared a look back to the front of the classroom and then turned to him with a shrug. "So, what'd I miss this morning?"

"We got out of class early so you didn't miss much at all, other than the professor," he replied. "He looked like a wild man just introduced to clothing for the first time. I've never seen an outfit so bizarre in all my life." She laughed, which was a good sign, and Petr allowed himself to relax. Her eyes were bright and her obvious disappointment at being in the class had vanished.

"Sounds like I missed out! I'll be there tomorrow, though."

"If you want to, you can look at the syllabus," he offered. "I managed to grab one off of the professor's desk after he left."

"Sure, I'd love one," she replied, so Petr dug into his bag, fumbled through his papers and handed it to the girl. That's when he noticed her expression had changed once again.

"You know, I think I should apologize," she began, surprising the young Russian. "I can't believe I just went off like that a minute ago about being in this class. I don't even know you and here I am complaining about the injustice as if you were a psychiatrist or something." She paused, looking pensive, and then asked, "You're not studying to be a psychiatrist, are you?"

Petr smiled, thinking this girl couldn't have offended him if she had picked up a two-by-four and hit him in the face with it. "No, no," he said quickly. "I actually want to be a writer. But don't worry about feeling upset about your situation. I know exactly what you're talking about. In fact, if you can believe it, I'm doing the same thing."

"Really?" she looked genuinely shocked.

"Yes," he answered. "The university here doesn't think a class taught in Moscow by a visiting professor from Oxford about English literature qualifies toward my English requirement, so here I am, the victim of bureaucracy just like you."

"I'm sorry for asking this, but I just have to. Are you from Russia?"

"*Da*, I'm from St. Petersburg," he said with a grin.

"That's great! I should have been able to tell with your accent."

Petr felt his smile fade a little. "Is it so obvious?"

"Don't worry about it," she soothed, understanding she might have touched a sore spot. "You speak excellent English and you're probably easier to understand than some Americans."

"Well, that's a relief," he said, relaxing again.

"I wish I spoke Russian as well as you speak English," she went on. "I only know a little bit."

"Really," he answered. "Say something to me."

"*Zdravsuitasya. Kak vas zovut?*" she said with a shy smile.

"*Menya zovut* Petr. *Kak vas zovut?*"

"*Menya zovut* Alex. Well, it's really Alexis, but everyone has called me Alex or Lex since I was a baby," she went on, smiling warmly. "Unfortunately, that's all the Russian I know. I had a friend in high school whose mother was from Russia and he eventually taught me a few words, but that's all I can remember. Oh, I can also say, *Da, eto dom.*"

"You just said, 'Yes, that's a house'," Petr said, laughing. "Very impressive!"

It was at that moment their professor walked in. The woman more or less fell into the room clutching a stack of crumpled papers and murmuring under her breath in some unknown language. She appeared quite startled to see only two students. She pulled herself together as quickly as possible, but it was obvious she would need a bit more time to recover from whatever she had just been through.

"Good evening," she said tiredly, running a hand through a tangle of dark hair. "Sorry I'm a bit late, but my computer crashed right before class. I'm rather surprised it didn't burst into flames and explode. I lost everything and I'm afraid I'm a little unprepared." She looked around the room. "Did everyone else leave?"

Petr responded, "Um, no ma'am, we're it. No one else has even come into the room."

Alexis nodded in agreement and the instructor looked as if the last straw had just been tossed onto the camel's back.

"You're kidding me," she said almost bitterly. "I have a class list with twenty-six names. This is the right room for English, isn't it?" When both Petr and Alex nodded in agreement, she went on, her agitation growing. "Well, that's what I thought. Okay, guys, I suppose there isn't much for us to do here today. I don't have any notes, and there's only the three of us. Why don't I get your names, I'll give you a syllabus, and we can try again tomorrow. Hopefully we'll have a few more students by then."

Five minutes later their professor was gone, presumably to yell at some poor, unsuspecting secretary tucked away in a basement somewhere, and the two students found themselves walking out of the building together.

"Are all American college professors like that?" Petr was asking, still shaking his head at the oddness of the day.

"No," Alexis answered. "Most are pretty decent, if tough. Sometimes, though, when they get out there, they really get out there, if you know what I mean."

"I suppose so," the Russian answered thoughtfully.

Alex chuckled as she looked over the syllabus for a bit and then turned to face Petr. "You know, it seems like there's going to be a lot of group-work in this course. If it's just the two of us and we want a decent grade, looks like we'll be spending a lot of time together. Maybe we should get each other's phone numbers and e-mail addresses."

Petr knew it was only for scholastic purposes, but was still thrilled at getting the contact information of a beautiful American girl. "That sounds like a great idea," he replied with a smile. "By the way, where are you walking? Maybe we could go somewhere for a drink and get to know each other a bit before class tomorrow." His heart sank a bit when Alex shook her head.

"Thanks, but I don't really drink," she answered.

He had heard there were many people in Utah who didn't drink alcohol, but he'd never assumed that included cute college girls. "I apologize," he said quietly. "Things are much different here than in my native country."

"Don't worry about it," she consoled him with a genuine smile.

"I'm pretty tired. I know it's early, but it's been a really long day and I've got to get some sleep. Maybe tomorrow morning we can get together after class and get some breakfast?"

"That sounds great," he said, brightening considerably. "I suppose it's time to brave the descent to my own humble home. I imagine the descent to hell wouldn't be much different."

"Sounds brutal," Alexis replied. "Where do you live?"

"On 4th South, at the bottom of the hill near the bagel shop. I'm in number twenty-seven."

"Shut up!" she exclaimed suddenly. "The brick complex on the corner? Are you kidding me? I live in number seventeen. You're right above me!"

Petr was simply dumbstruck.

"How did you end up there?" she asked.

Petr shrugged. "Luck of the draw, I guess," he replied. "The college set it all up for me."

Alex shook her head and frowned. "I know what that's like," she answered with a bite in her voice. "I had housing all lined up myself, but somehow it fell through. And if I didn't want to live in a house full of giggling sorority girls, I had to take what was left. It's a dump, but I like my privacy."

"It's certainly not the Ritz," Petr deadpanned and then smiled. "Did I get that right?"

Alex laughed. "Perfectly." They walked for a bit more before she spoke again. "You know, I think by the time the semester is over, we'll either be friends for life or hate the sight of each other!"

"Well, I very much hope the first," Petr said sincerely.

Alex nodded her agreement and then avoided an awkward silence by quickly turning the discussion back to the two courses they were taking. Petr was silent, happy just to listen to her voice. She then went on to tell him about the local happenings, specifically the disappearance of the star basketball player Gideon Sumbawanga and about preparing for the memorial. She explained how she'd gone to the memorial not because she'd known Gideon very well, but because her friend Owen did. Alexis went on to tell him how she'd missed their morning class because she'd spent it helping plan a charity basketball game that would take place in a few days. The idea was from Gideon's father, she explained, but there were a lot of people helping out with it.

They continued to talk about the game until they reached their building. Petr said goodnight as Alex got off the stairs on the first floor and he continued up to the second. He unlocked his door and entered, breathing a sigh of both relief and contentment, before collapsing onto a ratty, old, maroon lounge chair he had carried up from the side of the road the day before. A large centipede came whizzing out from under the chair and snaked across the floor, but Petr left it to continue on its merry way. Right now, he had too many other things on his mind to worry about pest control. If he was going to impress Alex, he was going to have to be smart in class and that meant keeping up with the homework. He paused as he realized how content he was and how natural it now felt to have cut the criminal ties with his family. He had to admit, it was quite a change from what he had been feeling that morning and Alexis had a lot to do with that. She'd talked to him because he was Petr, not because he was a Zhugravinsky, and that was a big thing indeed. He opened up his backpack, pulled out his Algebra and read for a little bit, smiling to himself all the while.

"You know," he said softly to himself as he flipped through the pages, while thinking about his day, "my life couldn't get any better, even if someone else was planning it all out."

CHAPTER 15

Tsarskoe Selo, Russia: Nikolai Zhugravinsky was sitting alone in his brother's old apartment outside of St. Petersburg, fuming. As he stroked his fingers back and forth across the mahogany table, he wondered why the city held such an attraction for Petr. While it was true the city had once held one of the most powerful courts in Russia, those days were long gone. Power was now situated elsewhere and there was very little of it to be had here anymore. Power, to Nikolai, was all that mattered, and thus it was impossible for him to wrap his mind around Petr's affection for a place that held next to none.

"This is no more than a tourist town," Nikolai mumbled to himself, letting his eyes scan the room as he picked up a small tumbler of vodka and tossed it back. There had to be some key that unlocked the mystery of his brother, but it was well beyond his grasp and it was that particular fact that angered him more than anything. Nikolai and Petr could have conquered the world together, but Petr had turned his back on him and things were rapidly falling apart. Every setback reminded Nikolai of his brother's disloyalty and made him hate Petr even more.

As he reached for the bottle to pour himself another drink, a knock came at the front door. With a start, Nikolai pulled his Makarov pistol out of a holster hidden under his black leather jacket, and inched toward the door. There had been three attempts on his life over the past year and he had long ago stopped trusting his own judgment as to the safety of any given situation. After several minutes of silence, he allowed himself to shift the nearby window curtain open just enough to peer outside, only to see the deck was completely empty.

Breathing a sigh of relief, he turned to go back into the dining room. That was when he saw the frighteningly large man, dressed all in black and wearing dark sunglasses, seated casually at the table as if he had been there for hours. Nikolai knew who the intruder was immediately, but rather than emptying his gun into the behemoth, the Russian's mouth curled into a smile and he quickly holstered his weapon and opened up his arms in a friendly greeting.

"*Privyet*, Hade! Welcome, my friend," he bellowed, forgetting all about Petr. "I was beginning to think you had forgotten your comrades in Russia!"

Hade, enjoying the private thought that he had completely surprised the skittish Nikolai and could have easily killed him, smiled widely. "Kolya, how could I forget you?" he answered easily, as one who would greet a long-lost friend. "You, who remind me so much of myself all of those many years ago. No, I'm with you always."

"I could have killed you," Nikolai boasted as he walked back to the table, grinning broadly and patting the holstered weapon for emphasis. "You should take care never to surprise a Zhugravinsky."

Hade only smiled, biting back his first words and instead laying on the honey that was needed with this particular worker bee. "You are both clever and cruel, which are two of the most important traits in a born leader. You are also young, which is always a problem, but you will grow into something special, of this we can be sure. But enough flattery, Nikolai. Come, sit down. Let us drink to your health and to that of your brothers."

"I have only one brother," Nikolai snapped bitterly as he took a seat at the table. He grabbed the bottle of vodka and poured himself another shot. He turned over a separate glass and poured one for the newcomer. "The world is out to get me, Hade, but I swear I'll destroy anyone who gets in my way."

Hade remained unmoved by the little speech and continued to smile. "A bit melodramatic, don't you think?" he stated, picking up his glass and sniffing at the liquor it held. "Besides, it isn't right to talk about your brothers in such a way. They're family, and family is hard to come by."

"My brother the betrayer is no family of mine and I do not wish to speak of him," Nikolai said. "But I do have a problem and I need your help."

"Why not ask your family?" Hade said, still smiling as he took a sip of his vodka. He savored the taste, which was not quite as good as his standard drink of choice, but quite passable. The Russians certainly got that right, at the very least.

"My family," he spat bitterly, slamming his shot glass down on the table. "They would give me a sermon and tell me to fix it myself."

Hade cocked his eyebrow but continued to smile, knowing that there were few things Nikolai hated more than cheerful people. "Maybe you should listen to a sermon or two," he replied smugly and took another sip of his vodka. "It could only help."

"You refuse me?"

"You are raw, Kolya," Hade answered, ignoring the challenge. "Talented, but raw and undisciplined. In times like this, you are like a ravenous dog that will attack any enemy, even if it opens you up to other enemies."

"What does that have to do with you helping me?"

Hade sighed and leaned back in his chair. "You have much to learn, Grasshopper. I am willing to give you the world, Nikolai, but only if you are willing to give me some time to offer it up to you. So in answer to your question, I will help you, as long as it coincides with the bigger picture."

Suspicion shrouded Nikolai's face. In their past dealings, Hade had never required anything of him other than the promise that one day, he would ask a favor and he must be willing to grant it, no matter the cost.

"What do you wish of me?" he asked unsteadily, wondering if that time had arrived.

"It's simple, really," Hade answered. "I want to know what your plans are for your, shall we say, non-existent brother."

"I think you know what my plans for Petr are," Nikolai spat his brother's name. "I swear I will catch him, I will torture him, and then I will kill him."

"And are you planning on doing this by yourself?" Hade's smile was gone, but he was still calm and showed no anger.

"No, no, I am sending Vanya to America to take care of him," was the Russian's reply. "Petr trusts him, so he can get close to him."

"Tsk, tsk, tsk, Kolya," Hade said, shaking his head in a scolding manner. "Your plan has so many holes in it, it is like Swiss cheese."

Nikolai slammed his hand down on the table and stood up, pulling out his gun and knocking back his chair.

Hade simply waved him off in that maddeningly calm way of his. "Oh, do sit down and put that away, Kolya, before you get hurt," the big man said with a smile. "Vanya is your right hand and you would cut him off just to kill your brother?"

"I would not cut him off!" Nikolai shouted again, refusing to sit.

"Think about it for a moment," Hade went on, ignoring the outburst. "Besides the cowardice of your plan, you forget that America is not Russia. Even if he succeeded, Vanya would be caught, you would be implicated, and your family would kill you. It is no secret they love Petr more than they love you, despite all you have done for them. I know this just as I know they conspire against you at this very moment."

"You say they conspire against me?" he stammered, anger and frustration clearly apparent. His only wish in life was to raise his family to the greatest heights of power in Russia, and now it seemed that his whole family was suddenly against him. "I love my family! I loved my brother! And they turn on me like this?"

"I want you to listen clearly here, Kolya," Hade answered calmly. "You will do as I say, no?"

Nikolai looked at him, eyes blazing.

"You know I do not repeat myself," Hade said dangerously.

The Russian quickly nodded, not wanting to push the man, for he knew very well what Hade was capable of doing. He had seen it with his own eyes and those visions were haunting even to someone as vicious as himself.

"Very good, Kolya" he replied, leaning back in his chair and smiling. He picked up his glass and took a drink, making an exaggerated act of savoring the vodka's flavor, before continuing. "To be honest, I don't understand exactly why you hate your brother so much that you would risk everything to destroy him. Are you so certain he has betrayed you?"

"Of course he has! He left this family and me, to go write nonsense in America. He has turned his back on me and on our family in our hour of need."

"Kolya," Hade said, shaking his head but smiling just the same, "you know I am on your side, but just because Petr went to America does not mean he has turned his back on you. In fact, perhaps it is you who has turned your back on him."

"Impossible!" Nikolai shouted. "How can you say that to me? Everything I do, I do for this family! Petr? He has abandoned us!"

"I think you might want to reconsider the situation," Hade countered. "He is soft, yes, but he is also very smart. Perhaps he has a plan in the works that will help you succeed. Perhaps he is in America right now looking for ways to get enough money to finance the next business venture of the family. Just because he told your family he was breaking away doesn't mean he actually is. Just because you think he is a traitor doesn't necessarily make him one. In the end, he may still be the one who helps you find your glory."

"So what would you have me do?" he finally seethed, his frustration bubbling over.

Hade shrugged. "I would have you leave him alone for the moment," he said matter-of-factly. "I am positive that the longer you let him live, the better chance you will have of completing your own goals. He is no traitor, Kolya. Of that, I can be certain. Let him live and you will see that I am right."

"I am to trust you in this?"

"Implicitly," Hade said with a smile and finished his vodka. "Besides, he is too important to us to continue to entertain thoughts of killing him at the moment. So let us move on, shall we, and talk about what I like to call the 'Big Picture'."

He pushed his glass forward and Nikolai obeyed the unspoken request and refilled it.

"You see, Nikolai," Hade went on, "there are things happening in the world today that you do not know about, but are about to have a sizable influence on your life. Strange things, bad things, just things, I suppose. And to be truthful, there are things happening that you simply don't want to know about, because you would never be able to sleep again."

"What is this you speak of?" Nikolai refilled his own glass and downed it. The alcohol was quite smooth and was beginning to calm him down.

"How can I put this so you will understand?" Hade sighed. "Listen closely, Kolya. The world is changing before your very eyes, but you cannot even see it. No one can really see it, which is part of the beauty of it all. The big picture is therefore hard to visualize. But I do need you to trust me that it is out there and you are a central part of it."

"I am a central part of it…," the Russian repeated, somewhat confused.

"Exactly," Hade answered, tapping his finger against his nose to illustrate the point. "And you need to realize that if you compromise yourself or Vanya by going after your brother now, it will destroy your very bright future and we wouldn't want that now, would we?"

Nikolai shook his head. "I suppose not."

"Trust me, there will come a day when I will give you a green light to do whatever you wish to your brother, but until that day, you will wait."

"How long?"

"However long I deem necessary," Hade replied coldly, indicating that there would be no further discussion on the matter. "You know, Kolya, I could tell you were visibly upset when I called you a coward. Do not forget that a true coward is someone who ignores the best advice for fear that their own judgment might be wrong. You must prove yourself a man tonight and accept my sage counsel."

"Very well," the Russian sighed. "I will do as you say and leave my brother be for now. But I want you to remember that the day will come when I will kill him."

"Excellent," said Hade, breaking into a broad grin. "Then we are agreed." He leaned back and lifted his glass as if he was ready to toast Nikolai's willingness to follow instructions. "Now that we have that settled, what else might I assist you with? And do sit down, Kolya," he finished, indicating the toppled chair.

"Very well," he sighed, carelessly tossing his Makarov on the table in front of him and slumping back into his chair. "There is indeed something that I can use your help with."

"And what is that?" Hade answered, a mischievous smile on his face as if he already knew the answer.

Nikolai cleared his throat, missing Hade's look. "A short while ago I had some associates eliminate several rivals of mine and, indirectly, rivals of my family."

"Indeed," Hade smirked. "Always quick with the gun, you are."

Nikolai gritted his teeth and ignored the remark. "After the business was complete, my associates seemed to have lost the bodies."

"And you are worried that these bodies may show up in the wrong place at the wrong time?"

"Not anymore," Nikolai answered with a frustrated grunt. "Whether they show up or not, Petrov is gearing up for a war now. His people could be alive and he would still want a war."

"Petr foresaw this?"

"Yes," Nikolai answered, biting back his anger.

"And you are certain Petrov can win a war with your family?"

The big Russian shook his head at that. "No he cannot," he answered proudly, before adding, "but the cost may be high."

Hade leaned back and smiled. "There is a saying in America, Kolya, about omelets," he said.

"Omelets?" Nikolai repeated in amazement.

"The saying goes," Hade began, "that if you want to make an omelet, you have to break a few eggs."

"Meaning?"

"Meaning that Maybe you should let things play out as they will."

"Let Petrov declare a war?"

Hade nodded and grinned.

"We will be weakened, perhaps to the point we cannot recover."

Hade continued to smile and leaned back in his chair. He held the glass up and swished the vodka around in it before answering. "I am counting on that, Nikolai."

"Are you mad?" Nikolai dared to snap back. "What are we without our strength, Hade?"

"My dear Nikolai, numbers alone do not equal strength. Strength comes from within. On the Savannah, who is the gazelle afraid of—the herd of zebras or the single lion?"

Nikolai stared at the man, having no idea where Hade was going with his remark.

Hade threw back his head and laughed. "My dear Kolya, you are no zebra. You are the lion."

"And that will be enough to stop Petrov?"

Hade nodded. "It was enough to remove a small part of the competition in the district, was it not? I think it was an excellent move on your part, by the way. But, of course, that did lead to the small problem of the bodies disappearing after the deed was done."

"Yes," Nikolai replied. "The hit was flawless, but someone snatched the bodies before we could take care of them. But what's worse is that bodies are disappearing all over the place now. Cemeteries and morgues are even beginning to place guards to stop the grave-robbing."

"Yes, yes, I am well aware of the disappearance of bodies," agreed Hade. "Did you know that this is a world-wide phenomenon, Nikolai? Well, mostly anyway."

"You seem pleased," the younger man said suspiciously.

"Of course I am," said Hade as if it was the most obvious thing in the world.

"But why? Papa was concerned that these missing bodies would be used by Petrov to start a war. Does that not worry you?"

"Truthfully? No," Hade stated flatly. "Should it?"

"I should say so!" Nikolai shouted, pointing his finger at Hade. "You know the danger we are in and you act like you do not care."

"I would care if I deemed the missing bodies to be a threat to you," answered Hade. "But they are not, because I have them. Or should I say, we have them," he added nonchalantly and made a show of examining his immaculate fingernails as if he were suddenly bored with the whole conversation.

Nikolai went red with rage and he reached again for the Makarov lying on the table. "You would betray me then?" he snarled, snatching up the weapon.

Hade only watched him, his eyes dangerous. "Will you take up your gun and shoot me now, Kolya?" Hade asked slyly.

Nikolai leveled his weapon at Hade's chest. "You would blackmail me? Blackmail my family?" he asked incredulously, stunned at the sudden traitorous admission. "I should kill you now."

"Then who would deal with Petrov?"

"I will deal with everything if I must!"

Hade stroked his beard and looked hard at the young Russian. Then he simply threw back his head and roared with laughter.

"You mock me," Nikolai said quietly, his voice low and dangerous. "No one mocks me."

The big man's laughter trailed off and Hade settled his dark eyes on Nikolai. "Kolya, Kolya, Kolya," he said, his tone suddenly paternal. "You show such courage at times. Now put away your weapon. I have no wish to harm you and will help you use all of this to your advantage."

Nikolai shook his head, not yet willing to believe the big man. "Then what do you want from me? And should I trust you enough to give it to you?"

"If I had wanted something from you, Kolya, I would have simply leaped out of this chair, grabbed you by the throat, and squeezed the life out of you until I had exactly what I wanted." Hade paused, before his voice suddenly dropped and his demeanor turned to ice. "Do you believe I could do that, young Nikolai?"

The Russian froze and then looked away, unable to meet the big man's hard gaze. Thinking back on what he had seen the man do in the past, his rage and bravado quickly drained away and he placed the weapon back on the table. Only after struggling mightily was he able to turn his face toward Hade. "But…"

"Answer the question," Hade said, his own voice almost a whisper now. "Do you believe I could do that?"

This time, Nikolai did not hesitate. "Yes," he answered in a shaky voice.

"Well then, I'm glad we could put that behind us. Now, I imagine you have questions?" Hade prompted, taking another drink. "This is extremely good, by the way," he added, holding up his tumbler and looking at the little bit of liquor that remained.

"Why?" Nikolai asked quietly after several moments of silence.

"Well, I suppose it is because the distillers have long perfected their work," Hade answered with a chuckle.

"Not the vodka," Nikolai said, daring to roll his eyes. "Why would you steal the bodies?"

Hade shrugged as if it was not a big deal. "We needed them," he answered. "And rest assured, if we did not actually need them, I would gladly give them back to you."

Nikolai started to protest, but Hade cut him off with a wave of his hand.

"Remember, Kolya. This is all part of the big picture and these plans have been in motion long before you even showed up on this pitiful planet. There is much more to this than just you and I. These plans are ages in the making and far beyond your current ability to comprehend."

"What plan?"

"A grand plan, my young friend," answered Hade, smiling his toothy smile again. "It is a plan that I promise you will see come to completion and when you do, you will become one of the most powerful men on the planet. But you must do exactly as I say if you are to live to see opening night."

"You speak in riddles, Hade," Nikolai snapped. "I grow very tired of them."

Hade's smile faded and he stared intently at Nikolai once more. "If I am to teach you anything, Kolya," he said coldly, "you are going to need to get rid of that five ton block of attitude sitting on your shoulder. This is no game I am talking about here. This is about you making it through the week alive. That might hold some interest for you, I would think."

"What do you mean?" Nikolai asked, his eyes narrowing suspiciously.

"Your family has secretly taken a hit out on you, Kolya," Hade answered coldly. "And you and I both know that officially makes you a dead man."

Nikolai was stunned. His hand shaking, he quickly drained his glass and stared blankly ahead. "That's not possible," he finally gasped. "I would know! It cannot be true!"

"Oh, but it is true," Hade corrected. "They can kill you and they will. It is already settled."

"But why?"

Hade smiled. "You already know the answer to that question, Kolya," he replied. "They believe you to be reckless. They believe you will drag them down to destruction. Looking at how you handled this Petrov business, it is hard to disagree with them. But it is more than that. They know that you would kill Petr if given the chance and they intend to make sure that does not happen."

"How could they do this?" Nikolai stammered. "After all I have done for them! I would give my life for the success of my family!"

"They are counting on that," Hade agreed slyly. "They believe they will be better off without you."

"And Sergei? Is he a part of this conspiracy, too?" Nikolai lamented.

"Sergei knows nothing because your father knows he would try to stop them," Hade answered. "They want you dead, Nikolai, and make no mistake, you will die." After a pause, Hade allowed a smile to creep back onto his face and then finished with an evil whisper. "Unless, of course, you get them first."

"You bring such evil news, Hade," he said quietly, shaking his head sadly. "Why do you tell me these things? Why do you tell me to kill my own family?"

"It is your only way to survive," Hade shrugged. "They will kill you if you do not kill them first."

"I could speak with them. I could convince them they are wrong."

"You know your family better than that," Hade admonished. "A death sentence by the Zhugravinsky family is never revoked."

"You won't let me kill my brother, who I despise more than anything in the world, but you want me to kill the rest of my family, including my own father?"

"You have free will to choose as you want, of course," was the icy reply. "But if you want to survive, you have only one real choice. You know who you can trust and who you cannot and it's about time for you to start separating the wheat from the chaff."

Nikolai sat there, unable to believe it had come to this. He knew his family did not trust him, but he never thought they would decide to kill him. It was an extremely difficult situation, even for a man as hateful and power-hungry as Nikolai. In the end, there was really only one choice and he was certain Hade already knew what his answer would be. "Will you help me then?"

"Of course I will," Hade nodded. "But as Emerson instructs, 'adopt the pace of nature: her secret is patience.' You must wait. Your family will not strike at you until after your mother's birthday, which is not for three days, so we still have a bit of time. But you must be careful, Nikolai," Hade said suddenly, holding a warning finger in the air. "You must not do or say anything that will make them think you have discovered their plans or they will kill you immediately, and likely Sergei as well."

"Sergei? But you said he knows nothing."

"He does not," agreed Hade. "But if they suspect you know, they will likely think that Sergei found out about the plot and warned you. Sergei would die for you, you know."

Nikolai nodded, but remained silent.

"In the end, you must decide whether you will kill him or not," Hade went on.

"I cannot kill Sergei," Nikolai said sadly. "Petr, yes. But not Sergei."

"That is a wise choice," Hade agreed, smiling again. "Sergei could indeed be useful to you. Whatever you do, do not involve him in your little coup d'état. That would ruin him and then you would be forced to kill him anyway."

Nikolai nodded again, but there was little happiness in him.

"You and Vanya should be able to take care of your family and do so quickly," he went on. "Meet with him tonight and plan it out. When you are all that is left, you will be in complete control of the family name and more, Nikolai."

"What of Petrov? He will see we are weak and move to eliminate those who survive."

"Of course he will. As a matter of fact, he is already moving," Hade replied with a perfectly evil grin. "He will move on your family in three days."

"My mother's birthday."

"Fitting, is it not?" Hade answered. "Your father wishes to spare your mother the tragedy of losing her son right before her birthday, so will wait until after the celebration before killing you. Petrov, on the other hand, intends to make his move on her birthday because to him, it will send a stronger message. In doing so, he will accomplish much of your work for you, by removing several of your family members that pose a threat to you—family loyal to your father and to Petr."

"Who does he intend to kill?" Nikolai asked somewhat nervously.

"It does not matter," Hade replied. "For you and Vanya, your task is to remove the head of the Zhugravinsky family on the evening before the birthday celebration. Petrov will, of course, learn about this and then move quickly to cripple your family even more."

"And then what? What of our family when few remain? Petrov will own everything."

"On the contrary," Hade countered. "Petrov will be dead, too. I will see to that."

"You will help me in this?" Nikolai asked, daring to hope.

"I said I would, did I not? With the heads of both families dead, you will step into the power vacuum and unite both families," Hade explained. "All holdings, assets, and the control of both families will then be yours, Nikolai, and you will have no enemies to oppose you. Your actions will prompt other influential people to join your cause and you will suddenly have powerful backers that you never even considered. You will be in a position to take your family name to heights never before dreamed of by your shortsighted father and his father before him." Hade leaned forward across the table, placing a hand on the Russian's gun. "You should be excited about the prospects of your future, my young friend. I am handing you more power than you can imagine and all it will cost is a little blood."

"Yet the blood is dear," the Russian countered. "You're asking me to kill my own family. Do not expect me to be overjoyed about it."

"Not overjoyed at the killing," Hade gently corrected, "but overjoyed at the path that will be laid out before you once you have completed your task. You will be a hero to many, Nikolai, when all of this is over. You do not see it yet, but trust in me when I tell you that this is simply part of the big picture. And the big picture will paint you as the most powerful man in Russia. In fact, in the end, you will be Russia."

"I do not share your optimism, Hade," Nikolai said bitterly. "You speak of this big picture, but yet I struggle with knowing what I have to do. How is it to be done?"

Hade sat back and shrugged his massive shoulders, not willing to push the young Russian any further on the matter. He had broken him down enough and Hade was a master at knowing when and where to push the right buttons with the people that he controlled. "I have to take a short business trip," he said. "In the meantime, you and Vanya must spend the next couple of days making plans before you strike."

"I will try and do as you say."

"There is no try, Kolya," Hade admonished. "Only do or do not. I always loved that saying, you know. Yoda said it to Luke in the Dagoba Swamp."

"Who?"

"Yoda," Hade said quickly. "Have you not seen *Star Wars*?"

"No."

Hade threw up his hands in disbelief. "I swear. First Victor and now you," he huffed. "Someone really needs to teach you fellows to get out more. George Lucas is a master story-teller of modern times and you sell yourself short by not experiencing the masters when given the opportunity."

Nikolai brushed the comments aside. "What I meant, Hade, is I will try to keep things under wraps. But what if they come for me first?"

"Nikolai, have you ever heard of the Diagonal Banded Sweetlips?" Hade asked, and then fell into his professor routine. "I know, it sounds peculiar, but it is a name for a kind of fish found off the Great Barrier Reef. These fish have a rather peculiar strategy for survival. They swim together packed tight for protection during the entire day without attempting to hunt for food. At night, once it gets dark, the school will break apart instantly and the fish will hunt individually. In this way they have stealth on their side when they can use it most. But when stealth is untenable, they band together and make sure everyone makes it through the day alive. So, while it appears during the day that these fish are doing nothing, in reality they are just patiently waiting for their moment to strike." Hade paused to see if the young man was following him and when Nikolai remained silent, he went on. "To put it in terms of the real world, the sun is still out, Kolya. So we must swim together, waiting for our moment to strike. But the night is falling fast, which means soon, very soon, I will let you out on your own to hunt by yourself."

Nikolai nodded his head in agreement and said, "Very well, Hade. I will wait."

"That is most reassuring, Kolya."

"You have given me much to think about, my friend, but I am up to whatever challenge you lay before me." Nikolai stood up and offered his hand.

Hade stood as well and accepted the Russian's handshake. Then he turned and exited through the door without looking back once or even saying good-bye.

Nikolai Zhugravinsky remained motionless for several minutes after the huge man had left, letting his eyes wander around the room before coming to rest on a large painting of the Zhugravinsky family covering much of the wall opposite him. With a sneer of finality, he let a single thought begin running through his mind, letting it come out in an audible whisper.

"I will go hunt, I will go hunt, I will go hunt…"

CHAPTER 16

Belle Plaine, Iowa: Father Michael Dalacourt let the facts sift through his head, looking for the common thread that tied them all together instead of unraveling into a tangled mess. Eight people had died here in this small town in the past few weeks. Six of those bodies had recently been taken from their graves. Two—both elderly—were left untouched. There had to be a plausible reason and when he found it, he would be that much closer to solving this riddle.

The first thing Dalacourt could think of was that someone, possibly a medical school, was in the market for relatively fresh bodies—and younger ones, at that. He had already considered that possibility and had done some research during his trip to the United States. He knew the University of Iowa was a major medical college and very close to Belle Plaine. It could be some rogue medical student, out to make some extra cash to pay for skyrocketing tuition costs or a drug habit. It certainly wouldn't be the first time such a thing happened.

Nevertheless, it didn't help answer the question about what had happened with Father Oliveira back in Rome, nor did it do anything to address the local reports of the man walking down the road several days after he had supposedly died. Was it possible the reports were erroneous, that someone had just seen a person who resembled the dead man? A practical mind would have to say yes and, Dalacourt was certainly practical, if he was anything. From what he could logically put together, beyond the actual tragedies, nothing really seemed that much out of the ordinary here. The missing bodies could be explained as grave robbing, even without proof, and there was no actual evidence the man seen walking down the road was one of the dead men. As far as Father Oliveira was concerned, Dalacourt would have to be content with the idea that Oliveira's death and subsequent resurrection was something entirely different than what was going on here in the States.

He wasn't sure how much further he could go regarding an actual investigation in Belle Plaine, so he would mark his time tomorrow talking with those who claimed to have seen the dead man alive and then he would make arrangements to return to Italy. There was much more to be learned from Father Oliveira and he was more than a little angry now he had been sent away when what was important was obviously happening back in Rome.

The ringing of the old rotary dial phone next to his bed jarred him from his thoughts and he picked it up, his mind still wandering. "Yes?" he answered almost absently.

"Father Dalacourt?"

"Father Sparrel," he answered, immediately recognizing the voice and quickly returning his thoughts to the present. "Did we forget something?"

"No," came the quiet reply. Father Sparrel hesitated before continuing, his voice low. "Do you have a television in your room?"

"Yes," Dalacourt answered, glancing at the old set, his brow furrowing at the odd question. "But I never watch the thing."

"Do so now," Sparrel said, his voice still quiet. "Switch it to channel nine, KCRG."

Dalacourt reached over to the dresser and the small television that sat on top of it. He switched it on and turned it to the correct channel and his jaw immediately dropped in shock. There in front of an ornate podium that Dalacourt recognized from the inside of St. Peter's Basilica in Vatican City, stood Archbishop Francis De Solei, hands held out before him in a grand gesture as he spoke.

"...are unprecedented occurrences," said the richly dressed figure at the podium, his voice fairly booming, "and can no more be ignored or shelved as the ramblings of the insane or the lies of deceivers. The Catholic Church has been aware of these amazing signs now for some time and, after much prayer and contemplation, I'm here to say as succinctly as possible the rumors are indeed true—the dead are rising from the grave. In one masterful stroke, God in heaven has replaced traditional and secular thought with that of the spiritual."

Dalacourt was stunned as the implications instantly became crystal-clear to him. He knew now without a doubt the objective hadn't been for him to learn more in Belle Plaine. No, De Solei had gotten him away from the Vatican and had then taken complete control of the situation and moved in the direction the church had decided to move in. What better way to assure there would be no dissension among those in Italy than to remove those that might be considered dissenters and troublemakers?

On television, De Solei went on, obviously enjoying the moment. "As spokesman for our beloved Holiness, I implore you to bring yourself back to God if you are lost. Those saints true to your faith, your vigilance and steadfastness shall be duly rewarded. The time of our Savior's return is at hand. For those of you who are still wandering or have strayed away from the fold, I urge you to seek out your local parish and come back to God the Father, where you will be welcomed with open arms."

De Solei looked down at the podium and opened up the huge gold-bound Bible that lay upon it. As he began to read from scripture, the scene cut back to the news desk where the two anchors sat, looking solemn. "Those words were spoken no more than thirty minutes ago and Archbishop De Solei—a man known to be very close to the Pope—is still addressing the growing crowd in Rome," said the male anchor. "The Catholic Church isn't the only denomination taking a stand on these reports. Other churches are making statements of their own as we speak. Generally, hearing reports of dead people walking and talking would be something you might find in the *National Enquirer*. But today, with so many faiths speaking out about the current happenings and the state of our nations and our world, people are beginning to open their Bibles again. Could this really be scriptural prophecy coming true?"

"Indeed, we may very well be on the brink of the greatest religious revival in all of history," the female anchor added, straightening the stack of papers in front of her. "The Baptists have gone on record as saying..."

Dalacourt switched off the television, stunned.

"I assume this was unexpected?"

Michael Dalacourt became aware he hadn't hung up the phone and shook his head, gripping the phone receiver tightly in his hand. "I beg your pardon," he sighed, closing his eyes and trying to calm his reeling mind.

"I said, I assume this wasn't expected?" Father Sparrel repeated.

Whether he heard Father Sparrel or not, Dalacourt gave no indication. "I'm in the wrong place," he muttered.

But Father Sparrel heard him plainly. "I have to disagree, Father," he said gently. "You're in the place God would have you. People are beginning to show up here at church already and many more will be here soon, wanting answers and seeking salvation. I can't do this alone, Father. I'm going to need your help."

Dalacourt took a deep breath and forced his mind to calm down. "Already?" he asked. "How can that be?"

"The newscast has been on for a little while now," Sparrel answered. "When the universal church tells the general population the end of the world is finally upon them, people are going to come running back to God. They're doing so now."

Dalacourt nodded, knowing Father Sparrel was right. His place was here and he would do what he knew he should do. "Then you shall have my services for as long as you need them, Father," he answered resolutely. "I shall come immediately."

"Thank you," Father Sparrel said. "I suppose we can be thankful for one thing, though."

"And what is that?"

"That Belle Plaine is indeed such a small town," answered the older priest with a weary sigh. "Imagine what the churches in big cities are going through right now."

"Amen to that, Father," Dalacourt said with a sad smile, and hung up the phone.

CHAPTER 17

Salt Lake City, Utah: The Jon M. Huntsman Center in Salt Lake City was a beehive of activity. Despite the rising concern for the increasing number of local missing people and the growing unrest in the world, the school had decided to go forward with the charity basketball event in Gideon Sumbawanga's honor.

"No one truly knows what's happening in the world around us," the University of Utah president had stated the day before in a public address. "Until we do, we will continue to live our lives to the best of our abilities and honor one of our own as we had originally planned."

People had turned out in droves to honor the missing and presumed dead basketball star. In reality, the event was for Chris Matthews as well, but there was no mistaking people had come for their favorite, Gideon. Tickets were ten dollars each and all proceeds were going toward funding officials in their continued search for the missing. The game itself pitted the starters against the reserves from the last season, sort of an encore presentation for the fans of a tremendous season from the Utes, even though the team was missing their marquee player.

David Sumbawanga was in attendance, sitting on the sidelines as he awaited his opportunity to speak at half time. Owen, Luke, and Chad were close by with prime seats right behind the second team's bench, courtesy of their friendship with not only Gideon but other members of the team as well. Alexis had also come, sitting a number of rows off the floor on the other side of the center. Her friend Libby was on the cheer squad, and both had helped with some of the setup, so their seats weren't all that bad. But with Libby performing on the sidelines, her other friends unable to come, and Owen near the bench, Alexis would have been alone in the crowd, and if there was one thing she hated most in the world, it was being out in public alone.

To remedy this, she had invited her new neighbor and study partner, Petr, to attend the game with her. Only after inviting him, however, had she thought to make her intentions clear. Her life was difficult enough without having a glorified foreign-exchange student getting the wrong idea, so she had gently let him know they were going just as friends. Petr, for his part, had simply been pleased she had asked him to go. He knew about Owen DiConte; had heard Owen's name come up more than a few times in the short time he had known Alexis and had seen the look in her eyes when she spoke of him. But he also knew he could be a patient man if it served his purposes. For the moment, he was more than content just to be near Alexis. He would be the perfect gentleman and choose his words carefully, control his actions at all times and continue to not only be the person she thought he was, but be the person he wanted to be. He had come to America for a new start and he was doing exactly that.

The two of them sat through the first half and chatted rather loudly in order to be heard over the crowd, their conversation covering such topics as their classes, the loss of Gideon, and all the hard work Alexis and her friend Libby had put in to make the charity game happen. Alexis had mentioned her anger toward another friend, Gen, because she had instead gone out with her creepy boyfriend. Petr had no idea who Alexis was talking about, so he merely smiled and nodded his head.

When halftime rolled around, they turned their attention to the tribute. The lights were turned down and, while pictures of Chris and Gideon were shown on the arena's video scoreboard, the president of the university offered a few words, followed by Chris' mother, Loren, and Gideon's father, David. Both parents spoke of their sons and the impact they had on their families and on the community. They stressed the need for unity and the need to remember good people as they struggled through bad times. The dual tribute was stirring and emotional.

As the presentation ended, the players started warming up again, turning the arena into a joyful haven once more. Petr offered to get Alexis something to drink, but before she responded, they were interrupted by a man moving toward the seat next to them.

"Mister Sumbawanga," Alexis said brightly, looking at Gideon's father in surprise.

"Good evening," he replied with a smile as he leaned on his walking stick, looking first at her and then Petr. "I hope I'm not intruding?"

"Oh, no," she said, motioning to the empty seat. "We'd love for you to join us."

"Wonderful," he answered, sliding into his seat with a tired sigh. He laid his mango staff on the floor and slid it carefully underneath the seats. "A mutual friend of ours insisted on getting me a seat up here beside you," he said with a smile. "I believe you know Owen DiConte?"

Alexis felt herself blushing slightly. "I do," she said warmly.

"He was under the impression you had wanted a word with me at the memorial, so arranged for me to have a seat next to you," David said easily, leaning back.

"Well, that was sweet of him," Alexis said, blushing slightly.

"I must admit," David went on, "it's nice to be out of the spotlight and relax for a moment. To say this week has been trying would be an understatement."

"I'm so sorry, Mister Sumbawanga. Please forgive my manners, but this is my friend, Petr," Alex said quickly, still standing and placing her hand lightly on the young Russian's shoulder as she introduced him.

"He's here from Russia. I thought it would be great for him to experience a little bit of American college entertainment."

"Wonderful to meet you," David smiled as he leaned past Alexis and shook Petr's hand firmly. "Another foreigner, like me. Can I ask a rather silly question, Petr? How do you find driving over here?"

"I don't mind it at all," he stammered, somewhat taken aback at the question. "I honestly haven't driven much, though. Everything I need is close by."

"Yes, they have a great transportation system here in America," David replied warmly, putting the Russian at ease as Alexis took her seat between them. "When I arrived, the college gave me a rental car to get around, but I haven't driven it yet. There are too many cars on the road here. I'm used to far less traffic."

"In Russia, it's worse," Petr said, warming up quickly. "You can't get anywhere without it taking forever and risking your life in the endeavor."

"Well, that's reassuring, I suppose. I've never been to Russia, although I studied in Denmark for a time. In those days, one didn't simply drive into Russia."

"I still wouldn't recommend it," Petr said and then caught himself. He had been about to talk about the crime levels, especially in certain areas where his family was responsible for much of that crime, but stopped. "Where I live, though, it's never been better." It was a lie, but he hoped they would believe it. Either way, he knew he had to change the subject before they started talking about Russia in depth. "I appreciated your comments, Mister Sumbawanga."

"Yes," Alexis agreed, "it was beautiful." Turning to Petr, she added, "I wish you could have been at the memorial service. Mister Sumbawanga is a truly gifted speaker."

"I'm grateful for your compliments," David said calmly, "but I simply speak the way any parent would speak of their child. And please, call me David."

"As you wish, Mister Sumba...I mean, David," she said with a smile. "I'm really glad you were able to be here tonight. I think it was important for everybody."

"It was cathartic for me as well," he answered softly. "I fear, though, closure will be a long time coming."

"I'm truly sorry for your loss," Alexis said, putting her hand on his arm. "Gideon must have loved having a father such as you."

"You're too kind," the elder Sumbawanga said softly, then raised his eyebrows inquisitively. "So tell me about Owen," he went on with a smile. "I've spent a great deal of time with him these last few days, but I'd be interested in your opinion."

"Well, he may not be much to look at and not altogether very smart," she joked, "but he treated your son with kindness. Seriously, he has a heart three times too large for his chest and he absolutely adored Gideon."

Mr. Sumbawanga's eyes narrowed and his lips snapped shut in a tight grin. Was he trying to suppress a laugh? Before Alexis could say anything else, he turned to look across the arena, spotted Owen, and spoke again, his voice wistful. "He stares into space like a dreamer—like my son. With all the sorrow I've felt the last few days, it's been a true pleasure to meet my son's friends. The true measure of a man is the company he keeps. If his friends have told me anything, it's that my son was indeed a great man."

The three of them continued to talk throughout the second half of the game, Petr joining in much more as the discussions spanned various topics. The young Russian felt more comfortable around the older man as they chatted. David was a good listener and he seemed to genuinely care about what Petr said. That was something Petr hadn't felt for a very long time, if ever.

Before they knew it, the final whistle blew. The game had been relatively close, with the starters beating the subs as expected. Instead of a loud celebration, however, people started filing out of the arena, somewhat subdued as reality washed back over them.

David politely excused himself, saying the fatigue was catching up to him and he wished to return to his hotel. Alexis and Petr said their good-byes to him, Alexis giving the older man a warm hug before he departed. As David left, leaning heavily on his walking stick, Alexis insisted they make their way toward the floor of the arena instead of going directly to the exit.

Approaching the large group congregating at midcourt, Alexis saw Luke and Clint first. They saw her and gave a quick nod to acknowledge her presence, but kept their attention on the players and coaches who were hugging, crying, and remembering their fallen friend. Eventually, Alexis found Owen nearby, who gave her a smile and a quick hug before giving Petr a cursory head nod and a polite, "How's it going?"

As Alexis and Owen talked, Petr found himself alone in a swelling crowd of humanity. Outside of Alexis, he knew no one, so he stood silently off to the side, hands in pockets, his eyes taking in everyone and everything. He began to consider slipping out quietly and walking home alone when he felt a tap on his shoulder. Turning around, he saw a man dressed in dark clothes and sporting medium length black hair that fell over his eyes. He had a crooked grin, and looked a bit older than the traditional students, but he seemed harmless enough and the camera in his hands broadcast his intentions.

"Hey, man," he said to Petr. "I'm with the school newspaper looking to get a few shots of fans for a story. Do you mind?"

"Not at all," Petr said innocently. He looked around and saw he had somehow distanced himself from Alexis. Turning back to the young man, he said, "I hope you're okay with just me."

"No worries," the photographer said, pointing toward where Owen and Alexis were talking. "Just step over there and I'll get you with everyone else."

Petr smiled and moved back to stand next to Alexis. He touched her arm, getting her attention as Clint and Luke sauntered over to them. "Hey," he said. "This guy wants to get a picture of all of us for the school newspaper."

Alexis turned and smiled. "Sounds great!" After a moment of wrangling, Alexis had Petr on one side of her and Owen, Clint, and Luke on the other.

Several snapshots later, the photographer thanked everyone and flipped Petr his card. "Email me and I'll get you a copy of the picture," he said, then turned and disappeared into the crowd. Petr smiled to himself as Alexis went back to talking to Owen. He waited a few more minutes for Alexis to separate from the group, but when it became obvious she wouldn't, he began to wonder if he should indeed act on his earlier impulse and slip away into the crowd.

He was turning to leave when Alexis stopped him. "We're going out for a bite to eat. Want to join us?" she asked.

A quick look at the men surrounding her told him it wasn't a good idea. A great general always chose the best ground to fight on, and this looked like losing terrain for him. It wouldn't do for Alexis to think of him as a third wheel.

"Thanks," Petr said casually, "but I'm going to call it a night. Maybe we can get together and study tomorrow?"

"Yeah," Alexis replied, twirling her hair between her fingers. "That would be great."

"Tomorrow then," the Russian replied with a smile. He gave Owen a brief nod and walked across the floor and out of the stadium.

As he walked home, enjoying the cool air of the late evening, he reminded himself he would simply be patient when it came to the beautiful young woman. If all went according to his plans, he would have her as his own sooner than later.

CHAPTER 18

Los Angeles, California: One of the many reasons people gravitate toward Southern California is that, even during the winter months, the temperatures are so pleasant that most nights it's possible to leave the house and enjoy what the cities have to offer. Tonight was one of those classic evenings where the sun had descended hours ago but people were still out walking the streets of Los Angeles. And yet, there were many streets with considerably less traffic—streets the more cautious types were wise to avoid.

It was on one of those side streets where the evening shadows muted the dim light from the few functioning street lamps, that a young girl walked purposefully along. She was likely no more than eight, with beautiful olive skin and deep-set eyes that framed a petite and perfect face. It was December, and yet she was dressed in a white knit shirt and a knee-length plaid skirt. She wore no smile of innocence, though; rather her look was singular, focused, and eerily determined. She glanced neither right nor left, eschewing all caution in her haste to reach her destination. The cool nights in this seedy and dangerous section of Los Angeles masked others with equal, if not greater, determination.

The young girl rounded a street corner, her stride never slowing, and as she slipped outside of the protective glow of a corner street lamp, a shadow detached itself from the other side of the street and moved quickly toward her, crossing the road with swift and silent strides. The man had timed his pursuit perfectly, giving her no chance to run or scream as his tattooed, needle-scarred arm slipped around her waist and a rough and callused hand clamped tightly over her mouth.

The man hoisted his young prey easily into the air, keeping his hand tightly pressed over her mouth. He had only taken three steps, however, when he let out a blood-curdling scream and immediately dropped his intended victim. He grabbed his hand in agony and held it up in the dim glow of the streetlight. He could see her little teeth marks in his palm. He began to howl wildly as the skin around the bite-mark blackened, festered, and seemed to rot away before his eyes. The man stumbled backward, tripped over the curb, and fell into the street. His eyes, previously hungry with intent, now reflected pain, torment, and abject horror. He clutched his maimed hand and stared at it, unaware of the child stepping slowly toward him.

"Oh no, Mister," she said quietly, a smile playing at her lips as she reached for him. "You look like you hurt yourself." She reached down and her little hand clutched at his face. Again he screamed, his cry a mixture of intense agony and pure terror. Her fingernails, suddenly long and razor sharp, dug deep furrows into the flesh of his cheek, peeling away the skin down to the bone. He broke away from her and crawled to his feet. As he reached up and touched his ruined cheek, he could feel the wound spread its rot across his face. He drew his hand back and it came away crawling with maggots. The vision in his left eye disappeared as the orb bloated with putrescence and then ruptured as the rapidly decaying flesh spread toward his scalp. His drug-tortured mind broke at that point and he turned and fled, screaming as he went. The little girl watched dispassionately as he disappeared, hardly noticing the pitiable wail of horror that trailed after him. She turned with a cold smile and resumed her trek toward her destination as if nothing had happened.

She soon reached her objective, the base of a short set of stone stairs that led up to a once ornate set of oaken doors, now weather-beaten and mostly covered with graffiti. The writing carved in crumbling stone above the doors indicated she was looking upon the entrance of St. Mary's Catholic Church, an older church with memories of a golden past long since forgotten. It had been decades since the building was one of the preeminent churches of Los Angeles, but as the neighborhood had gone downhill, so too had the church. They had closed it down for partial renovations years ago that had never quite gotten finished, but for now, at least the church was open and accessible. She smiled again, for she could feel her prey waiting inside.

She avoided an old homeless man in tattered clothes and worn sandals leaning against one of the doors as she mounted the steps of the church as quickly as her little legs allowed. She pushed open the other and entered the sanctuary, heading directly toward the confessionals. There were three of them and she knew the person she sought occupied the one on the left, alone in the church this night and more vulnerable than he might have ever believed possible. Still smiling, she entered the confessional and sat down. The panel opened and the priest cleared his throat to indicate he was listening.

"Forgive me, Father, for you have sinned," she said sweetly, thoroughly enjoying the prospect of the game she was about to play.

The priest stammered, trying to compose himself in the face of a seemingly innocent gaff. "I think you meant to say, 'I have sinned,' my child," he said kindly.

"Indeed you have," she answered, coating her voice with as much syrup as possible.

There was another pause before he spoke again. "You need to try again," he instructed calmly. "You must say, 'Forgive me, Father, for I have sinned'."

"Then I will hear your confession," she replied innocently, her eyes glittering in the darkness of the confessional. She was enjoying this. The priest remained silent, likely trying to decide upon the best approach to steer this obviously troubled young child. The girl pressed the priest for an answer. "Do you wish to confess your sins before

God?"

"I'm afraid you do not understand the confessional," he finally answered, his voice still calm. "Let me ask you, child, how old are you?"

"I thought you, of all people, would recognize the age of the body is of no importance, Francis," she replied evenly. "What's important is I'm here to listen to your confession and help you along the long and difficult road of repentance. As this might be your only opportunity for redemption, I suggest you take it."

"I beg your pardon," he shot back from the other side of the confessional wall, anger now in his voice. "How dare you insinuate..."

"I'm insinuating nothing, Francis," she interrupted, her sweet voice holding a sudden hint of disdain for the man on the other side of the screen.

"You mustn't call me by my first name, child," he said, straining to keep himself under control. "I am Father De Solei and you must address me by that title or simply, 'Father.' It is impudent and unsightly before God to do otherwise."

"My name is Francis De Solei," she mimicked. "I confess I have committed many sins and I must repent or be forever consigned to the fiery pits of hell with Satan as my master."

"Is this a joke?" the priest asked, all pretense of control gone. "If it is, I must ask you to leave..."

She cut him off, her voice becoming icy and menacing. "You will ask nothing of me, Francis De Solei. Rather you will listen very carefully to what I have to say." The power in her voice shocked De Solei so profoundly that the priest fell silent. Her voice had lost all sweetness, and she managed to contort the words in a way that made them sound as if they were coming from De Solei himself.

"Exodus 20:3, 'Thou shalt have no other gods before me'," the little girl went on in her pseudo-De Solei voice. "I confess I have placed other gods, mainly those of gold and precious stones and all other manners of worldliness, before God Himself. I have done this knowingly and willingly and will continue to do so all the days of my life."

"Now just a minute," he tried to interrupt.

"Exodus 20:4, 'Thou shalt not make unto thee any graven image.' I confess I have broken this commandment as well and have built up stores of graven images to be used for ill gain."

At this, the priest stood up on his side of the confessional. "You are lying," he said coldly.

The young girl failed to even register his complaint as she continued. "Exodus 20:7, 'Thou shalt not take the name of the Lord thy God in vain.' I confess I have taken the name of the Lord in vain, invoking His name to bring cursed damnation down onto all those who have opposed me. I have engaged in this repulsive practice for many years and enjoy seeing my enemies fall before me as the chaff before the scythe. But it's not God that answers my requests and lays low my enemies. God has long since turned His back on me."

Stunned silence.

"Exodus 20:8, 'Remember the Sabbath day, to keep it holy.' I confess I have failed to keep the Sabbath day holy, instead falling into idolatrous and damning behavior, particularly on the evenings of the seventh and final day of the week."

De Solei, still standing, found his voice and shouted, "You have no proof of any of this!"

The girl shook her head. "Don't be upset with me," she sounded sweet again, "after I give you exactly what you asked for." Her voice switched over again to her uncanny impersonation of De Solei.

"Exodus 20:12, 'Honor thy father and thy mother.' I confess I have failed to honor my father and my mother. I ignored their pleas for help and left them penniless and alone to die, forgotten and ignored by the son they worked so hard to help attain the lofty position he now holds in the church. Even now, I work diligently to erase the memory of them from the world."

"This cannot be," he whispered.

"Exodus 20:15, 'Thou shalt not steal.' I confess I have broken this commandment on many occasions," she continued, ignoring the pleading in his voice. "I have taken money from my parish and my flock and used it to better my already extravagant lifestyle. I have chosen to work here, in this poor section of Los Angeles, to shield my thievery from prying eyes and, in doing so, I have found it easy to rob my constituency blind."

"How..." his voice trailed off, horrified.

"Exodus 20:16, 'Thou shalt not bear false witness against thy neighbor.' I confess I have borne false witness against my neighbors, my brethren, and my family. I have used false words to break apart husbands and wives and to send the innocent to jail. I have lied to my superiors at every turn to protect my evil practices. I have become as the serpent in the garden, beguiling all those who would hear my voice."

"No..." On the other side of the booth, Francis De Solei sat down heavily and buried his face in his hands while the little girl continued to lay out his secret life in exact and damning detail.

"Exodus 20:17, 'Thou shalt not covet.' I confess I have coveted my neighbor's house, and have committed much wrong in the world to achieve status and wealth. Worst of all, I confess I have coveted my neighbor's wife. I have used my position to obtain relationships considered taboo for someone of my order. I confess I have made a mockery of my vows."

De Solei, his world crumbling around him, meekly asked, "How much more must I endure?"

The young girl smiled a delicious smile and responded tenderly. "Until I'm finished, Francis." Her voice deepened again as she resumed. "Exodus 20:14, 'Thou shalt not commit adultery'."

"NO! You have no proof!" De Solei had grown livid again.

The girl, for her part, showed no signs of slowing down. "I, Francis De Solei, confess to the most serious and evil practice of adultery. I confess to having used my position in the church to lure many women, both married and single, into my bed. I have broken marriages, I have ruined young girls' lives, all for my pleasure. Even this very evening, I have plans to meet Audrey McMillen, a member of my flock married to a prominent businessman in the community, and take her to my private chambers."

"How..." the priest stammered. "How can you know this? Who are you?"

The girl switched voices once more, responding, "No one of consequence. It is not important who I am, but who you are. So far, we have discerned you aren't a very nice man, Francis. But, we've only covered nine of the ten at this point. It wouldn't be like you to stop so close to the finish line, now would it?"

De Solei was openly sobbing now.

One last time, the girl transformed her voice into De Solei's. "Exodus 20:13, 'Thou shalt not kill.' I confess I have killed men and women who have gotten in my way. I have been responsible for the deaths of over fifteen people. I have paid members of my flock large amounts of money to take care of problems for me. I have killed husbands who found out about me, wives who have threatened to go to the police, and those who stood in my way in the church. I have even killed another priest with my own bare hands, suffocating him in his sleep so I could rise up and take his place here at St. Mary's. I have plotted with Audrey to kill her husband, but plan on killing both of them to cover my tracks. I am purely evil—the worst of all sinners—and will burn in hellfire forever for my great sins against the world. No amount of mercy could let God forgive me my trespasses now."

The little girl folded her arms and waited to hear what De Solei had to say about his fully documented confession. De Solei chose not to respond, but instead threw open the door of the confessional and ran out into the church. In his haste, he fell into a nearby pew, where he had one moment to decide: flee from the little girl who had just laid bare his life in all its wickedness, or kill her and silence her forever. Madness overcame him and with a roar, he shoved himself from the pew toward the confessional just as the little girl opened the door and stepped out. Murderous rage in his eyes, he reached for her throat and fastened his thick hands around her delicate neck. He had killed before to protect his lifestyle, one more would mean nothing. Mad with desperation and rage, he pressed his thumbs into her throat as hard as he could, collapsing her windpipe and cutting off her breath.

The little girl barely struggled, the calm look on her face suggesting she had expected the evening to come to this. In only a few seconds, a sickening pop of cartilage and bone announced her spine and neck had snapped. Her body went limp, her eyes open and staring, her last look of peace frozen on her delicate features.

De Solei maintained his homicidal grip, partly out of rage and partly out of shock at what he had just done. He stared down at the little girl's dead face, letting the fear and desperation slowly fade away from within. Finally, he released his grip and stumbled into a sitting position, his back against one of the confessional doors. His cold, calculating mind regained control and it took him no time to convince himself he had simply done what had to be done. He had silenced a blasphemer; eliminated an evil voice against God. Yes, he was a sinner, but he also did a great deal of good in the community that she hadn't detailed. Surely, he reasoned with himself for the millionth time, the two would equal out in the end in his favor.

Getting rid of her body would not be a problem. All he would have to do would be to dump her corpse in any one of the nearby alleys where it would likely remain, ignored by the bums and drug users who frequented them. Eventually a policeman would find the body, and De Solei could tip the authorities in the direction of one of the local homeless men who had "confessed" to the crime. It had happened before, it would happen again.

Francis De Solei closed his eyes and ran his hands across his sweat-streaked face, rubbing hard to release the stress of the incident. He took a deep breath and then froze as a deep and pervading sense of doom washed over him. His chest constricted in agony and he rolled to his side, thinking a heart attack had found him. With a groan of pain, he got his knees under him, hoping to get back to his feet and reach a phone to call for help. No! The girl! He had to get rid of the girl first!

Desperation took hold again and he began to crawl, before a wave of incredible despair engulfed him and stopped him cold. He felt a set of delicate fingers twine themselves in his hair and suddenly his head was yanked up so forcefully he thought his own neck would break. With sickening realization, he found he was staring into the glittering eyes of the dead little girl, a perfectly evil smile on her perfect face.

"That wasn't very nice of you, Francis," she said, her voice strangely distorted as she effortlessly held him before her. "But I offer you redemption. Look upon me, Francis. Look upon Letalis and be saved, for I am your savior."

He fought hard those last few moments to hold onto his soul, unable to tear his terrified gaze from the penetrating eyes of the girl who had reduced his life to shambles in just a few moments. As he looked into her eyes, he realized she was right; perhaps there was another way. He relaxed his body and she let go of his hair, all the while maintaining eye contact with the defeated priest. He had sinned and she had convicted him. He had killed her and she had risen and convicted him again. There was no doubt where his path now lay and all he could do now was accept his fate. The little girl, knowing she had caught her prey and was now his master, continued to smile.

The ring coming from the phone next to the bed of Father Michael Dalacourt instantly pulled him out of his deep slumber. In that moment where reality and the dream world mixed, Michael was unsure where he was and what the disturbing dream he had just experienced truly meant. The phone by his bed jangled again and he glanced at the bedside table, noting it was just after three in the morning. Shaking his head in an unsuccessful attempt to clear the disturbing dream from his thoughts, he reached out and picked up the handset.

"Hello?" he said, still somewhat groggy.

"Father Dalacourt," Archbishop De Solei's crisp voice came from the other end. "Why are you still asleep at such a late hour?"

"It's three in the morning, Your Excellency." Dalacourt realized that last comment might have sounded a bit frosted, but De Solei didn't seem to notice.

"Ah, yes, I forgot about the time difference. I have been at the Vatican too long, I suppose."

"You're in Rome?"

"Where else would I be, Michael?"

"I'm sorry, Your Excellency," Dalacourt quickly replied, shaking his head and realizing that while the De Solei in his dream had been in

Los Angeles, the real one was still at the Vatican. "Just trying to wake up."

"Very well," the archbishop replied. "How is God's work progressing?"

Dalacourt paused, trying to collect his scattered thoughts before answering. He had been in Belle Plaine for three days now, working with Father Sparrel of St. Michael's day and night as they attended to people, listening to prayers and confessions and doing their best to allay the rampant fears the world was coming to an end. Reports were coming in from all over the world now about mass vanishings and the dead rising from their graves, missing from their caskets and mausoleums in every city, every state, and every country in the world.

Religious fervor had reached epic levels and churches were swelling their ranks to unheard-of numbers. The previous night, he and Father Sparrel had met with several other church leaders from the small town in an effort to come to some consensus about what was happening around the world. In the end, all any of them could agree on was that perhaps in the coming days more light would be shed on the incredible events around the world and they might all have better ground to stand upon together. In the meantime, they would continue to care for their flocks and prepare as best they could for whatever might happen.

So it was a very tired Michael Dalacourt that answered slowly, "You could say His work is progressing how He wishes it to."

"You sound irritable, Father Dalacourt," said De Solei, abruptly changing the subject. "Is everything all right?"

"Yes, everything's fine," the young priest replied quickly, trying to push back the growing uneasiness he was feeling. "I'm just tired, nothing more," he lied.

"Well then, I shall get to business," De Solei went on. "You're being reassigned."

"Reassigned?" Dalacourt stammered, completely unprepared for that particular statement. "Am I returning to the Vatican?"

"No," came the reply, De Solei's voice awash with self-importance and unabashed superiority. "I've been personally charged by His Excellency with taking control of the church in the United States during these miraculous times. I'm flying to Los Angeles within the week and have requested you join me at the Cathedral of Our Lady of the Angels."

Dalacourt was stunned. Next to the Vatican, Our Lady of the Angels was one of the cornerstones of the church, serving the total Los Angeles archdiocese and the heart of all the nearly three hundred parish churches and communities in it. If De Solei was being assigned to oversee the church in the United States, Our Lady of the Angels was the obvious headquarters. However, even more disturbing in his mind was that De Solei was returning to Los Angeles, the same location in Dalacourt's nightmare, and the young Father could not help but feel very uneasy about the coincidence. Dalacourt had secretly suspected his mentor of placing his interests above those of the church on occasion, but his dream had taken things to a whole new level. Could his dream point to the truth?

"Father Michael," De Solei pressed again, his voice showing a bit of annoyance this time. "Do I still have your attention?"

"I'm sorry, Your Excellency," Dalacourt again replied quickly, silently cursing himself for not maintaining his composure. "Your news simply caught me by surprise. It's quite an honor for you and you have my congratulations."

"Yes, yes," agreed De Solei, the self-righteous superiority once again showing in his voice, as well as his impatience. "I asked specifically for your assistance and received permission from His

Holiness to bring you with me. I expect I won't be disappointed in my choice."

"Thank you," was all Dalacourt could manage to say.

"You will once again take a bus, Father Dalacourt," he went on smugly. "You've done what was necessary in Iowa and it will be a few days before I arrive. A long trip to Los Angeles should give you a chance to clear your thoughts and prepare yourself for what lies ahead. Now that you've seen the truth, I expect you will be more helpful."

"Yes, Your Excellency," Dalacourt answered quietly, by this point barely able to register what De Solei was saying due to his own mind spinning uncontrollably. "I shall be on the first bus tomorrow. If I may, I'm wondering why you're going to Los Angeles and not somewhere more central like the Holy Name Cathedral in Chicago or the Cathedral Basilica of St. Louis. Both would be excellent choices to serve the church in this country."

De Solei seemed taken aback by this question, but for quite a different reason than Dalacourt had expected. "My young Father," he answered, "you don't see the big picture here. The cathedral is the ideal location for a man of my stature to attend to the masses. In these trying times, the people need to see energetic, caring leaders demonstrating strength from great and holy places. Besides," he went on, misunderstanding the reasoning behind Dalacourt's question, "don't be too concerned with the bus trip. I know you'd prefer to stay where you are, but the ride will help you regain your focus. I'll be counting on you when you get here, Michael."

"I apologize for my impudence, Your Excellency," Dalacourt said, deciding it was best to end this conversation now before he said something he would regret. "It was unintentional. I'm quite happy to travel by bus to Los Angeles. I'll be ready for you when I arrive."

Any hint at a double meaning was lost on De Solei, who had

already mentally moved on to his next phone call. "Excellent. I shall see you in Los Angeles in three days."

Dalacourt listened to the click on the other end of the line and hesitated before hanging up, thinking hard on what his superior had just told him. He doubted De Solei's explanation on needing an able assistant, knowing there were many others far more qualified than him to aid the archbishop. Nevertheless, he would have a few days to ponder and pray over the dream he had witnessed and to search for its true meaning. Tonight, however, he needed sleep. Tomorrow would bring its own troubles.

Half a world away, Francis De Solei was putting the finishing touches on his own plans to limit the damage his enemies—enemies like Michael Dalacourt—could do to him as he began to consolidate his power and ready himself to become one of the most powerful men in the world.

CHAPTER 19

Monterey, California: Victor Emmanuel Legio sat perfectly upright while engulfed in an enormous black leather chair at the head of a slate black table in a lowly lit room surrounded by the members of the board of his corporation. He had forced them to be present here today—some with bribes, others with threats—because he needed their support in consolidating the entire business under his name alone. It wasn't going well. In fact, not only was it one of the worst possible things he could do if he intended to remain one of the wealthiest men in the world, but it was also quite blatantly illegal.

None of this mattered to Victor Legio, however, because he knew he wouldn't be around long enough to see his glorious wealth and power fade away or to find himself safely behind bars in jail. He had quite literally sold his soul to the devil, and he knew if he wanted his life to go on, he needed to follow the orders Hade had given him. And those orders had been clearly stated: put Legio Enterprises in one neat little package with his name on it.

"Gentlemen and ladies, I can see we're getting nowhere at the moment, and as we have been debating now for over four hours, perhaps we should recess for an hour for lunch. There are many layers to this new direction I have proposed and I can certainly understand why you might be skeptical, but I'm here to tell you it will be the best decision you'll ever make. This will put us in position to become the most powerful conglomerate in the history of the world and deep down, I know you all want to be a part of history."

Voices were again immediately raised in argument but Legio silenced them with a wave of his hand. "Not now," he said calmly. "Get some lunch, think about what has already been said here this morning, and return back in an hour. Trust me, you aren't going to want to miss this one for the world." His last sentence held, for the first time that day, a glint of the old Victor Legio who was always making and breaking deals, getting ahead at whatever the cost and making everyone who accompanied him rich in the process.

The board members acquiesced and began to rise slowly from their seats, some stretching, others grumbling, all fuming. If not for the fact that Victor Legio had made everyone on the board multi-millionaires, they would have voted him out as president and CEO of Legio Industries ten minutes into their meeting. However, he had proven them all wrong so many times before that they would all return to hear him out, even if they were utterly convinced he had lost his mind.

As the doors shut behind the last of them, Legio verbalized flatly, "Lights, ten percent," and the brightness level in the room dimmed immediately to almost nothing. The only other light in the room was Legio's tablet, sitting before him on the table, which gave his visage an eerie hue. Victor Legio was left alone with only one other individual: his right-hand man, for lack of a better description.

Legio's chief assistant was called Marmoset. His parents, in one of those disastrous instances where the cosmos came together to encourage someone to name their child a truly sad and ridiculous name, had chosen that their first and only child should go by the moniker of Callithrix Aurita Williams. Callithrix Aurita was the Latin scientific name for the buffy tufted-ear marmoset, an animal native to Brazil, arguably one of the cutest animals ever to roam the face of the earth. Unfortunately for Callithrix, his parents were in the Peace Corps and lived in an area where marmosets were everywhere. Sitting in the hospital in Belo Horizante after their son was born, they had decided to name their child after their favorite animal. His parents had returned to the United States shortly after his birth and Callithrix had indeed grown up an outcast, always referred to as "monkey-boy" or "marmosetta" or whatever other hurtful nickname his classmates could devise.

The even sadder truth, however, was that his parents hadn't been too far off the mark in naming him, for he did look strikingly similar to one of the small monkeys. This, of course, only distanced himself further from his peers. Shunned, he turned inward toward books and mathematics and eventually found himself at college, a struggling student without any friends and fewer prospects. Through chance or some higher fate, though, Callithrix Aurita Williams eventually found his way to Victor Emmanuel Legio and the two became friends of a sort.

It was a strange friendship, because deep down neither one of them had much affection for the other. On many levels, they actually hated each other immensely. But both of them were smart enough to know when they came across a fellow rogue, so they latched on to each other for a wild ride—a mutually beneficial union that put them both where they were today.

While they had worked together tirelessly over the years to build their fortunes, Legio had gotten all of the fame, glory, and riches. Marmoset was smart enough, however, to realize that without Legio, he might be back in his parents' mobile home in the desert on the outskirts of Perris, California. So while he was completely loyal to Legio, that didn't mean he was his yes-man. It was that rare quality in an underling that Legio was generally pleased with. But at this moment, what he wanted from his aide was unquestioning acceptance of the proposed new direction of the company. Unfortunately, that meant it would be the last thing the man would do.

"Are you crazy?" Marmoset blurted out the instant the two were alone, throwing his hands up in the air in exasperation as he fairly leaped out of his seat and stalked toward the CEO in a rage. "Are you trying to get yourself fired from your own company? Are you trying to lose everything you've worked so hard for? Everything we've worked so hard for?" He slammed his hands down on the table in front of Legio, forcing the man to look at him as he continued his rant. "Is it coke? Is that it? Are you high? You always say you never touch the stuff and yet here we are! And as you are always so fond of saying, Victor, 'actions speak louder than words.' So logically, you have to be high on something."

Legio, who had spent all of his energy attempting to convince the board to accept his plans, slumped further into his chair and waved the infuriated man off. "Calm down, Marmoset. You'll have to trust I know what I'm doing. After all these years, after all these years..." He trailed off and looked as if he was ready to cash in his chips, when that familiar glint in his eyes returned just enough for his next sentence to carry a little weight. "I've never lost a deal yet, or have you forgotten that already?" He looked up briefly and made eye contact with Marmoset.

"What I haven't forgotten is how you should still be in jail, but you got out of your little problem over twenty years ago and never told me how," he said, hands still on the table. "I haven't forgotten how you have nearly bankrupted us five times and how you had Steve McMichael killed so he wouldn't blow the whistle on us. I haven't forgotten the bribes to congressmen and third world leaders, the threats to competitors, or the fuzzy accounting. You know they invented the phrase 'cook the books' due to your financial magic, but no one has ever caught you. I've seen you grow from nothing to everything and take a lot of people with you." He paused and straightened, folding his arms across his chest and his voice softened as he continued. "But then, I also haven't forgotten how for the past week you've pulled yourself away from everyone and everything. Look at you, Victor. You've lost weight, your eyes are glazed over, and you mutter constantly. Did you think I wouldn't notice these things?"

At this, Legio smiled. "I don't have an answer for you, if that's what you're wondering. All I know is for us to continue our climb to the top, we must continue to make up the rules as we go. This is how it has to be and if you aren't with me, I suppose it's time to part ways."

Marmoset's jaw nearly hit the floor. "What?" he exclaimed, his face turning red. "Are you saying you would break your ties with me after all we've been through? Don't forget I know enough to put you away for lifetimes upon lifetimes."

Legio only smiled. "Very true," he admitted. "But even if you did, your own time behind bars would far outlive your remaining days. No, Marmoset," he said with a knowing nod, "you are as tied to this direction as I am, you just don't see it yet."

Marmoset stood perfectly still, his features working in a rage while Legio watched him closely. After what seemed like an eternity, Marmoset relaxed. "Fine, fine," he said with a dismissive wave of his hand. "If this is how you want it, then I suppose we can survive one more major bump on the highway."

"Excellent..." Legio began, but Marmoset leaned forward again, interrupting him.

"But, I warn you, Victor," he growled menacingly. "Don't think you can get rid of me so easily. I can do things you can't and it would be wise to remember that. If you want to get rid of me, you'll have to kill me. But don't take that path too quickly. I have friends, too, you know."

"I'll be sure to file that away for future reference," Legio sighed. "While you're onboard for the wrong reasons, you're still onboard and I'll content myself with that. The wolves are circling, Marmoset—

circling, circling, ever circling. This is my only chance to keep them at bay. I have to do this or…" he trailed off, before finishing in a voice barely above a whisper. "Well, there is no 'or'."

Marmoset wrinkled up his nose and skewered his face enough so that he looked even more like a monkey. He straightened and made a spitting motion toward the floor. "Screw you, Victor," he snapped. "I'm on board because, quite frankly, I still want my hands in the honey pot. It'll be that much easier to take control when you lose it." With that, he turned and stormed out of the room, leaving Legio alone.

For the longest time, Victor just stared at the door. How could he convince some of the smartest people he knew that what he was doing was in everyone's best interest, when he himself knew it was not? As he sat there, desperately trying to figure out a way to accomplish the task Hade had set before him and thus save his own life, he felt the hair on the back of his neck begin to prickle and a cold surge of terror ran through him.

"Hello, Victor," Hade said from the shadows at the back of the room. "My nose was itching, so I figured someone must be thinking about me. Was it you?"

Legio fought back the panic at the man's sudden and silent appearance and he gripped the edge of the table for support. "What are you doing here?" he snapped, his fear changing to anger. "How did you get past security?"

"Victor," Hade said, spreading his hands in a mock gesture of peace, "why would you want to keep me away?"

"I'm doing what you want," Legio fumed.

"Are you?"

Legio paled, wondering if Hade knew he was trying to discover a way out of this mess. But he kept his voice firm as he replied, "I'm not stupid, Hade. I know what my orders are and I intend to see them through. Now, get out of here before someone sees you and ruins everything."

"How do you know I don't want everything ruined? How do you know there's anything here I care deeply enough about to be concerned about it becoming ruined? How do you know I'm not just here having a bit of sport with an old compadre?" Hade stood up and walked down the length of the table to where Legio was seated at the other end. With exaggerated slowness, he pulled out one of the plush chairs next to the billionaire, before falling into it and kicking his dirty boots up on the table.

"Ruined," Hade ruminated. "That's such a subjective word. Usually when one man is ruined, another is made anew. You know that, don't you? But of course you do," he said with a knowing smile. "Personally, I prefer the words 'immense pain and suffering'." He looked at Legio and raised an eyebrow. "You see, when someone says, 'If things don't get wrapped up within three days, another certain someone will only know immense pain and suffering for the last thirty years of their life,' it's hard to see any wiggle room on that one."

Up until this point, Victor Legio's only possible future involved staving off death for as long as possible. Now, however, it dawned on him that, as bad as death sounded, it was suddenly second on his list of dreaded outcomes. He couldn't make it through that kind of suffering, of that he was most certain. His chest hardly moved at all and his mouth appeared to remain closed as his words seeped out. "I understand what you mean," he finally answered meekly.

"Good," came the reply.

"You mean to make this as hard for me as possible, don't you?" Legio went on with a resigned sigh. "So tell me, Hade, what exactly is it you want me to do now?"

"I want you to finish what I sent you to do, Victor," he answered contemptuously. "It's taking too long. According to organized religion in general, the end of the world is upon us. So, tell me, Victor, how are you going to solve our little problem in a timely manner?"

"I have no idea," Legio responded in annoyance. "I've just spent four hours talking to the board and they are refusing to sign off at the moment. You know I can't make this stick without their approval, even with my majority holdings. If you had any idea how difficult this is, you would give me more time."

Hade stood up so fast his chair flew backward and hit the wall with a loud bang. "Do you take me for some kind of a fool?" Hade fairly roared as he slammed his hands down on the conference table, causing a large crack to appear and run the length of it. "Do you think I'm making up this deadline for my own enjoyment?"

Victor Legio was speechless, his eyes riveted on the crack that had just ruined his immense and incredibly expensive boardroom table. He always knew Hade was a strong man, but this simply defied explanation.

"I'm not," Hade went on, leaning closer, his voice dropping to a dangerous level. "This deal *has* to be closed immediately, no excuses. I thought you would have realized that by now."

Victor Legio tore his eyes from the split down the table and looked at the big man towering over him. "I'm doing the best I can," he finally said, his voice barely above a whisper.

"Then do better," Hade snapped and sat back down, his anger seeming to fade as quickly as it appeared. He laced his fingers behind his head again, relaxed his posture, and sighed. "You know, I'm amazed you're treating me like this, Victor. I know more about your company than you do, because when you're gone, I'm going to be the one running it. So, as long as you can get your board to agree, we can all live happily ever after. Well, everyone but you, of course," he finished with a perfectly depraved smile.

"Would you stop talking about my death as if it's already happened?" Legio pleaded. "It's hard enough concentrating on this mess without that being waved in my face all the time!"

"I prefer to call it a motivational pep-talk," Hade answered slyly. "People with problems either fix them or put a bullet in someone's head."

"So I should fix it in order for *you* to put a bullet in my head?"

"That's one of several easy ways we can do it, but we're getting ahead of ourselves here, Victor. You're still alive and, while you're alive, you need to be working. So, where are we on the matter?"

"It's fairly simple," Legio explained, somewhat glad he could concentrate on something else other than torture and dying. "Once they're in agreement, I can have everything else done in a matter of hours. The problem is, I have no idea how to get them to agree."

"So, persuade them."

"How am I supposed to do that?" Legio shot back. "These people aren't stupid, Hade. They're cold, calculating business men and women and they know a sham when they see it."

"Let's look at the assets then," Hade said with a smile, reaching into his coat and pulling out a cigar.

"You're not going to smoke that in here, are you?" Legio said, looking at the huge man incredulously.

"Why not?" Hade asked, biting off the tip and spitting it onto the floor.

Victor Legio just sighed, too tired to even argue about it. "Never mind, you just do whatever you want," he said wearily.

"I intend to," Hade grinned. "One of the perks of being me." Hade said with a nod as he pulled out a matchbook, struck a match on the pack and lit his cigar. He snuffed the match out on his pants, puffed on the cigar a few times to get it lit properly, then leaned back in his chair again. "Did you ever read *The Hobbit*, Vic?"

Legio just stared, unable to fathom where Hade was going with this new conversational twist.

"It's certainly not Latin," Hade went on, waving his cigar in the air. "I just liked the way old Gandalf blew smoke rings in the shape of dragons and ships and the like. I think maybe someday after all this is over, I might try and elevate my own talents."

"What does that have to do with anything?" Legio snapped.

"Oh, do calm down, Vic," Hade answered easily. "You'll give yourself a heart attack. Sometimes you just have to mix pleasure with business, that's all. So, who's on your side?"

"Marmoset is, of course," Legio answered, grateful to be back on topic.

"Excellent. Good man, that Marmoset. I've got plans for him."

"And then there's Eikmeier and Morris who would go along with it pretty easily if the others caved. Both of them are single and have no ties here in the States. If they're in, I think they could shift the thinking of Emanuel and Ridgeway, although the price would have to be extremely high."

"Is that it?"

"Unfortunately, yes. Everyone else, I'm afraid, is against this thing whole-heartedly and that leaves us hopelessly in the minority."

Hade sat and stared for a moment, stroking his long beard and puffing on his cigar thoughtfully. "So, how many more do we need?"

"Well, there are seventeen on the board and twelve need to agree to it, which is the first problem because I'm only halfway there. The bigger problem is there can't be a single person voting against it or the whole thing is sunk. There can be abstentions, but no negative votes."

"So many of our dreams at first seem impossible, then they seem improbable, and then when we summon the will, they soon become inevitable," Hade said importantly. "Christopher Reeve said that, Vic. I know you've had a long day, but I need you to focus here, okay? Summon up the will and stick with me. Are you with me, Victor?"

"Yes, yes, go on. What am I to do?"

"It's really quite simple when you think about it. We just need to ask ourselves which five we need to kill to convince the other twelve to go along with it."

"Are you insane?" Legio hissed loudly. "We can't just kill five members of the board of directors! If you think two or three of them dissenting from this would look bad, what do you think killing off five of them would look like?" He threw up his hands in disgust. "For the love of God, Hade, I thought you said you knew what you were doing?"

"I'm quite beyond God's love, Victor," Hade replied, "and I certainly do know what I'm doing. You'll just have to trust me."

"Trust you?" Legio fumed. "You're going to kill me and now you want me to take five people along for the ride! And I'm supposed to trust you? Give me one good reason."

"Well, for starters, I think in a few short days, very few people are going to be concerned with five dead rich guys. I can assure you that there will never be an investigation."

"We're talking about very high profile individuals, Hade," Legio explained dryly. "These people have their names in the paper at least every other week. Killing them off would feed the conspiracy nuts and newsmongers for a year."

"Victor, you know there are people missing all the time these days and those numbers are rising every day. Why, just yesterday the entire national baseball team in Cuba was spirited away without anyone knowing where they went or what happened to them."

"That's a baseball team," Legio countered.

"A very good baseball team, Victor," Hade answered.

"Regardless, they're all missing together," Legio pointed out. "That means lots of unanswered questions, but none directed at any particular individual. Unfortunately, we can't make five people who went out to lunch separately simply disappear. There would be all sorts of questions asked and every single one would be directed at me. They would have to be dead and it would have to be public."

"Didn't you just say killing them would bring the newshounds descending down on you?"

"Depends on how it's done," Legio answered. "But dead people are certainly better than missing ones."

"Now you're getting the picture," Hade said with a knowing smile. "You know, you can be pretty smart when you want to be, Vic."

While Legio was startled by the direction of the conversation and by his own participation in deciding on the deaths of people he knew, he quickly became determined to take the path of killing his associates to the logical conclusion. It was the only way, even if there were a lot of unanswered questions. "What are you going to do to deflect accusations, Hade? This company is like a child to me, Hade. I won't have my legacy destroyed."

"That won't happen, I promise you," Hade replied seriously. "But just because five men must die, it doesn't mean we need a media circus. I'm not suggesting we bring them in here, invite the press to cover the event, and then execute them all while the cameras are rolling." Hade paused, looking thoughtful. "Although that does have a certain flair to it. No, the trick is to kill them all discretely while convincing the others we did line them up and execute them."

Legio sat back in his chair and thought for a moment about Hade's words. "Must we kill five?" Legio asked, trying to minimize the carnage and preserve the integrity of his company. "Ramirez could go and I wouldn't mind at all. We'd probably be doing a favor for his trophy wife and cavalcade of lawyers."

"Ramirez goes, then. No problem." Hade smiled to himself.

"Weston could go as well and so could Borgen. Isn't that enough? If we kill five, then the others know each of them is safe because they would know we needed all of them to get this done. If we leave room for one or two more of them to go, then our position would be stronger."

Hade mulled this over for a bit before responding. "Stronger, yes. I suppose you're right," he finally said. "You know, Victor, for someone who is most assuredly on the fast track to hell, you're doing a fine job making things right at the end. I've managed to convince you the only way out is through the death of your associates, but ever the dealmaker, you've managed to make all sides come out better than before. I have to say, I'm impressed."

"Don't patronize me, Hade. I just think we can do this with a minimum of bloodshed."

"Oh, I wouldn't dream of patronizing you, Victor," Hade answered smugly. "So, Ramirez, Weston and Borgen it is."

"And how do you intend to do this?"

"Oh, don't worry about that. I knew Ramirez and Weston would be on your short list, so Weston is presently getting run over in a carjacking gone wrong and Ramirez is dying of a heart attack. He really should never have eaten so much food high in cholesterol, you know."

"You can't be serious," Legio exclaimed.

"Oh, I'm quite serious, Victor," Hade went on. "Now, I didn't figure on Borgen, but I can pull my man off of Stevenson and Borgen can be the one who dies from a very nasty strain of food poisoning. If you don't mind, I need to make a quick call. Hope I'm not too late."

Hade opened up his jacket and pulled out a sleek, black Smartphone. He pronounced in a monotone, "Tuono," and Legio could see the bright light from the screen radiate through the darkness of the room as the video chat opened. Hade slid fluidly into Italian as he spoke to someone on the other end. *"Cambi l'obiettivo da Stevenson al Borgen."* A moment passed and Legio heard a voice say, *"Certo,e fatto."* Hade pinched his forefinger and thumb together and swiped his hand sideways, indicating "perfect" in Italian sign language, and ended his call. He took another few moments to read a text message and shook his head at what he saw, then turned his attention back to a stunned Legio. The whole thing had taken less than sixty seconds.

"You should be happy," he explained, working on his cigar again. "You just saved Stevenson's life—at least for the moment. Borgen will die shortly, and Ramirez and Weston are already dead. I couldn't get to Hajaan before he was shot dead by an angry husband whose wife he was allegedly having an affair with. Of course, I had to set that one up earlier so it's just as well. The really sad thing is, Hajaan was as faithful a husband as they come, so he didn't even get to enjoy what eventually killed him. But, so goes life for so many in this world, I suppose. That said, I'm afraid your margin for error is down to one. Is that good enough for you?"

"Yes, I suppose it will do," Legio sighed.

"You can get the other seven on board?" It was asked as a question, even if it wasn't one.

"We can wrap this up fairly quickly, I think," the businessman nodded.

"Good. When Marmoset gets back, give him the news of the premature demise of his colleagues and make absolutely certain he's on your side. If he isn't, he should be the fifth."

"Marmoset?" Legio asked, not wanting to go that far, despite their current animosity.

"I'm serious," Hade pointed out. "If he shows any hesitation at all, call me as soon as you can and I'll take care of it." Hade opened up his jacket, took out a red, white and green striped Smartphone and slid it across the table. "Reach out and touch me."

Legio picked the phone up, turning it over in his hands.

"Listen to me, Vic," Hade said, taking a long pull on his cigar. "The heavy lifting is done. When the others return, all they need to know is one of them can still die, which should make them all want to sign off immediately. I want their signatures tonight, am I understood?"

Legio looked into Hade's eyes, saw the burning fire of a man with a mission, lowered his own eyes and finally said quietly, "Yes. Yes, of course."

"Wonderful. I'll see you in three days and I expect everything to be in order. Do you have any last questions before I leave?"

Legio sat for a moment, contemplating whether to ask his one burning question. Eventually he decided there were no longer any real repercussions for his actions so he might as well throw caution to the wind. "I suppose just the one," he finally said, "which I can only assume you knew I'd ask anyway. Is there any way of me getting through this thing alive?"

Hade sat in silence, puffing on his cigar before eventually answering. He shook his head slowly and said softly, "No." He stood up without looking at Legio and walked out of the office.

Legio sank into his chair and buried his head in his hands. It was one thing to know you were going to die. It was quite another to know you were going to die in three days.

Hade had only been gone for a few minutes when the door opened and Marmoset walked into the room. Legio quickly pulled himself together. He still had one last deal to make, and even though it was going to end in his death, he was going to make sure it went through. He'd finished every other deal he'd ever been involved with before, and he wasn't about to ruin his perfect record on his last one.

Marmoset stopped and wrinkled his nose. "Nasty habit, smoking cigars," the monkey-faced man said. "Those things can kill you, you know."

Legio only smiled hollowly and began to think about how he wanted to spend his last remaining days. One thing for certain was that he wanted to live out his final hours as far away from here and as far away from Marmoset as possible, so he had to make sure everything was finalized that afternoon. But how do you get away from evil when you've courted it your entire life? How does one get the devil out of your home when you've invited him in and fed him all these many years? It was only now he realized he could never break with the devil. He had made his bed and now he had to die in it.

"Marmoset," he said quietly as his index finger idly glided back and forth along the visible crack in the table. "We need to talk."

CHAPTER 20

Salt Lake City, Utah: All paths on the university campus lead eventually to the north entrance of the library. They converge from all directions, meeting in a concrete plaza speckled with islands of grass and trees, and pyramids of tinted glass that provide natural light to the underground levels of the building. On the north end of the plaza, an artificial waterfall splashes into a U-shaped pool. Trees fill the concavity of the U, along with concrete seating at the water's edge. It's a place of contemplation, where studious minds can relax and soak in their surroundings.

Owen preferred this locale because it reminded him of Ferguson Canyon, and he came here often. With the consistent hum of the waterfall to mask the noise of the outside world and the nearby grove of trees to obscure its sight, Owen almost felt that same sense of dissociation. He savored those rare places where he could find the solitude necessary for introspection because there were so few places he could be alone with his thoughts. Today, however, he was there with Alexis, on whom the effect of this perfect morsel of man-made nature was thoroughly wasted. She shouted loudly in her fourth attempt to initiate conversation, highlighting one of the differences Owen had always felt existed between them. Alexis loved to talk—Owen loved to think and do.

He knew she didn't understand why he loved this spot, but smiled as he thought he didn't understand how she could eat the things she ate. Shaking his head and grinning, Owen looked at the sandwich he held. Yet again, he had let Alexis talk him into something he knew he wouldn't like. This particular experiment was a bagel with four different kinds of green leafy vegetables.

He had asked himself many times during their friendship why he went along with Alexis' suggestions. He'd eventually come to the realization that it was simply too much work to say no. She never acknowledged a "no" the first time, disbelieved the second, and invariably challenged the third. Under normal circumstances, such a personality would drive Owen crazy, but Alexis was different. She asserted herself without being overbearing, treated others with kindness, and fit in well with Owen's circle of friends. Besides that, she was beautiful. Her dark hair spilled in perfect ringlets to her shoulders, providing a wonderful contrast to her bright blue eyes and her rosebud lips that had a permanent upturn at each corner.

Owen's eyes followed the progress of his thoughts from Alexis' hair to her eyes and then to her mouth. Abruptly, she stopped talking and looked at Owen with a wide-eyed gaze. Thinking she had caught him admiring her, Owen looked away quickly and bit down too hard into his sandwich. When he looked up again, Alexis was brushing at the corner of her mouth as if searching for something, a questioning look on her face. She spoke again, and of course, Owen heard nothing. Realizing he wasn't going to enjoy his surroundings with Alexis in tow, he motioned with his head toward an opening in the trees and the two gathered their things and left.

Strolling onto the open space of the plaza, he finally heard Alexis ask, "Did I get it?"

"Get what?"

"The mustard. Is it still there or did I get it?" Owen's blank look answered her question for her. "I don't have mustard on my face, do I? It's just I thought you were looking—oh, never mind," she finished, embarrassed.

Her blue eyes narrowed and Owen knew her quick mind would discover the intent of his stare if he let her think long enough. "So," he began desperately, "tomorrow's the big day—my annual road trip to

San Diego. Heaven knows I'm ready after everything else that's happened." Just thinking about the trip made Owen feel like a kid in a candy store. He imagined himself sitting on his surfboard, the sun beating on his back and the sea rolling beneath him. Next to the mountains, the ocean gave Owen the greatest sense of the overwhelming power of nature. Surfing gave him the chance to harness some of that power.

"Hello?" The obvious irritation in Alexis' voice popped the bubble of Owen's thoughts and brought him back to the present with a sheepish grin. "Have you been ignoring me on purpose or are you just absent-minded today? I really want to know why you're even considering this now."

"Why not?" Owen answered, getting ready to defend himself. "We go every year."

"This isn't every year, Owen," she replied.

"Look, I'm not going to stop living my life because every religious person on the planet is screaming 'this is really, truly the end, we swear.' Besides, I need to do something to clear my head, to find my normal again. You probably wouldn't understand."

In truth, she did understand and felt it as keenly as Owen did, but she had learned to trust her instincts and didn't feel good about their upcoming trip. Over the past couple of weeks, she had been arguing to join them with a couple of her friends, but now she simply didn't want Owen to leave at all.

"Look, Alex," Owen continued. "I know you want to go, but I just can't let you come. It's nothing against you," he finished, trying not to hurt her feelings. This trip gave them a week to do whatever they wanted without worrying about schedules, responsibilities, or most of all how they appeared to the opposite sex. If they spent two days surfing and playing volleyball on the beach without bathing, so be it. If

Alexis went, Owen knew he would spend his time worrying about things that shouldn't matter on a trip like this. Which was ironic, of course, because it was worrying him now.

Over the last few months, he had found himself acting differently around her. If he knew she would be at a particular event, he took more time on his appearance and made sure there would be no other girls with him. His excitement over anything would pique more if Alexis was somehow involved and he had started going out of his way to spend time with her. Alexis was becoming more than just a friend or "one of the guys" and therein lay the issue. The theme of this road trip was to surround himself with those he didn't need to impress and just have a good time. For that reason alone, Owen couldn't let her come.

The silence between the two extended. Usually, if Owen kept silent, Alexis would forge ahead and, when she did this time, it wasn't what Owen was expecting to hear. "You still don't get it. I don't want to go any more," she said softly, "and I don't want you going, either."

He sighed. "Look, Alex, if the world is going to end, it'll have to either wait until I get home or it'll end with me on the beach. There's worse ways to go."

A light touch on his shoulder interrupted his thoughts. He heard the intoxicating voice to whom the touch belonged and the bottom dropped completely out of his world. "Owen? It's you!"

For a moment, Owen forgot all about Alexis and the trip. After all, Windy's hand rested on his shoulder and *she* was excited to see *him*. Their first meeting had left Owen with little information about her, so he had spent a good portion of that evening imagining the personality accompanying such disarming beauty.

While Owen stood stunned, Windy continued, "Imagine running into you again. I come to this waterfall almost every day and I've never seen you here. What are you up to?"

She removed her hand from his shoulder and the sudden loss of her touch helped him calm down a little. "Just chillin'," he said as casually as he could. "I'm glad to see you looking happier."

Windy must have agreed as her smile broadened and her eyes sparkled. "I am, thanks to you. I did what you told me. I'm taking a long-term economics course right now and today I sat in the back row of class with someone who always sits alone. It's what Chris would have done and I think he appreciated it."

Owen thought any man with even half a pulse would have appreciated it. Refocusing his thoughts, he reminded himself this girl had come to him the other day looking for a friend, not a boyfriend. Her speech and actions appeared without guile to Owen.

Windy smiled and said, "I can see you're as talkative as usual. I wish I knew what was running through that brain of yours that kept the rest of you so occupied."

The way she looked at Owen sent lightning through him. He had no idea how to respond, when Alexis, whom he had completely forgotten, spoke for him. "Mainly nothing—boyhood fantasies of becoming Batman or the first man to do a three-sixty spike in the national volleyball championship. On those rare occasions when he entertains more serious notions, he breathes slowly and exclusively through his nose and closes his eyes."

Owen felt himself redden and turned to face her again. When he did so, he expected to see her wearing the face he called "the thunderhead." After all, he had ignored her presence the instant Windy arrived. However, she just looked at him—or more precisely, near him. Her gaze focused on a spot just in front of him. Owen had never seen Alexis react this way when he spoke to other girls. Although she hid it well, he could usually see the subtle ways she changed when other girls approached. She would stand closer to him, fidget with her hair, or laugh a little less at his jokes. This time, however, there was something more going on.

Without a glance at Alexis, Windy responded, "There's something boyish about you, Owen." With a deep sigh, Windy cast her gaze about and said in a bored tone, "Well, I'm done with my class for the day. I wonder what there's to do around here on a Friday night."

Alexis came up with an idea first. "Owen has a lot of packing to do, but maybe you and I could hang out. By the way, I'm Alexis."

She extended her hand to Windy, who still hadn't graced Alexis with so much as a glance. With a slight hesitation, Windy turned to Alexis and the two shook hands, but she said nothing. Admittedly ignorant of female behavior, even Owen saw nothing congenial in the greetings exchanged between the two. They looked like two lionesses about to devour each other. Then Owen noticed Alexis' gaze. She looked sharply at Windy's hand and hesitantly released it. Then she renewed her invitation to hang out together for the evening.

Windy turned back to Owen and, ignoring Alexis' question completely, asked, "So what are you packing for?"

"My friends and I are hitting the road for a few days. It really doesn't take much packing; some gear for Fishlake, golf clubs for Vegas, a volleyball and swimming trunks for San Diego."

Windy's face lost some of its excitement. Without noticing, Owen continued, "If you're looking for something to do, Alexis' offer is probably the best you'll get. Just don't let her feed you. She has a cool group of friends, though, and I'm sure they'd love to get to know you."

Each girl's face soured at the suggestion, but both suppressed their reactions quickly.

Windy spoke first. Again, she steered the discussion towards Owen's trip. "A road trip? When will you be leaving?" The words hurried out in a tone that made him uneasy, and he wondered what could disturb her poise like that.

"We leave for San Diego in the morning," he answered almost blandly. "But I'll be back in a week. I'd be more than happy to help set you up with some friends when I get home."

"A week," she said in a breathless voice, "that'll be too late."

Mercifully, Alexis broke the silence. "That'll be too what?" She appeared to have cast pretense aside and asked bluntly. At the same time, she moved a step closer to Owen and curled her arm under his. She had never done that before and the shock of the apparent intimacy caused Owen to steer his gaze from Windy to his own arm. Her touch warmed him, which surprised him even more.

"I… I need to go," Windy said breathlessly, bringing Owen back to reality. "I have someplace…I need to be."

"Are you okay, Windy?" he asked.

Windy extended her arm with the palm forward as if she feared for Owen's safety if he came too close. After several seconds of this, she inhaled deeply, regained her regal posture, and looked at Owen with the powerful presence of someone once more in control. She managed a smile. "Sorry, it's asthma," she confessed breathlessly. "I've had it since childhood, but it sneaks up on me occasionally. Nothing to worry about."

Alexis' face regained its strained smile as she spoke, "Are you sure you don't need to sit down or anything? If you feel like you're going to pass out, I could give you a ride home. Where did you say you lived?"

Owen looked at Alexis with a doubtful expression. "I thought you said you had a study date now."

Alexis shot Owen a look that expressed anything but appreciation. "Come to think of it, you're right," she said with a bit of snap to her voice. "So I should get going, since Petr is probably expecting me." She then slowly slid her arm from underneath Owen's and backed away with an impish smile and a glimmer in her eye. "Petr seems like the type who would worry about me if I were late."

Something about the loss of her touch made Owen pay special attention to what she said. But he kept up a nonchalant appearance and replied jokingly, "If this Petr knew you at all, he wouldn't worry about you even if you were in the middle of a pack of wolves."

"Of course you wouldn't worry about me," Alexis said coldly, "especially since you're too cool to worry about anything. Just be careful you don't wander carelessly into a spider's web." Her smile returned and she leaned forward and whispered her familiar catchphrase into Owen's ear. "You can do better than that." She brushed her lips lightly against his cheek, then turned and walked toward the library, not looking back.

Owen knew exactly what she meant by that last statement, but her tone was different this time. And did she just kiss his cheek? What possessed her to do that? But before he could make sense of everything, Windy called his attention back to her.

"She has a bit of a jealous streak in her." Windy had regained her composure, and her sideways grin confirmed Alexis' attitude didn't threaten her in the least. "How long have you been together?" She maintained her smile as she asked the question, as if she knew the answer.

"We've been good friends for a while, but we're definitely not 'together.' Besides, Alexis doesn't think of me that way. Of course, I think you two would really click, since you're already off to such a good start." Now it was his turn to smile sardonically.

"Watch out, Owen," she said. "No girl latches onto your arm like that without reason. That was classic 'mama bear protecting her cub.' I bet you're just so accustomed to having girls fawn over you that you don't even notice." She took a step toward Owen and her smile became mischievous, her eyes deepening. "Trust me, I know these things."

"Right," Owen brushed it off, rolling his eyes. "You've got the wrong guy for that."

Windy laughed and looked at Owen as if he were a lost puppy.

"What's so funny?" he asked.

"You really don't recognize what's right in front of you, do you?"

Owen thought she was speaking in generalities, but something in the statement caught him off guard.

"I just hope the first time you notice, it isn't wasted on the wrong one," she added.

Owen could only shrug off the comment as he usually did when girls said things he didn't understand. Taking a breath, he forced the conversation to something more tangible. "So what's this thing you have to get to?"

"Just a meeting," she answered evasively. "I really should get going, too, since I'm expecting a phone call. Would you mind walking me to my bus stop?"

Truthfully, Owen would have carried her to her bus stop, just to spend a few more minutes in her presence. "Where's your stop?" he asked innocently, trying to play cool.

Windy flashed him a knowing smile and said, "Don't worry, it's over by Lot A."

"Hey, that's right by where I'm parked," Owen laughed. "What a coincidence!"

It wasn't a coincidence at all, but Windy was feeling much better today about keeping her secrets to herself and so she kept smiling as they walked across campus. "So, this trip you're taking is kind of like a guy's night out, right? Only for a week?"

"Yeah, something like that," he answered, not altogether thrilled to be back on the subject of his trip. "We just like to get away to relax and unwind. We need that now more than ever."

"I understand," she said softly.

"I'm glad someone does," he replied under his breath, then continued normally. "This year, it feels especially necessary. Everything's so different. Life feels…heavier, darker."

Windy only nodded, understanding all too well what Owen was feeling.

He continued talking. "Ever since Gideon disappeared, things feel like they're out of control. Even the mountains seem like they've noticed it."

Windy's expression changed from dubious to confused and she let her gaze stray to the peaks. "You speak like a poet sometimes, Owen," she said softly, her voice almost distant. "But I think you must be projecting your feelings about something personal onto the mountains. They actually look tranquil to me. Maybe you're still upset about Gideon."

"I suppose that's part of it, but it's still only a drop of water in a wave that's about to break." Looking to Windy, he saw no indication she understood his feelings, so he quickly changed the subject again. Putting on a casual smile, he nudged Windy with his elbow. "So what about you?" he asked. "Where do you live?"

The question broke Windy's visible tension and her shoulders and face relaxed. "Park City," she answered, relieved to be talking about something innocuous. "It's not the easiest commute to campus when it snows, but it's cheaper than moving here."

This surprised Owen. Park City stood a good thirty minutes west of campus and, from what he knew, it was a lot more expensive to live there than in the valley. Not to mention, to arrive there, one had to drive through Parley's Canyon and up into the mountains. The commute would be downright treacherous in the snow. Still, it was a beautiful town and Owen could see the allure of living there. "So, do you need a ride or anything?" he asked. "I wouldn't mind the scenic drive."

Windy's normal, poised self regained control and she gazed at Owen. "So what you're saying is you wouldn't mind spending some more time with me?"

"Mind? Well, it is out of my way," he answered lightly. "I'll just call it my good deed for the day. Besides, my car is pretty weak. It'll be good to have a passenger to help me get out and push it up the steep parts of the canyon."

That light-hearted response got the best laugh he had heard yet from the woman. "How about if I just point the air conditioning at you occasionally, as you push it up the canyon? It would be a good work out." She squeezed his upper arm.

"Be careful," he joked, "I wouldn't want you to hurt your hand on that."

Wrapping her arm underneath his, she laughed again. "All right, He-Man, where's my chariot?"

It didn't take much longer to get to Owen's car, and soon they were on their way to Park City. As he drove, Windy asked question after question about his upcoming trip. Why was he going? Where in Las Vegas was he staying? When would he be back? In general, she sounded excited for Owen, but she punctuated her questions with several warnings about the dangers of Las Vegas and California girls. Owen wondered why girls warned him about other girls. As far as he could tell, they were all a lot nicer than the warnings predicted.

Finally, Windy ran out of questions. "You're not like the other men I've met," she stated matter-of-factly. "They just stare until they think I look back. Next thing you know, they try some stupid pick-up line and expect me to swoon."

"I wouldn't be too hard on guys for that," he replied. "You just have to see things from our perspective. The pretty girls aren't going to ask us out and they've heard every pick-up line imaginable, so we have to approach them with the hope something we say will separate us from the pack. It's a lot of pressure to put on one sentence."

Windy looked skeptical. "As if you know about that. From what I've seen, I'd bet you've never had to approach a girl in your life."

"Maybe if you hadn't spoken to me at the memorial, you could've been the first," he joked.

"Really?" Her eyebrows rose and she looked up at him through thick eyelashes in mock surprise. "And what would you have said?"

"Well, I would have asked you what you were looking at during Gideon's eulogy. When the rest of the congregation was completely focused on what Gideon's father was saying, you stared toward the front exit." Owen thought the question was innocent enough, but the levity of the conversation disappeared. The blood drained from Windy's face before she turned to look at the green slopes of the canyon.

She spoke quickly, almost accusingly, her face turned away from his. "I could ask the same question to you. Why weren't you paying attention?"

Chuckling, Owen held his hands up in a gesture of surrender. "Relax. I didn't mean anything by it. Now we know how successful my opening line would have been. I'd have been lucky to get away without you dumping the punch bowl over my head." He paused before finishing. "Realistically though, I never would have approached you anyway."

Windy whirled back to face him. "Oh? And why not?"

"Girls like you always have a boyfriend or two already," he explained, trying to defuse the situation. He thought that comment would agree with Windy, but the fire she displayed a moment before quieted only partially and now smoldered like the last coals of a fire. Her eyes focused on something unseen again, as they had at the memorial. Owen suspected he knew what caused her mood to deflate and what unseen image she looked for, so he moved the conversation along those lines. "You left a boyfriend behind when you moved here, didn't you?"

Avoiding his questioning look, Windy shook her head. "No," she replied curtly. "There's no boyfriend. And why do you think I just moved here?" She continued without waiting for a response, her agitation evident. "If I had a boyfriend, I'd have asked him for a ride home. That's what a boyfriend does, right? They do nice things for their girlfriends and say nice things about them. At least I'm sure you'd be that way." Her last comment sounded like a compliment, but her voice had an unabashed acidity to it. A brief, musical tone came from her bag, bringing a halt to the discussion. Owen recognized the sound because it was the same one his phone made when he was out of service range. Windy withdrew her phone and looked absently at it, then placed it back in her bag. "If you could just drop me off up here at the outlet mall, that would be perfect."

Owen's head was spinning from trying to follow Windy's dodging moods, not to mention her shifting conversation. Without argument, he pulled off the freeway and turned into the outlet mall parking lot, stopping in front of a shoe store.

Windy made no motion to leave, however, and just sat in the car with Owen in silence for some time after he parked. In her lap, she held her bag as if trying to strangle it, wringing it between tightly clenched hands. She was looking at each passerby, each car in the parking lot, every store window, as if searching for a familiar face. Finally, she whispered. "No one is here."

"Are you supposed to meet someone?" he asked tentatively.

She turned to face him again. Her demeanor expressed an inner conflict, as if she was debating whether or not to say what she wanted to say. Finally, she leaned closer and spoke in a hushed, yet clear tone. "Be careful on your trip, Owen," she whispered. "Especially in Las Vegas. I fear the shadows are growing, and this time they're coming for you."

Coming from anyone else in the world, that statement would have made Owen look for a hidden camera. Coming from Windy, he found himself believing every word. Over the past several weeks, the vague sensation of unease that had settled upon him had become concrete—a palpable feeling of dread looming over him. His mind raced back to the odd sunset seen from Ferguson Canyon, the disappearance of Gideon Sumbawanga, the comportment of the mountains—everything seemed to be heralding some dreadful impending event. And her words had just confirmed it.

"What's going to happen?" he asked, looking deep into her troubled eyes.

For a moment, he thought she was going to tell him, but instead she reached for the door handle. "I'm out of time, Owen." She quickly leaned toward him, pressing her lips to his ear as if to kiss him. "I promise, that's all I know," she whispered in his ear. "I have to run now. I've taken too long." She pulled away and a tear rolled down her cheek. Owen reached for her, but she pulled away and got out of the car. And then, as if on cue, her demeanor changed dramatically again. She stood up straight and her beautiful smile once more appeared on her face. "Remember what I said," she scolded mockingly. "Stay away from those California girls! Thank you for the ride and I'll see you when you get back!" She shut the door and hurried toward the shoe store and disappeared inside.

Shaking his head in bewilderment, Owen started up his car and pointed it home. He took a meandering course homeward so he could ponder the day's events and attempt to put things in perspective. He got home just as the sun touched the Oquirrhs to the west and he felt his shoulders tense, as if somehow the world was going to end with this evening's sunset. He sat outside for a while, watching as the mountains swallowed the sun and the world rested once again. As the shadows deepened, Owen went inside. Tossing his keys on the kitchen table, he picked up his iPad, unlocked the screen, and checked the most important thing first—the weather in San Diego. Sunny and in the eighties all week. Fishlake? Upper seventies. Vegas was calling for the lower nineties. Perfect.

He opened up his e-mail and his eyes immediately went to a message from Alexis that had arrived less than an hour earlier. Of course, the bulk of the message was blatantly critical of Windy and every type of libel was used, including a comment about her being named after the wind blowing between her ears. He found most of her comments over the top, but several of them caused him to laugh out loud. Owen wondered why Alexis cared so much, when it struck him that perhaps she really was more interested in him than she let on. Otherwise, why would she act so jealous? Owen had himself been struggling over his own feelings and whether or not he should ask her out. Maybe she was doing the same?

Lost in his thoughts, he was pulled back to the present as he finished Alexis' email. He frowned as he read about how she was going to go study for her class with Petr. Owen had met Petr at the charity basketball game and hadn't been impressed. More curious than anything, he decided to do a little detective work on Petr. A quick check of Facebook showed him to be one of Alexis' three hundred plus friends. Looking further, he wasn't overly surprised to find Petr

Zhugravinsky had but one friend, Alexis.

Now armed with a last name, he did a quick Google search, and was shocked to find the first page listing a variety of links detailing the lives of one of the most prominent mafia families in Russia. There were websites detailing their legitimate businesses, but there were also news articles and exposés about the unsavory part of their business affairs. A quick scan of several of the stories showed Petr had been mentioned in connection with numerous murders and disappearances over the past several years, all related to the family business. The most recent article talked about police suspicions regarding Petr's involvement in the disappearances and murders of several members of a rival group—the Petrov family—and how he was wanted for questioning by local police who feared he had recently fled to America.

Owen felt his blood run cold. For the longest time, he stared blankly at the story as he tried to work through everything in his mind. If Petr was the criminal the internet made him out to be, what was he doing in America and why was he connecting with Alexis? Worse yet, what was he capable of doing here? Wearily, he turned off his iPad and leaned back on the couch and closed his eyes. He would make certain he had a talk with Alexis before he left on his trip and warn her to stay away from Petr. Without a doubt, he knew the Russian was bad news.

CHAPTER 21

Salt Lake City, Utah: Petr Zhugravinsky sat by himself at the Training Table restaurant, waiting for David Livingston Sumbawanga to arrive. He was ten minutes early for their lunch meeting, but he'd hoped David would have been early as well. It had now been fifteen minutes, which meant that while David was only a few minutes late, Petr felt like he had been waiting for hours. If there was one thing he hated, it was waiting. It was a trait inherited from his upbringing, one not so easy to part with.

He was anxious to find out why David had called him the evening before, asking for a lunch meeting. Petr had said yes, and not just because he was curious. He had felt a connection with David as they conversed during halftime of the charity basketball game. The venerable African had seemed genuinely interested in what Petr had to say and that impressed the young Russian, as a father would impress a son. Petr had never had the kind of father he could feel proud of, or relate to. With his own, he had learned the art of the gun before anything else. But something about Gideon Sumbawanga's father resonated deeply within him.

Still, Petr was realistic, and he held no pretentions that his relationship with David would amount to much in the long term. He knew that spending time with David would only improve his standing with Alexis and that was the final goal, was it not?

Petr looked up at the clock and noticed it was now seven past the hour when he saw David finally enter the restaurant. He waved to catch the man's attention, then shook his hand when David walked over to him.

"Hello again, Petr," David said warmly, setting his walking stick up against the table. "I apologize for my tardiness. I've been so busy since

I arrived in America." He sighed wearily, but seemed quite calm for a man who had gone through what he had experienced. "On one hand, I'm glad my son touched so many lives. On the other, I still need at least an hour or two of sleep each night." He finished with a wry smile.

"I'm sorry, Mr. Sumbawanga," Petr said, searching for the right words. "If this is too much, perhaps we can arrange to meet another time?"

David held up a weathered hand to silence him. "Please, Petr, call me David. And I arranged for this luncheon, so it is definitely not too much."

"Only if you're sure," Petr replied uncertainly.

"I insist," was the warm reply. "I have actually been excited about coming. I wanted to tell you I enjoyed our conversation the other night and would very much like to continue it."

Petr smiled, visibly relaxing.

"Besides," David went on, "I could actually use a little company now." He picked up the menu and looked around. "Has the waiter been here yet?"

Petr smiled again. He had only been in the country a few weeks but now, for the first time, he actually knew more about something than the person he was with. "When you're ready to order," he explained, indicating the intercom on the table, "you press this button and just talk into the speaker."

David allowed himself to grin. "America. Always looking for ways to do things quicker."

The two shared an easy laugh, and as Petr looked at the man sitting across the table, he recognized why people respected David so much. The man carried himself with a solemn, but noble bearing, and in better times Petr could easily see him as a great leader. He had a degree of *auctoritas* rarely seen in society that allowed him to take control of any room and any situation. Unfortunately, it was easy to see the deep sense of sorrow he had just passed through, as well, and Petr wondered if the man would ever recover from his loss.

David picked up a menu and studied it for a moment before leaning over and questioning, "So, if you don't mind me asking, what brought you to America, Petr?"

"I'm here to further my education and to continue my journey to become a writer," he replied. He left out the part about separating himself from his ruthless family.

"A writer?" David repeated, sounding pleased. "What an excellent goal. I applaud you, Petr. A good piece of writing can change the world. You should do well."

"I hope so."

David continued to smile and, when Petr didn't say more, he added, "But that isn't all, is it? I wonder if you've come searching for something or if you're running from something, as well?"

"You're very perceptive, Mr. Sumbawanga," Petr admitted after a few moments of silence. "Perhaps the answer to your question is both. I do have dreams of a noble future here in America, but I'm also a victim of a past that's not my doing."

David watched him closely as he spoke. "We are defined by our actions, Petr, not by the actions of others." He paused before finishing. "Even if those are the actions of our family."

Petr's heart sank. David knew. "You're aware of my family then?" His last name tied him to the dark side of humanity like an anchor and now, more than ever, he felt he was drowning.

David shrugged. "The name Zhugravinsky is not unknown to me," he answered plainly. "During my years in Europe, I occasionally heard about the exploits of your kin. However, if one is to believe the news out of Russia these days, your family doesn't appear quite as cruel as it once was."

"If my brother has anything to do with it, that might change," Petr said with a frown, thinking of Nikolai's frightening lust for power.

"And yet, you are not a part of that life, Petr," David continued, knowing the young man was agonizing about his past. "You strive to put it behind you, and that's not an easy thing."

Petr looked up. "I'm not as strong as you might think," he admitted sadly. "I fear in the end I'm no better. I've done terrible things as well, things I'm deeply ashamed of but in the right circumstances could do again."

"I don't believe that's the case, Petr," David replied, smiling warmly. He leaned back in his seat and ran his hand absently down the polished wood of his mango tree staff. "A great man makes his own path, regardless of those who would help or hinder him."

Petr was silent, digesting the words. He knew David was right. When he considered these were the words of a man who had just lost his only son, he keenly felt the frustration over his own past and the helplessness of having to rely on himself. It was a fine and noble thought to want to strike out on one's own; it was another thing entirely to actually do it.

"Petr," David added. "You were born and bred for strength, and despite the disquieting history of your family, your parents raised a strong son. Be proud of that and use it to be the person you want to be."

Petr looked at David with great relief. "Thank you," he said quietly.

David smiled. "I've been around a long time, Petr. Long enough to know when I see a man of quality, even if he can't see it in himself."

Petr returned the smile, feeling as if a great weight had been lifted from his shoulders. "Again, thank you," he said and then leaned back in his chair, much more relaxed. "Not to change the subject, sir, but do you mind if I ask you why your wished to meet me here today?"

"Of course, of course," David replied. "Our time together at the basketball game was short and with all the shouting and cheering going on, it was rather difficult to hear you. What I heard was most interesting, though, and I decided I'd like to learn more about this young man from Tsarskoe Selo."

"I enjoyed our time together as well," Petr said. "But that's not all, is it?"

David was silent for a few moments, somewhat taken aback at the direct question. He had been impressed with the man's insight the other night, which was the other reason he had asked for this meeting. "Now who's the perceptive one?" David finally said.

"I've learned to read people," he said with a shrug.

"Very well," David said slowly. "So tell me then what is the other reason I have asked you here for?"

"You continue to search for your son, no?" Petr knew he was correct, but he winced at the heavy Russian inflection that slipped into his words. David didn't seem to notice, though.

"I'd like to," David answered, sorrow etching his features, "but I'm not sure where to begin. I feel I must do something to find my son; to at least allow him to rest in peace."

"And you feel I can help?"

"Petr," David answered plainly, "I need your assistance. The answers are out there. I can feel them. But I'm an old man and new to this country, and if I'm to find what I most sorely need, I'll need help. The police are overburdened. They have no resources to apply to a missing person's investigation. My son was well-known, yes, but he's one of hundreds missing just here in Utah. I ask for your assistance out of the selfish need to discover the truth about what happened to my son."

"I understand," Petr replied, "and I give you my word, I'll help however I can. Where do you intend to start?"

"I must start at the end," David answered thoughtfully. "I've prayed for guidance and feel I must visit the place where Gideon's blood was shed. I hope to find answers to many questions there."

"I know where the tunnel is," Petr said, "and I'm free tomorrow evening. I'd be happy to meet you there."

"I would appreciate that, Petr. My son was taken from me at night. To truly connect with what happened, I feel I must go at night as well."

"Understandable. Tomorrow night at ten, then?"

"Thank you, Petr," David said, great relief in his voice. "It's odd," he went on. "Here I am, having resigned myself to the fact I have lost one son, when another arrives to be brought in. Both your paths have taken you on far different journeys, Petr. But remarkably, both your paths have led back to me—one ending in grief, the other continuing in hope. Perhaps it's grief that tempts me to accept that, perhaps it's pride. For whatever reason," he finished with a sigh, "I pray some good might come of it."

"As do I," Petr said firmly. "I don't make such decisions lightly, either. I've always been one to follow my heart and this is no exception."

"Spoken just as Gideon would have said it," David said, a tired smile playing at his aged face. "Now to be honest, I'm quite hungry. Let's order and we can talk while we eat."

"Agreed," Petr stated with a smile as he picked up his own menu. He found the possibilities in aiding David to be intriguing, as much for strengthening their mutual friendship as it was for his own possible future. Growing up a Zhugravinsky, he was used to understanding how situations could benefit him in the end and this would be no exception. Usually, though, helping someone in need came back in the form of wealth, future favors, or power. Tonight, it looked like it was going to bring him closer to a mentor/father figure and perhaps the girl of his dreams. This could not have worked out better for him. Perhaps America was going to turn out okay in the end after all.

CHAPTER 22

Park City, Utah: Windy sat in the parking lot outside her apartment building in a state of shock. She'd had some time to think about what had happened between her and Owen and she cursed her weakness. She couldn't believe what she had done, or more directly, what she had allowed Owen to do to her. He had caused her to feel true emotion and then she had gotten so flustered—her, of all people!—that she had only been able to breathe out some cryptic warning before fleeing in panic. And yet, despite her best efforts to ensure no one could eavesdrop on that warning, she knew her handler would eventually discover she had betrayed him, if he hadn't discovered it already. That would get her killed.

Unless, she dared to think, someone could save her.

The momentary flight of fancy was quickly brought to a halt as the cold, logical side of her brain once again regained control. She knew she couldn't allow herself any hope for a different future than the one she'd already forged.

Countless times over the past few years, Windy had considered her death and wondered how it would come. She had never feared it, though. Most of the time, she welcomed the prospect. She knew she was living on borrowed time, both with her boyfriend and with her handler—whoever he truly was. But now? Of all the pain she had gone through over the past eight years, perhaps this was the worst of all. There was nowhere lower to fall to than holding onto a hope one knew to be hopeless.

While she was twenty-seven years old now, the version of Windy who had gone after Owen with the intent to ruin him was created eight years ago in a hotel room in Park City, Utah. She was icing the black eye her longtime, drug-addicted boyfriend Cole had given her the night before, feeling about as low as she ever had. Cole had started her wild plummet from the high of his latest fix, claiming in his haze that she was sending messages to the FBI by the sequence in which she changed the channels on the television. For her betrayal, he punched her squarely in the face. She had apologized for hours, not knowing what she was apologizing for, but sure she was guilty of whatever it was. He eventually passed out and slept for two days.

On the second day, she gathered the courage to leave the room and find some food for the both of them. Upon her return, she found Cole awake and terrified, hanging from a noose tied to a large metal hook screwed into a ceiling joist. He was still breathing, since the length of the rope allowed him to stand on his toes, but a look of madness and rigid fear shone from his bulging eyes. Horrified, Windy rushed to his aid but before she could help him, she noticed the note pinned to his shirt with a safety pin.

Terror paralyzed Windy and she stopped. Cole had faked suicide before, an attempt to prevent her from leaving him, but this looked nothing like a suicide. Conflicting emotions ravaged her. Reflex told her to save her abusive boyfriend and nurse him back to health, something she had done so many times before. But her mind screamed for her to run; run from Cole and all he had ever done to her. He would surely die here; nobody could stand forever. Nobody would find her or accuse her of wrongdoing. She had become an expert at moving, hiding, existing without the world realizing it. She could do this. She could break free.

In the same instant she claimed her freedom, her will broke. Amidst the maelstrom of thoughts, reflexes, and emotions, her heart saw a man in need whom nobody else would help. She couldn't abandon him. She could save him.

The note changed all that. In large block letters written in red marker, it read, "ANSWER THE PHONE FIRST."

Upon reading the message, she had just enough time to wrinkle her face in confusion before a strange cell phone lying on the bed next to Cole began to ring. It wasn't her phone, nor was it Cole's, and the sound sent her entire body into a convulsion. Windy backed away from the phone and from Cole, unsure of what she should do. The phone rang again, sounding more insistent, a third time, a fourth. Finally, her nerves shredded and her strength gone, she ran to the phone and snatched it up, putting it to her ear.

"Hello, Windy," the voice on the other end said quietly, the first of many times she would hear it. It was a deep voice, one of limitless depth and almost palpable danger. Losing control, Windy burst into tears and curled up on the bed at Cole's feet, somehow keeping the phone to her ear. "There, there Windy. No need to cry. I bring good tidings to you in this, your darkest hour. You've been chosen, Windy; selected for a new life. You've certainly succeeded in wasting the life originally given you, but I can help you turn that around. It won't be easy and it won't be fun, but I feel it's always best to be honest about things from the beginning. Wouldn't you agree, Windy?"

None of those words penetrated the girl's frantic cries and, after a few seconds, the caller recognized this and adopted a less patient tone. "I know you can hear me, Windy, and if you hold any hope of either one of you leaving the hotel room alive I suggest you listen very closely to what I'm about to tell you."

Hearing the threat, coupled with the absurdity of the situation, Windy choked, sputtered, and fought back her tears.

The voice softened. "Good. It appears you can follow instructions. Now, I have a proposition for you. I'm going to help you get the one thing you've always wanted, and you're going to do the same for me."

The shattered young girl found the strength to respond in a barely audible whisper. "What do you want?"

"I want what you want, Windy," the man answered easily as if he were her best friend. "I want a healthy, cleaned up Cole Banyon."

"Cole?" she repeated, completely dumfounded as she looked at her boyfriend, noting his bulging and terrified eyes. "Who are you?" she asked quickly, feeling panic well up within her as Cole swayed dangerously from side to side, attempting to keep his balance.

"My identity isn't your concern. What you need to focus on right now is that I'm offering you hope, Windy," he went on. "Isn't it enough to have hope?"

"No." Windy startled herself with how cold the word came out, but it was the most honest answer she had provided to any question asked of her in quite some time.

"I know, Windy. I know," the voice spoke with compassion. "I'll be in contact in a week. Keep this phone. Don't show it to anyone and never tell anyone you've talked to me. Oh, one bit of advice. I'd wait until Cole passes out to cut him down. Since he thinks you're the one that had him trussed up, he might give you more than a black eye if you cut him down now. I'll be in touch."

A week later, the voice did call back. Windy had just gotten out of the hospital from the beating Cole had given her after he came to, but she remembered the message as if it had just been spoken to her. Her handler, as he would quickly become, told her the only way he could help her was if she was willing to better herself in ways she had never considered. Only by doing exactly what he said, could she have any hope of finding salvation for herself and, more importantly, for Cole. Knowing she could save Cole had awakened powerful feelings of regret and self-loathing. Apathy and numbness would have been much better, she told herself, but she couldn't become apathetic no matter how hard she tried. She loved Cole too much for that, so she agreed to the demands the voice placed upon her.

Over the next year, Cole managed to get cleaned up and even stopped beating her, causing her to wonder what was driving him to make the changes in his life. He stopped using hard drugs, got a part-time job, and was talking about going to a local community college. Of course, the good changes didn't come without a price, and her handler's price for helping them was steep. At first, she was puzzled at the demands made of her, but she dutifully underwent a series of training exercises meant to strengthen her both physically and mentally. With success came rewards, with failure there were always punishments.

When she was successful, money would show up in her bank account, enabling her to comfortably provide for her and Cole. When she wasn't successful, the punishment was usually physical and self-inflicted. In the beginning, it was often sleep deprivation, but after she adapted to that, her handler turned to fasting for lengthy periods, extensive workouts, or marathon-like runs. She remembered clearly the day she stepped out of the shower, looked in the mirror and saw a stunning body reflected back at her—her body. It was then she realized that, while her tasks had aimed at improving her mind, the punishments had been physical and had been aimed at perfecting her physical form.

As she grew stronger, both in mind and in body, her tasks became more difficult, as she expected they would. Her handler had quietly molded her into a modern day Mata Hari, young and strong. He had given her passports, new identities, and plenty of money—to use in seducing men of international importance into giving away secrets, money, power, and occasionally, their very lives. She was a diamond, used by her handler to wow her marks, but she was always comfortably away when the end came. She knew many men had died after she was done with them.

She had never been asked to do the truly dirty work and she fervently hoped she never would. However, over the years, she had been trained in handguns and in martial arts, and she knew how to kill someone if needed. If the time came that she would be called upon to do so, she would deal with it then. For now, she simply allayed her concerns by telling herself that her victims were all people who deserved their fates, nothing more.

Then, just as her world was starting to fall into place, Cole began to regress. He sought out some of his old friends against Windy's wishes and began to use again. Soon, he had lost his job and all ambition to go to school. He had threatened to beat her and kill her, but he hadn't yet raised a hand against her. So she stayed with him, trying to get him back. However, the tears were long gone. Windy Covington had no more to shed.

And that brought her full circle to the present. She had finally given up hope of ever getting Cole back and she was beginning to seek a way to leave him, when her mysterious benefactor had called her with her current assignment. She was informed this particular assignment was to be her last and, if she completed it satisfactorily, she would have everything she ever wanted.

That mark was Owen DiConte.

The assignment itself had sounded absurdly easy—meet the young man and get him to fall in love with her. Use that attraction to follow him, report on his actions, and set him up so that, when some future plan was enacted, he would be easily trapped.

The dossier she had received on Owen was incredulous and she immediately doubted the information. She had read Owen carried himself with confidence and integrity. The reports described him as disarmingly handsome, steadfast in his beliefs, athletic, and intelligent. This young man was special. People gravitated toward him—he attracted people by his innocence and sincerity and he inspired trust. He wasn't to be taken lightly, and she was urged to be cautious in all her dealings with him. Windy Covington could handle anyone. Powerful, popular, rich—all men bent to her will. This college volleyball player with dreams of attending medical school and no history of a serious girlfriend would be cake.

Or so she had thought.

Her handler had feared she would fail, expressed those fears to her repeatedly and made certain she knew how important this assignment was. She had given his warnings little thought and, in the end, his concerns had turned out to be prophetic. She had found Owen to be everything described in the file and then some. In turn, it was she who had fallen into a trap that she had unknowingly set for herself a long time ago.

She realized with startling clarity that she no longer needed Cole; she no longer needed her handler. She wasn't going to win Owen for any other reason now than that she wanted him for herself. Owen and his innocence could rescue her from her life; rescue her from everything wrong with her world; rescue her from herself. She would make Owen love her. She would use everything she had to convince him to save her.

And if she failed? Well, Owen would still be her salvation. Without knowing it, he had given her the strength to take that final step if it was needed. Success or failure in this meant the same thing now. If he rescued her, so much the better. If she failed, she would simply take her own life before her handler did. In the end, Windy would finally be free.

No sooner had that thought of freedom ran through her mind, when her phone alerted her that her handler was calling. She fought back the terror the R.E.M. song brought, telling herself she would not be a slave to it, but she had to answer, and as she did her feelings of renewed hope began to die. Swearing silently, she grabbed her phone out of her purse. "Yes," she answered, trying desperately to keep the hate and anger out of her voice.

The voice on the other end of the line replied with exaggerated sympathy. "My dear Windy, did I call at a bad time? I can call back later, when it's convenient for you."

Windy knew not to respond and was inwardly grateful that her handler was likely calling for an update. At this point, though, all he wanted was her silence and she knew how to give that. "Good," the voice on the other end said quietly after a few moments. "Now tell me how your car ride with our dear Owen went."

She grimaced again at his ability to know where she was at all times and who she was with. Her handler always required that Windy first state her original orders. She then would report the execution of her work in chronological order, with priority given to the chief objective, but without omission of every possibly relevant detail. Concise, complete, and chronological were the three "C"s that kept her alive. She was to render no opinion during the factual report. That was saved for her concluding assessment, and redundancy was abhorred, which is to say it was severely punished.

Inhaling deeply, Windy proceeded to give her account, leaving nothing of the conversation out, except for her own final whispered warning to the young man. She recounted her frosty interaction with Alexis and her success in planting the seeds of jealousy within the other girl. When she had finished, a long silence ensued.

He asked no questions and she could hear him breathing on the other end of the line, the sound of someone concentrating. "Impressive," he finally said in a low tone, but giving no indication of what exactly impressed him. "Do you have anything more to add?"

"No," she replied a bit too hastily, but then was all business as she continued. "He's as you described him—charming, attractive, and innocent."

"Mr. DiConte sounds like a challenge," he said somewhat off-handedly, putting Windy on her guard even more. "Even for you."

"I have it under control," she replied icily.

"Do you?"

Windy bit her lip and kept her voice even. He knew. He had to know. "I do," she lied.

"You understand how important this is to me?" he went on, his voice dripping with malice.

"Yes," she answered softly. "I understand."

"Good," he answered. "I'll be in touch."

A moment later, the line went dead as her handler abruptly ended the call. Sighing, she looked up and saw the front door of her apartment and reality sank back in. Whatever else was going to happen, she still had to deal with Cole and she knew he was waiting inside. All the sacrifices she had made for him flooded back into her mind, forcing out her hopeful thoughts of Owen and making her bitter beyond compare. Steeling herself against the rage that threatened to overwhelm her, she pulled herself out of her Jaguar and walked slowly up to the front door.

As Windy walked through the front door, she noticed Cole must have awakened and actually moved around the house some since she had left. There was a half-eaten bowl of cereal and an almost full jug of milk sitting out on the table. She felt the milk jug, realized it was warm, and knew Cole had been up for a while. She fought back the irritation in her voice and called out, "Cole? Are you here?" She found him sitting on the sofa, watching their sixty-inch LCD HDTV. It was a fishing show, which struck Windy as humorous since Cole had never gone fishing, nor had he ever shown the slightest interest in doing so.

"Cole, I called for you," she went on, laying on as much sweetness as she could stomach but finding it left a horrible taste in her mouth. She started to say something else, but noticed he wasn't watching the program, but was talking on his phone. She hated that phone, as it was typically one of his friends inviting him out for a night on the town or asking if he had scored any drugs. Usually those trips ended up with him back home either sick or deliriously high and her nursing him back to health or down to reality.

Cole finished his call and tossed the phone on the couch beside him. "Why the long face, babe?" he asked, smiling up at her and showing his snake charmer face. It was meant to disarm, meant to manipulate, meant to gather favors from her. She knew it was also meant to warn her not to ask questions about where he was going. However, Windy wasn't going to play along this time.

Crossing her arms over her chest, she gave him a dark look. "What are you up to?"

"Wouldn't you like to know?" he smirked nastily.

"Actually, I would," she snapped, feeling her blood begin to boil. Dangerous or not, she wasn't backing down this time. Not today. Not ever again. "You're hiding something," she accused. "I want to know what it is and I want to know now."

Cole smiled again, obviously enjoying the game he was playing. "I'll tell you what," he finally said, lounging back on the couch and putting on an air of utter superiority. "I'll tell you if you promise you can keep it a secret."

"Cross my heart and hope to die." The words came out too quickly and cut her as she realized what she said.

"Fine," he went on, not noticing the brief flash of pain that crossed her face. "Your cell phone friend just called me again."

Windy went absolutely bone-cold.

"I thought that would get a reaction," he chuckled, looking at her knowingly. "I know all about the guy that calls you and tells you to go to Monaco and seduce rich bankers or some crap like that."

One word echoed through Windy's mind. How? She had always been so very careful as per orders and she had never let her secret be known. There was no way he could know. Unless...

With shattering clarity, it all came into focus for her.

Cole had always known.

He saw the look on her face and correctly guessed what she was thinking. "Looks like we've got ourselves a winner, Johnny," he laughed. "Cat's out of the bag now, I say," he continued, standing up and stepping around the couch, moving toward her.

Windy felt her body tense.

"You little minx, you," he went on spitefully, taking another step toward her, fists clenching and unclenching at his side.

"Why…are you doing this?" she finally found her voice, her tone as cold as she was feeling.

Cole gave her an exaggerated wink. "Can I tell you another secret?"

"You know I hate secrets."

"You're right," he said and then his own tone changed to mocking anger and bitterness and—what was it—pain and anguish? "But that hasn't kept you from keeping all these secrets from me over the years, has it? That hasn't stopped you from doing things any whore would do to make a buck."

"Stop it," Windy said dangerously. It was enough to surprise Cole and he stopped moving toward her.

"Doesn't make you feel too good, does it?" he snarled. "Secrets, secrets, everybody has secrets, don't they, Windy? But no, not you.

You've never kept a secret from me. I've always known."

"I don't care what you know, Cole," she snapped. "I did everything for you! I paid with my sweat, my blood, my love, and most of all, with my dignity!"

Cole shrugged, his body seeming to relax. "Nice analogy, and I suppose it's true," he agreed, his voice still menacing. "But sometimes we're asked to pay in ways we don't mind. In fact, sometimes we look forward to paying. Maybe that's the difference between me and you."

Suddenly, the last piece of the puzzle fell into place and Windy went cold inside. Cole had known because her handler had told him. "Cole," she warned in a voice barely above a whisper. "You have no idea what you're getting yourself into. You have no idea who you're dealing with."

"Oh, I think I know plenty," Cole replied with a shrug as if it was no big deal. "I've been trapped here with you for a long time, living your lie, having to pretend it didn't gall me to know what you were doing all those times you were away. I had to accept it! I HAD TO LIKE IT!" he finished in a sudden scream of rage that caused her to visibly cringe.

"I did what I did for you, Cole," she whispered miserably. "It was always for you."

Cole spit on the floor in front of her, his face a mask of disgust and fury. "You make me sick," he snarled. "And I don't have to take it anymore. I don't have to live in your shadow. It's my turn, Windy. Time to square the deal."

"You'll pay, Cole," she warned, unable to think of anything else to say. "Whatever you think you're getting, whatever he told you he'll give you, you'll always have more to pay. It will never end."

"I don't think so," he replied. "You don't pay later when you're doing the kind of job I'll be doing."

"Job?" she repeated, but the word left her cold. She knew exactly what he was being asked to do. It was in his eyes, an almost gleeful light. Cole was being asked to become a killer.

"You heard me right, Windy," he went on casually. "Knock off a few people, square the debt, and I'm home free. I'll be free of you and I'll have everything I ever wanted."

Windy's shook her head sadly. "I knew you were a lot of things, Cole, but I never thought you could be a murderer."

He shrugged. "What's the dif? This is a lot better than waiting for you to come back from your latest affair."

"Don't do it," she started to warn, but her voice was hollow and lifeless. She was beaten. Her whole world had crashed down around her and she did the only thing she could think of doing. She launched herself across the room at a speed that took Cole completely by surprise, managing to land the first punch straight to the side of Cole's face. But her momentum took her into his arms and both tumbled over the back of the couch.

Cole recovered quickly from the attack and twisted his body on top of hers as they fell, coming down hard on her and driving the breath from her lungs. Taking advantage of the moment, Cole fastened both hands tightly around Windy's throat and squeezed her windpipe closed. Windy's eyes immediately went wide and she clawed frantically at his hands, her long nails tearing into his flesh.

Cole ignored the bloody furrows she was opening up on his hands and arms and leaned closer to her face, his grip like iron. His voice dripped with venom. "He always said the day would come when you'd do that," he hissed. "Seems he knows a lot about you, Windy." He squeezed harder, the rage clear on his face. "But he also said I wasn't supposed to kill you yet. That's too bad." He leered at her and then, after several more agonizing seconds, finally released his grip. Windy gasped, sucking air into her starved lungs as Cole stood up. He looked down on her, his voice pure contempt. "Before I forget, he has a message for you, Windy. He wanted me to tell you that you're not done with Owen yet." Cole's last words were delivered with as much hate as he had and he then spun on his heel and walked out.

Windy lay in stunned submission, unable to think or move. She heard the front door slam and the Jaguar's engine roar to life before he was gone, smoking the tires in the street. Windy was alone. After long minutes of emptiness and pain, she finally climbed to her feet. She searched deep within herself and found the tiniest spark that still flickered in her shattered soul. Her mind settled on one word, one person, one hope.

Owen.

CHAPTER 23

Salt Lake City, Utah: Libby Davis looked over at her friend Genevieve Abramson. "Text him again, Gen. I'm telling you, he's not at work."

"No," Genevieve replied flatly. "And could you wait at least two minutes since the last time you asked? For the last time, if Todd says he's at work, he's at work. Drop it okay?"

"Calm down, both of you," Alexis intervened, holding both hands up. She turned first to Genevieve. "Libby is right, Gen. You need to know the truth." She then turned to Libby. "And Gen is right, Libby. You could have waited at least two more minutes before asking." She laughed, getting a giggle from Libby, while Gen just sighed and crossed her arms, looking back out on the field and ignoring her two best friends.

The sun was directly overhead and the weather was just right for a day at the ballpark. The Triple A minor league baseball team—the Salt Lake Bees—were playing at Spring Mobile Ballpark. Gen's boyfriend, Todd, had a cousin who was a hot prospect working his way up in the Florida Marlins' organization and was currently with the Albuquerque Isotopes. Todd had invited them to the game, but at the last minute, he had bowed out, saying he'd been called into work at his job with a local internet technology firm. Alexis and her friends went on without him; three girls rooting for the Isotopes among a sea of Bees.

The friends had first met the night Alexis started college and had immediately hit it off. Gen was tall, topping five-foot-ten inches, and about as uncoordinated as a person could be. Constantly sporting a Band-Aid, if not a splint or a cast, her wide smile and large, hazel eyes drew people to her, particularly the opposite sex. Her perfectly-styled dark brown hair certainly didn't hurt, either.

Liberty, known as Libby to everyone but her parents, was considerably shorter than Gen and Alexis, with red hair usually pulled back in a ponytail and an abundant supply of freckles. Her engaging manner and supreme self-confidence made her a favorite with the boys, as well as a leader on the Utes cheer squad. She knew exactly what she was looking for in a man, however, and discarded boyfriends left and right as soon as one flaw—no matter how minor—appeared. Yet despite what most people might consider extreme shallowness, Libby was well-liked by everyone, even her many ex-boyfriends. At the moment, she was wondering when Gen would officially make Todd an ex-boyfriend.

"Fine, gang up on me," Gen finally replied, knowing Libby wouldn't let it go. "Todd really wanted to be here. Why else would he invite us to see his cousin play and pay for the tickets?"

"You realize the tickets only cost seven dollars each, right?" Libby pointed out.

"Look, we're glad Todd invited us and it really is a perfect day for a game," Alexis interjected. "But getting called into work at the last minute? The last time he got called into work he wasn't really called into work, was he?" The last sentence hung heavily in the air, but Alexis continued. "Gen, you just have to understand we're concerned about you, that's all. He does have a history of cheating and we don't want you to get hurt again."

"Yeah," Libby chimed in. "I think we had twelve ice cream and movie nights in a row last time it happened. I put on six pounds. My wardrobe can't put up with that again."

Despite the topic, Gen laughed. She knew that while her friends could be a little pushy when it came to Todd, it was only because they loved her and wanted the best for her. She leaned over and gave Libby a hug. "You won't have to. We're good."

Libby smiled mischievously. "So why can't we text him?"

"Alright," Alexis intervened. "We've made our point. As long as you're happy, Gen, then we're happy too."

"Do you really mean that?" Gen asked.

"Or course not!" Libby answered gleefully.

"Well, I'm glad we ironed that out," Gen said as she rolled her eyes. "So, now everyone is okay with my life, maybe we should get into yours," she finished, looking directly at Alexis.

"What do you mean by that?" Alexis asked, quickly turning her attention back to the game. The last thing she wanted today was to talk about her love life, or lack thereof.

"Don't take this the wrong way," Gen said slowly, "but you haven't had a boyfriend in what… forever? I know you don't want to make the same mistakes I've made, but you'll never catch a fish if you don't go fishing."

"Touché," Alexis said quietly. She looked to Libby for help, but could see immediately she was going to agree with Gen on this one. "I thought this was supposed to be an intervention for Gen," she went on. "How did I become the focus so quickly?"

"Well, she's right, you know," Libby replied. "How can you be happy without love?"

Alexis could only shrug. "It just isn't that easy for me, I guess. I have to finish my degree next year and then get into med school. I barely have enough time to volunteer at the homeless shelter. I just don't have time for a boyfriend."

"That's not true," Gen pushed. "You need to make time for important things, and this is important! Normal people date other people. They kiss them, marry them, have babies with them, grow old with them, and live happily ever after. They connect with the world!"

"I connect with the world! I just can't afford to connect too much right now."

"Then connect a little, okay?" Gen kept up the pressure. "Look at Libby! She'll go out with any guy who has his own car! She's never been serious with anyone but she's had a lot of fun and gotten a lot of free meals and watched a lot of free movies!"

Libby laughed. "For your information, Ty didn't have a car."

"Libby," Alexis shook her head and couldn't help but smile, "he had a boat. And you dumped him as soon as it got too cold to go out on the lake!"

"You say that like it's a bad thing," Libby joked.

"All I'm saying, Alex, is that you need to think about getting out a little more. When are you going to ask Owen out, anyway?"

Alexis' heart sank. She had hoped to avoid the subject. "I know, I know," she sighed, cringing because she had said those exact words many times already to her friends. She also knew what their response would be—that it really wasn't as complicated as she thought, and up until last week, they would have been right. However, what they didn't know was it had gotten complicated recently. Messy was more like it.

She looked at her two friends and shook her head. "If you must know, there's a problem."

"Problems typically have names," Libby pointed out. "What's this one's name?"

"Windy," Alexis said glumly.

"Well, that kind of a problem certainly changes things," Gen added.

"Exactly," Alexis agreed, relieved to get it off her chest. "You should see this girl! Tall, gorgeous, with these amazing blue eyes; her figure is perfect, her walk is perfect, her smile is perfect. She's intelligent and funny and charming and strong, but vulnerable at the same time. I hate her!"

"Who wouldn't? I haven't even met her and I hate her," Libby said.

"How long has this been going on?" Gen questioned.

"She met Owen at the memorial for Gideon and has been 'bumping' into him a lot. Like, more than just a coincidence a lot. Yesterday all she had to do was pout and the next thing you know Owen is giving her a ride to Park City. You should have seen how he looked at her."

"I don't know how he looked at her, but I've seen how he's looked at you before, sweetheart, and I've heard how he has talked about you, too. Trust me, this isn't a lost cause," Libby maintained.

"Well, if anything, we've had a breakthrough here," Gen pointed out. "If I'm not mistaken, you admitted you want to be with him! Like, maybe you have deeper feelings for this guy than you've been letting on?"

Alexis bit her lip, thinking hard about the danger in answering that question. In the end, she realized the best way to answer it was truthfully. So she did. "You know something, I think you're right. I think I do want him," she said, her voice a little stronger. Her face lit up as she heard herself saying something aloud she had been thinking for a long time. "Wow, that sounds really good to say out loud!"

"And trust me, it's great to hear," Gen grinned. "This is real progress! But this is no time for baby steps. There's a wolf on the prowl and if you want Owen, you need to go after him now!"

"But he's leaving for his San Diego trip tomorrow," Alexis pointed out, her excitement quickly ebbing.

"So?" Libby asked.

"Well, that kind of puts a damper on me asking him out, don't you think?"

"Why wait?" Libby went on. "They're gone for a week, aren't they?"

Alexis nodded.

"So make him miss you."

"She's right," Gen agreed, her eyes twinkling. "Give him something that will keep his mind focused on you!"

"Are you kidding me?" Alexis stammered. "Do you know now how incapable I am of pulling something off like this?"

"Where there's a will, there's a way," Libby chuckled. "I think you should write him a letter and give it to him just before he leaves."

"Oh, that's a great idea," Gen agreed. "And don't forget a hint of perfume!"

Alexis looked like she was just shy of bolting in panic when Libby reached over and patted her best friend on the knee. "It all comes down to this, love. Do you want him or not?"

Alexis looked hard at her two friends, her mind working furiously. "I'll do it," she finally said with a smile.

"Now we're getting somewhere!" Gen said gleefully. "Nothing like a little competition to stir the pot!"

"Yeah, Alexis, go get your man!" Libby added.

"Don't worry, I'll get him," Alexis said with a nod and a wink.

Libby looked around at the stadium and pursed her lips. "You know, I just realized I hate baseball. Can we get out of here? I think Alexis has a heartfelt letter to write anyway."

"Absolutely," Gen replied, standing up. "Let's go help Juliet get her Romeo."

Minutes later, the three friends were walking out of the stadium, talking excitedly. As they did, Alexis realized her life was about to change.

She had no idea just how much.

CHAPTER 24

Parque Nacional do Pico da Neblina, Brazil: The small chemical plant lay on the outskirts of the city of Sao Gabriel da Cachoeira, which in reality meant it was lost deep in the Amazon forest and almost entirely isolated from the rest of the world. The area was only accessible by the Rio Negro or by a small plane from the local airport. The clouds that covered Brazil's largest mountain to the north kept the area almost constantly obscured. For the past decade, enough money had been paid to grease the right wheels, from local government all the way up to the Brazilian president himself, to maintain its isolation.

Of the few local residents and business owners of Sao Gabriel da Cachoeira who did initially complain about the location of the plant, all had allegedly moved away, leaving the factory comfortably unbothered. The key phrase was that the dissenters had *allegedly* moved away. The man standing just down the road and looking toward the guarded gates knew differently.

It was a relatively small operation as factories go. The English-printed sign above the chain link gates read simply: "Legio Industries Water Purification Plant," but its operation was anything but small to those in the know. For the past fifteen years, the plant had been the only location in the world engaged in refining, producing, and stockpiling a specific chemical compound created by combining the right plant-based ingredients found only in the rainforests of Brazil.

For the last fifteen weeks, that chemical compound had been secretly and steadily introduced into most of the bottled water produced across the globe.

In the next fifteen minutes, all traces of the factory and its workers would cease to exist.

Hade reached into his trench coat and fished out a cigar. With a smile, he bit off the ends and then clamped it between his teeth. From another pocket, he pulled out a lighter. Instead of the cheap Bic he usually used, this was an expensive brushed palladium Gatsby. This particular lighter he had taken from a high-level Washington politician just two days ago, a man who had thoroughly disappointed him and would now no longer be needing it.

Ever.

He thumbed the flint, letting it flare to life, fully cognizant of the fact that it would be visible to the two men in the guard shack just up the road from him. He kept the flame hot and high for nearly fifteen seconds, lighting up the darkness around him, before finally looking up. Nothing moved from the shack. Frowning, he flipped the lighter closed and slipped it back into a pocket. Then, taking a long drag from the cigar, he started forward, walking down the middle of the road toward the gate.

He had nearly reached the guardhouse when the two soldiers on duty finally reacted to his presence, one of them stepping from the booth, his Kalashnikov pointed at the ground, but his finger resting on the trigger. The plant seldom got visitors and never a visitor on foot at night. Hade had wondered how the man would react.

"E aí, irmão?" the guard asked casually. Hade couldn't help but smile. Who else but the Brazilians were that casual and welcoming, even among the ranks of security guards? It was a cloud-shrouded night of the darkest black and a tall, imposing figure had appeared out of nowhere at the front gate of what was supposed to be a secret and secure factory, and the guard had simply asked him what he was about. He'd even called Hade his brother!

"Tudo beleza, amigão." Hade replied in flawless Portuguese. *"Estou andando para fora, mas tou um poco desligado, sabe?"* No one could have

believed a man dressed in black alligator skin boots, a long black leather coat and wearing sunglasses in the dark was out for an evening stroll in the middle of the forest at midnight and gotten lost. But he went with it, clearly amused.

With his voice friendly and his manner relaxed, the guard looked back at his companion and joked, "*Achou que o Alemão está chapado, não é?*" Apparently the idea of a drunk traipsing through the forest was a comical one. He turned back to Hade and motioned him along, letting the man know he should just go home.

"*Vixi Maria,*" Hade replied. "*Estou quebrado, mesmo, Nossa, preciso um cerveja!*" He came a bit closer to the guard, walking haltingly as if he had indeed had too much to drink.

"*Basta, amigo. Tenho uma arma …*" The guard held up his rifle, indicating his patience was now wearing thin and the only option besides leaving involved the wrong end of his rifle.

"Yes," Hade replied, flexing his muscles as he switched effortlessly to English, his voice dropping dangerously and his eyes narrowing in focus. "But are your arms as powerful as mine?"

The guard blinked once and died without ever seeing Hade move. The big man was only a blur as his right hand lashed out, the heel of his palm slamming into the guard's face. The man flew backward like a rag doll, instantly dead from the raw strength of the blow. Hot blood splashed from his shattered face, spraying across Hade's boots and coat, causing him to growl dangerously as the coppery scent of fresh blood filled his nostrils.

Turning, Hade saw the other guard inside the shack raising his weapon, a look of stark terror on his face. Hade was quicker, pulling an enormous Desert Eagle from his shoulder holster, its metal gleaming gold in the night. The hole that appeared in the guard's chest was large enough to place a cantaloupe in. The hole the expanding bullet left in the back wall of the guard booth was large enough to crawl through.

For a moment, Hade's visage rippled and changed into something found only in the darkest of nightmares, as the very dead guard slid down the wall and out of view. But a moment later, it was gone, replaced again by the hardened face of a bad leather-clad biker chomping on a foul-smelling cigar.

Hade chuckled and holstered his weapon as he made his way to the door. Using a fifty caliber Desert Eagle was overkill, he knew, but Hade loved his weapons and he hadn't had a chance to use the Eagle in a while. Tonight's little offensive gave him the opportunity to haul it out and put it to work. It made for good fun. He stepped inside the guardhouse and took a long drag off his cigar. He enjoyed this particular vice immensely, particularly for the soothing effect it had on his baser instincts. Savoring the feeling, he blew it out as he looked around.

The guardhouse itself was small, but technologically advanced. A bank of flat LCD screens filled one wall, showing the plant and the surrounding area from a variety of different camera angles. Nothing moved around the outside of the plant. It even appeared that the animals had vacated the premises. It was the perfect night for business.

"All quiet on the Western Front," he muttered to himself and turned his attention to the large, stylized desk adjacent to the door. The mid-portion of the desk was actually a forty-inch Samsung Surface screen, which allowed security to run almost all of the functions of the compound from one access point. Hade needed more than that, however. He needed admin access to the data center buried deep below the plant. Hade pulled up a chair, cracked his powerful fingers, and got to work.

First came the fingerprint scan. Hade placed all ten of his fingertips on the screen. A blue line scanned up and down his hands and he was through stage one. Next, the retinal scan and facial recognition. Hade leaned over and let the greenish glow of the screen envelop him. A chime let him know he had completed those two stages and should proceed to the next.

He cleared his throat and projected, "Quoth the Raven, 'Nevermore, Nevermore'." With the voice recognition stage passed, the final test appeared as a small black square emerged in the middle of the screen. The first levels would have been enough security for almost anyone else in the world, but this plant was too important to his plans to take any risks, no matter how remote.

Hade stood up and pulled his massive right arm out of his black trench coat, exposing the incredibly intricate tattoos that decorated it. The artwork was a masterpiece of the highest order, as spectacular as anything Michelangelo or Da Vinci were capable of. The center of the work showed four individuals, covered in darkness, chained together and encircled in flames. Surrounding them were demons, devils, dragons, and all manner of the most horrible of monsters imaginable. Below two of the figures, on the inside of his forearm and almost imperceptible to anyone otherwise mesmerized by the rest of the tattoos, was a small blue heart wreathed in a white glow. Hade placed his arm on the table, centering the tattooed heart in the middle of the square, and a message on the top of the screen popped up. *"Cobalt aluminum oxide saturation level, 82.3%."* One of the main components of his blue tattoo ink, Hade had created the last stage of his security clearance to be a scan of the exact amount of cobalt in one of the most obscure but important tattoos on his entire body.

"Excellent," Hade said as he steepled his fingers and the screen came to life.

Within a few seconds he was watching a live feed of the large laboratory inside the plant. The overhead lights were either dimmed or shut down, throwing into stark contrast the individual Surface screens at the desks. Several white-coated lab techs were moving around the room, talking to one another or working over their stations.

Hade counted them. Seven. "Looks like all my little piggies are ready for market," he rumbled quietly. He opened up a schematic of the building as a reminder of how the rooms were laid out and then started moving around virtually throughout the plant. He moved to the security room and quickly disabled the entire plant's security system, including all cameras. A tap on the basement and a few more touches and the entire plant was ready to be reduced to a smoking crater. Finally, he typed in a series of commands and enabled the interference system that would keep anyone from calling in or out. Satisfied, he swiped the logout icon with his pinky finger and the Surface screen went black.

"Time to have a little fun," Hade said to himself with a smile. He picked up a clipboard near the edge of the desk and scanned the names on the list. He already knew who would be in the plant, and the deceased guard's sign-in list simply confirmed it. Seven on the list—seven in the lab. There would be no loose ends after tonight.

A grand total of forty-eight people were employed by Legio Industries in this plant, all of them working directly for Victor Legio and indirectly for Hade. On any given day or night, sixteen or more of those workers would be on duty. Tonight, there were only those seven—the first time the plant had been operating with so few on duty. Everyone else on the employee roster would never work another day at the plant. Some would never work another day anywhere.

Most of the plant's forty-eight employees were of little consequence—mindless workers who had little if any knowledge of what actually went on at the plant. They were safely home in their beds or burning through their last paycheck in some nearby bar or bordello.

Seven of those forty-eight employees were considered a potential risk with only one containment solution. A half a dozen bullets and a surprise promotion to one lucky individual would finalize those loose ends perfectly.

He tossed the clipboard back on the desk and stepped over the guard's body, pausing only for a second to look down at the fixed and staring eyes of the dead man. He wouldn't have to worry about cleaning up. The plant had been waiting for this moment, the moment of its utter destruction, since it had first been built. The architectural plans had included large cavities in the concrete foundation supposedly for a geothermal heating system. However, in actuality they had been carefully packed with enough C4 explosives to make the plant nothing but a memory. It wasn't the first time he had designed a building specifically to be destroyed from within, but he never got tired of watching his buildings go up in fire. To Hade, it was the most beautiful form of creation: destruction of something old so something new could emerge in its place. Devastation with a purpose. It could have been his motto.

His plan for the evening very much still on schedule, Hade walked out of the guardhouse and sniffed the night air. Ignoring the heady scent of fresh blood, he walked up to the gate and placed a hand on the chain link fence, curling his thick fingers around the metal links. With a flick of his arm and a screech of metal, Hade tore the entire gate from its moorings and tossed it aside as if it was nothing but paper. Puffing on his cigar, he walked through the newly opened gate, his stride long and purposeful, the structure at the end of the factory compound his destination.

The building was a non-descript steel and concrete bunker with a set of labs, offices, and only one way in or out. Opening the door, he stepped inside and wrenched the door closed, his strength bowing the metal inward and jamming it into the reinforced steel frame. He couldn't take the chance of any of his piggies getting out before market time. Now it was locked to everyone but him.

As the noise of twisting metal filled the air, seven sets of eyes looked up in alarm from their work, alarm changing to fear when they beheld the strange and wholly frightening intruder. While everyone at the plant in effect worked for Hade, none of them knew him. No one here had ever seen him. All were filled with terror.

"*Boa noite, senores,*" Hade's voice boomed in Portuguese, breaking the silence. "*E claro, senora,*" he finished, raising an eyebrow as his gaze locked on the lone female in the room who sat looking at him questioningly from behind her workstation.

"Who the hell are you?" one of the men said, his English heavily accented, his voice stressed. He stood up from the station he had been seated at and took a step forward.

Hade simply laughed, a sound like rolling boulders. He took a moment to suck in a lungful of cigar smoke before blowing it out in an acrid stream. "You know, I'm fairly certain that hell knows me quite well," he answered. The man started to say something else, but Hade waved him off. "Yes, I know," he went on easily. "I didn't answer your question. So, I'll indulge you." Spreading his arms wide, he announced, "Believe it or not, I am your boss."

No one said a word.

"Now I know you all think you work for Victor Legio, but I'm the one ultimately responsible for your paychecks," he continued as he took another puff on his cigar. "And I'm here to tell you that, as of tonight, your services are no longer required by Legio Industries."

"Mr. Legio is the head of this corporation and this plant," the man replied, his voice even more tense, but with a hint of frost now. "I hardly think he works for you."

"Well, it's a good thing I'm not overly concerned about what you think, Ricardo," Hade laughed dangerously, the foul-smelling cigar smoke wreathing his head.

The man, Ricardo DeSouza, blanched. "How do you know who I am?" he stammered.

Hade continued to smile, chewing on the cigar. "You should pay a little more attention, Ricardo. I already explained that you work for me. Do try to keep up." Letting his gaze sweep the room, he continued. "Now that we have the pleasantries out of the way, let's get down to the business of severance packages, shall we?"

"Are you terminating us?" another man spoke up, his voice slightly nervous, but indicating he was from the States.

Hade smiled, his teeth gleaming in the gloom. "In a manner of speaking, yes," he chuckled. "Tonight is both an ending and a beginning. As of this moment, this factory is no longer necessary. It has fulfilled its purpose and done so wonderfully. Really, I couldn't be happier with everything you've done. You should all be very proud of your accomplishments."

"Wait just a second," the man continued, his anger growing. "What gives you the right to barge in here and tell us we've all just lost our jobs?"

"Hello, McFly!" Hade said, still smiling and then tapped his chest with both hands. "Me boss. You worker bee," he finished, throwing his hands out to encompass the rest of the room. "But fret not. All is not lost. You'll be pleased to know that, as a result of your hard work and dedication to the cause, I'm here to engage you all in a job interview for a future endeavor."

"An interview? But why?"

"Well, George," Hade began, placing the cigar back between his teeth, "an interview, generally speaking, is for a job, and I need to know

I'm getting the best man or woman for this job. But we both know that's probably not going to be you. Am I right, George?"

"I don't…I mean…"

"Come now, George," Hade cut him off as he stepped toward the middle of the room. "I've been reading the reports of your little office spats with Almeida. You don't seem to play well with others, George. Where is Almeida anyway?" he quickly asked, making a show of looking around before his eyes settled on another man, short and dark-complected with tight, wiry gray hair, who had been peering at him from the shadows of a darkened office doorway. "You," he stated, pointing directly to him. "You're Jorge Almeida, right?"

The man nodded and slowly stepped into the main lab. "*Sim*, I am Jorge Almeida," he answered, his voice fairly shaking.

"Jorge, come here," Hade said, motioning him forward. "I want to talk to you."

The man hesitated, as a child would hesitate before stepping to the front of the class to be addressed by an angry teacher.

"Come on, Jorge," Hade said, smiling widely again. "I won't bite. I promise." *If only the man knew the truth about that*, the big man thought to himself, chuckling inwardly.

Jorge Almeida shuffled forward, casting his eyes about nervously. Reaching Hade, he paused, looking up. He could not have topped out at more than five-foot-five, while Hade stood a good foot and a half taller. Acting like the small Brazilian was one of his good friends, Hade reached out and patted the man on the shoulder, nearly knocking him down. Pulling him closer, he spun him around and laid his massive left arm across the terrified man's shoulders.

"Jorge," Hade said, his tone light and easy. "I understand that you and George aren't getting along real well right now—a little friction between North and South America here, am I right?"

Jorge hesitated and then nodded. "*Sim*," he said, his voice very quiet.

"So what about the rest of these guys, Jorge? Do you get along with them?"

The Brazilian nodded.

"All of them?"

He nodded again, this time vigorously.

"So it's just ol' George—the American—that you're not clicking with, right?"

"*Sim*," Jorge said, slightly emboldened. "*Meu problema…*"

"I'm not interested in your problems, Jorge," Hade quickly cut him off. "You see, if I listened to you, then I'd have to listen to George's rebuttal and quite frankly, I just don't have the time or the patience for a long drawn-out workplace intervention. This is an interview, Jorge, and I'm already behind schedule."

With his right hand, he reached into his coat and pulled out the Desert Eagle. There was an immediate reaction as the workers shouted or screamed, all of them diving for cover or hiding behind computer stations. Hade simply smiled, leveled the gun, and pulled the trigger. With an ear-shattering boom, the fifty caliber bullet smashed through a large LCD screen and reduced George Davidson's chest to hamburger as the force of the gunshot slammed the man's body over another work table and to the floor.

Hade waited for the screaming to die down and then looked down at Jorge Almeida, who had fallen to the floor in terror, his arms clamped protectively over his head. "You know, *Celebrity Apprentice* would be a whole lot more interesting if they let Donald Trump carry a weapon like this," he said with a laugh. "I really should have my own reality show."

His musings were answered with a rapid-fire stream of pleas in

Portuguese that came out so fast, it was impossible to understand. "Come now, Jorge," he said jovially, still looking down at the babbling man. "Obviously George wasn't the man I'm looking for. Are you?"

"You…killed him," the room's only woman stammered, standing up from behind the desk she had taken cover behind. She must have realized hiding would do her no good and now she was screwing on a face of courage as she stepped around her desk, looking directly at Hade.

"And?" Hade pushed. "Do you have a point, Sarah? Or are you just throwing out meaningless banter as you inch closer to me, hoping to scratch out my eyes with your well-manicured nail extensions?"

Sarah Kanan froze.

"I'd give you points for bravery," he continued, "but I'm looking for a survivor tonight, not a martyr."

Cold understanding slowly dawned on the woman's face and she turned to run. Hade shot her in the back. She was dead before her body slid down the wall in a smear of blood.

"Seven little monkeys jumping on the bed," Hade mocked. "Two fell down and broke their heads."

"Enough!" another of the men screamed, poking his head up from behind a file cabinet he hoped would give him a little more protection from the massive firearm. "Enough! Please don't kill any more of us!"

"Marcos Vida," Hade said, focusing his gaze on the man and smiling. He paused to puff on his cigar, letting the smoke leak out of his mouth. "I was wondering when you would speak up. You know, I've got my money on you tonight, Marcos."

"Why are you doing this?" Marcos cut in. "Why in God's name are you doing this?"

"In the first place, Marcos," Hade answered, his smile vanishing.

"This has nothing to do with God."

"But you killed George! You killed Sarah!"

"I prefer the term 'culling the competition'," the huge man replied and then walked to the nearest work table and laid down the Eagle. "The reality of your situation is that I'm here to hire the best. You seven—well, five now—were chosen as finalists for this job."

"You must be joking!" Marcos said incredulously.

"I'm quite serious," Hade replied evenly. "And you, Marcos, are the front runner." Hade looked around the room. "Let's see, with George and Sarah terminated, that leaves you and Ricardo." He hooked a thumb behind him at Jorge Almeida, who was huddled on the floor in terror. "Jorge is a long shot, but we knew that before we even started, and then there's Sven Hjellen and Alexander Johansson, our two Norwegians." He nodded toward the two men who hadn't spoken yet. "This is how it's going to work."

"No," Ricardo snapped.

"No to what, precisely?" Hade asked, an amused look on his face.

"No to all of it," Ricardo said, his voice getting louder. "You've murdered our colleagues. This ends right now! There has to be another way to deal with this!"

Hade smiled and drew in some smoke. Blowing it out, he looked pointedly at Marcos. "Better be careful, Marcos," he warned. "Ricardo is getting a head of steam and might be our new front-runner."

"What are you talking about?" Marcos' nerves were fraying and it showed.

"Work with me here, Marcos," Hade replied. "We're still in the interview process and I'm running out of time. So let's get started," he finished, holding up both hands to keep anyone from speaking up. "Any further interruptions will lead to your immediate resignation."

"I said no!" Ricardo screamed.

Hade calmly picked up the gun and pulled the trigger. Another hollow boom filled the air and the top half of Ricardo Juarez' head vanished in a crimson mist as his body was flung backward into the wall by the force of the bullet. "Looks like you're back to being the front runner, Marcos," Hade said easily as if his actions were the most normal thing in the world. He looked around at those that remained. "I'm sure you've all heard the old business maxim: last one hired, first one shot. Any more interruptions?"

No one moved. No one even breathed.

"Good, now let me give the rest of you some free advice. Don't ever play a game you don't know in your heart you can win. Otherwise, you're just going to be disappointed when it doesn't go your way. Now, are the rest of you ready to hear the rules?" he asked, continuing to look around.

Three men, all of them terrified beyond words, simply nodded their heads. Hade turned to look at the fourth, who still lay on the floor in terror behind him, and he shook his head. "Not sure Jorge is going to make it, but we'll give him an opportunity and see. Who knows, maybe he'll surprise us all," he said with a grin and then turned back to the others. "Now, the rules of the interview are simple," he explained and laid the gun back down on the table. "I have three bullets remaining. There are four of you. I have a single position available within my organization that I'm looking to fill, and each of you has a chance to fill it."

"H…How?" one of the other men dared to speak up, a man of blond hair and blue eyes, his accent heavily Norwegian.

"I'm glad you asked, Sven," Hade answered and then held up the gun and looked at each of the three men in turn, while ignoring Jorge, who still hadn't moved. "As if it wasn't already obvious, I'm going to shoot three of you. When I'm out of bullets, whoever is left alive will be my new number one, as it were."

No one moved.

Hade cleared his throat. "You know, if I had just been told I was about to be killed by someone with a very large caliber handgun, I might consider running. You're only going to get out of here alive if you are the furthest from the man with the gun when the interview process is over." His eyes narrowed and he began to level the Desert Eagle. "So run," he finished, his voice low and laced with danger.

They did.

Sven Hjellen and Marcos Vida went left. Alexander Johansson went right. Jorge Almeida went nowhere.

"I'm going to count to one hundred," Hade called out loudly enough to be heard. "And then it really is survival of the smartest." Hade hopped up into a sitting position on the table and looked at Jorge with eyes that glittered coldly. "One! Two! Three!" He paused. "You know, I really hate waiting. Let's count by fifties instead and get this thing moving. Fifty! One hundred! Ready or not, here I come!"

He hopped down off the table and walked slowly over to Jorge, whose eyes were open and locked on the huge killer. Tears formed in his eyes as Hade loomed over him and then looked down at him. "Sorry, Jorge," Hade said without feeling, aiming the gun downward. "But rules are rules. Better to find out you aren't upper level management now than later."

The gun went off, the force of the bullet's impact bouncing Jorge's corpse a few inches off the floor.

Whistling the theme to *Mission Impossible*, Hade turned and smiled. It had been a long time since he had such sport. Even if he had been a slave to feelings and emotions like the meat sacks that he dealt with every day, he would never have felt any regret about killing these men. They had all signed on to help him create and manufacture a compound that would, in all likelihood, be responsible for the eventual deaths of more than a billion people the world over. Hade understood the reasoning and the rationale and he knew the ends justified the means in this case. But these men had agreed to do something they knew could only end in one way and they had done it for greed and avarice.

Hade went right, mentally checking Alexander Johansson off his short list. The man had darted into a hallway that led directly to several offices. Foolish, but not unexpected. All of the data on Alexander proved that while he was brilliant, he was also very short-sighted and had problems seeing the bigger picture. Tonight, that would prove fatally problematic for the man. Hade stepped into the hallway and stopped. Six doors were spaced evenly down the hall, three on each side. All were open, save one.

"Predictable," he mumbled, shaking his head in annoyance. He walked down the hall and then stopped, turning to face the closed door. He paused for a moment, then raised his head and sniffed the air. Anyone else would have been taken unaware. But Hade was not anyone else. He spun around and caught Alexander Johansson's wrist as the man attempted to drive a letter opener into the middle of his back. The man had been waiting in the open office opposite the closed door, hoping for just that opportunity.

With a smile and the sound of popping bone, Hade crushed the man's wrist in his grip. Johansson dropped to his knees, screaming in agony as Hade placed the muzzle of the gun against the man's forehead. "Nice try, Alex, but I'm afraid we're going to have to go in a different direction."

He pulled the trigger.

As the last tremor died in the dead man's legs, Hade held the man's lifeless body up in a kneeling position for a moment, before flinging it unceremoniously to the side. At that moment, he heard an angry yell from the other side of the bunker.

"One more bullet to go," he shouted loud enough to be heard through the entire complex, "and two more little monkeys! Your chances are now fifty-fifty, which is as good as anything you'll get in this world! Someone is about to get lucky!"

He heard some sounds coming from the opposite hallway and frowned. "These monkeys aren't doing a very good job keeping a low profile," he said to himself as he walked across the lab, pausing for a moment to admire his handiwork on George Davidson. "It's a flat screen for a reason, George," he told the corpse with a smile, quickly surveying the wreckage of the LCD panel that had done nothing to spare the man from the killing bullet. "Not a chance it's going to stop a fifty."

There was another crash and he looked up. Shaking his head, he continued across the lab and into the hallway. The door at the end of the hall caught his attention. It opened into a large storage room where many of the base chemicals and ingredients were stored. From that storage room, he heard a low moan, followed by a quick scuffling sound. Hade cocked an eyebrow and listened, but the sounds weren't repeated.

"Well, this could finally get a little interesting," he said to himself as he began walking down the hall toward the room. A few moments later, he reached the open doorway and, without hesitating, stepped into the room.

Sven Hjellen lay face down just inside the door amid the wreckage of a shattered desk and an overturned chair. A yellow cord was wrapped tightly about his neck. His cheek was pressed against the floor and Hade could see the man's eyes, open and bulging nearly out of their sockets. Sven had been viciously strangled. To complete the interesting crime scene, a box cutter lay near his body, along with copious spatters of blood.

The blood wasn't Sven's.

"Good ol' Marcos," Hade said, looking up. "I knew you had it in you." Looking down, he saw the blood spatters leading away from Sven's body and into a darker part of the storage area. A few steps around several stacks of boxes and barrels took him to where Marcos was hiding. The man was leaning up against a large chemical drum, his hand pressed tightly to the side of his neck. Blood covered his hand and shirt, and the man's skin was already pale and drawn.

"Hello, Marcos," Hade said, crossing his arms in front of him, the Desert Eagle loose in his right hand, his cigar in his left.

"Did I make it?" the man asked softly.

Hade looked around. "It appears you're the last man standing. Or slumping would be the better word, from the looks of you. Rough night at the office, huh?" he smirked.

Marcos sighed with relief, leaning harder against the drum. "Just help me, please," he stammered. "I'm going to bleed to death."

"Now hold on a second there, hoss," Hade replied. "Give me a sitrep first."

"The…what?"

"Sitrep, Marcos. Situation Report." When the man still didn't respond, Hade rolled his eyes and shook his head. "What went down here, Marcos?"

"Sven came at me with the box cutter…and slashed my throat," Marcos explained breathlessly. "Next thing I know, I slammed him into the desk. The cord was right there and I…I guess I strangled him."

"You guess?"

"Well, it was either him or me," Marcos pleaded. "I did what I had to do."

"I know, Marcos," Hade answered. "It's a cutthroat world, isn't it?"

"Please," the man begged. "I'm the last man standing; I won your game."

"Well now, that's the rub, isn't it," Hade countered, putting his cigar in his mouth again and holding up the gleaming Desert Eagle. "You see, the rules of the interview were pretty specific. I distinctly remember saying when I ran out of bullets, whoever was left alive would get to keep their job. Do you remember me saying that, Marcos?"

"But…well, yes," the man stammered and then looked at Hade in blank confusion. "I don't understand."

Hade very slowly placed the muzzle of the gun against Marcos Vida's forehead. "I still have one bullet left in my gun, Marcos," he explained quietly. "The interview process isn't over until there aren't any bullets left. Do you understand?"

"But…but he would have killed me!" the man nearly screamed in terror.

"If he had, then I'd be having this discussion with Sven instead of you."

"Please, no!" Marcos begged, falling to his knees, the barrel of the gun against his forehead the whole time.

"I'm sorry, Marcos, but I'm a man of my word," Hade said coldly and then shrugged. "I always have been. And if a man gives that up, well, what else does he have?"

"But I have a family!" the man sobbed.

"And I have kings to make and a world to win," Hade said flatly.

Marcos Vida died mid-scream.

Hade slid the huge gun back into the shoulder holster under his duster and looked down at the still twitching body. "Why won't people listen to what I actually say instead of what they want to believe I said?" he sighed. He turned and strode out of the storage room, pulling out his phone as he walked. "Wilson," he said absently. The iPhone put the call through immediately and Hade waited for it to pick up. It did after only one ring.

"*Bom dia*, Wilson, *como vai?*" he said loudly.

"Hello, Hade, what can I do for you?" Jose Maria Wilson Nunes da Silva dos Santos replied from the other end.

"I'm afraid I have bad news, Wilson," Hade went on. "There's been an accident at Victor Legio's water purification plant in Brasilia. Nothing is left. It was unfortunate, but not wholly unexpected, knowing the volatile nature of the chemicals they were working with."

"A disaster, I'm sure," Wilson replied, a clear sense of understanding in his voice.

"Indeed," Hade said. "I'd appreciate it if you'd keep a lid on things. Just for a few days, anyway. I don't care what the media says, but keep the authorities grounded. I don't want anyone poking around for now."

"*Claro*, Hade, of course! After all you've done for me, how could I say no?"

"*Obrigado, presidente del futuro*. I'll be in touch." He reached the door of the bunker he had jammed closed and placed his hand on the bent metal. He took another puff from what remained of his cigar and, without even the slightest strain, shoved the ruined door outward, forcing it to break away from its hinges with a screech of twisting metal. Once outside, Hade tossed the stump of his cigar to the ground and breathed in the evening air. The night was silent. Nothing moved.

He began walking across the compound toward the front gate and pulled out his cell once more. "Vittorio," he said as he left the compound. He had Victor Legio in two rings.

"Victor, my friend, did I wake you?" he asked disdainfully.

"You know I don't sleep," came the reply in cold and clipped tones. "What can I do for you?"

"Straight to the point, Vic," Hade said easily. "That's what I like about you."

"There's a lesson there for you," the old man couldn't keep the satisfaction from his voice.

Hade only smiled. "Yes, yes, I'm rarely brief, Victor, which you certainly know. But I shall be concise for the purpose of this call. You have a water purification plant in Brasilia, no?"

"I assume this is a trick question? What did you do, blow it up?"

Hade reached into another pocket and pulled out a battered old pocket watch on a polished sterling silver chain. He flipped it open and noted the time before answering. "In about thirty seconds, yes," he replied.

"How many had to die?"

"Not as many as could have," the big man answered.

"I suppose that will have to do, then."

"We do what we have to do, Victor," Hade went on. "But that doesn't mean I can't have fun in the process. Of course, in a few days it won't matter anyway."

"It won't matter to me or to the rest of the world?"

"Both," was the answer. "Don't worry about it, though. I just want to make sure no one in your company cares too much about what happened for a few days. *Capiche?*"

"*Capisco*, Hade. Don't worry about it, it never happened."

"*Bene*, Victor, *molto bene*. Are we still on for our date?"

"Of course, master," Victor Legio replied icily. "I'm in Italy. I'm sure a man of your talents can ascertain my exact location when you wish."

"*Fantastico. Ciao.*" Hade finished with a grin and then ended the call and pocketed the phone. Victor Legio had served him honorably. He could afford to give the man a little freedom before they met for the last time.

As his footsteps took him around a bend in the road and out of sight of the plant, he stopped and then held up three fingers, then two, and finally one. As he dropped the final finger, the ground began to shake and the night was torn apart by the sound of an enormous explosion. Night turned to day as the fireball that was once Legio Industries Water Purification Plant roared up into the sky, obliterating anything and everything in the factory compound and beyond.

Hade paused to look up, the fire flickering against his dark shades. He smiled for a moment and then, with a bored expression, turned away from the flames and looked down at his boots. They were black, alligator-skinned, and about as rare and expensive as any item of clothing he owned. They were a pain to keep shiny, and blood was always tough to get off them. Too much could even ruin them. They were comfortable, however, and he had such an affinity for how he looked in them that he put up with the hassle. He had worn them tonight hoping he would accomplish what he needed to without getting too much blood on them.

"Well, I don't suppose I can claim a victory in everything I do," he lamented, shaking his head sadly at the fact that his boots were almost completely covered in blood. It was an occupational hazard and Hade had more pairs where those had came from. He had to. In the coming days, he knew he would need them all.

CHAPTER 25

Salt Lake City, Utah: Sitting on the porch in front of his parents' home, Owen waited for his friends to arrive. Elbows rested on knees as he stared admiringly at the mountains and the blue sky above. Between him and the mountains lay only the thin, weightless Utah air, which on mornings like this, was of perfect temperature and humidity. While the sun had not yet fully risen, its rays had just begun to beam over the shoulders of the mountains.

The noise of an approaching car stirred Owen from deep thoughts, but he was surprised to see it wasn't Luke, Chad, or Clint, but Alexis pulling into the driveway. He didn't wonder why she had come—he had left her three messages the night before asking her to give him a call. He hadn't wanted to leave without telling her what he had found out about her study partner, Petr Zhugravinsky. She hadn't called, though, and he had resigned himself to speaking with her about it when he returned. He had decided it was for the best anyway, as knowing Alexis it would be a discussion that could last a while. Sitting on his front step waiting for her to come to him, he promised himself he wouldn't get drawn into an argument.

"Good morning!" Alexis greeted him with enthusiasm as she strolled up the walkway with a plastic bag in her hand and a demeanor suggesting her presence was expected. Owen kept his expression blank, which only compounded the silence.

Unruffled, she sat down next to Owen on the porch step and continued. "I know what you're thinking, but you can relax. I didn't come to argue with you about your trip."

If this was her plan, it was a strategy Owen hadn't seen her use before. But he decided silence was still his best ally until he could decipher her intentions. She spoke again, a little irritated this time.

"Fine, ignore me then. You know, you're lucky to have a friend like me who'll overlook such rudeness and still give you this," she tapped the bag. "Here," she huffed and shoved it into his hands.

Suspiciously, Owen kept his eyes on Alexis while taking the sack. Alexis' smile had disappeared. Where she had initially presented the bag with excitement, she now handed it over begrudgingly. "I didn't have time to wrap it," she grumbled as he went to work on the knot, "so you'll have to be satisfied with opening a plain old bag." Leaning forward, she rested her beautiful cheeks on her clenched fists.

While observing those amazing features, he noticed her cheeks were more pale than usual. Beyond Alexis' temporary appearance of disappointment, she also looked exhausted. It concerned Owen enough to break his silence. "Are you feeling okay?" he finally asked.

"Fine, I'm just a bit tired." She smiled to minimize her statement, then pointed at the bag in his hands. "Come on! Open it already!"

Owen smiled and put his ear to the bag, shaking it as if he thought that would help him divine its contents. "Is it a new Mercedes?" he joked, peering inside. He broke out into a grin and then reached inside. "What's this?" he asked with a laugh, drawing several vintage handheld electronic games out of the sack.

"I know your mastery of conversation all too well," she winked. "And when I think of poor Luke, Chad, and Clint stuck in that car with you for an entire day? Trust me, you'll all want something else to do."

Owen smiled warmly, his relief overwhelming. The bag's contents constituted neither crux nor distraction after all. It was merely a gift. "Electronic football! Baseball! I haven't played these since elementary school, Alexis." He remembered with fondness the excitement of playing those exact games on family road trips as a child—Coleco football, Mattel baseball and basketball. They were woefully outdated even then, but they were great memories for him. "Thank you," he said with a twinge of guilt, remembering his suspicions about the motive behind the gift. "You know I love this vintage stuff."

With a shrug of her shoulders and a playful smile, she continued. "Of course, *I* converse with unrivaled alacrity and longevity, so my company..." she stopping and laughed as Owen pointed an accusing finger at her, his eyes wide with mock indignation.

"So now the other shoe falls," he laughed along with her. "Very funny, Alexis. But you're staying here." As she laughed, he saw her color brighten slightly and he caught himself admiring every part of her, something he had done countless times in the past. "Seriously, though, thanks for the games."

She nodded, but her smile disappeared and her mood became heavier. Owen felt it keenly. She drew her breath and sighed. "It's just that I'll miss you, Owen," she said softly.

Now Owen knew something was different. Alexis never expressed herself to him in that way. Not knowing how to respond and afraid of the consequences if he did, he avoided the subject. "I'm just a boring ol' regular guy," he said with a self-depreciating smile.

"On the contrary, you're fascinating! Who else on this earth can fall asleep in every lecture and still be knuckleheaded enough to keep going? You even look like you could fall asleep right now."

"I only slept for a couple of hours last night," he said truthfully. With little coaxing, his mouth generated a believable yawn he hoped would assist him in drawing attention to the new subject—his insomnia.

Alexis' face changed visibly. "So you didn't get much sleep either?" Her eyebrows rose innocently, almost appearing concerned. "What did you do instead?"

Owen knew there was more to the question and an image of Windy reared up unbidden in his mind. Trying to look innocent and confused, he decided to ask a question in return. "What did I do instead?" It was a trick he had learned a long time ago—repeat what was said in the form of another question.

By the way Alexis' eyebrows tightened in consternation and the fact that she played more vigorously with her hair, he knew she saw through his ploy. With a sniff, Alexis looked away and appeared indifferent. "Oh forget it, Owen," she said. "I mean, most people who don't get much sleep have a reason; like they were doing something, somewhere, with someone…" she shrugged to emphasize her new disinterest.

The words spun through Owen's head. That was it! The last time Alexis had seen Owen, Windy was with him, asking about things to do on a Friday night. When Owen complained of his sleepless night, Alexis assumed it might be due to a long night with Windy! Could she be jealous? Of course, when she left yesterday, she was on her way to "study" with her new Russian friend, Petr, whose song of praise she had sung rather loudly. Thinking of the Russian caused a surge of tension within him that he refused to believe was his own jealousy.

Owen's tongue caught pace with his thoughts at just the wrong moment and he blurted out, "Speaking of certain 'someones,' I wanted to talk to you about that Petr guy you've been hanging out with." He tried to bite his tongue, but it was too late. He had just done what he had promised himself he wouldn't do.

Alexis looked confused and almost appalled by the sudden line of questioning. "We have a couple of classes together, Owen, that's it. I don't know what the problem is. He's a perfect gentlemen—intelligent, handsome, and modest." Owen had no idea why she emphasized that last word with a look hard enough to crush stone. "And don't change the subject, Owen."

Ignoring her question, Owen persisted. "I'm not sure I am," he replied, still thinking she was zeroed in on Windy. "It's just I found out some things you need to know."

With a gasp, Alexis inhaled the fuel for her tirade. "Found out some things? Are you telling me you invaded his privacy, hoping to dig up some dirt and make him look bad?"

"I didn't invade anyone's privacy," he snapped more forcibly than he had intended, causing Alexis to twist her hair with renewed fury. "I just ran across some information that makes me concerned about you hanging out with him."

That stopped Alexis and she stared at him, suddenly still.

Owen didn't expect that, but forged ahead. "I think the guy could be dangerous, Alexis."

In a very innocent tone, Alexis responded, looking up at him this time through her eyelashes. "You're concerned?"

Owen shook his head and couldn't help but wonder if she was getting it. "I think he may be here in the States because he's unwelcome in Russia, Alexis. Did you know he comes from one of the top organized crime families in Russia? Apparently, he's wanted for questioning for a couple of murders. This is serious stuff."

She continued to play with her hair, staring at a stray lock, her mouth turning up into a half-grin that Owen always found irresistible. "So, you're concerned?"

"You haven't heard a word I've said!" Owen sighed. "Of course I'm concerned. I'd worry about anyone in his company."

"Anyone?" Alexis snapped, her sudden change in posture startling Owen. "I'm glad I receive as much concern from Owen DiConte as the average person," she went on, angry and hurt all at once. "I'm sure your information comes from the most credible sources, too. I mean, Petr looks, sounds, and acts quite dangerous and I've had my suspicions from the start."

The sharp edge of her sarcasm cut Owen deep and he was surprised at how badly it had hurt him. When Alexis resorted to sarcasm, it meant her arguments were emotional and had no place for logic and that was unfortunate for him.

Unrelenting, she pressed on. "The fact is, Owen, you could learn a thing or two about how to treat girls from him."

Owen started to say something, but couldn't find the words so he just looked at the ground, wondering how it had all blown up in his face so badly.

With a rounding of her shoulders, Alexis exhaled angrily. "There's a letter in that bag of games, Owen," she added. "I'm not sure you'll even care to read it. It tells…" She trailed off, not certain how to phrase her comment. Eventually, she just said, "Well, you know what they say." She gave a dejected sigh and looked away.

Before Owen had a chance to respond, the honk of Chad's horn interrupted them, shattering the intensity of the moment and startling Alexis enough to make her jump. As she turned to face the intruders, her expression was a mixture of extreme disappointment and profound relief.

All three of Owen's traveling companions—Clint, Luke, and Chad—were in the car. They pulled into the driveway with the windows rolled down and rap music playing loud enough to wake the neighbors. With his head hanging out of the driver's window, Chad pointed at the two of them and yelled out, "Wuddup? Lookin' good this morning, Alex," he said with a wink and a smile.

It was common knowledge Owen and his friends were unabashedly loud when together. They joked constantly and laughed without restraint, and of the group members, Chad was the loudest. A handsome young man with an imposing stature, he focused all of his efforts on finding his future wife, or so he professed. He lived in a state of perpetual conflict, though, as he suffered from a malady from which Owen, Luke, and Clint also suffered—they were happy bachelors. They enjoyed dating different girls, playing hoops whenever they wanted, and watching sports until their brains melted. They valued the freedom and carelessness of singlehood thoroughly. Some of those traits rubbed Alexis the wrong way, but in the end, she liked them, and to Owen, that was the most important thing.

Alexis was on her feet before Owen was and walked toward the car, purposefully swaying her hips as she walked. Reaching the car, she tapped Chad's outstretched fist with her own. "Wuddup, handsome?"

Alexis decided to play with the young men a bit more as Owen walked around her and threw his backpack into the trunk of the car. "So Owen tells me you guys decided to let me come with you," she said with an absolute poker-face. "I even brought my own fishing gear and golf clubs, too, so I won't need to be borrowing any of yours." She followed that with her sweetest smile and had all three of them slack-jawed and wide-eyed with panic.

Luke and Clint looked to Owen, their eyes silently pleading with him to deliver them from the evil that suddenly loomed. Owen shook his head and rolled his eyes, smiling as he did so. "Relax, gentlemen," he reassured them, aiming to get a little payback on their behalf. "The wench doth joust with thee."

"Wench?" Alexis' hands were on her hips and she glared at Owen.

"Ouch," Clint said, drawing a line in the air with one finger. "Don't get us wrong Alex, you know we're cool with you. It's just..." he trailed off, trying to figure out how best to explain.

"Don't worry about it," she said with a dismissive wave of her hand. "I really didn't want to go anyway—guy stuff and all. I suppose it would be this way even if we were married, right?" She finished with a smile and a blush, surprising even herself she had purposefully said what she just did. A quick glance at Owen showed her he hadn't heard her comment and she shot a quick wink to the others.

As Owen came around the car, she quickly put her arm under his and grew serious as she spoke to all of them. "You'll drive carefully, won't you?" She ignored the chorus of "Yes, Mom" from the others and turned to Owen. She spoke directly to him, her voice soft but filled with great urgency. "I mean it, Owen; I want you guys to be careful. I'd be lying if I said I wasn't worried, given everything that's been happening lately."

"I know, Alex. You've warned me before, and I quote, 'Those California girls...'"

"I'm not talking about that this time, punk," she interrupted him, putting her fist in his gut. "I'm serious. We've all been through a lot, Owen, you know that. The world has been through a lot."

"You know I don't spook that easily. We'll be fine." He spoke with bravado, but was surprised to find that he was actually a little uneasy about the trip. "Nothing is going to happen to us," he finished with his most confident smile, hoping to convince himself as much as Alexis.

"You'll call me, though? To let me know you are okay?"

"Alexis, you know we stay as far away from the outside world as we can on these trips," Owen replied.

Alexis frowned worriedly. She reached up and put her arms around his neck, hugging him close. It was a brief embrace, but enough to make Owen believe he could survive on that feeling without food or water for years. Just as quickly as she initiated it, she ended it. She looked at Owen once more, then forced a smile to her face. Waving to the other guys, she turned and walked to her car without another word. A few moments later, she was gone.

Owen watched her car turn the corner and then with a deep sigh, turned to get into Chad's car. Three ear-to-ear grins and a cavalcade of congratulations and high-fives greeted him. Chad shifted the car into reverse, unsuccessfully fought the urge to leave black marks on the street, and the four of them started on their journey.

Ironically, Alexis rendered her own hypothesis null that they would need something in the car to keep them busy. Her conversation-ending hug spurred a new talk between Owen and his friends, which eliminated the immediate need for electronic games. "Owen, she's so into you!" Chad exclaimed. "What happened to finally break down the 'just friends' barrier?"

Despite his willingness to be loud with the guys and voice his opinion on any subject, Owen liked to keep his feelings private. "Are you trying to say we're more than just friends?" he said, his voice almost bored. Inwardly though, he fervently hoped the hug meant exactly that. He just wanted to be absolutely certain before letting his feelings out of the bag.

"Face it, Owen. She's the one," Clint went on. "And why shouldn't she be? She has everything you're looking for and then some. Why wouldn't you go for her?"

"You ought to just be happy to have found someone like her," Chad added. "I don't know what more you want from a girl. I mean, what does she have to do? Pay a pilot to write 'I LOVE YOU, OWEN' up in the sky?"

"Dude, that hug said it all," Luke interrupted. "She's fallen for you."

"Yeah, I get so misty-eyed thinking about it, I think I might have feelings for you myself!" Chad joked, busting them all up.

"Look, it's not that simple," Owen finally said. "This is new territory for me. It would be for any of us." The others nodded silently in agreement. They had each had girlfriends before, but none of them had ever been in a serious relationship. While eager to push their friend in a new direction, they all knew none of them were really willing to taste their own medicine. "You're right, though. She's perfect," Owen went on. "And that's the problem."

"What are you talking about?" Chad asked.

"I mean, she's so amazing I wonder if I'm even worthy."

"I never thought I'd hear you say that," Chad commented and then smiled widely. "I'll tell you what we're going to do, gentlemen. This trip is now officially a bachelor party! When we get back, we're going to do everything in our power to ensure Owen is never single again. Enjoy the trip, buddy, for it's going to be your last taste of freedom."

"Stop it, guys. I'm serious. I mean, what do I have to offer? She's never given any indication she harbors feelings for me—well, nothing concrete anyway." Owen hated admitting these things to his friends. He felt it made him look weak somehow.

"Nothing concrete?" Luke said in disbelief. "That hug looked pretty concrete to me. Your problem is you've always dated girls who asked you out and rarely the other way around. But now? You've met your match, my friend. You've met a girl as confident and patient as you."

Owen's thoughts scanned recent events and he came up with two possible explanations for Alexis' decision to show her feelings more plainly. Either she was crazy, or she really was falling for him. Either way, he thought, they all pointed in the same direction. His bachelor days could very well be ending. A wide smile broke out across his face as he finally accepted the situation and his three friends caught on immediately, once more high-fiving him and talking excitedly.

Owen shook his head happily and opened the bag Alexis had given him. He quickly dealt out the hand-helds and withdrew the letter for himself. He had great friends and no one could tell him otherwise.

They all saw the letter and gave him a knowing look, then offered him all the space he needed. Their work was done. As the blips and beeps of the games filled the car, Owen opened the letter. His heart soared as he read:

"My dearest Owen..."

CHAPTER 26

York, Nebraska: Father Michael Dalacourt yawned and looked out of the tinted window as the Greyhound bus pulled into York, Nebraska, one of the many stops he would have along the way to Los Angeles. The priest had already traveled for hours, but had enjoyed precious few of the missionary opportunities De Solei had suggested he would find. For the most part, the world was getting caught up in the paranoia of people disappearing and the dead rising and they were staying home because of it. He could hardly blame them. He made a couple of half-hearted attempts at breaking the ice with several passengers, but an older well-dressed woman simply turned up her nose at him and a tough-looking man traveling with a much younger woman—a daughter, he hoped—simply mumbled he wanted to sleep and turned away. So with a sigh, he had resigned himself to a long and uneventful trip.

Things changed dramatically, however, in York. It was only a fifteen-minute stop, but as the few passengers straggled back onto the bus, Dalacourt recognized a new traveler walking down the aisle. He smiled from ear-to-ear as he watched the old man shuffle toward him.

"Good afternoon, Michael," the old Indian greeted him with a grin and a tip of his weather-beaten hat.

"And to you, John," Dalacourt answered cheerfully and then motioned to the vacant seat next to him. "Please sit down."

"Thank you," John replied, lowering himself into the seat, his bones creaking all the way.

"What on earth are you doing here?" Dalacourt asked, trying to keep the hundred or so immediate questions in his mind from coming out all at once. His first meeting with the man had given him much to think about and now that fortune had brought them together again, he could hardly contain himself.

John sat back, tipped his hat over his eyes just a bit, and stretched. "Just traveling," he answered easily.

Dalacourt continued, unperturbed at the man's way of redirecting a conversation where and when he would. "Do you do this often?"

"For the past several years I've been all over the world and then some. You might say I have an itch I just can't scratch. I'll stay someplace for a while, sometimes even a long while, but there's as much wanderlust as calcium in these old bones and there's no getting rid of it now."

"Where do you call home when you're not traveling?"

"You're mighty inquisitive, aren't you?" the old man smiled. "The last place I suppose I called home was Arizona."

"Really?" Dalacourt asked. "So what brought you here?"

"A bus," came the straight answer.

Dalacourt couldn't help but chuckle. There was something warm about the old wanderer and the priest could feel it acutely. "If you don't mind, I've had a question running through my thoughts since our first meeting. I'd like to ask you about it."

"We have a long road ahead of us, so why not?"

"Wonderful," the young priest smiled. "The first time I saw you, back in the cemetery, I got the distinct feeling our meeting wasn't a coincidence. It felt like you were waiting for me."

John tilted his hat so the top half of his face was totally covered. He placed his hand behind his head and yawned. "You don't believe Father Sparrel told me about you?"

"Should I?"

"That depends on how trusting you are," John answered with a wink. "Tell me, Father. What makes you think I know anything about you in the first place? I'm just a weary old traveler, trying to find a quiet corner in the modern world. I don't know much about myself, when you come right down to it, so just how could I know anything about you?"

"The things you said to me…" Dalacourt trailed off, not sure how to wring the answer out of John that he knew was in there.

"I've found in life that a person should look at all the facts, then look deep into their heart, and somewhere in there they'll know the truth. That's where belief lives, and once you believe something, well, you have to believe in what you believe."

"That makes sense," Dalacourt replied thoughtfully, thinking that was what drove him to question what he was hearing from De Solei. He had indeed been searching his heart, and his heart told him that things were much different than what his mentor was telling him.

"Let me put a question to you, Father," John went on. "What do you think of the world today?"

The young Vatican emissary sat back in his seat and folded his arms. "That depends on what context you are talking about," he finally replied pensively. "I suppose it would be easy to say that, in general, the world isn't the brightest place in God's universe anymore."

"No, it isn't and hasn't been for a while now," agreed John somberly. "But what about specifics?"

"Such as?"

"Let me rephrase the question," said John. "Do you believe Archbishop De Solei's claim that the purported second coming of Christ is upon us?"

"What do you know about that?"

"Only what I hear on the news," answered John, "and what I have gleaned from talking to both you and Father Sparrel." He winked a wink that said he knew more than he was letting on and that Dalacourt should not press him any further.

"Do you believe we are in the last days, then?" Dalacourt asked.

"What I believe is irrelevant, Michael," John answered softly. "What you believe is of far more importance."

"And why is that?"

John paused again, purposefully avoiding the priest's question. "Tell me what you believe, Michael," he finally said. "Let's start from there."

Father Dalacourt pursed his lips in minor annoyance. He might trust the man, but he was also somewhat irritated by him at the moment. "Very well," he said almost curtly. "I'll answer your questions and then you answer mine. Agreed?"

"Fair enough."

"Then I believe we are seeing an aspect of the last days," Dalacourt began. "I believe there is something supernatural about what is going on with so many people vanishing and the dead supposedly rising, but I don't believe it is associated with God."

"At least not in a divine way?"

"Precisely," the young priest agreed. "There is something more at work here, but what that is, I do not know."

"You are well-versed in the Bible, are you not?"

"I am," replied Dalacourt. "I am, after all, a priest in God's Holy Church."

John wrinkled his nose, but thought better of saying what was on his mind. Instead, he asked, "How extensive is your understanding of the Book of Revelation?"

"Enough to know that what is happening with the dead rising is not what John meant when he wrote it."

The old man nodded his head almost imperceptibly. "And what do you believe John meant when he wrote the Book of Revelation?"

"Hard to say," Dalacourt answered, absently reaching up and

rubbing his still-healing neck, the result of his earlier encounter with the risen Father Oliveira. "I had the misfortune of meeting one of these recently risen dead people and it was an experience I do not care to repeat."

"But you will," John sighed sadly.

Dalacourt turned to face the old man again. "What do you mean by that?"

John waved him off. "Nothing. It's just that these are trying times we live in," he answered. "We are swamped with reports about the dead rising, but most of those reports are not proven."

"Meaning what?"

"Meaning that graves are reported opened, the living say they see formerly dead men and women walking about, but the majority of it cannot be proven. What you saw in Belle Plaine was only a tiny whisper of what's going on all over the world right now. Yet most of what we hear is only rumor and innuendo, people saying things because they are hearing others say it."

"That doesn't mean it isn't true."

"Oh, I didn't say it wasn't true," answered John. "There is no doubt that it is indeed happening. But ask yourself how many of these risen dead people have you heard give their side of the story?"

Dalacourt paused, giving some thought to the old man's question and wondering about Father Olivera's unwillingness or inability to answer that specific question before he attacked him. "I don't suppose I've heard of any."

"Have you seen any of these risen dead yourself?"

Again Dalacourt hesitated before answering. "Just the one."

"So what about all the others?" John asked, spreading his hands in the air. "Every day now, the news is replete with instances of the dead rising from the grave, yet where are all these people? In a town as small as Belle Plaine, there were at least six dead bodies that had vanished from their graves, yet there was only one mention of someone seeing the person walking along the side of the road. Where are they going? Where are they at?"

"I guess I don't know."

"Neither does anyone else, Michael, and that's the missing piece in all of this. Don't you think that should be cause for worry?"

"Slow down a bit," Dalacourt said. "I think we agree that what's happening around the world isn't as divine as some would say, but I fail to see what you're getting at."

John leaned forward and said softly, "They're gathering, Michael. Somewhere, someone is gathering the risen dead."

"Gathering?" Dalacourt asked, shocked, and in a soul-searing moment of illumination, he suddenly understood exactly what was happening. He knew why Father Oliveira had attacked him. He knew what was causing the rising feeling of dread within him. He knew…and he was deathly afraid. "Oh, my Lord God in heaven," he whispered in horror, quickly crossing himself.

"Yes," agreed John, looking hard at Michael Dalacourt. "Your thoughts are correct. The dead are indeed rising, Michael. They're rising the world over and what you're hearing in the news is only a fraction of the number of bodies actually being raised. But this isn't the resurrection spoken of in the Book of Revelation. This isn't of God. This is of Satan. This is an army specifically created for a war that's about to begin."

As the highway hummed beneath the Greyhound's tires, Michael Dalacourt sat in absolute silence, too stunned to utter a word. What was being suggested was almost too fantastical to believe, yet he knew the old man was right. But how was it even possible? Could the dead literally be massing into an army? Was the world actually on the brink of the final war of good and evil? Even if it was plausible, it was still difficult, if almost impossible, to accept.

"The enemy has been moving for thousands of years, working toward this day with all his evil scheming. He's close, Michael, close to accomplishing his goal of overcoming the earth and banishing God." John's voice trailed off into a wearied whisper.

Dalacourt turned a stunned face to John. "Banishing God? What do you mean by that? The Bible states that in the end, Satan will be cast down. Certainly the last days are going to be incredibly dangerous and difficult for the righteous, but how can you say God will be banished? That's blasphemous!"

"How much of the Book of Revelation have you read, Michael?" John asked calmly.

"All of it," countered Dalacourt, his voice still sharp. "Nowhere does it talk about God being banished."

"Then I put to you that you haven't read all of the Book of Revelation."

"Of course I have," snapped Dalacourt. "Why would you say such a thing?"

"Because not all of the Book of Revelation has been given over to man to read. A small portion has been kept hidden for just these very days. Do you recall what Revelation 10:4 says?"

The young priest paused for a moment to draw upon his mastery of end-times scripture. "'And when the seven thunders had uttered their voices, I was about to write: and I heard a voice from heaven saying unto me, 'Seal up those things which the seven thunders uttered, and write them not','" Dalacourt quoted. "I'm well aware of the scripture, John. Are you implying that what was sealed up speaks of God being banished from the earth?"

"In part," John said solemnly.

"I'm afraid your credibility is falling quickly with me, my friend. You're talking about scripture that has never been printed—has never been made part of the Bible. John supposedly sealed it up so that no eyes could ever be upon the words. How, then, would you know what is said in those passages?"

Now it was the Indian's turn to smile. He leaned down and picked up his battered backpack. After rooting around inside, he withdrew his hand. In it, he held an old wooden tube, stoppered on both ends with wax and intricately carved with ancient text and symbols.

"What's that?" asked Dalacourt, intrigued.

"It's a scroll tube that has been in my possession for a very long time."

"And I suppose you have the lost scriptures within?" Dalacourt scoffed.

"I didn't tell you this would be easy," John answered, his face deadly serious. "But, I ask you to indulge me and listen to what I have to say before passing judgment. I've been around for a very long time, Michael, and I've seen many, many things. I know a great deal you don't and you can gain much wisdom from listening carefully to my council."

"I don't wish to be disrespectful, John, but what you're saying is virtually impossible to believe."

"Is it?" the old man challenged. "A very short time ago, seeing the dead rise up in front of you, let alone being attacked by one, would have seemed impossible to you, as well."

"True," Dalacourt agreed slowly.

"And now here you are, far away from home, investigating reports of the same. The dead are truly rising and you accept that as fact."

"I do," answered Dalacourt, "because I have seen it happen with my own eyes."

John arched his eyebrows sharply. "You believe because you see it, because it is there in front of you."

"Yes."

"Do you view God in the same way, Michael? Do you find it hard to believe in Him because you have not seen Him?"

Dalacourt whirled on the old man, his voice suddenly angry. "That is unfair and I resent your implications," he began, but John waved him off.

"Relax, Michael," John said gently, patting him on the shoulder. "I'm certainly not accusing you of not believing in God. I know a God-fearing man when I see one, and if ever there was one, it's you. I am only trying to get you to apply the same mindset you have toward God to what I am about to tell you."

Dalacourt relaxed a bit, but his scowl remained and John went on.

"We have a long bus ride in front of us, Michael, and many miles to talk," he said. "Just listen to what I have to say before you make any decisions about my sanity. At the very worst, perhaps it will turn out to be a good story for you to pass the time. What have you got to lose?"

"Very well, John," he said, still incredulous but certainly intrigued. "Tell me your story and we'll go from there."

"Thank you," John replied, carefully digging the wax plug out of one end of the tube. "This has not been opened for many years," he went on. "I am careful to keep it protected at all times."

"These are the original scrolls?"

"Not at all," John laughed. "That would make them more than two thousand years old. Besides, I'd be hard pressed to explain why they're transcribed in English. It was hardly the accepted language of the early Christians during the time of the Caesars."

Dalacourt smiled. "Point taken. So tell me, what proof do you have these are authentic? How am I to know these words are truly words from St. John the Divine?"

"I offer no proof other than what your heart tells you is true. That's where faith comes in, Michael," he answered. "Just read what I give you and listen to what I have to say and you can decide for yourself. In the end, I trust you to make the right decision."

"Very well."

John slipped two fingers into the scroll tube and gently eased out a roll of parchment. The pages were aged and yellow and the young priest was reminded of the ancient parchments he had seen in the vaults of the Vatican. The old man carefully peeled off the outer page and handed it to the priest. He rolled up two other pages and placed them back in the tube. "Be careful now. The parchment you hold was transcribed almost three hundred years ago."

"By you?" Dalacourt asked with a mischievous smile.

"Now that would be even more difficult for you to believe," John answered with a chuckle. "Let's just say they've been in my family's possession for a very long time."

"I can accept that. So, why don't I get the whole thing?"

"Perhaps someday you'll get to see the other pages, but not today, my young friend. Not today." His voice trailed off, as if already deep in thought about when that day might come.

Dalacourt shrugged his shoulders and turned his eyes to the yellowed parchment. As John had said, the words were penned in English, the script spidery, yet neat and readable:

In the age of the last dispensation, shall the anointed of the Beast arise from the shadows and come forth upon the earth, and Death shall be his name. And he shall bear before him the sword of War, and Famine shall be his chariot, and Pestilence shall be his shield. And war shall be brought to the lands all around and death brought to the people.

And the earth shall give up her dead, insomuch that the dead shall stand with the Beast. And they shall march forth upon the earth and shall slay the living and shall rend the ground from whence they came.

And then the anointed of the Beast shall gather his people to him and shall give them power over the night. And they shall seek the living and shall slay them and shall drink of their blood and shall enslave their souls.

And then all about the lands, shall her prisons be opened, and her dark pits, and her secret places. And those within shall be made over according to the desires of their hearts. And they shall gather forth, and shall be his right hand, and shall do according to his will.

And the anointed of the Beast shall stand forth among his people and shall command them as unto an army, that they should go forth and slay all manner of living thing throughout the land. And the army of the Beast shall march forth and shall slay all manner of living thing, according to his word.

And the earth will be made desolate and all manner of iniquity and abominations and wickedness shall prevail and the Almighty God shall weep for His creation for a thousand years.

Dalacourt read and reread the scroll twice, his feelings alternating between stark disbelief and deep understanding. Finally, after a lengthy pause, he spoke, "If what you've shown me is indeed true, then the answer is before us."

"In part, yes."

"I have to wonder, though, that the dead—particularly those who were righteous in their lifetime—would rise up and serve Satan."

"We aren't speaking specifically about Satan here," countered John. "These scriptural passages speak of one whom he has anointed to stand in his stead."

"The anointed of the Beast," agreed Dalacourt, handing the old parchment back to John. "The Antichrist?"

"Perhaps," was the reply. "Or perhaps one of his minions. I

cannot say for certain."

"But why would the righteous serve him? That's what I don't understand."

"They wouldn't," the old man replied as he carefully rolled the scroll back onto the others and then slid them back into the ancient tube. "But Satan has many unseen followers. They're ever present on this earth and hate the living with a passion, for we have what they desire."

"A body," Dalacourt answered immediately. It was well-known and much discussed in many religious circles that evil spirits, if that's what they could be truly called, lacked the one thing they truly desired—a physical body they could call their own.

"Exactly," answered John with a nod. "They want what we have, but can't have it while we yet live. Therefore, it's the dead they seek."

"You're talking about possession," Dalacourt stated.

"In a matter of speaking," John replied. "These spirits can inhabit a physical body vacated by its rightful owner and are capable of rudimentary movement, actions, and perhaps even limited speech. The righteous spirit is gone, awaiting the first resurrection, but in the meantime, the body is being used by the spirit of another, one that is vile and evil. And in possessing a body, these spirits end up hating the living even more. They know what they have is a farce—a hollow representation of what having a mortal body is truly like."

"So when Father Oliveira attacked me, it wasn't actually him."

"I wouldn't think so," answered John. "I don't profess to have all the answers, Michael, but I do have enough to understand that what's happening is the beginning of the end as spoken of in the Book of Revelation. The dead are indeed rising, but it's actually the followers of Satan who are in control, taking up the bodies of the dead and following the anointed of the Beast here on the earth. They've been waiting for this moment for thousands of years."

"So what you're saying is the world is being threatened by zombies."

"I wouldn't quite call them that," cautioned John. "Traditionally, zombies are thought of as mindless creatures. However, these particular abominations are evil spirits fully capable of thought. They're intelligent, some of them quite so, and are consumed by hatred and constrained only by the limitations of the body they're currently inhabiting."

"In what ways are they limited?"

"Depends on the body, I would imagine," the old Indian answered. "In the first place, they certainly aren't accustomed to what an actual physical body can do, so they would likely not be nearly as dexterous as you and me. Though they likely don't feel pain, injuries and damage would inhibit them as they would a living person. For example, a body with two broken legs isn't likely to be of any use to them."

"So they need someone recently dead and in fairly good shape," said Dalacourt with a snap of his fingers. "That would explain why the four softball players and the father and son were dug up in Belle Plaine, yet the two elderly people were left alone."

"Exactly. The terrible thing is, all of these people who have gone missing lately are probably being carefully killed for their bodies. That would afford the invading spirit the best possible vessel in which to inhabit. This is a horrible, horrible thing we are witnesses to."

Dalacourt sat back, a puzzled look on his face. "But what I don't understand is, how are they pulling it all off? How is this happening today and why not earlier? If they've been waiting for thousands of years, wouldn't they have done this millennia ago?"

"That, my young Father, is the million dollar question, as they would say," John answered. "I don't have an answer, but I have a theory. My guess is it has something to do with a medical advance of some kind. I'd think for a spirit to take control of a physical body, there has to be something working on the inside, even if it's at a very low level."

Dalacourt looked hard at John. "So you're saying someone discovered a way to reanimate a body?"

"That would be my guess," answered John. "But like I said, it's only a guess. I might know a lot about what is happening, but how it's happening is another matter entirely."

Dalacourt hesitated before speaking. "As incredible as it may seem, what you are saying has a ring of truth to it. The Bible tells us we'll see things in the final days that simply are not believable. I've felt deep in my heart the time was coming and have wondered if I'd see it in my lifetime." He paused and looked straight at John and there was an almost desperate look in his eyes. "I can't help but wonder how you know all of this. Who are you, really?"

The old Indian shrugged his shoulders. "I am who I am," he answered simply. "I was living in Arizona, and now I'm traveling westward on a Greyhound with a young Vatican priest who asks many questions. I have the scriptures and I have wisdom. What else matters?"

"I think a great deal more matters, personally," Dalacourt pressed on. "For example, how is it you have in your possession the supposed lost scriptures of the Book of Revelation?"

"They have never been lost, Michael," John answered, "merely hidden. That's just semantics, I suppose, but let me ask you this. Do you believe them?"

"I already said that I did," answered the priest, "even if it's a stretch. I can't explain it other than to say those words and yours seem to hold more truth in them than I've read or heard in a long time. I'm just curious to know how you came by them."

"If you believe them, then what does it matter where they came from? They exist and they speak truth. I know this isn't what you want to hear, but I need you to trust me that, for now, too much information is more dangerous than no information at all. Understand my aims are honorable, I'm led by God, and my only intention is to help you to the best of my ability."

"You speak like you intend to accompany me to Los Angeles."

"Salt Lake City," John corrected.

"I change buses there," Dalacourt explained, "but I travel on to Los Angeles."

"Ah," John said with a knowing nod of his head. "Francis De Solei has requested you join him at the Cathedral of Our Lady of the Angels."

If any part of their previous conversation had shocked Michael Dalacourt before, it was nothing compared to the bomb the old Indian had just dropped on him. "How could you know about that?" he stammered, his eyes wide with amazement. "It's one thing to claim wisdom about mysteries enshrouded in the past. It's quite another to know something that only happened yesterday and only I should be privy to."

"Let me tell you something you should always remember, Michael," John explained, leaning close and quickly changing the subject. "Not every ally is really your ally."

"And where does that leave you? I have known you only a few days and you have said very little to me that I can understand. Do I trust you to be sincere?"

"Your heart tells you that I am sincere," John answered easily. "Yet your heart tells you differently with Archbishop De Solei."

"Are you saying I should ignore his request to report to him in Los Angeles?"

"That's precisely what I'm saying," John explained. "Archbishop Francis De Solei is a powerful man, which also makes him a dangerous man. He'll be given important choices in the upcoming conflict, and I'm afraid he won't be up to the challenge. He turned down that darkened path long ago, and the days to come will plunge him deeper and deeper into that forest until he will be forever lost. Yet despite his power within the church and the sway he will soon hold over the masses, he's still only a pawn to higher powers."

Dalacourt turned to look out the window, his mind reeling. John's words had brought all of his previous misgivings concerning his mentor boiling to the surface. The dream from the other night filled his thoughts and again he saw De Solei in the confessional, being accused by a little girl of breaking every commandment given by God. The dream was utterly bizarre, but his heart told him John's words should be believed. "What can I do?" he pleaded, struggling to keep himself on an even keel even as he felt everything he'd ever known or believed in was churning and swaying beneath him.

"I understand your feelings, Michael," John said warmly. "You feel your life has been a waste, that you've been deceived all these years. In truth, you have been deceived, but you mustn't think it's a reflection on you. And certainly your life hasn't been wasted. On the contrary, it's prepared you for the dangerous road that lies ahead."

"I certainly don't feel prepared," Dalacourt sighed, casting a glance out the window as the bus passed a large wind farm.

"You're more prepared than you could imagine," replied the old man. "Yet you have much more to learn. The enemy has been working for thousands of years and his power is broad. He has soldiers in every aspect of business, religion, and society the world over. Francis De Solei is but one of many and he's being used and controlled like thousands of others, through the seductive allure of riches, power, and glory."

"That's hardly comforting."

"Take heart, Michael," said John reassuringly. "The war will be a long and brutal one, but this is only the beginning and the outcome is far from decided. Many have been deceived and many more will yet be deceived before the war is ended and a victor emerges."

"I just don't understand," Dalacourt said quietly. "How could it have come to this? How deep does it go?"

"It goes deeper than you would care to know," John answered gravely. "It has been brought about by an organization in existence for thousands of years, whose sole purpose is to bring about the millennial reign—not of Christ, but of Satan—upon this earth."

"Is that what the verse means about God weeping for a thousand years?"

John nodded.

"Will they succeed?"

The old Indian shrugged. "No one truly knows. God says nothing of it in any personal revelation to anyone or in any of the known scriptures, because ultimately all God's children have free agency. I will say that evil can succeed. That's why the scriptures you have just read have been kept secret. While not pretty, the Book of Revelation as it is, has a happy ending. Evil is put aside and the world lives happily ever after for those who ally themselves with God. It's a fairy tale in a way, only it's a preordained fairy tale. It has to happen that way."

"As the world understands it today."

"Exactly," said John somberly. "But now you know it doesn't have to happen that way at all."

"That's an extremely frightening thought," Dalacourt said with an involuntary shiver.

"Indeed it is," John answered. "How many people, when faced

with a choice between good and evil, choose good because they know without a doubt good will prevail in the end?"

"Many, I would imagine," Dalacourt answered.

"And what would it do to society to find out that, not only does evil have a shot at overwhelming good, but it will be extremely difficult for the forces of good to withstand the coming storm? I shudder to even think about it myself," John answered his own question quietly. He leaned close again. "Michael, the additional scriptures I have tell the truth, but it's a truth the world can't deal with. It's only given to those who have enough courage and hope to overcome the fear that almost certain defeat comes with. People like you."

"But why me?" Dalacourt whispered, desperation again in his voice.

"Because you are strong enough, no matter what you might think, and you will continue to do the right thing, no matter what," John answered. "The forces of evil, led by the anointed of the Beast, are in a position to begin the final battle. Many are already under their sway and many more will fall under their sway as each day passes. The world is at a tipping point and mankind teeters on the brink. The next days will tell us everything. You will be a leader, Michael, because you'll be one of the few who can withstand the first blow. That's why I shared this with you, to further prepare you for your destiny."

Michael Dalacourt's brain spun out of control. This was so far beyond anything he had considered that he did not know if he could ever be the person John apparently thought him to be. "So what would you have me do?" he finally asked.

"You must do what you feel best," John answered simply. "If you choose to go to Los Angeles, I won't stop you. I don't think you'll make it, though. I'm not overly sure we'll even make it to Salt Lake City. The storm very well might break before you get to either port."

"What do you mean? It could start today? It could start this afternoon?"

"Think about what we have spoken of," John said. "The dead are gathering. They are building strength so that, when they strike, chaos will reign. This is the goal of the adversary, for in chaos, he grows stronger. For the past few weeks, the dead and missing have been all over the news, helped in large part by media empires that are completely within the throes of this organization. But to what end? There are no solutions, no helpful hints, nothing to prepare the average man for what lies ahead. But people are starting to take more notice," he went on, waving his arm around to indicate the few passengers on the bus with them. "Look around you, Michael. It's on everybody's mind now and the murmuring is growing louder. The enemy cannot wait much longer, for his greatest success lies in striking with as much surprise as he can."

"But, a war?"

"A war," John affirmed. "Or at least the beginning."

"What of De Solei?"

"I believe the church knows much about what is happening, or at least suspects as much, and the Vatican has sent De Solei to Los Angeles to help stabilize the people," John answered. "But while the church might understand the bigger picture, they do not see what is happening in their own house. They do not see De Solei for who he truly is. The church acts in good faith and the Pope is a good man, but I believe that ultimately the archbishop has been sent to Los Angeles to help establish a new world order at the behest of someone outside the church."

"But how can this be allowed to happen?"

"It is not the Catholic Church that is the problem here and De Solei's true orders were not given by anyone within your church organization," answered John. "De Solei is a man controlled by another power and his God is not our God. Man is not a loyal creature; man can be tempted, subverted, and turned into someone who is wholly evil. Francis De Solei long ago surrendered to the whisperings in his head and the allure of power that was presented to him."

"Can the church do anything about him?"

"It's far too late for that, Michael," was the answer. "De Solei is too entrenched and his move to Los Angeles signals a great change in his direction. For those few who know him well, he is taking off his mask and making his move for power. For the rest, he is simply doing what a man of God should do. Unfortunately, this will have dire consequences for your church."

"What are you saying?" Dalacourt exclaimed, horror washing over him.

"Calm yourself, Michael," John soothed. "This has been in motion long before you were born. De Solei, while he is but a pawn to higher powers, will hold much power in the coming months. He will become the driving power behind the church and I'm afraid that numerous good people will fail to live up to their potential because of his lead. That is the reason I am talking with you today. I do not want you to fall into a trap that I'm afraid will capture many others."

"But how can one man wield so much power over so many people?"

"Because he is not one man. He is a willing part of a cabal whose sole purpose is to enslave humanity. They will stop at nothing. Just think how powerful they will be, controlling both sides of the conflict, both government and religion."

"I... I just can't get my mind around all of this."

"You will, in time," John answered gently. "There is much yet to play out."

"So where do I go? What do I do?"

"I am going to Salt Lake City, Michael," John answered plainly. "I ask that you accompany me, but I know in the end, the decision must rest with you."

Father Michael Dalacourt was silent for a long while, staring out the window as the miles continued to roll beneath them. Could it all be true? He found himself believing everything John had told him, except perhaps the size of his role in the war that was to come. Finally, he turned and looked directly at the old man. "I'll go with you."

John nodded, smiled, and then pushed his hat over his eyes. Within seconds, Dalacourt could hear the heavy breathing that came with a sound sleep. He decided he might as well try to get some sleep, too. If the onslaught was as imminent as John predicted, he would need every advantage he could muster. He leaned back and looked out the window, watching the Nebraska cornfields and wind farms rush by, willing sleep to come, but failing. His thoughts were too jumbled and his mind wandered desperately. Then he heard something that confirmed everything John had told him and he wondered if sleep would ever come to him again. He almost didn't hear it at first, but one of the other passengers had a radio and had turned it up as the breaking news story was being reported.

"…reports are still sketchy, but it appears the explosions have decimated many of the structures in the complex. We repeat: the Vatican has been struck by multiple bomb blasts, thought to be the work of unknown terrorists. Casualties are high. Emergency personnel are on the scene…"

As the reporter went on, Michael Dalacourt crossed himself and began to cry.

It had begun.

CHAPTER 27

Salt Lake City, Utah: David Sumbawanga paused at the mouth of the tunnel and leaned heavily on his mango tree walking stick. His breath came in shallow puffs and he felt as if his heart was being squeezed in a vise. He knew he should be better able to overcome the oppressive feelings that threatened to tear him down and that fears and doubts shouldn't find victory over him so quickly or easily.

But they were.

Taking a deep breath, he focused on steadying his breathing and calming his nerves. In a few moments, David was master of his emotions once again. He wouldn't be beaten by fear. With a deep, cleansing breath, he peered into the tunnel. The single lamp that lit the underpass glowed orange, casting a sickly pall over the floors and the walls. David stood just outside the glow and wondered what his son had felt before descending into the tunnel. Had he sensed anything amiss? Had he seen or heard the demon that would take him?

Steeling his resolve, David stepped forward, determined to feel what his son had felt. It was late evening and the concrete walls in the empty tunnel amplified his slow footsteps as he walked toward the spot that bore witness to the end of his son's life. He froze and turned his head to look back the way he'd come. Had he heard something? Was the demon waiting to claim him as it had claimed his son? Or, had Petr finally arrived?

No one was there. He was alone.

The Russian had promised to meet him at the entrance to the tunnel, having told him he knew exactly where it was. But perhaps it was just as well he hadn't arrived yet, as it gave David a few precious moments of silent contemplation he felt he needed. He wanted to touch the walls, smell the scents, breathe the air, connect with what was left.

The light beckoned to him, calling him forward to witness, to see the final moments of Gideon Sumbawanga. He closed his eyes tightly to steady himself once more and when he opened them again, the demon was there. Huge and imposing, the monster blocked his way. Arms, corded with muscle and covered with unspeakable tattoos, were folded across a massive chest. Long black hair was pulled back into a ponytail and a matted beard covered half of his scarred face. The creature looked at David and smiled, teeth gleaming white in the darkness.

David hadn't been alone after all. Death had been waiting for him, the same way it had been waiting for Gideon. He closed his eyes and waited for the inevitable. There would be no escape. The end was upon him. His breathing slowed and acceptance quickly came. He would not give into fear. No, he would embrace whatever fate had been decided for him. Taking a deep breath, he opened his eyes to face the specter.

David Sumbawanga was alone again.

The tunnel ran straight and true underneath the road and toward the stadium. The orange lamp buzzed. Nothing stood in his way. Only the memories of what he'd seen in his vision remained with him. Heaving a weary sigh, he slowly walked forward to the middle of the tunnel. This was where it had happened. The crime scene had been processed, the yellow tape collected, and the concrete scrubbed. But as David knelt reverently on the path, he could see the faint brown stains where blood had once pooled—Gideon's blood.

David had long felt that blood was a sacred gift and the spilling of it was the greatest of sins. He recalled Leviticus, 17:11, which read, "For the life of the flesh is in the blood; and I have given it to you for making atonement for your lives on the altar." Here, in small amounts spread thinly over a concrete wall, was the life of the flesh of his son.

His son was gone, never to return.

But David was a man of deep spirituality and convictions and it was his faith that told him he must do what he could to find Gideon and bring him home. David Sumbawanga wanted to tell his son one last time that he loved him, that he was proud of him, and then to finally say good-bye. In short, he wanted closure.

He bowed his head, a prayer on his lips, and the tears finally came. He sobbed quietly, oblivious to everything but his own grief. How long he knelt, he didn't know, but he never heard the approaching footsteps until they were almost on top of him. Looking up, he saw their source. It appeared as if three demons were advancing on him. Blinking furiously to clear the tears from his eyes, he realized they weren't demons. They were men. And they weren't friendly.

"Look at what we have here," the first man said, coming to a stop mere feet from David. He was dressed in tattered jeans and a filthy t-shirt. A dirty, red bandana was tied around his shaved head and his eyes were hollow and sunken. He looked at David in hungry anticipation.

David slowly pushed himself to his feet, leaning heavily on his walking stick. He realized he must have been kneeling for quite some time because his legs and his knees ached to the point of barely moving.

"Don't get up on our account," the man said as he kicked his foot out, knocking David's walking stick away and sending the African tumbling to the concrete. All three men laughed as David sprawled on the ground.

"I'm sorry," David said, rolling painfully to his knees. "I don't want any trouble. I was just paying respects to my son."

The thug looked around with a smile. "This ain't no cemetery. You lost or somethin'?"

David shook his head as he climbed back to his feet. "My son was killed here," David answered sadly. "It seemed a sensible thing to come."

"Bad news, Pops," the punk replied with a harsh laugh. "The sensible thing would have been to stay home." He took a step closer, his voice dropping dangerously. "So how 'bout we make this easy. Just give me your wallet, anything else you got, and we won't hurt you."

"Much," another of the thugs added with a snicker.

"I'm sorry," David replied, his eyes going to each face and back again, gauging their intent. "I have only a few dollars on me, cab fare back to my hotel."

"Wrong answer, Gramps," the lead punk said, a truly nasty look passing over his face. He drew back his fist and threw a punch toward David's face, but the older man was less a victim than they might have hoped and he stepped to the side and shoved his attacker's arm out wide, throwing him off balance. The assailant recovered quickly and whirled back to face him, his face reddening with anger.

"Not smart," he snarled and drew back again. But it was only a feint, enough to keep David's attention while one of his cohorts threw a vicious blow to David's kidneys, driving him forward against the wall. Before David could recover, the leader laced him across the jaw with a closed fist, sending him to his knees. "Now, you're gonna pay," he added angrily.

The man pulled his arm back, but before he could launch his fist at David, a new figure appeared from behind, hooking an arm around the attacker's neck and throwing him violently to the ground. The other two thugs immediately moved toward the newcomer with shouts of rage, one of them reaching for something tucked into the back of his pants. But Petr Zhugravinsky had lived his entire life around violence, and he drove his hand forward, fingers stiffened into an edge that smashed into the mugger's throat.

Choking and gagging, the man spun around and fell to the ground, trying desperately to scream from a smashed windpipe while the second attacker, shorter but more solidly built, shouted a string of curses, lowered his shoulder and charged. Petr neatly sidestepped him and shoved the man hard, allowing his momentum to carry him into the concrete wall.

By that point, the leader had regained his footing and came at Petr in a fury, leading with both fists. Petr threw out a lightning quick jab that caught his opponent in the nose, breaking it. Blood streamed down the man's face as he staggered backward. Petr followed in a boxer's stance, hunter versus prey, and snapped out two more straight jabs. Both connected, the second one breaking numerous teeth. The assailant stood for just a second more before his eyes rolled back in his head and he toppled to the ground.

"Petr," David's voice said shakily.

Adrenaline coursing through his body, Petr ignored David's call and whirled around just as the shorter, bulkier thug was getting back to his feet. Petr gave him no quarter, grabbing the man's head and holding it while he drove his knee up and into his face, breaking his nose.

David was leaning against the wall, trying to catch his breath. But he saw what was happening and was alarmed. "Petr," he said more forcefully, but Petr wouldn't be denied. With the bigger brute bloody and staggering, Petr drew back and fired a punch nearly straight down at the back of the man's neck. The assailant's legs immediately folded and he dropped heavily to the ground, a low moan escaping his bleeding mouth.

The thug he'd chopped in the throat was on his hands and knees, still trying to get air through his damaged windpipe. Petr stepped up behind him and yanked the cheap 9 millimeter handgun out of the man's waistband. With a practiced hand, he swung the barrel of the pistol to the back of the assailant's head. His finger tightened on the trigger.

"Petr!" David shouted, desperate to stop him from falling into the pit that was opening up before him. "Stop!"

The Russian finally heard him and froze, turning slowly to face the old African. The look on David Sumbawanga's face cut through him deeper than any knife could, as the realization about what he'd just done struck home.

"David," Petr said softly, the energy draining from him. He quickly looked down at the man on the ground before him and then to the gun in his hand. His eyes found David's again and he hated what he saw there.

"That's enough, Petr," David commanded, his voice hard, his eyes even harder.

"Sir, I'm…sorry," the Russian stammered. "I only wanted to…"

David held up a hand for silence and shook his head. He bent down and picked up his walking stick, then slowly straightened, wincing in pain as he did. He looked around at the three would-be muggers, all on the ground and not likely to get up for some time. Then his eyes went back to the Russian. "Violence is not the answer, Petr," he said, disappointment in his voice. "It's never the answer."

Petr lowered his head in shame. "You needed help," he said softly.

"And I thank you for that, Petr. But once the threat was over there was no need to continue," David pressed, stepping toward the younger man. He reached out and placed a hand underneath Petr's chin and pushed his head up so their eyes could lock. "If you can't learn to control your anger when it matters most, you will become that which you abhor."

The Russian looked up, his eyes stung by the rebuke. "I'm sorry, Mr. Sumbawanga," he said again, a little more formally. "You were in danger, sir. I was only trying to help."

David stared at him for several moments before his visage softened. "What kept you?" he sighed as he began walking back up the tunnel.

Petr fell into step beside him, absently taking a handkerchief from his pocket. "I would have been here a half hour ago, but I was pulled over," he answered as he released the gun clip and slipped it into his pocket. He worked the slide, ejecting the chambered bullet, ignoring it as it bounced along the tunnel floor. Then he proceeded to wipe down the weapon as he continued. "The officer said I was speeding, but he sat in his car for fifteen minutes and never even wrote me a ticket."

"He just let you go?"

"Yes."

David said nothing more, but his jaw tightened in thought.

"May I ask a question, sir?"

He was answered with an almost imperceptible nod.

"Did it help?" Petr asked.

"Coming here?"

"Yes."

"This is where it happened," David said as they emerged from the tunnel and back into the cool, dry night. "Gideon was last here. I had hoped to get some sense of what happened."

Petr paused momentarily to toss the now harmless gun into a nearby public trash can as they walked by it. With the clip in his pocket—which he would throw into some random dumpster on the way home—he didn't have to worry about someone finding the weapon and putting it to use. "Did you learn anything?" he finally asked, his gaze going back to David.

"I don't know," David answered quietly after a few moments.

The two of them walked in silence for a while, Petr letting David lead where he wished. He followed, silently berating himself for allowing his baser instincts to take over during the fight in the tunnel.

"Sir?" he finally broke the silence.

David continued walking, looking neither left nor right.

"About what happened back there," the Russian continued. "I'm deeply sorry for my actions."

David stopped and turned around. His face was no longer hard, the anger having left it. He was simply tired and his face was lined with sadness. "We will speak no more of it, Petr," he said. "I'm not so angry with you as I'm just confused by everything that has happened here. I wish to go back to my hotel and think on these things in solitude."

"I'd be happy to drive you, sir," Petr offered.

"That won't be necessary, Petr," David said and then resumed walking again. "It's a pleasant night and I wish to walk for a bit and clear my head. I'll catch a taxi back to my hotel when I'm ready. Thank you for coming tonight. I do appreciate all the help you've given."

Petr nodded silently and watched as the old man walked slowly into the darkness. At that moment, Petr hated himself more than ever before. In just a few moments of violent anger, he had quite possibly destroyed everything he'd hoped to attain: helping David, becoming more than his family name, and using it all to win Alexis for himself. In the end, perhaps it was all a waste of time. Perhaps he was nothing more and nothing less than a Zhugravinsky.

CHAPTER 28

Telve di Sopra, Italy: At a population of less than seven hundred people and situated high above the green valley below, the picturesque community, Telve di Sopra, was one of a series of small towns in the Trentino-Alto Adige region still recovering from the devastation of being on the Eastern Front between the Italian and Austrian armies during much of World War I. Isolated in the Italian Alps, and struggling a century later to rebuild in terms of both buildings and population, the villages in the region had the appearances of places and times the world had long ago forgotten. As such, Telve di Sopra was about as unlikely location as possible for the meeting now taking place. And yet, to the two men sitting together on a park bench, watching the storm clouds churning off on the horizon under an already dark gray canopy, it would be hard to imagine taking care of this one last business deal anywhere else.

The first man leaned back on the bench and let his eyes roam the little Italian town and the valley below. He was dressed in a light blue running suit and expensive tennis shoes, the kind someone with money would gravitate to, as well as a pair of coal black sunglasses that seemed to cover half his face. His hair was not slicked back as was his usual style, but instead fell in curls around his forehead. He had not shaved for a few days, but even his facial hair did not look out of place. He looked just as he wanted to—a tourist passing through a small Italian villa without a care in the world.

He had come to the village hoping to avoid, at least for a little while, the very man sitting next to him. Truth be told, the two could not have looked more dissimilar to any passing local. The second man was enormously tall, dressed in black jeans and a white t-shirt that accentuated his powerful physique. Intricate tattoos covered his bare arms, disappearing beneath his clothes. The first had wondered since the day they met long ago what the designs meant, but had never felt comfortable asking and certainly didn't feel comfortable asking now. Another day, he had thought to himself, but then he had remembered that there would be no other day.

"I don't know if I've ever seen you so happy, Victor," Hade said with a smile as he leaned forward and tossed a few scraps of bread to the small group of pigeons gathered at their feet. "Or perhaps happy isn't quite the word I'm looking for."

Vittorio Emanuele Legio stared hard at the man's face, trying to see if he could read Hade's emotions at all. But his vision seemed to slide away from Hade's visage the harder he looked, making it impossible to read anything. The only thing he could really see were the dark clouds reflected in the man's sunglasses. It was an ominous sign and not one he liked. There would be no reprieve, he knew, no last minute stay of execution.

"I don't know if I'd use the word 'happy' either," Victor replied, shifting his eyes back to watching the birds mill around them. "I think a better word would be resigned," he went on.

"Yes, our last bit of business indeed," Hade answered, his voice almost melancholy. "But I think not yet." He reached into a paper bag sitting at his feet and withdrew a bottle of water. "Here," he offered it to Legio. "Let's have a small toast instead, as we reflect on the journey that's brought us here." He reached back into the bag, pulled out a few baguettes, and broke them apart. "At the very least, perhaps we can fatten up a few of these sickly looking birds."

Legio accepted the bottle and twisted off the cap. He hoisted a mock cheer to Hade and took a sip. Putting the lid back on, he said softly, "Colette once said, 'What a wonderful life I've had, I only wish I'd realized it sooner.' I feel the same, now that I've had time to think about it."

Hade looked at the man, one eyebrow rising in surprise. "Why, Victor, I didn't realize you knew Colette!"

Legio shrugged. "I've always been well-read, Hade," he replied evenly, "even if you never thought so."

Hade studied Legio for a minute before turning his attention back to the pigeons. He tossed a few more crumbs of bread to them and watched them peck at their meals before replying. "I like this look on you," he said, changing the subject. "I'd say it brings out the gray in your eyes, but I can't see your eyes," he finished with a chuckle.

Legio managed to smile and reached up and took hold of his oversized sunglasses without removing them. "I'll show you mine, if you show me yours," he dared.

Hade smiled back, his teeth gleaming. "Not today, Victor," he answered easily, making a show of adjusting his own black shades. He reached into the bag and pulled out another few scraps of bread, which he flung to the gathered birds. "You really do look at peace, though. I suppose I could almost find some joy in knowing I've helped you put aside all your earthly cares. In some ways, I'm like a Jacob Marley to your Ebenezer Scrooge. I've managed to save you at the last moment from falling into the abyss."

The businessman stared off across the park, his eyes catching up to a couple of joggers as they trotted past, perhaps hoping to reach home before the storm broke. "You know I would have killed you if I had the chance," he finally said, feeling no more need to mask the desire of one day freeing himself of the man sitting next to him.

Hade only smiled. "Come now, my old friend," he said. "You had plenty of opportunities to do the job yourself or pay off some hired goons to do it for you. But in the end, you must have realized that you could not have gone through with it." He paused and idly watched the same runners as they vanished around a bend. "Don't feel bad about that, though, Victor," he went on. "Truthfully, there isn't a man alive who could have pulled the trigger."

"Well, one can dream," Legio stated, taking another small drink from his water bottle.

"There's no harm in dreaming. You've been a dreamer since I first met you back in college," Hade replied with a smile. "The difference between you and every other dreamer out there is that you had the temerity to see those dreams come to fruition. You had the drive to do whatever it took to win. That's why I like you, Victor."

"Oh, come now," Legio scoffed. "You're talking to a master manipulator here, Hade. I know the game well and, with the exception of you, I probably played it better than anyone else in the business world. So forgive me for not believing you liked me. You manipulated me just as I manipulated hundreds, perhaps thousands of others, for my own gains as well as yours."

"Now don't get bitter on me, Victor," Hade soothed. "You built an empire and despite what waits for you, there are still rewards to be had, even if you can't currently see them."

"Rewards?" Legio asked incredulously. "I know what my 'reward' is and while resigned to it, that doesn't make me welcome it."

"Then you don't know everything you think you do," Hade replied, still smiling. Legio started to reply, but Hade held up a hand and silenced him. "Death isn't always the end, my friend. Now please, let's not talk business just yet. Let's just sit, as old friends, and talk about the weather and our aching feet and what is happening to the stock market."

Legio could only shake his head. "Conversations between friends don't usually end with one friend killing the other."

"Of course they do, Victor, more often than civilized people would like to believe. So let's chat, shall we? Have you seen many of the sites since you arrived last night?"

"Yes, Hade," Legio replied tiredly. "I went to mass last night at the Chiesa di Santa Maria Maddalena in Scurelle. I haven't been to mass in years, but there was something soothing about being there. I woke up early this morning and only just returned from visiting the graves of relatives at the cemetery."

"Ah, yes, dead relatives are always the most interesting to talk to, I think. More interesting than the live ones, at least for those of us who know how to listen. You didn't happen to catch the big sign on the large enclave in the cemetery, did you?"

"It's hard to miss," Legio replied. "It said *Risorgeremo*."

"It means, 'We will revive.' A nice reminder for the living that death isn't the end of our journey on earth," he trailed off knowingly, looking back up at the growing storm clouds hanging low in the sky. The air was cool, yet electric, and even in the absence of the sun, his skin felt quite warm, as it always did when he was away from the shielding darkness of nightfall.

"And, we're back to my death. Thank you for the nice chat, old friend, as short as it was."

"It's hard to ignore the topic, isn't it?"

"You know," Legio went on, "I keep thinking about this tiny villa and I find myself wondering what the people here would do if they knew one of the richest men in the world had his roots here. I doubt anyone here even knows they have such a wealthy and famous son." He looked around and then chuckled. "Maybe that explains the lack of a parade."

Hade laughed as well, but caught himself as he noted a figure approaching from down the cobbled street. "Don't speak so quickly, Victor," he said with a smile and a nod of his head. "You wished for a parade and here it comes now."

Legio followed Hade's gaze to the solitary figure walking toward them from across the park. His features were distinct and along the handsome side, but his eyes were dark and his forehead was creased with an almost vicious scowl.

Hade raised a hand in greeting as the man drew nearer, ignoring Legio's questioning look. "*Zdravsuitasya*, Nikolai!" he hailed the newcomer. "Come, sit with us, my young protégé." The few remaining birds scattered as the man approached and Hade looked around as he finished. "I'm afraid we have already fed the pigeons, but perhaps you aren't here to enjoy the relaxation that comes from aviculture."

As Nikolai Zhugravinsky came to a halt before them, Hade turned his attention back to Legio, purposefully baiting the young Russian. "I apologize for this pitiful excuse for a parade, Victor," he said with a sly smile. "He's not even throwing out candy. Oh, well, you get what you pay for, I suppose." As Nikolai continued to glare at the big man, Hade made the introductions. "Vittorio Emanuele Legio, sixth richest man in the world, I'd like you to meet Nikolai Zhugravinsky, eventual ruler of all Russia."

Both men nodded politely toward each other, but neither said a word.

"Now, Kolya," Hade went on, oblivious or uncaring at the discomfort of either man. "Tell us, how was your flight?"

Nikolai cringed, as he always did when Hade used the familiar form of his name around others, but he responded quickly and, as usual, not to the original question. "Would you care to explain to me why I'm here?"

"Come, come, Kolya," Hade said in a patronizing tone. "Would I have dragged you all the way to *Bell' Italia* if it wasn't important?"

"Yes," he snapped. "I'm busy at home as you well know, so I trust you have a good reason for pulling me away from the business you personally told me to see to."

"Mind your manners, boy," Hade scolded in a mocking tone that held a glint of steel underneath. "Do you have any idea who this man is?" he asked, motioning to Victor. He didn't wait for an answer. "He's one of the world's most powerful men, risen from the depths of poverty by his own indomitable will. Surely, spending time with someone such as this must serve some purpose for you. At the very least, he deserves a modicum of civility."

Nikola glared, switching his gaze back and forth from Hade to Legio, but he stayed silent.

"So I'm a self-made man, now," Legio chuckled.

"Of course," Hade answered immediately. "I might have steered you down the path once or twice, but it was a path you had already chosen. And you handled it quite well, which was to be expected. You had everything, Victor: you were powerful, intelligent, and motivated. And most importantly, you had a deep-seated fear that everything you had could be taken away in an instant.

"It is interesting, though," the huge man went on, "that as I look at the two of you, I seem to be shifting my aim just a bit. I'm trading in an intellectual I turned into an executioner for an executioner I hope to turn into an intellectual. But while you are the nearly completed project, Victor," Hade continued, switching his gaze from the businessman back to the young Russian, "Nikolai here is the block of marble ready for the master's touch. He is wild, impetuous and power-hungry and knows little more than the way of the gun. But I have high hopes for him and what he can become."

"You speak as if I'm not here, Hade," Nikolai spat angrily, shifting his stance. He still stood, refusing to sit down, his arms folded across his chest in a defiant manner.

"Kolya," Hade went own, adopting his professor-like tone. "Have you heard of Confucius? He was Chinese, in case you didn't know." He smiled that patronizing smile of his, further agitating the young man. "He wrote 'Ignorance is the night of the mind, a night without moon or star.' Do you know what that means?"

Nikolai remained silent, watching the big man closely.

"It means," Hade explained without missing a beat, "that without any light at all, there's nothing to guide us, nothing to show us the way." He stopped and turned to Legio before continuing. "Victor, perhaps you can give him some advice on the importance of thinking."

"I suppose I can offer your new pupil some guidance, but when I am through, you might wish I had not."

"Victor," Hade chuckled. "We have come so far, you and I. If I feared your words would harm my new protégé, I would not have asked for them."

"Very well, Hade," Legio nodded. Facing the Russian, he continued. "Do you really not know or even suspect why you are here?"

Nikolai continued to glare, but finally shook his head. "No, I do not. I seem to only be wasting my time here."

"No," Legio corrected quietly. "You're not wasting your time. In fact, you're being given a gift only a few get the chance to see in their lifetime. You're being afforded a private screening of your future."

"My future?"

"Indeed," the older man went on, casting a glance at Hade as he spoke. "Hade brought you here to show you how high he can take you. Do you realize I have enough money at my fingertips to buy a small country? I may have done well myself, but there's no way I'd have reached the pinnacle, the heights I stand upon today, without Hade at my side."

"And what does that have to do with me?" Nikolai asked.

"It has everything to do with you," Legio answered almost sadly. "Hade sees in you what he saw in me many years ago. He sees potential. He sees where he can take you. And make no mistake, Nikolai, with Hade as your friend there is no limit to what you can attain. That is, of course, until he has no further need of you."

"What are you talking about?" Nikolai snapped.

But Legio wasn't looking at him anymore. He was looking at Hade. "I wonder, Hade, if your pupil will ever realize that nothing given is ever given freely. Just as you've planned my death for many long years, so is his death by your hands already foreordained. Do you think this toy will last as long as your previous one before you break it as well?"

"So you would use me then," Nikolai accused, his eyes flashing dangerously. "You would use me for your ends and then kill me when I have served your purpose?"

The Russian's hand slipped toward his jacket, but Hade merely chuckled. "You would do well to understand, young Kolya," he warned easily, "that there is indeed a bullet with your name on it housed in the chamber of at least a few of my guns, including the forty-four Magnum I'm carrying with me right now. Would you like to meet it? I can arrange an introduction."

Nikolai's hand froze. The thought of gunning down Hade had occurred to him on more than one occasion, but he knew enough to know he would die first in any shootout.

Hade recognized the hesitation and played on it. "I'm glad we have come to an understanding, Kolya," he went on, his voice changing to ice. "Now if you would be so kind as to put away your violent fantasies and speak nothing else until I tell you, then I can finish up this transaction," he continued, acting as an exasperated parent might with an unruly child. "It might interest you to know that I'm in the middle of perhaps the biggest business deal since J.P. Morgan slipped a napkin to Andrew Carnegie saying he would hand over four hundred ninety-two million dollars for his steel company."

It looked as if the veins in Nikolai's forehead were about to explode, but he simply nodded mutely. Nikolai was impetuous, but he was far from stupid.

"Good," Hade went on. "Now I suggest you take a little walk through town. See the sights—the fresh air will do you good. You may return in about thirty minutes. Then our real work will begin." Hade waved his hands at the young Russian. "Now shoo!" he said and turned to Legio, who had watched the whole thing with a slightly bemused expression on his face. "It's so difficult when they are so raw, Victor. Some days it's like working with a monkey, only an infuriatingly slow monkey."

Nikolai Zhugravinsky stalked away, leaving the two men alone again on the park bench.

"Still, that boy has potential," Hade added after Nikolai was well out of earshot. "It's his brother the family prefers, but they don't see what I see. Nikolai will rule more than his family ever thought possible. If he would just relax a bit, he might enjoy the ride." Clearing his throat, he turned back to Legio. "So, Victor, where were we? Oh, yes," he answered himself. "You were just about to make me the sixth richest man in the world."

Victor Legio sighed as the weight of the current moment settled back on his shoulders. The brief interlude with Nikolai Zhugravinsky had made him almost forget the real reason he was there. "I suppose that's a way of phrasing it, Hade," he said quietly. "The work is done, as you instructed. You're more than comfortably wealthy now."

Hade laughed softly. "You have a gift for wit, Victor. I'll give you that." He reached into a pocket within his trench coat, which was hanging neatly over the back of the park bench, and pulled out a long cigar. He bit the ends off and spit the pieces on the ground, then retrieved his lighter.

Legio shook his head in irritation. "If you don't mind, Hade, I am in Italy in a beautiful little village. The last thing I want to do in my final hour is smell the acrid smoke that billows out of those awful cigars you smoke. If you're going to smoke, could you at least find something a bit more pleasant smelling?"

"Ah, it's a habit of mine and a bad one at that, I suppose," Hade replied with a grin. "I grow my own leaf because I just can't stand all the additives the regular manufacturers put in them." He pulled the cigar out of his mouth and looked at it thoughtfully. "If it bothers you, I can wait."

"Thank you," Legio replied. "At least my last few breaths will be pleasant."

Hade chuckled and tucked the cigar back into his coat. "It's a shame, isn't it, when one becomes enslaved to a power and no longer has any control?"

The older man nodded. "'No cause has he to say his doom is harsh who's made the master of his destiny'," he quoted. "Friedrich von Schiller. I suppose we all chose our own doom in one way or another, regardless of how long ago we gave up being our own masters."

Hade smiled. "The Sophists have nothing on you, old friend. Ah, but what I wouldn't give to someday hear young Kolya speak like you."

"Maybe you will," Legio said softly, "if you let him live long enough."

"Well, I let you live for many years, Victor," Hade replied. "Surely that must account for something. Now," Hade said as he slapped both hands down on his legs, "let's talk about the money."

"Spoken like a true stick-up artist," Legio said. He reached into his pocket and pulled out the red, white and green Smartphone Hade had given him a few days earlier in California. He pressed his right thumb to the screen and a fingerprint scan confirmed it was Legio. A second later an encrypted square "Quick Response" code appeared. He tapped the three larger squares within the QR code and the square changed ever so slightly. Below the QR code, an image of half of a vintage Jell-O box top appeared. He looked over to Hade, who held up his own Smartphone with a QR code and the other half of the Jell-O box top. Legio handed the phone to Hade, who slid the two phones together using barely visible grooves, syncing both phones and bringing the metadata embedded in the QR code to his phone. He then slid the phones apart and handed the Italian-themed one back to Legio. A menu appeared on Hade's Smartphone and he touched "process." He then sat back as a blue upload bar slowly filled in.

"This might take a few minutes to transfer." Hade grinned. "It's a lot of money."

"A life's work, a fortune gained, an empire built, and all handed over in a matter of seconds." Legio said forlornly, incredulous at just how easily Hade had taken complete control of his conglomerate in such a short time. "It's all yours, Hade. I hope you enjoy it. You should have enough to buy half the world with some change left over."

"I'm not interested in half the world," Hade replied

Legio ignored the comment, so Hade continued speaking.

"You've indeed done well, my old friend. Now, while we wait, I don't think there's any harm in letting you in on a little secret."

"A secret?"

"Sure," Hade replied. "You can't tell me that you've never wondered why I've asked you to do all of this."

Legio sighed again. "The thought had certainly crossed my mind a few times," he answered.

"And yet you never thought to ask?"

"There really wasn't any need," the businessman said with a shrug. "In the long run, it matters nothing to me."

Hade leaned back on the park bench and cast his gaze skyward again. The clouds were going from gray to black and an occasional lightning flash could be seen in the distance. This was his kind of weather. "Look around you, Victor. This world is like a giant puppet show and we all have our parts to play. We each have strings attached that force us in directions we wouldn't normally take but can't avoid because of the whims of the puppet master. Some people call these strings fate, others call them human nature, and still others refer to them as the results of the stars. But do you know something, Victor? In reality, it's none of those things. You didn't give me all your money because the stars decreed it or it was your fate. And it most certainly isn't in your nature to give away everything you've worked so hard to build up.

"No, Victor, you did all of this because I made you do it, plain and simple. I bent you to my will, as it were. You spent a number of decades amassing the sixth largest fortune on the planet, becoming one of the most powerful businessmen of all time, only to give it away over the past couple of weeks simply because I told you to." He paused for a contemplative moment before finishing. "In the end, my old friend, there is no such thing as fate. But there is Hade. And while the world might not know the difference yet, trust me, they will." He was silent for a few moments, before adding a final thought. "Of course, I have my strings, too, or didn't you know that? We all do, Victor."

"The great Hade has strings?" Legio said in an almost patronizing tone. "I find that difficult to believe."

Hade smiled. "There are forces in this world you can't even begin to comprehend. There are secret worlds and dark maneuverings where the creatures of the night cringe at any light. There are ways around this mortal realm. As I said, this isn't all about the money, Victor. It's the power you wield. It's the name, Legio Industries. If I simply wanted money, I'd walk into any branch of the First National Bank of Suckers and take it. But Legio Industries and all of its power, influence, and potential? That's the true gift here."

"A gift for whom, then?" Legio asked, sensing something he hadn't caught before.

"Let's just say it's for the cause," Hade answered. "It's for ensuring the right people are in power in the right places and they have the right tools to do the right things at the right time. You're a hero for doing all of this, Victor, and you'll be remembered for your efforts here. You might not get the parade today, but you'll get yourself a statue someday where people will come and talk about how important you were in creating the world anew. That's what this is all about—a new world order with an invincible army and strong leaders. It's all been for the greater good, and today we're on the cusp of achieving what was put into place thousands of years ago."

Legio laughed. "You speak as a megalomaniac, bent on utter subjugation of the world."

"Not a megalomaniac," he corrected. "I'm the director, seated in the director's chair, preparing for the greatest performance of all time."

"That's a pretty expensive performance."

"You have no idea," Hade replied with a knowing smile. A chime from Hade's Smartphone interrupted the conversation before Legio could ask any further questions. Hade simply checked the screen and scrolled down to view the information. After a few moments, he nodded satisfactorily, tapped out of the application, and put the phone back into his coat pocket. "So it comes to this, Victor," he said. "Shall we begin the final act?"

"My finale…" Victor Legio replied nervously as the long-awaited prospect of his demise finally became a terrifying reality. He took one last drink of water—his last, he realized—and then placed the bottle on the ground by his feet.

"As it were," Hade nodded slowly. "You know, I have to admit you moved me quite a bit this morning, Victor. I'm glad young Kolya isn't here or he might lose the little respect he has for me. He thinks I'm weak because I speak Latin, read poetry, and use metaphors about fish to explain the future. He doesn't understand, as you and I do, that true power doesn't come from a gun. True power comes from tying your strings to others and making them dance to the music you play. True power isn't a tangible thing that can be bought and sold—although admittedly with enough money, one can buy a lot of puppet strings."

"All that power and money," Legio said quietly, "and yet it's not enough to buy my life."

"We all must do what must be done," Hade affirmed. "There's a storm coming, Victor. I can feel it, but I can also smell it, see it, hear it, and most of all, I can taste it. It's intoxicating and sumptuous. It's ambrosia and nectar, sugar and spice. People would kill just for a taste. In fact, I've killed for my taste and it's indescribably sweet. It's sublime, not in its modern sense but in how the romantics of the nineteenth century used to describe the cosmos. It's nature, humanity, and divinity carefully converging, and it brings whoever sips of it to an unfathomable level of clarity and understanding." Hade paused and looked hard at the older man. "If there's one thing I can say for you, Victor, it's that you have proven you belonged with the best of us."

Legio, knowing his moment had finally arrived, said, "'And now the time has come when we must depart: I to my death, you to go on living. But which of us is going to the better fate is unknown to all except God'." Legio looked up at Hade. "So this is it?"

Hade nodded.

"Very well, then. I'm ready. I just ask that you make it quick."

Hade sat up and reached into his coat again, this time pulling out something wrapped in a white cloth. He handled it gently and began to slowly unwrap it as he spoke. "I wouldn't think of doing it any other way." Hade finished unwrapping the object and held it up. It was a long-needled syringe filled with a dark green liquid. "Do you want in on one last secret before you go, my friend?" Before Legio could answer, Hade quickly flipped the syringe around in his hand and plunged it into Victor Emmanuel Legio's chest. He forced down the plunger and injected the entire contents directly into the old man's heart.

"This isn't the end."

Victor Legio's eyes flew open in shock and agonizing pain and the whites turned red as the blood vessels burst. His back arched in agony, his spine cracking like a rifle shot. For a few moments, violent spasms rocked his body. Then, suddenly, it was over. Victor's eyes fluttered shut and his body slumped. It had taken less than ten seconds.

"Good night, old friend," Hade said quietly, pulling the needle out and wrapping it back in the cloth. He slipped it into his coat and pulled out his phone. He tapped the screen and waited for only a moment. "It's done," he said, then returned the device to his coat. He turned back to Legio. "Fitting, Victor, that in the end you would quote Socrates. I can't deny the similarities: accepting death for the good of society, ingesting the poison peacefully, and never attempting to escape it. I'd like to add that your death will mean a great deal more to the fate of humanity than Socrates' ever did. Hard to believe, I know, but it's true."

He noticed then that Nikolai was returning, walking back across the park toward him. Hade looked down at Legio's lifeless form and whispered almost reverently, "You know, I feel like a small child on Christmas Eve. The anticipation of all the presents I get to open tomorrow is killing me, and yet I've done all I can for now. I hate to wait. And you'll have to wait a bit, too, I know. But it will all be worth it, my friend."

Hade stood up as Nikolai approached. The Russian took immediate notice of Legio slumped over on the park bench and eyed Hade suspiciously. "Is this what you've planned for me then, Hade?" he asked point-blank.

Hade smiled. "No, Kolya," he replied. "Victor is a special case."

"In Russia, we say it's good luck to stand over a corpse, but I think there's no good fortune here. Not even I would do something this bold."

"Well, I'm not you. If nothing else, we're in agreement on that," Hade countered. "Cervantes said, 'There's no taking trout with dry breeches.' If you want the world, you're going to have to spill some blood."

"Then that's what this is about?"

"More than you know, Kolya," Hade answered. Behind him, a small unmarked box truck rumbled to a stop in the street and Hade spared the briefest of looks toward it as two men quickly got out. "Come, my young friend," he said, getting to his feet. He picked up his coat and slipped it on. "The time is near, but not quite yet. There are still things to do."

"You're leaving the body here?" the Russian asked incredulously.

"No," was the reply. "My associates will take care of him."

Nikolai looked shocked. "Why? Do you have a trophy room where you keep the bodies of all your victims?"

"No, Kolya, for who could build such a building?" Hade retorted and then began to walk back in the direction the young Russian had come from. "Now, are you going to join me or should I have my associates prepare for two bodies?"

"No need to threaten, Hade," Nikolai said quickly. He watched the two men take Legio's body and load it into the truck.

Hade looked over at Nikolai and smiled. "I must admit, I'm famished. There's a great little *ristorante* named Alle Betulle just up the road in Torcegno. I know the owners and I'm sure they would love to give us a spot to eat. We can be there in five minutes if we take my Harley."

Nikolai eyed at him doubtfully. "You have a motorcycle in Italy?"

"A 1989 FLSTF Fat Boy, to be exact," Hade laughed, "though I prefer my 2006 Night Rod. It's always nice to know I have one nearby when I truly need one."

Nikolai didn't know how to respond, so they walked on in silence to Hade's bike. True to the man's word, they were at the restaurant in under five minutes. They were welcomed right in and immediately shown to the small, private dining room just to the right of the front door. Breakfast arrived soon, consisting of eggs, muesli, grapes, toast with marmalade and croissants with Nutella, along with orange juice and coffee latte. "*Bellissima,*" Hade bellowed, gesturing with his hand.

Nikolai watched as the big man began heaping his plate with food, before taking a single croissant for himself. Setting it on his plate, he looked at Hade. "So what was the point of all that?" he finally asked.

"The point of what?" Hade asked back, shoveling a large fork-full of eggs into his mouth.

"If you were going to kill Legio, what was the point in all the discussion beforehand? Why not just shoot him and be done with it?"

Hade enjoyed several more bites before replying. "I suppose it might have appeared a waste of time since Victor's demise had been carved in stone for quite some time, but I can promise you, Kolya, it was not. You see, I've worked long and hard for today, longer than you can even imagine. George Bernard Shaw wrote, 'The real moment of success is not the moment apparent to the crowd.' Today might not go down in history as anything special to the many-headed hydra that is the common masses, but trust me on this—this is my real moment of success. These are the days I have waited forever for.

"In a thousand years, the storm that will soon cover the earth will be remembered as the days that changed the world. But today will always be my own. After today, Hade will come washing down on the world, and the world will never be the same. After today, people will sing songs about me. They will make statues and monuments. My face will be carved into the side of a mountain and I'll live forever in the hearts and minds of humanity. It's perhaps too much to ask for out of this life, but when given an opportunity at glory beyond compare, who am I to turn aside as if it was but a trifle? It's worth the death of every living thing, if it's worth a cent."

"You speak in riddles," Nikolai said with frustration.

"I speak clearly enough for those who listen," Hade answered, looking sharply at the Russian. "The storm is about to break, Kolya. We'll ride it and all the savage fury it contains until we are masters of the human race. Is that not noble in and of itself, to ride out the storm and emerge unconquered? You don't like me now, Kolya, but once you find yourself on the crest of the tsunami, you will."

"I do not understand you at all, Hade," Nikolai said quietly. "I don't know that I ever will."

"It is enough right now to simply trust me," Hade replied in an almost fatherly tone. "The understanding will come later."

They finished their breakfast in silence, Hade wolfing down several large platefuls of food, while Nikolai sipped at a glass of orange juice.

When they were finished, Hade pushed his chair back and let out a window-rattling belch, before dabbing daintily at his mouth with a linen napkin. "That hit the spot," he said easily. "Now, we should be on our way, Kolya. This is the last time we will speak face-to-face for some time, as I have urgent business elsewhere. But I will be in touch by phone. I want you to return straight home and attend to your business. Oh, and no holidays in London."

"London?" Nikolai repeated in confusion.

"Correct," Hade replied. "London is about to become a real hot spot. Now, I trust you have planned everything out back home?"

Nikolai nodded. "Everything," he answered.

"Very well," Hade said. "Tomorrow, the world is going to experience something extremely horrendous. Pay it no mind for it is not aimed at you."

"What's going to happen?" Nikolai asked, feeling suddenly nervous.

"Just stay out of harm's way," Hade replied knowingly. "The time has come to remake the world. Follow me, trust me, and you will help rule it."

Nikolai nodded.

Hade continued. "Before you depart, I would give you some final advice."

"And that is?"

"You have a good family, Kolya. Despite your misgivings, your family deserves to know that their deaths will serve a higher purpose. They deserve good deaths— quick deaths. I expect you to give them that."

The Russian nodded again. "Agreed," he said shortly, having already planned it all out.

"The future is yours, *Tovarish*," Hade said, leaning back in his chair and reaching for his cigar. He popped it into his mouth, fished a match out of one of his many pockets and struck it alight with his fingernail. He lit the cigar and then paused a moment to sniff the smoke-laden air. "Victor was right," he muttered off-handedly. "They really are unpleasant." He turned back to Nikolai and tapped his forehead in an informal salute. "*Dosvadona*, my friend."

Nikolai stood up, nodded slightly in reply, and walked out of the small dining room. Hade watched him go and smiled. The boy did indeed have potential, but he was impetuous and impatient. Hade shuddered to think how that impatience could wreck so many of his well-laid plans. He would have to be careful with this particular set of puppet strings.

The huge man puffed on his cigar, then lazily blew a smoke ring and watched it drift over his head. "My crown of glory," he remarked quietly as he watched it float in the air above him like a cloudy halo. "It's time for the emperor to unleash the tempest. It's time to crown my kings."

With that, he stood up, put his cigar out in a glass ashtray and walked out the door as thunder rumbled overhead.

CHAPTER 29

Las Vegas, Nevada: Half a world away, the emergency room at Valley Hospital Medical Center was busy as the afternoon deepened toward dusk. As the world seemed to be descending rapidly into anarchy, victims from an increasing number of accidents and assaults throughout the city were pushing the double-shifted doctors and nurses as hard as they had ever been pushed. And from what Dan Weatherly had heard, Valley wasn't the only hospital to be hit. Not that it bothered him much—he was just an orderly and not a very well-paid one, at least according to him.

Readjusting the temperamental right ear bud of his iPod so that he could better listen to Nine Inch Nails, he went back to pushing the sheet-covered gurney down the hall toward the morgue. The body under the sheet did not concern him. For him, taking bodies to the morgue was part of his job. He had pushed enough dead people down this long stretch of hallway that he had been over the heebie jeebies for a long time now. After all, it was Las Vegas. People died here every day and enough of them kicked off from unnatural and downright weird causes that they had even made a television show centered on the city's Crime Scene Investigation unit.

Cursing under his breath as his ear bud shorted out once again, he stopped and pulled the equipment from his ear. Had he not spent a few seconds fiddling with the wire entering the tiny ear piece, he might have caught the slight movement under the sheet. As it was, he missed it, popped Nine Inch Nails back into his ear, and pushed the gurney around the corner—and right into another person.

He began to mumble an apology until he realized that the man he had just ran into simply stood there staring vacantly at him. Then he realized the man was wearing a bloodstained hospital gown. Finally, he saw the ragged bullet hole in the man's neck.

Daniel Weatherly had no time to scream as the man's hands fastened themselves tightly around his throat, closing off his airway. He was pulled over the side of gurney, sending the gurney, the dead body, and Daniel crashing to the floor, with his killer coming down on top of him. His attacker drove his thumbs harder into his throat, crushing his trachea. His diaphragm strained, pulling against the closed door of his windpipe. His cells begged for oxygen. Daniel's eyes went wide and stars began exploding behind them. Terminally ischemic, his heart finally stopped. The last thing he saw was the body that had been on the gurney sit up. The sheet fell off and revealed the dead face of a young woman who looked at him with a vacant stare. A few moments later, Daniel Weatherly was dead.

Daniel's dead body leaked lactic acid from every cell into the stagnant bloodstream where it encountered the catalyst. An enzyme awaited that converted the lactate to an oxygen substitute. A cascade of biologic reactivity ensued as glucose once again converted to ATP and cells sprang back to life.

Finally, an impatient spirit entered the vacant body.

Five minutes later, Daniel Weatherly and his new friends were heading deeper into the basement levels of the hospital to wait.

They would not have to wait long.

It was time.

CHAPTER 30

Echo Resort, Utah: Father Michael Dalacourt stirred, not wanting to open his eyes, but another strong nudge to his shoulder finally brought him awake. "What is it?" he mumbled, trying to stifle a yawn and stretch as much as the cramped bus seat would allow.

The enigmatic John had been sitting beside him since the Greyhound pulled out of York, Nebraska, and now pointed past him to the window. "Echo Resort," the old man answered softly, his voice oddly strained. "We're about an hour out of Salt Lake City."

"So why wake me now?" Dalacourt mumbled, trying to force a half-smile to his face, but failing. The revelations of the past day had been nearly too much for him. "Another hour would have seemed like manna from heaven."

"Look," John commanded, his face grim.

Dalacourt saw the old man's worried expression and he snapped fully awake. He turned to follow his gaze, trying to discern what had him so anxious. "What do you see?"

"Shadows," John answered cryptically. "It's beginning."

Dalacourt saw nothing but deep gloom and shook his head. "It's early," he argued with little conviction. "You must be seeing something that's not there."

"I assure you, Michael," John said nervously as he quickly stood up. "I'm seeing quite clearly. It has indeed begun." He strode down the aisle, passing the half a dozen other passengers and knelt down beside the driver's seat. "Are we stopping here?" he asked softly, peering ahead.

"Yes, sir," replied the bus driver in a southern drawl. He was a grizzled, but smartly dressed older man with a broad smile and kind eyes. "Flag stop," he went on. "Shouldn't be but a couple of minutes."

"How soon will we be there?"

"It's just down the road here a little more," he replied as he slowed the bus down and moved onto the exit ramp. "We get off I-80 right here and swing around onto Echo Canyon Road. If no one's there, we turn around and get right back on the highway."

John watched intently as the driver swung the bus off the interstate and onto the blacktop road. He noted the dual set of railroad tracks running parallel and then felt his skin crawl as he noted several shadowy figures off to the edge of the tracks.

The bus went left then, following the road and running next to the tracks. "It's just right down here," the driver said again, then paused before adding with some surprise, "Well, I'll be buggered."

"What is it?" John asked sharply.

"Looks like we've got some riders getting on," he answered, pointing down the road. "I don't think I've ever picked up more than one or two at a time on a flag stop like this. Must be a family or something."

John noted, with mounting alarm, four people standing on the side of the road, all of them looking toward the oncoming bus. "Don't stop," said John quietly. "Something isn't right."

The driver turned to regard John for just a second when all hell broke loose. One of the bus passengers sitting just behind the driver screamed, "Look out!" and the driver turned around just in time to see a figure dart directly in front of the bus. With a shout of alarm, he yanked the steering wheel hard to the left to avoid hitting the person. Tires squealed loudly and the big bus bounced up onto the curb, several of the tires blowing out on impact. The driver frantically brought the wheel back around the other way, trying to regain control. It was a futile effort, though, and the overcorrected Greyhound slid sideways before the wheels caught on the pavement and the bus rolled over onto its side with a scream of metal and breaking glass.

John was thrown hard against the roof of the bus, bounced off, and landed where the driver's window should have been. Concrete scraped against his thigh as the bus slid several more feet before coming to a rest. He immediately got to his knees, ignoring the shattered glass shards, and reached out to help the stunned driver who was still securely belted into his seat, hands gripping the steering wheel in white-knuckled terror. The rest of the bus was deathly quiet.

"Are you hurt?" he asked hurriedly, reaching up and unbuckling the driver's safety belt.

The driver shook his head. "What did I do?" He moaned to no one in particular, his voice trembling.

"It wasn't your fault," John replied, helping the driver into a standing position behind him. "Quickly now. We have little time."

As if to punctuate his statement, one of the passengers screamed. He whirled around and saw the four people from the bus stop coming toward them. The lead person held a baseball bat menacingly in one hand. John focused on the man's dead eyes, saw the somewhat lilting and awkward gait, and his fears were finally and irrefutably confirmed.

It had indeed begun.

He looked back into the bus at the frightened passengers. "Everybody out!" he commanded, his voice strong. "Run!" He turned again, stepping through the broken windshield to meet the oncoming threat.

The bat-wielding attacker came on strong, bringing the weapon down in an overhand strike, attempting to crush John's skull. But the old man moved with surprising swiftness and caught the bat cleanly, pushing the blow aside. He used the momentum of the missed swing to throw the attacker off balance and into the bumper of the overturned bus. The man's head slammed into the metal edge with an audible crack of bone and he slumped to the ground motionless, the baseball bat rolling from his limp fingers.

John turned to face the other three. He sidestepped a clumsy punch from the next enemy and swung his arm out, catching the man in the throat and sending him flying. The third managed to get his hands around John's wrist. It was enough to break his momentum, allowing the fourth assailant to quickly close the distance. In his hand, he held a jagged piece of metal.

A deafening boom sounded from the back of the bus and a ragged hole appeared in the attacker's forehead. The man stumbled sideways until a second shot caught him squarely in the chest and sent him flying backwards, the piece of metal clattering harmlessly to the pavement.

John used the moment to twist his arm down hard, breaking the other man's grip and grabbing him by the throat. With all his strength, he squeezed, crushing the man's windpipe, but his enemy seemed unfazed and raked a hand across John's face, clawing for his eyes. John quickly turned his head to protect his face and changed tactics. He threw a vicious elbow to the side of the man's head, cracking the jawbone. Another blow followed, crushing the cheekbone—and still his enemy came on. But a third shot rang out behind him and the enemy buckled, his knee blasted away. John shoved the wounded man backward and threw him to the ground where he lay motionless, eyes rolling back in his head.

The old Indian let out a heavy sigh of relief and turned around as one of the passengers stepped through the broken windshield to stand beside him, a nine millimeter Beretta handgun in his right hand.

"I'll bet that hurt," the man said matter-of-factly, a crooked grin gracing his unshaven face. He was middle-aged, his short cropped hair shot through with gray, but there was a strength in the way he carried himself.

John could only nod. "Thank you," he said, trying to catch his breath.

"Don't mention it," the man said. At that moment, a very shaken Michael Dalacourt stumbled out of the bus and onto the pavement. He looked at John, then at the man who had just saved John's life. He tried to say something, but the words wouldn't come. Still smiling crookedly, the man stuck out his free hand. "McCain," he introduced himself. "Tom McCain."

"Father Dalacourt," the priest finally stammered weakly as he accepted the man's firm handshake.

"A priest, huh? That's good," McCain added. "We could use some old-time religion here." McCain reached behind him and started to tuck the gun back into his belt holster when another voice stopped him.

"How'd you get a gun on my bus, anyway?" They all looked back to see the bus driver climbing through the shattered window, eyes on McCain.

"Would you rather I didn't have it?" McCain asked. "Don't worry, Pops. I'm a New York City police officer."

The bus driver looked at them for a moment, still somewhat in shock, before finally relaxing his shoulders. But as he looked off to the horizon, he tilted his head and spoke in a quizzical tone. "How many rounds you got in that gun, officer?"

"A few. Why?"

"Because you're going to need them all," the driver answered, pointing past them. "Look!"

John, Dalacourt, and McCain looked up to see another group of people walking down the road toward them, various weapons—and items that could be used as weapons—held dangerously in their hands.

"Those aren't friendlies," McCain said and raised his gun again. He yelled to the young woman he'd been sitting with in the back of the bus. "Stacia, we've got more company! Get everybody out now!"

John laid a hand on the officer's arm. "There are too many, Tom. We need to go."

"Will someone please tell me what's going on here?" the bus driver asked fearfully, looking past them to the oncoming people. "Has everyone gone completely nuts?"

"It's the end of the world!" an older woman in the back of the bus wailed, tears streaming down her cheeks, mixing with blood that ran from a nasty cut across her forehead. "Lord Jesus, it's the end of the world!"

John ignored her. "Everyone out!" he shouted. "Quickly! We have no time!"

Everyone but the old woman obeyed as they gingerly picked their way forward as fast as they were able, helped along by a slender young woman with blonde hair pulled into a ponytail. She was wearing dark clothes and running shoes and looked ready for anything.

"Are we going to fight or run?" she asked, helping one of the passengers step through the hole that used to be the front windshield of the bus.

"We run," John answered quickly. "It's our only hope."

All of the passengers but one were outside of the bus as the new group of assailants drew closer, shuffling along the pavement toward their intended victims. The crying woman from the back of the bus, though, would not budge as she sat amid broken window glass, her arms wrapped tightly around her handbag. Her desperate wailing rose in pitch.

"Come on, lady," another passenger called back to her. He was dressed in a business suit, somewhat rumpled from a long trip and maybe more so now due to the accident. He had a bruise swelling beneath one eye that was already turning purple, but he seemed invigorated by the action. "We need to get out of here!"

She ignored him and only cried louder.

"Let's go, people!" McCain shouted back over his shoulder, raising his gun toward the oncoming horde. There were at least a dozen of them now and drawing closer. "We're out of time!"

"Follow me!" John ordered as he led them away from the oncoming attackers, but he immediately froze when he realized who was missing. Dalacourt had gone back into the bus and was kneeling beside the terrified woman, talking gently to her and trying to calm her down.

"Michael," John called to him, urgency in his voice. "There's no time for this."

The priest looked up, his eyes wide. "We can't leave her."

"You have no choice," John said again, his voice hard. "You can't save her, Michael, but there will be others you can."

There was a gunshot, followed by McCain bellowing. "Beautiful Oprah moment there, gentlemen! But now would be a great time to move out!"

Dalacourt stood and offered a quick and silent prayer for the woman, then hurried to the front of the bus just as McCain fired again, taking down another of the approaching mob.

"Follow me!" the man shouted, squeezing off one more shot before rushing around the bus. The others obeyed, seven individuals desperate to escape the madness.

They wouldn't go far.

Several more attackers were converging on the bus from the opposite side and, as McCain looked around for another escape route, half a dozen more came out of the trees, effectively trapping them.

"I'd say we're officially screwed here," McCain said grimly above the terrified screams of the doomed woman in the bus. He turned to face the closest group and fired several more times, emptying his clip. By then, the attackers were on top of them.

"Hand-to-hand!" shouted the middle-aged businessman, who appeared excited at the prospect of fighting for his life. He lashed out at the nearest attacker, a younger man with a skull tattoo on the side of his blue-tinged face. The businessman's punch broke the would-be killer's nose, but the attacker took it without slowing, grabbed him by the other arm and flung him backward into the teeth of the approaching mob. The businessman went down under a flurry of limbs and weapons, his dying screams muffled by the onslaught.

John grabbed the tattooed enemy by the hair before he could fully recover and drove his foot into the side of the man's knee, crushing the bone and tearing the cartilage. The attacker fell backward, his eyes closing in death. "Go for the legs!" John shouted as another attacker lunged forward with a long bladed hunting knife. He side-stepped the blow and the blade dug into the metal roof of the wrecked bus with a metallic clang. John struck forward with one hand and snapped the man's arm above the elbow. He spun around and his elbow crashed into the side of the man's head with a resounding crack and knocked him to the ground. John smashed his foot down hard on his shin with a loud crack and the attacker slumped back and didn't move again.

At the same time, McCain met another enemy head on. The New York City cop dropped his gun and slapped away the attacker's blows in order to grab him by the head. With a shout of anger, he drove his forehead into the man's face, shattering bones and sending the enemy sprawling to the ground, where he twitched feebly before going still. But even as one fell, another took his place. McCain grabbed the next foe by the hair and drove his head into the hard metal bus roof with a crack of bone. He saw the hunting knife still quivering in the metal nearby, wrenched it free and whirled back around to face the mob.

To his right, John fought a pair of unarmed foes, a middle-aged man in a jogging suit and a young woman who had probably been in high school yesterday. To his left, Stacia had adopted a batting stance with the baseball bat she had retrieved from one of the first attackers, and as another closed in, she swung with all her might. The bat connected solidly with the man's head and with a crunch of bone, the body collapsed to the ground.

The fight was terrifyingly vicious and before it was over, another bus passenger had fallen to the pavement, clutching his ruined throat as he lay dying. His attacker held a bloody hay hook and brought the pointed end down violently, burying it in the old man's skull. He got no further as a young male passenger, not even out of his teens, stepped forward and snapped a straight kick directly into the killer's upper arm. The bone shattered and ruptured the skin and the young man drove his knee into the face of his enemy. The assailant dropped to the ground in a heap. It was enough to give the dwindling group a narrow window of opportunity.

"This way!" the young martial artist shouted even as he jumped into the air. His foot landed solidly against the chest of another oncoming adversary.

The few surviving bus passengers quickly followed him between the narrow gap in the attacking mob. They rushed toward the tree line on the other side of the road, but only John saw the sudden danger to the young man running full speed in front of them. John's warning died in his throat as their young leader let out a grunt and was lifted completely off his feet, before he was slammed back to the ground, the blade of a garden shovel buried deeply in his chest.

McCain got there first and leapt past the fallen young man, grabbing his attacker by the throat. The cop lifted the overall-clad farmer off the ground and shoved him backward, his legs churning with momentum. A broken tree branch directly behind him brought them to a crushing halt as the branch pierced the assailant's back and burst through his chest. The impaled farmer struggled feebly before slumping forward, and McCain whirled around as the others caught up to him. He knelt down and wrenched the deadly shovel out of the injured young man's chest, angrily throwing it aside. He then hefted his mortally-wounded comrade up and slung him across his shoulders. Looking at the others, his face said it all. "Let's move."

The six survivors—John, Father Dalacourt, the bus driver, Stacia, Tom, and the injured young fighter he was carrying—hurried along the road before John led them into the trees. They crossed the railroad tracks and headed west, tearing through the timber quickly, leaving their attackers behind. John finally brought them to a halt as he looked back to see McCain laboring under the weight of the injured young man still slung over his shoulders. The cop's shirt was soaked with blood from the horrendous wound and, as he lumbered up, he dropped to his knees and gently laid the youth on the ground. John knelt beside him and looked into the dying teen's terrified eyes before turning his own eyes to the bubbling wound.

"Can he survive until we can get help?" Stacia asked, kneeling beside them.

It only took John a moment to understand the severity of the savage wound. The shovel had been driven into the kid's chest, had severed bone and sliced through his right lung. How the young man was still alive, he had no idea.

"It…hurts," the teenager croaked, a gush of blood running from his mouth.

"I'm sorry, my son," John said softly, placing his hand on his sweat-beaded forehead. "I truly am."

"What can we do?" Michael Dalacourt asked helplessly. "Can we get him to a hospital?"

John looked at the priest, his eyes saying what his mouth couldn't. The young man was beyond help.

McCain, still seated on the ground nearby, looked up. "You're not going to leave him for those butchers," he cut in, still breathing hard from the exertion of their escape.

John looked into the eyes of the teen. "No, I won't leave him to that," he answered and then looked up at McCain. "Can you get them to safety?"

"Well, we're sure not going to sit around and wait for more of those things to show up," the cop panted, slowly climbing back to his feet.

"Good," John went on. "Head west toward Salt Lake City and go as quickly as you can. I'll catch up to you shortly."

"You can't mean to kill him yourself!" Dalacourt exclaimed in disbelief.

John looked up, his eyes hard. "Michael Dalacourt," he said forcefully. "You would do well to understand the world of today is not the world it was yesterday. You, me, all of us, will be called upon to face things we never dreamed possible; to do things we never dreamed we could do. If we're to survive, we must be prepared to do what is necessary. Do you understand me?"

Dalacourt shook his head, but John reached up and grabbed the young priest by the back of the neck and pulled him close. He locked his eyes with those of the terrified priest, their noses almost touching. "Listen to me, Michael," he said softly. "Remember our discussion on the bus. Know that many are already dead and many more will die before this is all over. You will be a witness to things that you fear you cannot handle. But you must be strong. You must survive! You cannot know how important that is! Do you understand me?"

"I'm not ready for this, John," he pleaded.

"You have no choice," John finished coldly and pushed him away. He looked at McCain. "Now go. All of you. Protect them as best you can, Tom. The enemy won't give up the chase."

Without a word, McCain nodded and took the shell-shocked priest by the arm. "Come on, Father," he said gently as he turned them toward the trees. Along with the others, they set off into the timber without looking back. When they were out of sight, John turned his gaze back to the young man.

"I'm...scared," the teen gasped, his breathing ragged and bloody.

"I know," John said softly, tears gathering in his own eyes. "But fear not, my child. Your Father in heaven is waiting for you. You saved us, son. You're the hero." He placed a hand over the young man's eyes and his other hand over his mouth. Tears streaming down his face, John did what he had to do and a few moments later, it was all over.

John caught up with the other four a short time later as they were resting beside a small creek. They all looked at him as he slipped out of the trees and their gazes held the unspoken question. "He died quickly and peacefully," was all John offered. "Now it's up to us to go on."

"Where?" McCain asked pointedly.

"We need to find help," the bus driver said. "All these crazies running around? There must have been a prison break somewhere or something."

"This is no prison break we're dealing with," John countered. "It's far worse. Whatever is happening here is likely to be happening everywhere else, too."

McCain held up his cell phone. "You got that right," he said. "I've got full bars, but I can't get a call out to save my life right now. We're on our own here, Cochise."

"Just what the devil is happening out there then?" the driver went on, his voice strained.

John draped an arm over the driver's broad shoulders. "What's your name?"

"Stanley," the driver replied. "Stanley Hotchkiss."

"Well, Stanley," John said wearily, "it's a long story."

"It's a long walk to Salt Lake City," McCain interrupted as he looked off in the direction they had been running. "If that's where we're still headed," he finished.

"It is," John replied somberly.

"I don't know, John," McCain said doubtfully. "If the whole world has gone bonkers, what kind of safety do you think we'll find in a big city? At least out here, our enemies have smaller numbers and we've got cover and places we can hide."

"I understand," John replied somberly, "but the city is where we have to go and it's imperative that we do so as quickly as possible."

McCain shrugged. "Well, if you're certain. We sure could use reinforcements," he chuckled sourly as he pulled out his gun. He deftly popped out the empty clip and shook his head in disappointment. Slipping it into his pocket, he took a full one out and snapped it into place. "Last one," he mused. "Ammunition would be nice, too."

"Where are the spare clips?" Stacia asked, her gaze stern and reproachful.

"Back on the bus."

"You didn't grab them?" she asked incredulously.

"Well, we were kind of rushed, in case you've forgotten," he went on. "That and the fact that they're in the under-compartment and the bus was on its side, kind of made it impossible to grab them."

"You should have had that bag with you, Dad," she scolded. "You know that."

"Not a chance," he replied. "Stan here probably would've kicked me off the bus," he finished, giving the bus driver a wink and a smile. "Besides, I didn't think I'd need them this early." Before his daughter could say anything more, he turned to John and changed the subject. "Salt Lake City is a good forty miles on foot. We'll never make it by nightfall."

"We'll go as far as we can and take shelter before dark," John replied.

"Do you think we'll find anyone out here we can trust?" Dalacourt put in. He'd mastered his terror, at least for the moment.

"We're in the heart of Mormon country," McCain answered. "If there's anyone still around, chances are we'll be able to trust them, if we could get them out of their basements and storage rooms. But I'm not sure we'll even find anyone."

"How do you figure that?" the bus driver asked.

"Just listen," McCain pointed out. "We're only about a half mile from the highway and we should still be able to hear cars and trucks. But, there's nothing." They all did just that and noticed it was indeed quiet. They only heard the sound of the breeze rustling the long grasses and tree leaves, as well as the occasional bird, although now and then they could hear a faint echo like thunder in the distance to the west. "No," McCain went on, "anyone around these parts is either long gone or hunkered down in their locked fruit cellars waiting for the end of the world. More importantly, we're still not that far from the bus. If you don't mind, I'd like to put a few more miles between us and those loonies."

"Do you really think they'll follow us?" the priest asked.

It was John who answered. "They'll track us easily enough,

Michael," he said quietly. "Tom is right. We should move out."

Within a few minutes, the five of them were on their way again.

The sun was nearly setting before they found what they were looking for. They had traveled the entire day through timber and fields along the base of the mountains, staying well clear of the road after a near disaster. Initially, the interstate had indeed been eerily deserted and offered the path of least resistance, even with numerous empty cars still on the pavement or yanked off to the side of the road. So they had hiked along, making good time until they found an abandoned Toyota van that was still drivable. Unfortunately, they had only driven for less than two miles, weaving around other wrecks, before they came to one that involved several cars and a couple of trucks, leaving the highway blocked in both directions. Several bodies were lying nearby. It was the first sign of people they had seen—living or dead.

Two of the "bodies" turned out to not be dead and, like the mob at the bus stop, came at the little group with every intention of killing them. John, McCain, and his baseball bat-wielding daughter made short work of them and it was quickly agreed upon that they would be better off staying away from the highway and any other signs of civilization until they reached the city.

John then led them back into the trees, and they had stayed there the rest of the day. Several times they heard sounds within the brush around them as they hiked, but they had no idea if the sounds were from animals or if their pursuers were closing in on them. Determined, they had pushed on, everyone lost within their own terrified thoughts.

As the sun began to set, John finally brought them to a stop just inside a tree line and was peering through the deepening shadows at a small farmhouse just across a dirt road. It was an older dwelling and not in the best of shape. A dilapidated barn sagged behind it. There were no lights that showed through any of the windows and no vehicles sat in the driveway.

"Doesn't look like anyone's home," Stanley whispered, looking past John.

McCain stepped up beside him. "We need to be sure," he said quietly. "If there's someone there, I want to make sure they aren't nuts like everyone else we've had the pleasure of meeting today."

"Agreed," said John, taking a step forward. "I'll check it out. The rest of you wait here."

McCain clamped a strong hand on the old man's shoulder. "Hang on a second there," he said with a tight smile. "This sort of thing falls under my job description, not yours. Let me handle this."

John hesitated before nodding his head. "Just be careful, Tom," he cautioned.

"Roger that," he said quietly. McCain pulled his gun and darted across the road, keeping to the shadows as much as possible. He dashed across the yard and up onto the porch, where he flattened himself against the wall next to the front door. When there was no movement in or around the house, he reached over and tried the knob. Finding it locked, he quickly hopped over the porch railing, slipped around back, and disappeared from view. Fifteen stressful minutes later, he was standing on the front porch, a newly acquired shotgun in his hands and motioning for the others to join him.

"House is clear, but abandoned," he said as they hurried up to him. "Electricity is out. No one's been here for a while."

Gratefully, they all went inside, leaving Tom on the porch. For several minutes, he cradled the shotgun as his eyes scanned the dark shadows of the trees, searching for some sign of pursuit. Eventually, satisfied they were safe for the moment, he went inside, carefully locking the door behind him.

As the front door clicked shut, a single figure stepped out of the shadows of the trees and stood motionless, watching the house with cold, dead eyes.

As night deepened to blackness outside, the group gathered around the kitchen table. They had found a couple of working flashlights in their search of the house and one of them now provided their only illumination as they enjoyed a few cans of Spam.

"I never thought this stuff could taste so good," Tom said, taking another big bite. "Glad Farmer Bob had a little left."

"That's pretty much all that's left," Stacia reminded him. There was little else in the house in the way of food; some cans of Spam and fruit cocktail were all they had come across in the cupboards. The refrigerator was completely empty and had a dank, musty smell, but the house was fairly tidy and there were a few items of men's clothing folded neatly in a small dresser in the bedroom, allowing McCain to trade his blood-stained shirt for a clean one.

If the house had been abandoned, it hadn't been abandoned for very long. McCain had immediately claimed the shotgun and a cache of shells from an unlocked gun cabinet upstairs when he'd first broken in. When the small group had settled in, he'd given his handgun to his daughter with the express command to save the bullets for when she really needed them. They had also found an old radio on a dresser in the bedroom, but with no electricity they were still cut off from knowing what was happening in the world.

"Do you think the owner will come back?" Stacia eventually asked, casting a glance out the window. The night was completely dark now, with low hanging clouds masking the moon and stars. She realized someone could be standing in front of a window and she wouldn't know it. It was a chilling thought and she quickly returned to the others.

"Let's hope not," John replied. "We could use the rest without any complications."

"So tell me, John," Stanley said after a while. "You seem like you know what's going on out there. What do you know that we don't?"

"What makes you think I have the answers, Stanley?" John asked.

"Come on, John. I'm a bus driver. I've seen all kinds get on my bus and I don't miss much. I saw you talking with the Father there for a long time and you seem to have some idea about these crazy people running around."

"Very well," John finally said, pushing his chair back from the worn table. "Let's get ourselves set up for the night, then I'll tell you what I know."

It was an hour later before John finished his story, aided considerably by Father Dalacourt. Tom McCain had a few comments of his own while he modified his shotgun by duct-taping one of the flashlights to it, but Stacia had been quiet throughout the whole tale. In the end, John and the priest related much of the story from the Book of Revelation and spoke in-depth about formerly dead bodies being taken by evil spirits. It was a sobering discussion and did little to raise anyone's spirits, but at least they had a better idea of what they were up against.

They settled in for the night, everyone curled up with a blanket on the floor or a chair—Stacia took the couch—hoping to get some sleep. They got two hours of rest before the attack came. It was McCain's newly-claimed shotgun that woke the others, and each of them yelled in fright and confusion as the gun roared. McCain jacked another shell into the shotgun's chamber and aimed it at the kitchen doorway, the muzzle-taped flashlight shining into the kitchen. Lying across the table was a body, a hole blown through its chest, while two more figures came around the kitchen table, intent on reaching the occupants in the living room. McCain fired a second time, taking off the top half of the head from the nearest one, then loaded and fired again, dropping the third attacker.

"Looks like we've got company!" he shouted as the others scrambled to their feet and grabbed whatever weapons they had.

"These are the same ones from the bus stop!" yelled Stacia, grabbing her baseball bat. "I recognized the one you just shot!"

McCain swung the shotgun around and pointed it at the front door just as two arms thrust through the door's window and sent shards of glass flying into the room. One hand brandished a large knife, while an arm snaked around the throat of Stanley Hotchkiss, who had been standing near the door. Before McCain could shout a warning, the knife plunged deep into the bus driver's chest. He screamed once as the knife was wrenched free and then screamed a final time as it was driven home again. The attacker tore it free once more before McCain shoved the shotgun past the bus driver's head. He pulled the trigger and blasted the killer backward into the night.

Stanley sagged to the floor and Dalacourt rushed over to pull him out of harm's way, praying he was not too late. The battle raged on, the only light coming from McCain's shotgun-mounted flashlight. John fought with another invader who had come through the kitchen, and McCain shot another that had tried to crawl through the shattered front door. Stacia moved across the living room toward John, then stumbled in the darkness and screamed as she felt an arm wrap around her waist.

McCain whirled and shone the light in her direction. The young girl was being lifted off her feet, one of her assailant's arms wrapped around her waist and the other hand clamped firmly on the baseball bat she still held. What shocked McCain the most was the attacker. It was the wailing woman from the bus, her face bruised and broken, her eyes flat and dead. With a feral growl, the woman flung Stacia viciously into the wall and wrenched the bat from her grasp as she did. She raised the bat high as McCain took aim. But before he could fire, he was grabbed from behind as another killer came through the front door. He never saw the bat fall, but he heard the sickening thud as it connected with flesh. Rage roared up within him and he twisted around and slammed the stock of the gun into the face of his assailant, breaking the man's hold on him. He brought the barrel around and smashed it into the side of the man's face, shattering bone. Before the enemy could recover, the barrel of the gun was under his chin. McCain didn't hesitate to pull the trigger.

With his assailant dead, he whirled back around as John grappled with the woman from the bus. Both the old man's hands were on the bat as he tried to push her backward, but she brought a knee up hard into his groin and doubled him over. As John dropped to his knees, McCain fired. The shotgun blast took the woman's arm off at the elbow. He ratcheted another shell into the chamber and his next shot caught her in the chest and slammed her into the wall. She stood there for a moment and then sank slowly to the floor.

McCain spun back and forth several more times between the kitchen and the front door, but it appeared there were no more attackers. Inwardly sick at what he might find, he shone the flashlight toward the floor where he knew his daughter was. He expected to find her bludgeoned to death, but he was instead surprised to see the young priest lying on top of her. Astonished and confused, he took a step forward just as Dalacourt slowly raised his head. The young man winced as he tried to pull himself up, but then collapsed back to the floor beside the girl.

John was next to him in an instant. "Are you all right, Michael?" he asked anxiously.

Dalacourt managed to nod his head, his breath wheezing. "Took it...in the back," he gasped.

McCain knelt down beside his daughter and lifted her up, cradling her in his arms.

"How is she?" Dalacourt gasped, turning his head painfully to look at her.

Tom felt the pulse in her neck. It was strong. "Ought to be okay," he said. "Just had her bell rung." He looked at the priest struggling to his knees. "That was a nice move, Father. Seriously, I owe you one."

Dalacourt winced again. "It was nothing," he wheezed. "What about Stanley?"

The cop cleared his throat and shook his head.

"We should move on," John said sadly, standing over them. "It's just not safe here."

"On the contrary," McCain answered grimly. "I don't think there's any place safer in these mountains right now. Those were the same punks that attacked us in Echo Resort."

"There were a lot more than just those," John pointed out. "And they had no problem tracking us."

"True," McCain answered. "But not all of them came after us. They're mindless killers and they aren't organized. If there were any more out there, they'd be coming through the house right about now."

"Nevertheless, we must go," John said quietly, looking around at the carnage in the room. "The sooner we can get to Salt Lake City, the better."

"You're the boss," McCain said. "If you say we go, we go."

A short while later, they set out in the darkness, heading towards the flickering lights of the city. They had no time to bury Stanley Hotchkiss, so they had wrapped his body in a blanket and laid him peacefully on the couch. Stacia was shaken up but had no discernible injuries, and while Michael Dalacourt had a nasty purple bruise across his back and possibly a cracked rib to show for his heroism, he was otherwise fit to travel. More importantly, the priest had finally broken through the barrier of fear that had threatened to engulf him. He was glad, because if even a fraction of what John said was going to happen actually happened, he was going to need to be as strong as possible. They all would.

CHAPTER 31

Salt Lake City, Utah: Colors shot out of the sky like a burning rainbow, showering debris all around. It was as if the world had just been ripped asunder in front of them, and turned a nightmarish situation into utter hell. Genevieve Abramson screamed and wrenched the wheel of the car to the right, driving up onto the sidewalk as the roaring flames scorched the metal and blackened their windows. A moment later, they were through the conflagration and speeding on. Alexis Kennedy couldn't even think about what would have happened had their windows been down.

None of it made any sense. Alexis frantically fought to piece together the last few minutes of her life in a desperate effort to figure out what to do next. She was sitting in the back seat of Gen's old Honda, trying to stop the flow of blood from their other friend's head wound as they raced to find shelter from the sudden chaos that was rapidly engulfing the city. Libby's breathing was shallow and ragged and Alexis spurred Gen on with a sharp, "Hurry!"

The morning had started out innocently enough and nearly as perfect as she could have hoped for. After saying good-bye to Owen the day before and giving him the letter she'd written, Alexis and her friends had decided to have a girl's day out. They were up early to hit the big sidewalk sale at the Gateway Center and had spent the rest of the morning at the mall. After lunch, they were in high spirits as they walked toward Northgate Apartments, where Gen had parked her car.

It was there that their world had turned upside down.

A terrified scream sounded loudly from an open front door of one of the apartments as they walked past. All three of them froze, unsure whether to rush to the person's aid or call for help. Libby was the first to move and opted for the latter choice by pulling out her cell and dialing 9-1-1. She was surprised to get a busy signal, so she tried again, wondering if her cell had just glitched, but she got the same flat tone telling her there was no one to take her call. Before she could try a third time, a man staggered out of the front door of the house, blood streaming down his face from a deep gash across the top of his head. He stumbled and fell to his knees, holding out his hands helplessly toward the three young women, his eyes wild and terrified.

"Help...me," was all he managed to say before a second person, a heavyset woman in curlers and a flowered bathrobe, followed him out of the house with a bloody hammer in her hand. With frightening strength, she raised it high and slammed it down into the back of his head with a crunch of bone. His eyes rolled back in his head and he pitched forward on the front walk, his body twitching.

The woman turned her lifeless eyes on them and began slowly lurching toward the girls, still brandishing the bloody hammer dangerously in her hand. Screaming in terror, the girls turned as one to flee, as Libby fumbled with her phone in an effort to call 9-1-1 again.

From across the lot, they heard another scream and saw two men drag a young woman out of a parked car. Hands grasped at her throat and her screams were quickly cut off as they began to strangle her. It was, to Alexis, a certain sign they needed to get to their own car immediately. She spurred her two friends on, screaming, "Run!"

The three of them ran through the lot as fast as they could, arriving at their car just as another scene of violence played out before them. A police car speeding down the street toward the apartment complex swerved violently to the side as a young boy of about ten or eleven staggered out into the street in front of it. The vehicle collided with a parked car and ricocheted off, clipped the boy, and threw him thirty feet down the road before the cruiser's tires caught on the pavement and flipped it. The car landed on its top and slid down the street, coming to rest against the curb. There was no movement inside.

With fear threatening to incapacitate her, Gen worked her key fob to unlock her car doors.

At that moment another terrified resident, frantic to escape the growing madness, jammed his car in reverse and roared backward into the lot. Libby never had a chance. The rear of his car clipped her leg and flipped her upside down before her head slammed back to the pavement with a crack of bone on concrete. The terrified man paused only a moment to see what he'd done, then took off, tires smoking.

Alexis rushed to her fallen friend, blood already beginning to pool on the asphalt under her head. Libby had been badly hurt. Her right leg was bent at an odd angle above her knee and blood ran freely from a long split in her skin along the side of her head and down behind her ear.

"Help me!" she shouted to Gen.

Genevieve was frozen, her eyes seeing the danger coming toward them from all sides. People of all ages were everywhere, some walking toward them and some pursuing others who were attempting to flee in terror.

Alexis followed her gaze and then, fighting back her own overwhelming fright, she quickly worked her hands under Libby's broken body. "Help me, Gen!" she screamed.

The girl shook herself out of her terror-induced paralysis and quickly knelt down to help. They pulled Libby to her feet and, half dragging, half pushing, they managed get her into the back seat of Gen's car.

"We have to get Libby to the hospital!" Alexis yelled breathlessly. "Now!"

A new cry of terror drew their gaze across the street as a teenager in a basketball jersey had pinned down a frantically-struggling young mother, his hands fastened tightly around her throat while a child of about one lay in the grass nearby and cried desperately. Alexis felt like dying inside, but there was nothing she could do. She jumped in the back seat with her injured friend as Gen slid behind the wheel. In less than a minute, they were speeding down the road.

"What's happening?" Gen sobbed, desperately swerving her car around a group of people.

"I don't know," Alexis replied, trying to keep herself together. "Find a radio station and see what they're saying."

Gen quickly turned the radio on, but was immediately met with an emergency broadcast signal. She hit the scan button and the radio dutifully ran through the stations, giving the same result every time. Gen cried harder.

"Pull it together, sis," Alexis coaxed her from the back seat, her own voice trembling. "Just get us to the hospital."

Looking down, she noticed a small duffel bag of clean and folded laundry on the floor. She quickly grabbed a towel and pressed it to her friend's wounded head, hoping to stop the bleeding. Libby had lost a lot of blood, soaking the shoulder and arm of her tee-shirt. Alexis prayed they would make it to the hospital in time.

"Will she be all right?" Gen asked shakily as she thumbed off the radio.

"I don't know," Alexis replied, noticing her injured friend's pasty white complexion. She pressed harder with the towel, ignoring the blood that began to soak through it. "Just keep driving," she finished.

Gen sped down the street, doing her best to avoid people and other cars, but just as traffic seemed to clear a bit and the girls had a moment of hope, a tanker truck that had been unloading fuel at a convenience store exploded. Gen had no choice but to drive straight through the inferno.

They burst through the flames on the other side, choking on the fumes of burning gasoline that filtered in through the air vents. It took a few moments for the reason for the explosion to register with Alexis. Cars coming from the other direction had been forced to a stop for the roaring flames, only to have attackers pull them from their vehicles and murder them in the street. It was an ambush set up to trap helpless victims for the growing mob of killers.

"We can't get out!" Gen screamed in desperation.

"Stay with me!" Alexis shouted, knowing Genevieve was close to breaking. "If we're going to get Libby to the hospital, you've got to keep it together!"

Gen swallowed thickly. She swerved around several cars and careened down a side street, avoiding murderers and victims alike. It was nearly impossible to believe that less than an hour ago, they had been sitting in the mall having lunch. Now they were in some horror movie come to life. What had caused people to go crazy and start cutting down other people in broad daylight in the streets?

Alexis Kennedy, always so logical and pragmatic, could only shake her head in complete confusion.

The muffled sound of Gen's cell phone brought her quickly back to the present and Alexis listened intently as Gen raised it to her ear. "Todd!" she exclaimed, bursting into tears. "Yes, we're okay. No, we're not okay," she quickly amended. "Libby's hurt bad. We're trying to get her to the hospital." She paused again, listening, then quickly looked to her left as they went through an intersection. "We're on South Temple, just coming to Third West." She sobbed and then quieted. "Yes, you're close," she replied. "And Todd?" She trailed off, but apparently he'd hung up or the call had been cut off. Crying softly, she dropped her phone on the seat next to her. At the next intersection, she turned without a word of warning.

"Where are you going?" Alexis asked, alarmed.

"To get Todd," Gen replied evenly, fighting to get her emotions under control.

"Are you crazy?" Alexis snapped, anger rising within her. "We've got to get Libby to the hospital!"

"He was in an accident. He's only a few blocks down," Gen replied defensively. "We need help, Alexis."

Alexis bit off her reply, shaking her head. She was livid at Gen for detouring off their route to the hospital, but she couldn't argue with her logic. They were two women with an injured friend in a world gone stark raving mad. She wished somehow they could get to Owen in all of this, but he was in Vegas. She grabbed her cell phone just so she could hear his voice and make sure he was okay, and felt a surge of relief when it rang, but it continued to ring without him answering and eventually went to his voice mail. She was about to leave a message when the call was disconnected. She quickly tried again, hoping he hadn't gotten to it in time. This time, she got the message that all circuits were busy. In despair, she looked out the window. She felt alone.

Several blocks down, they turned a corner and saw the accident. Todd's car was up against a telephone pole, its front end pushed in.

"How'd he get here?" Gen asked almost to herself as she slowed down.

Alexis knew why immediately, but she didn't answer. They were nowhere near Todd's job. They were, however, very close to where Todd's ex-girlfriend lived—the one whom Alexis suspected he had never really left. She and Gen had had words many times before about how unfaithful Todd was, but Gen had chosen to follow hope rather than reality. Alexis saw Todd standing with a young lady beside his car and her thoughts were confirmed. It was indeed Emily. "What a jerk,"

Alexis muttered under her breath.

Gen set her jaw and pulled over. Both of the women saw the look of concern on Todd's face and Gen prepared to break into an angry outburst. But when he opened the passenger door, it was Emily who said nervously, "This isn't what you think, Gen."

"Just get in," Genevieve said quietly, turning her eyes forward and biting her tongue. "What happened?"

Todd swung into the front seat as Emily squeezed into the back seat with Alexis and Libby. "Some idiot just ran out into the middle of the road," he said quickly. "I tried to swerve to avoid him and ended up hitting the pole."

"Where did he go?" Gen asked, her voice still very quiet as she drove around the wreck and headed back toward the street that would take them to the hospital.

"Is that him?" Alexis asked, pointing to a body lying in the street. They had not seen him when they pulled up.

"Yeah," Todd answered in a voice that mixed disgust and a little bit of fear. "When I got out of the car, he came at me and we got into it. I ended up pushing him down and he cracked his head on the curb. He never got up. It was an accident, I swear." He turned to look at Gen, trying to get all his explanations out at once. "Look, Gen, I can explain this," he began, but Alexis cut him off from the back seat.

"This isn't the time, Todd," she snapped, her voice angry. "Libby's hurt and the whole world is going crazy! For once in your life, think of someone besides yourself."

Gen turned a corner to get back on the main road and immediately slammed on the brakes. About a block ahead at Pioneer Park was a much larger group of people—men, women and even children. Some were looking in their direction while others were walking slowly down the middle of the road toward downtown. Some carried weapons like rocks, boards, and knives, others had nothing but their bare hands. Beyond the crowd of rioters, the buildings of downtown Salt Lake City were growing hazy, obscured by a thickening pall of smoke. Here and there, they caught bright flashes of fire. Salt Lake City was burning.

"Oh, Lord, what do we do?" Gen asked, a panicked edge to her voice, her hurt forgotten.

"We'll never get to the hospital through all of that," Todd answered grimly, turning around to look at Libby's still form.

"What do you suggest then?" Alexis asked bitterly, aiming all her anger and frustration at Todd, even though she knew he was probably right.

"We have to find shelter," he began, but he was interrupted by a loud bang of metal on metal. Everyone whirled around to see one of the rioters, a teenager, with a metal pipe in his hands. He was shirtless, with a large purple bruise under one eye and bruising all around his neck. Raising the pipe high, he brought it down on the back of the car a second time, this time shattering the rear window. Emily and Alexis both screamed as glass showered them. From the front seat, Todd yelled, "Go!"

With a wail of desperation, Gen shifted the car into reverse and gunned it, mowing down their teenage assailant. The car bounced wildly over his body and Gen quickly turned the wheel to get them pointed in the opposite direction. "Where to?" she shouted, slamming the accelerator to the floor. As the car sped back the way they came, they all became aware of more and more people around them. Some had the dead, blank look of the rioters. Others were fighting for their lives or attempting to flee the chaos

"My apartment is nearby," Emily said quietly. She knew she was not well-liked by the other women and, in a normal situation, it would never have been a consideration. Things being what they were, it was their best hope and everyone knew it. "It's a security building," she explained. "We can take shelter there. I work at the hospital. Maybe there's something I can do." She finished, looking at Libby's pale face with genuine concern.

"Where's your apartment, Emily?" Gen asked, fighting to keep herself under control.

"Just a few blocks down Broadway, then turn right," Emily replied meekly. "It's the Renaissance Suites, about a half-mile down the road on the right hand side."

They drove in uncomfortable silence, arriving at their destination in only a few minutes, trying to ignore the scattered scenes of insanity happening along the way. Genevieve whipped the car into a parking space and jammed it into park. Without a word, she opened her door and jumped out. The others joined her.

"Help me with Libby, Todd," Alexis said, her voice carefully neutral.

Todd merely nodded and ducked inside the car, sliding Libby out of the backseat as gently as he could. He straightened up, then slipped his arm behind her knees and swept her up into his arms.

"Oh, no!" Emily said pointing toward the apartment building. Three other sets of eyes followed hers. The security door to her apartment complex stood ajar, the outside of it smeared with blood.

"We don't have any choice," Todd said, pushing by them with the wounded Libby in his arms. Wordlessly, the others followed him into the complex where they stopped just inside the entryway. From down the hall, they heard shouts and screams coming from numerous apartments.

"Upstairs," Emily pointed as she started up the stairway.

They climbed two sets of stairs to the top floor and hurried down the hall, which was thankfully empty. Emily pushed ahead, pulling out her apartment key as they reached her door. A moment later, they were inside and Emily locked the door behind them. "Take her to the bedroom and lay her on my bed," she told Todd and then hurried off to the bathroom. She returned a moment later with a small first aid kit and a wet towel and followed him into her room, Gen and Alexis right behind her. Sitting beside the pale girl, she gently peeled the blood-soaked towel away from Libby's head and went to work.

After a few minutes of cleaning the blood from her face, she started applying bandages to the wound, trying to pull the torn edges of skin together as best she could. "It's a scalp wound," she said quietly, "which is why it bled so much. It's pretty big, though, and she'll obviously need stitches." There was a sigh of relief from Alexis and Gen, but Emily held up her hand. "She's still in bad shape," the young woman cautioned. "She's unconscious and most likely has a serious concussion and maybe even a skull fracture. Her leg is broken, too, and we'll need to splint it before we move her again. We definitely need to get her to a hospital and the sooner, the better. If she has bleeding on the brain, she could be in serious trouble."

She picked up the bloody towels and the kit, then stood up and left the room without looking at any of them. Gen wheeled around angrily and walked out, too, going the opposite way into the living room. Alexis knew why. On Emily's bed stand were several pictures of Todd in small frames, and on the wall over her dresser there hung an eight-by-twelve inch glossy photo of her and Todd in each others' arms somewhere in the mountains amid a sea of wildflowers.

Shooting Todd a final glare herself, she stalked out of the room, leaving him standing alone. A sudden, frantic beating on Emily's front door sent him running after her. In the front room, Gen and Alexis stood there, hands over mouths in fright as they stared at the front door. The pounding on it was followed by the voice of an older lady, pleading for her life. *"Por favor,"* she screamed in Spanish. *"Me ayudan!"*

Emily rushed past all of them to the front door, her hands fumbling with the locks.

Todd reached out to stop her. "What are you doing, Emily?"

She angrily shook her arm free and finished unlocking the door. "She's my neighbor!" she shouted back.

Emily yanked the door open to find the old woman standing in the hallway, her eyes wide with terror, but they were already too late. The first of her attackers, a man in a business suit, was already on her. Todd leaped forward, knocking Emily down, and began pounding on the man's arm with his fist. The old woman let out a strangled cry as she was pulled backward. Lip split and nose broken, the enemy would not release his hold on the woman. As he fought, Todd saw more of the murderous mob coming down the hall toward them. "Run!" he shouted.

Behind him, Emily staggered to her feet. "Hide in the bedroom!" she yelled, rushing to the kitchen. She was back out in a moment, a butcher knife in her hand and a long-bladed steak knife in the other. "Both of you get to the bedroom with Libby and lock the door!" she said, slapping the hilt of the steak knife in Alexis' hand. She turned and rushed forward, slashing at the intruder with her butcher knife.

Alexis had never felt fear the way she felt it at that moment. She pushed Gen backward and both of them rushed to the bedroom. Inside, they locked the door and slid slowly to the floor. Shouts and screams sounded from the living room and beyond as the fighting raged. Both women cried silent tears, eyes shut tightly against the terror that washed over them. There were several crashes against the wall on the other side of the bedroom. One knocked the picture of Todd and Emily off the wall and the glass face shattered as it impacted with the dresser.

A high-pitched scream, that sounded like Emily split the air, followed by a roar of rage. Another crash followed and then there were new shouts, strange voices shouting curses and encouragement. Finally, a few moments later, there was silence. The fighting was over.

Alexis and Gen didn't move, holding tightly to each other. The silence stretched into a minute. Then two. Finally, there was a soft knock on the door and a strange voice sounded from the other side. "It's over out here," someone said solemnly. "It's safe."

Alexis stood up, tentatively unlocked the bedroom door and slowly opened it, coming face-to-face with a stranger. She almost screamed, but the young man held up a finger to his lips. "Shhhh," he said sadly. "You're okay. We're the good guys. I'm Greg. My friend Danny is guarding the front door." He paused, his features gentle. "Look at me," he said softly. "I'm not one of them. I promise."

Alexis did look at him. The man didn't appear to be any older than she was. He was tall and blond, with haunted blue eyes that peered at her from under bushy eyebrows. There was a smear of blood on one of his cheeks, and a bloody strip of cloth was wrapped around his left bicep. In his hands, he carried a piece of metal pipe, streaked with gore, that had been put to grim work. He moved away from the door, letting them pass, and the two women walked out into the living room.

There were a half-dozen bodies strewn about, most of them showing signs of having been severely beaten, and Alexis fought down the urge to throw up. The front door was still open and the old woman was propped against the hallway wall, her eyes closed and the front of her dress stained with blood. Another stranger was kneeling beside her and shaking his head.

And then she saw Todd. He was kneeling beside the body of Emily, his blood-soaked hands pressed vainly against her ruined throat.

Her eyes were open and unseeing and Alexis knew she was dead. The body of one of their attackers lay nearby, the man still clutching a hooked weed-cutting knife that glistened wetly with fresh blood.

Walking gingerly into the room, Alexis shook her head in grief, crying. "I'm so sorry, Todd," she whispered, and meant every word. The young woman had died trying to protect them and a terrible guilt welled up within her. Alexis had no words. She sucked in her breath and turned away, her body shaking with sobs. Genevieve dropped to her knees beside Todd and threw one arm around his neck and clung to him, her own desperate sobs racking her body.

Embarrassed and defeated and feeling as low as she could remember, Alexis walked away from them, her eyes coming to rest on the stranger. She knew he and his friend had saved them at the very moment all should have been lost. "Thank you," she said, her voice breaking.

The young man just shook his head, his face sad. "It's nothing," he replied quietly, heading toward the door. He paused and looked down. Todd had not moved, still trying to hold together Emily's slashed throat, even though she was dead. "I'm sorry about your friend, but I wouldn't stay here any longer than you need to," he said and then turned away. Without another word, he joined his friend in the hall. A moment later, they were gone.

Alexis knelt down beside Todd and placed a hand on his shoulder. She was saved from having to find the right thing to say when Todd's cell phone, which was still attached to his belt, began ringing. Todd cried silently, either not aware of it or wishing to ignore it. On the fifth ring, Alexis reached down and gently unhooked it from his belt. She slid her finger across the screen and tapped answer. There was a rush of voices on the other end and she held it up to Todd's ear.

His far-away look vanished and his eyes refocused. Reaching up, he took hold of the phone, not caring about the blood covering his hands. "Yeah, I'm here. Calm down," he said, strength returning to his voice. "No, we're okay for now." A pause. "Yeah, I can get there." Another. "I know where that's at." A longer pause before he finished. "Keep yourself barricaded in. I'll be there as soon as I can." He slid it back onto his belt.

"That was my sister," he explained, climbing to his feet with renewed purpose. "She can't get in touch with her husband. She and her kids are hiding out in the basement of their house listening to the radio. She said this is going on everywhere and the announcers are listing some shelters in the city that are taking people in for safety. There's one nearby, the Road Home on Rio Grande."

"That's the one I volunteer at," Alexis said quickly. "I think we can make it."

Todd looked down at the body of Emily, then he focused on Gen. "I'll drop you two off at the shelter with Libby and then I'm going to get my sister."

Gen shook her head. "No, Todd," she said. "I'm going with you." Not bothering to wait for him to speak, she looked at Alexis. "We'll take you and Libby to the shelter and then we'll go after Todd's sister."

Alexis could only nod mutely as the weight of what had happened began to press down upon her. Would the shelter truly be safe? She'd never felt less safe in all her young life. The words of her online conversation with Rebekkah just a few days ago flashed through her mind. The world was indeed going crazy, she thought bitterly. How much crazier would it get?

Less than ten minutes later, they were in the car, heading for the safety of the shelter. It wouldn't be long before she found out just how insane the world had truly become.

CHAPTER 32

Salt Lake City, Utah: Petr Zhugravinsky sat silently, brooding as he absentmindedly stirred his Coke with a straw. His decision to use his connection with David Sumbawanga to help show Alexis his value had blown up in his face in three near-fatal minutes inside the tunnel on the University of Utah campus. To say it had not gone well was an understatement. As they had parted that evening, Petr had been convinced David no longer wanted to see him again, so he was surprised when David had phoned and asked for another meeting. He couldn't imagine anything positive coming from it, but he still said yes. He had agreed to meet him at the Rodizio Brazilian Grill at Trolley Square in downtown Salt Lake City. He knew he was in trouble when he arrived fifteen minutes early and saw David was already seated. After a brief interchange, the two had eaten in near total silence.

After they had finished their meal, Petr knew he could no longer avoid the discussion. "I'm sorry about what happened in the tunnel," he finally said, contrition clearly evident in his eyes.

"What has happened, has happened, Petr," David said quietly. He was tired and his voice was strained. "We can't change the past, but we can learn from our mistakes and go forward."

"I'll admit that what happened wasn't a new experience for me, David. But in the past, I could control myself. But something happened this time. I was…I…" he trailed off in thought.

"Would you have killed those men had I not stopped you?"

"Without a doubt, and that's what frightens me. I fear I'll lose myself."

"Then there is still hope for you," David said, nodding sagely.

"Hope?" Petr asked incredulously.

"Certainly," he replied, letting a small smile come to his face.

"Petr," he went on, leaning forward and reaching out to the young Russian. He patted Petr's hand with his own. "A wise man knows that you can only find yourself if you have lost yourself first. Your words tell me the truth of your heart."

Petr shook his head in confusion. "I don't understand."

"It frightens you. You do not embrace it as others might, and that speaks of a man who understands his shortcomings and wants to better himself."

Petr's visage began to soften. "So, what you're saying is now that I've seen what I can become, I can more easily resist going to that place again."

"Exactly," David answered. "Things didn't end as badly as they could have and I'm a firm believer everything happens for a reason. The important thing is to understand that reason."

"You speak as if you know the reason."

"It would be prideful of me to think I know everything, but after a restless night, full of examination and prayer, I think I've come to the answers I've been seeking. I saw where my future will lead me, Petr. For me, it was a vision of hope, though not hope as the world would see it. Rather, I finally came to understand my son is truly dead."

"You believe this?"

David paused, grasped his walking stick and leaned forward, touching his forehead to the smooth wood before looking up. "I've felt it since I first became aware of his disappearance," he replied, envisioning the dark shadow that had loomed over his son. "For reasons I cannot explain, though, I feel his journey isn't complete yet. Therefore, mine isn't complete, either."

"I don't understand," Petr said honestly, trying to comprehend the man's message.

"I'm not certain I do, either," David replied thoughtfully, "but I know I have to continue, both for my son and for myself, and whether I comprehend it or not is inconsequential. There are still answers to be sought and I trust in God. He will see me through, and Gideon's journey—whatever it may be—can be completed."

Petr hesitated again before speaking, wanting to make certain he stated correctly what was on his mind. "You speak of God," he said "I've never considered myself a religious man, but for the first time in my life, I'm starting to believe that maybe there is something more out there—something worth believing in."

"I believe mankind is connected to God in mysterious ways, and it's up to each individual to wake up to that connection," David said. "It's like a radio and it's up to us to tune into the correct station. I've always believed that God speaks to us, so perhaps it's easier for me to accept this for what it is. I'm impressed you're able to see it for what it is as well."

David had guessed correctly that faith in anything other than oneself was a new concept for Petr, but it was clear he was trying to open himself up and embrace the changes within and around him. Whether it was faith, hope, or a spiritual understanding, David knew Petr had been touched by something new.

"If you're willing, I'd still like to help you, David," Petr offered sincerely.

"I don't know that it would be a pleasant journey," David replied. "There's something nebulous and dark that stalks the path I must tread. I sensed it in the tunnel and it tells me nothing lies beyond this journey. I feel things are going to get much worse, and I fear I won't be around to see them get better. It's quite possible my life will end when I've discovered the answers I seek."

"You believe you're going to die?"

David shrugged. "If it's God's will, then yes. I do not fear it, though," he went on. "But I fear for anyone who accompanies me."

"I can appreciate that," Petr said and he truly meant it. Despite everything that had happened, despite his serious transgression, Petr was being given a second chance. It was more than he could have hoped for. "But ultimately," he added, "the choice is mine and mine alone and I have made it. I wish to help."

At that moment, one of the waiters hurried over to them. "I'm sorry," the teenager said, looking and sounding frightened. "We're closing up and you gotta go. We're locking up right now."

"Closing so soon?" David asked in mild surprise.

"Yeah," he replied hurriedly, pointing to one of the restaurant televisions.

David and Petr both quickly looked up at the silent television screen, focusing on the grim-looking anchor and the closed captioning text scrolling across the screen.

"...are not yet certain if these riots have been elaborately coordinated or if the unrest is, in fact, unrelated and simply spreading. We'll be cutting live to an address from the President of the United States soon, as the White House moves to handle this disturbing situation."

David and Petr looked at each other in shock.

The news anchor went on, his face strained. "Reports continue to come in concerning violent outbreaks all over the world. Moscow, Beijing, Paris...these are just a few of the many major cities experiencing this terrifying calamity. There's no word yet on a death toll, but preliminary reports are that the final tally will be staggering."

"What on earth..." Petr began, but he was drowned out by a loud wailing sound.

"It's the emergency warning system!" another waiter shouted, running toward the kitchen. "Better get out now," he said, just as the television changed over to pictures taken from a helicopter of a roaming mob in the streets. The caption at the bottom said it was live from New York City. It was unlike anything they'd ever seen.

"Just got a phone call!" shouted a man from behind the counter. "There's rioting breaking out right here in town!"

David stood up quickly, his face grave. "Come, Petr. We must leave." He grabbed his walking stick, took Petr by the arm, and quickly herded him toward the door. "Hurry," he added as he and Petr stepped outside. Both men quickly put their hands to their ears trying to muffle the sound of the warning sirens.

Petr turned to David and had to almost shout to be heard. "What next?"

David looked around, trying to focus on the moment. Despite the loud wail of the sirens, everything around them seemed calm. There were no rioters and very few vehicles on the road. It was hard to make sense of what was happening.

"Look, my car is parked two streets over," Petr said, while keeping a lookout for any trouble. "Let's get to it and decide what to do from there."

David gripped him by the arm and drew him close. He didn't like to yell, but the sirens made it all but impossible not to. "I'm staying downtown at the Red Lion! Do you know it?"

"Believe it or not, I do," the young Russian nodded. "But why the hotel? It could be dangerous downtown!"

"It's much easier to go unnoticed in a crowd," David answered. "One thing you learn living in Africa—when danger threatens, it's always smart to take the target off your back."

"Okay, let's get moving then," Petr agreed. He started off in the direction of his car at a brisk pace, but slow enough that David and his walking stick had no problem keeping up. As he walked, he pulled out his cell phone and called Alexis' number four times in quick succession, each time getting the recording that all circuits were busy. Muttering in Russian, he thrust the phone back in his pocket as they turned the corner.

They walked right into chaos.

A car was stopped in the middle of the street and a young woman was backed up against the passenger door, holding a tire iron in both hands but shaking so badly she was likely to drop it before she ever got the chance to use it. She screamed in terror while a middle-aged man in a business suit wrestled with a large man who looked to be a cab driver a few feet in front of her. Several other people were closing in on the car from all directions. None of them looked friendly.

"Hey!" Petr shouted and hurried forward.

"Petr!" David called out in alarm.

The young Russian did not seem to hear him, his focus on the drama that was playing out before him. "Hey!" he shouted again as the cab driver threw the businessman to the ground and followed him to the pavement, hands reaching for his throat. Petr Zhugravinsky was well built, physically capable, and at that moment he acted out of instinct.

Oblivious to the others closing in, he sprinted forward and lowered his shoulder, slamming into the cab driver with all his weight and knocking him away from his intended victim. A cry of pain from the young woman had him pivoting quickly to take on the next threat. Two men had reached the young woman. One had tangled his hands into her hair and pulled her onto the hood of the car while the other clamped his hands tightly around her throat, choking off her next scream. The tire iron dropped uselessly from her hands.

Petr lunged forward and thrust his hands under the would-be strangler's arms. Using moves his brother Nikolai had taught him as a young teenager, he yanked upward and locked his hands behind the killer's head in a full nelson, breaking the man's grip on the woman's throat. She immediately started screaming again, her voice blending in with the siren. "What's wrong with you?" the Russian shouted at the top of his lungs as he threw the man to the pavement.

But the attacker did not answer. He simply stood up slowly, empty eyes staring at Petr.

"Petr!" David yelled over the clamor. "Behind you!"

The Russian whirled as a middle-aged woman with a battered face and bruised neck lunged toward him with a shovel aimed at his midsection. He easily sidestepped the attack and clamped his hands down on the handle. Muscles bulging, he flung the much lighter woman to the side. Off balance, she crashed to the street, her head smashing against the pavement. She twitched once and lay still.

He had no time to dwell on her death, though, as a body blow from behind caught him in the kidneys and drove him painfully to his knees, the shovel dropping from his nerveless fingers. His attacker, a powerfully built man in a t-shirt and tattered jeans, leaned down and clamped a muscled forearm around the Russian's throat. He pulled Petr roughly to his feet, tightening his grip, and Petr began to see stars. Before he lost consciousness, though, there was a crack of wood on bone, followed by a wordless grunt from his assailant, and the pressure was gone. Coughing violently, Petr looked up and saw David standing with his walking stick in both hands, a grim look on his face.

"Thanks…" Petr gasped, but he had no time to continue speaking as several more of the rioters moved in. The woman's attackers were back at her and the cab driver was back on the businessman, his own arms bulging as he strangled him.

At that moment, another woman, this one in a jogging suit, lunged at Petr with a butcher knife, and a teenage boy clad in grunge clothing came at him with his bare hands. Petr caught the knife thrust from the woman and with a hard snap, he shoved downward on her arm, sending the knife clattering to the ground. Spinning around, he caught the woman across the jaw with a powerful roundhouse, sending her crashing to the pavement. But, amazingly, she immediately pulled herself back to her feet, her jaw broken and sickeningly askew. She made no sound, her dead eyes locked on the Russian.

Petr had no time to contemplate the significance of that as the grunge rocker was on him, fists swinging toward his face. Petr caught a glancing blow to the side of his head that sent him reeling. Knowing he was in desperate trouble, he lunged forward and drove his knee solidly into his attacker's groin. His enemy never even flinched and swung again. The Russian could not get an arm up to block in time and the blow sent him crashing to the ground.

The teen continued advancing relentlessly as Petr's hand closed around the handle of the knife the woman had dropped. As the would-be killer began reaching for Petr's throat, the Russian slammed the knife into the young man's stomach. Petr locked eyes with his attacker and then, with a primal roar of rage, he viciously tore the blade upward, putting an end to the threat. Petr let the body slide to the ground. He looked up as the woman charged back in and, without a thought, he put the knife through her heart and shoved her slumping body aside as she went limp.

The beast within had taken control.

Petr—now fueled by an intense rage—saw David doing his best to help the young woman. He had dispatched her first two attackers and now fought with the cab driver who had successfully strangled the businessman. Petr stepped up and caught him from behind, one arm clamping across the man's chest and his other arm coming around his neck. He cupped his hand tightly onto the attacker's chin and then violently wrenched his head sideways, snapping the man's neck. With a curse in his native Russian, he shoved the body to the ground and then turned around, looking for more.

But for the moment, it was all over. None of the attackers on the ground moved, and there were no others nearby that he could see. David was holding the young lady tightly now, her head pressed against his shoulder as her body shook with sobs.

Petr didn't know what to say. Had this really happened? Had he just killed these people? He looked up at David questioningly, but David shook his head sadly.

"We must leave," David said, visibly shaken. "How far away is your car?"

Petr started to reply, but he saw David freeze and his eyes go wide as he looked over the Russian's shoulder. Petr whirled around and came face-to-face with the middle-aged businessman whom the cab driver had just strangled. The man had purplish bruising on his neck and his face was pale blue, splotched with red where blood vessels had ruptured. His chin was coated with spittle and his tongue lolled out of his mouth, but he stood, impossibly, facing the Russian. Petr could only stare in horrified shock as the man's hands grasped for Petr's throat and pushed him back against the car.

Shock gave way to survival and Petr swung his body out of the way at the last moment. He grabbed the man's head from the side and smashed it into the side of the car. He could tell by the loud crack of bone that the threat was ended, but something inside Petr snapped. Grabbing the man by the hair, Petr slammed his head into the side of the car over and over again, turning the killer's face into a misshapen lump of ruined flesh and shattered bone. He would have continued the onslaught had he not felt a hand on his shoulder. Whirling around, rage in his eyes, he raised his fist to strike, but found himself face-to-face with David. The fury drained out of him and he found himself suddenly reeling from guilt.

"It's all right, Petr," David said calmly, answering the Russian's unspoken plea.

"I killed them," Petr gasped breathlessly, dropping to his knees and trying to comprehend what had just happened.

"No, Petr," David corrected, a commanding tone in his voice. "I believe they were already dead."

"Already dead," Petr repeated in a daze. David stood patiently next to him, gathering the terrified young woman in his arms once more, watching him carefully. At last, Petr looked up, his face stricken. "What in God's name is going on here, David?" he rasped, pain and bitterness threatening to overwhelm him.

"You must take us to your car," David answered. "We can talk later. But we must find shelter first."

Petr hesitated before finally nodding in understanding. Now was not the time to figure out what was going on. "All right," he breathed. Climbing to his feet, he set his jaw and led them away from the carnage and down the street. Just over a half a block away they came to Petr's car, an old Dodge Intrepid, its dark blue paint visibly chipped and a large dent in the right front fender. Petr slid into the driver's seat as David helped the young woman into the back and then got in himself. A few seconds later, the car roared to life and they were soon driving toward the Red Lion Hotel.

Petr was the first to speak. "What did you mean when you said those people were already dead?" he asked.

David was silent at first, watching the buildings go by as Petr sped west. There were very few vehicles on the road and most of those were heading in the opposite direction, which was a thoroughly discomforting thought. Here and there, he also saw people milling about. Some looked normal, talking excitedly with each other while they looked around in fear, stupidly standing outside the shelter that their homes might provide in case of an attack. Others looked like those they had just fought with; shambling along with one purpose, their lifeless eyes looking for victims.

"I don't know what's causing this," David finally replied, "but whatever is happening, those people were not alive."

"How does a dead man get up and try to kill me?" Petr snapped, his voice cracking.

"Do you read the Bible?" David posed the question quietly, sparing a look back at the young woman they had saved. Her cheeks were wet with tears, her clothes torn and dirtied, but her jaw was clenched tightly in determination and her eyes were alive.

Petr was silent, but the woman answered. "I do," she replied quietly. "You're talking about the end times."

David nodded. "It's a distinct possibility, but I am not learned enough to speak with any authority. The Bible does speak of the dead coming back to life in the last days, though."

"You think that's what happened?" Petr asked incredulously.

"That man died trying to save the young lady back there," David pointed out, giving a nod to their passenger. "Then he came back and tried to kill you."

"But how?" Petr asked.

"I couldn't even begin to answer that question," David remarked, before turning to look at the young woman in the back seat. "I'm truly sorry, my dear," he said as he composed himself. "I've forgotten my manners. My name is David. My friend here is Petr."

"Rene," she answered with a nod, her voice tight with fright. "Rene Camiliere."

"Petr is taking me to my hotel, the Red Lion," David explained. "Is there anywhere you need to go?"

"Not really," she answered shakily. "I just moved here two weeks ago. I'm alone and my apartment is all the way over in Sandy. If you don't mind, I'd rather stay with you."

"I think that would be wise," David said, his voice quiet. "I only wish we could have saved your friend."

"I don't even know who he was," she said, closing her eyes and placing a hand on her forehead, reliving the horror. "I stopped the car when those...those people walked into the street. I didn't want to hit them and then one of them opened my car door and two of them dragged me out and...and..." she trailed off, sucking in her breath as she tried to master her emotions.

"I understand," David said gently. He shuddered to think of his own daughter in the same situation and wondered if perhaps Chuike was in as much danger as they were. He pushed the thought out of his mind, knowing to focus on that now could only distract him in the chaos around them.

A lengthy silence ensued and Petr took the moment to reach into his pocket and pull out his cell. He scrolled to Alexis' number. Putting the phone to his ear, he was again greeted with a recording that all lines were busy. With a look of disgust, he tossed it on the dashboard. "I'll drop you off at the hotel and then I have to go back to my apartment," he said with determination.

"Petr," David said kindly. "You don't even know if she's there."

"And I don't know that she isn't, either," Petr snapped.

"You must do what you feel is right," David gave in, not wanting to fight over an eventuality he believed was doubtful. The city was falling apart around them, and he was concerned they might not even make it to his hotel, let alone have other options after that. "Turn left at the next light, I believe," he said, praying they could make it before anything else went wrong. Unfortunately, David's worst fears were about to come true.

Petr slowed the car, turned the corner and drove straight into hell.

CHAPTER 33

Las Vegas, Nevada: Owen snapped awake and, in that panicked moment between sleep and wakefulness, he had no idea where he was. But as his conscious mind took full control of his brain, it quickly came to him. They were staying at the Circus Circus, comfortably resting in their rooms on the thirty-fourth floor of the newer Skyrise Tower. It was an upgrade from their usual stay at the Manor rooms, which were right next to the Strip's only RV park, and thus not quite as high class as other parts of Vegas. But high class or not, the four young men loved the place.

After gorging themselves to near immobility at the buffet after checking in, they had retired to their rooms—Owen rooming up with Clint and Luke with Chad. Had any of them bothered to switch on a television before bed, they would have seen report after report about what was happening in the United States and abroad. They would have tried to reach family and friends on their phones. They would have immediately abandoned their trip and set out for home. However, television had been the last thing on their minds and, in minutes, all four of them had fallen asleep.

Now, he was greeted by a cacophony of sound, none of it good. He heard pounding up and down the hall, as well as muffled shouts. Worse, he could hear sirens out of the window and the more ominous cracking of what had to be gunfire, with an occasional thunderous boom thrown in. He turned to look at the digital clock on the bed stand, but saw nothing. Reaching over, he switched on the light. Still nothing.

"Power's out," he said, throwing his feet over the edge of the bed. "Clint, get up!" he said loudly.

Clint moaned and rolled over, pulling a pillow over his head.

"What do you want?"

"There's something going on," Owen answered. "I'm going to see if Luke and Chad are up." He'd barely reached the door when there was a frantic banging on it.

"Owen! Clint!" Luke yelled from the other side of the door.

Owen had it open a second later and his friends charged in, both of them dimly backlit by the fire strobes flashing in the hallway. "What's going on?"

"Get dressed," Luke said and hurried to the window. "There's rioting all over the city. We need to get out of here."

"A riot? What are you talking about?"

Rather than answer, Luke ripped the curtains open, eliciting startled gasps from Owen and Clint. The windowpane was lit up with flickering light.

Las Vegas was in flames.

"It's worse on the other side," Luke went on grimly, hurrying back toward the door. "Get dressed and get your gear. We're getting out now!"

Neither of them needed any more urging and they were dressed in a matter of seconds. Less than a minute later, the four men were running down the hallway, heading for the stairs, passing more and more people heading in the other direction.

"Elevators will be out," Owen said, as they got to the door. "You parked on five and we're almost thirty stories up."

"So it'll be a long run down," Clint added sarcastically.

No one argued and, as Clint reached for the handle, the door slammed open, almost breaking his hand. A wild-eyed man in his twenties wearing a bathrobe and untied tennis shoes burst out. Owen grabbed him by the shoulders, stopping him from running away. "What's going on?" Owen shouted at him.

"Can't go that way," the man panted. "They're coming up the stairs!"

"Who is?"

"Them!" the terrified man yelled. "Run!"

"Who's them?" Clint yelled at the man, but at that moment, he broke away and ran pell-mell down the hall shouting at the top of his lungs.

"He's nuts," Luke put in. "Still…" he paused and looked at his friends. Both had the same look on their faces. The stairs were out of the question. "Yeah, we'll try the other end," he finished.

They took off again down the hall. They had almost reached the other end when a shriek sounded out behind them. They stopped as one, and all four of them whirled around. The scene down the hallway was surreal, lit by the flashing strobes of the emergency lights. Several figures had dragged a woman from her hotel room and thrown her to the floor. One of them raised what looked like a fire axe high in the air. It seemed to fall in slow motion, ending the woman's scream with a strangled gurgle. The figure wrenched the axe free, then started toward them at a loping run, the bloody axe carried loosely in its hands. A white lab coat flapped behind him.

"Run!" Luke shouted, shaking them all out of the horror-induced trance they were in.

Once more, the four of them were moving. They hit the stairwell and started down rapidly, following some of the faster hotel guests and passing some of the older and slower ones.

"Glad you decided to park on five, Luke," Clint chided breathlessly. "It'll save us a few flights of stairs and a heart attack or two." But there was no humor in his voice. He was as terrified as the others. They continued down, the muffled sound of gunfire outside echoing in the stairwell. A dozen flights down, they were brought to an abrupt halt by a pair of uniformed police officers, their backs braced against a landing wall, handguns held at the ready and pointed toward them.

"Whoa!" Owen yelled, his hands going up in the air automatically. "We're not the bad guys!"

"Move it out, sir," one of the officers replied quickly. "All guests are to evacuate the premises immediately."

"What's happening?" Clint asked quickly.

"Riot," the other snapped. "It's happening everywhere. The quicker you get out of Vegas, the safer you're going to be."

"Are there any others behind you?" the first officer asked. Another cry of terror rang out above them, not more than a few floors up.

"Yeah, the old and the weak," Luke snapped angrily as he pushed past the officers. "You probably shouldn't stay here, guys." He hurried down the stairs, followed closely by Owen, Clint, and Chad. They had put another eight flights behind them when gunfire opened up above them.

"Fifth floor," Clint finally panted, stopping to lean against the wall, severely winded. "I swear..." he trailed off, unable to finish.

Luke pulled open the door to the parking garage. "We're on the opposite side of where the car is parked," he said quickly. He was in much better shape than his friend and had stamina to burn. "You guys bring Clint. I'll get the car and pick you up," he shouted, already on his way.

"Hurry!" Owen shouted after him, placing his hand on Clint's shoulder. "Let's move, buddy," he said, turning back to his winded friend. "We've got no time." Above them, as if to punctuate the statement, they heard footsteps coming down the stairs. Many footsteps. They would be on them in a matter of minutes. A figure appeared at the top of the landing and took the last few stairs five at a time. It was one of the police officers.

Owen noticed the grim expression on his face and the absence of his partner. The cop grabbed the radio mic from his shoulder. "Ten-Adam-Six," he spoke rapidly. "Cleared to five. If you're going to do it, you better do it now!"

"Roger that," came the reply from his radio. "Better move, Steve. They ain't gonna waste time."

"On my way," he said as he reached the door. Looking at the three young men, his look hardened. "You guys better move, too," he snapped. "The army isn't worried about collateral damage right now. They're going to bring this whole place down."

"Our car's on this level," Owen said quickly. He was very conscious of the pounding feet growing closer and he fought to push back the terror that was threatening to overwhelm him.

"Forget it," the officer said, heading toward the next flight down.

"But our friend is out there!"

The officer paused for just a moment to give Owen an almost pitying look. "Then he better have a fast car, son." A moment later, he was gone, disappearing down the stairs.

Owen swore quietly under his breath and yanked Clint away from the wall. "Run!" was all he said and the three of them were through the door, running hard through the empty parking garage in the direction Luke had gone. A few moments later, they heard their friend scream, a long drawn-out wail of agony and terror.

The scene before them was enough to freeze their blood. They could see Luke at the far end of the garage, near his car. But he was on his knees in the middle of the garage, his arms outstretched and his back to them. His head was tilted upward, facing the shadowed blackness of a robed figure that towered over him, reaching out to him.

Owen shook off the chains of terror and screamed, "Hey!" He

took a faltering step forward, then froze again as the figure raised its head to look at him. Shrouded in the darkness of the garage and shadowed in a deep cowl, Owen couldn't see the figure's face. If he had felt desperation before, he now felt a despair so complete it was as if his very soul was withering away. Only the sudden sound of their pursuers entering the garage behind them brought him back from the brink of utter hopelessness.

Tearing his gaze away from the apparition, he whirled around to see the first of the attackers lurch through the door. One man looked like a doctor, but his white lab coat was spattered with blood and, if he'd been saving lives earlier, he was certainly taking them now. The gore-covered fireman's axe was still in his hand and he took a step forward, before he stopped and stared at Owen with flat, dead eyes. More figures began coming through the door, surging around the doctor. But they, too, stopped.

Confused, Owen turned back to face the strange figure at the other side of the garage, only to find the phantom was now gripping Luke's head with both hands. A slow, pitiable wail began to come from their friend, rising to a shriek of pure terror that would forever chill their souls—the sound of a dying man.

"No!" Owen yelled and rushed forward. Behind him, Clint and Chad snapped out of their own stupor and quickly followed. It was fight or flight for the three of them and they had all decided to fight. "No!" Owen shouted again, closing the distance with the terrifying figure.

Perhaps it was the force with which Owen had taken over the situation. Perhaps it was the sight of three young men in the prime of their lives, converging on a single solitary attacker. Whatever the reason, the towering shadow released its grip on Luke and began to back away. Owen hurtled toward the shadow, intent only on eliminating it, but the specter would not be caught. It reached the edge of the garage, vaulted over the railing, and was gone. Owen ran after it, throwing himself against the railing. Looking over the edge, he saw nothing. Five stories up with a straight fall to concrete, the mysterious figure was nowhere to be seen.

That was when he saw it. It was peripheral at first, but as he raised his head, he was astounded and terrified at what he saw. All around him, Las Vegas was burning. Flames roared from casinos; office buildings were belching smoke. The streets were littered with bodies, and troops were moving with purpose everywhere he looked, shooting without hesitation at mobs of people. Before him, arrayed across the road, were a number of troops, weapons trained on the Circus Circus casino. A pair of tanks stood center stage, turrets pointed his way. As he looked, a huge gun on one of the tanks thundered. The shell hit the main tower of Circus Circus, and that was all Owen needed to see.

Spinning away from the edge as the shell detonated inside the building, he sprinted back toward his friends. "There's no way this is happening!" he shouted at the top of his lungs as he ran. The concussion of the explosion threw him painfully to the ground, skinning his knees and elbows, but he was right back up and running for all he was worth. Clint and Chad both knelt beside the prone Luke, their expressions dazed and their faces ashen. Owen caught a glimpse of Luke's ruined face and paused, but only for a moment. Survival instinct drove him now. Whatever had been holding back the attackers had gone with the disappearance of the dark man. The rioters had moved toward them from the stairwell and the army was about to bring down the building. If they had any chance at all, they had to give a whole new meaning to the word "flight".

"We have to get out of here now!" Owen roared.

"Look what they did to him!" Clint yelled, jumping to his feet, ready to fight.

Owen grabbed him by the shoulders and shook him violently as a rumble ran through the concrete under their feet. "We stay together, Clint!" he shouted over the rising sounds of destruction. They were far from the main tower, but the garage floor was starting to sway. "Keep it together," he went on. "We need you!"

"Luke's still alive," Chad said as he leaned over his friend, "but he's in bad shape. We need to get him to a hospital."

Owen grabbed Luke's keys from the floor of the garage and shoved them into Clint's hands. Clint stared at his friend for a split second, then yanked open the car door and slid into the seat. The car roared to life as Owen helped Chad pick up Luke's limp form. He was shocked at just how light his friend was. He tried to ignore the uneasiness and tried not to look at the horrible wounds on Luke's face, but there was no avoiding it. Where the phantom's hands had been, Luke's face looked as if it was made of parchment. The skin was desiccated, stretched and brittle over protruding cheekbones, and his eyes were open, unseeing and milky white. He looked for all the world to be dead, but breath still rattled in his chest.

Chad and Owen practically threw Luke into the back seat as they piled in. "Go, go, go!" Owen yelled. Clint grabbed the wheel and roared out of the parking space, straight toward the advancing rioters. For a split second, Owen caught the look of their leader. The expressionless face—the dead eyes. It was a vision that would always haunt him.

His hospital lab coat covered in the blood of numerous victims, Daniel Weatherly stared at Owen as the car bore down on him. Clint never hesitated. He stomped on the gas. The car shot forward and slammed into the man, throwing the broken body of the former hospital orderly against a nearby concrete pillar. The axe flew forward and crashed into the windshield, sending a spider web of cracks through the glass. A few moments later, they were circling down the ramp as fast as Clint could drive and still maintain control of the car on the slick garage floor.

They had reached level four.

"What in God's name is going on?" Clint asked as they were finally clear of the mob of rioters that had been pursuing them. Before anyone could answer, another tank shell slammed into the hotel with a deafening explosion. This one hit the garage just above them.

"That takes care of one problem," Owen said under his breath, even as the floor beneath the speeding car began to shake considerably more.

"Let's hope it doesn't take care of us," Chad said from the back seat. Even as he said it, there was a prolonged roar as the west tower began to collapse on itself. Weakened by several tank shells, it was finally giving way.

Teeth gritted in concentration, Clint expertly swerved the car around chunks of falling concrete and sped on. He hit the third level and smoked the tires.

Ahead, there were a few more people milling around the garage. They had the same look about them as the other rioters—dead and unfeeling. Clint mowed down anyone who got in his way. "I'm going to miss our road trips," he said under his breath, not even flinching as the car thump-thumped over the body of a young woman who never moved from their path. He hit the second level and the debris cloud from the collapse found them. Clint floored it down the ramp, the car scraping the walls with a screech of metal as he drove in nearly blinding conditions.

"Oh man, this is messed up," Chad said from the back seat.

As the dust cloud rushed past them, the car began to shake as a rumble sounded from above them, gaining volume. It rocked the parking structure more violently with each successive quake.

"Gun it, Clint!" Owen said frantically, the realization of what was happening dawning on him. "It's coming down! The whole thing's coming down!"

"I am gunnin' it!" Clint yelled back over the deafening chaos. Pulling onto the final straightaway of the ground floor, they could now see the exit through the swirling dust. "Hold on guys!" he exclaimed. "This isn't going to be pretty!"

Gas pedal mashed to the floor, the car shot forward at a rapidly increasing speed. The three young men stared at the exit, each of them silently praying the structure would hold out just a few seconds more. Owen looked back and saw the furthermost concrete pillars, which supported the upper levels, buckle as the ceiling dropped, a process repeated by the next closest set of pillars and continuing toward the car with terrifying speed. White-faced with terror, he willed himself to look forward as the force of the collapse generated a powerful wind behind them that shot dust and debris back over the car and completely obscured their vision of the exit.

Progressively larger chunks from the upper level rained down on the car, denting the body and cracking the windows. Within one hundred feet of the exit, the storm of debris enveloped the car, leaving the men inside in utter blackness. Completely blind, Clint hit the brakes out of sheer panic.

As desperation overwhelmed them, Owen flashed back to the times in his life when he had hung by a tired finger on a difficult climb with no rope. With that familiar thought came the familiar feeling of immortality—he wasn't going out this way. Reinvigorated and encouraged, he yelled, "Don't stop or we're dead!"

With a wild yell, Clint stomped on the gas one more time and the car shot forward through the dust and debris. The dark outline of a human being appeared in front of them, but just as suddenly, it was gone as the car nailed it and threw it to the side. Clint continued to yell and the voices of Owen and Chad joined him as they plowed on. Three more times in rapid succession, someone appeared in front of them before quickly being run down. As the third body was cast aside like a ragdoll, the blackness lightened to gray. Roars of defiance changed to shouts of victory.

They never saw the last man at the end of the ramp. He was suddenly there—his body slamming down on the hood of their speeding car, his face pressing on the already spider-webbed windshield. They could see that, where one arm should have been, there was little more than a ragged stump. But the other arm was whole and well-muscled and the man slammed a meaty fist down on the fractured windshield. The second hit punched it in. The fist blasted through the safety glass on the third hit. A powerful hand reached for Clint, seeking his throat, but at that moment, the car careened off the guardrail of the parking attendant's station. The force threw their assailant to the side and the car shot back across to the other side, sparks flying as it sideswiped the wall. The man went the other way this time, falling off to the side as the car whipped back against the wall and slammed the man's body between the car and the wall with a stomach-turning crunch.

A moment later, the car shot out of the collapsing parking garage and they were free. Assuming they were now out of the ramp—the dust still hung too thick to see—Clint whipped the car to the right and slammed down on the brakes, throwing all of them forward as the car came to a sudden stop just inches from the underside of what looked like an overturned bus.

"We're in the RV park!" Owen yelled, looking around desperately.

"How'd we get here?"

"Just be glad we're out!" Clint yelled back, shifting into reverse and burning the tires as he backed away from the wrecked vehicle.

"Get us out of here, Clint," Chad said urgently.

"You want to drive?" Clint snapped back. Wearing more tread off the tires, he whipped around the wreckage and sped through the park. Smoke and flames were thick around them, the destruction of the nearby hotel only adding to the devastation that had already been wreaked upon the park. Clint took the car through a small opening on the right and ended up on the grass by a laundromat where they found it a little easier to see. Driving in concentric circles and looking for a way out, all three of them couldn't help but stare at a world gone completely insane. Time seemed to slow to a snail's pace, giving the horrible images plenty of time to imprint themselves permanently upon their damaged psyches.

All around them, the truth was painfully evident. Las Vegas was a war zone. Thousands must certainly be dead. Good people were dying and bad people were killing them. And the National Guard was apparently killing both. Clint took them between two trailers and emerged on another street. Street lamps flickered, but stayed lit and Clint limped the damaged car down the street, looking for a way out. "What do we do?" he finally broke the silence, his voice sounding broken and despondent.

Owen shook his head. "I don't know," he replied softly. "I really don't."

Chad spoke up from the back seat. "They were after us, you know," he said, his voice distant.

Owen turned to look at his friend. "Us?" he repeated skeptically. "The whole city is gone, Chad. They were after everybody!"

"Think about it, Owen," Chad went on quietly, ignoring his

friend's skepticism. "We were on the thirty-fourth floor. Those people came up the stairs to the thirty-fourth floor and chased us back down the other side. They came after us in the garage on five, while most of the other guests that got away went further down. Why else would they do that?"

"So, what are you saying?" Clint interrupted angrily. "That somehow, we four guys are responsible for Las Vegas getting wiped out? No way! Not a chance!" Clint yelled, slamming his hands down on the steering wheel hard enough to shake the car. "None of this makes any sense!"

Chad shook his head. "I'm only stating the obvious, Clint," he answered, his voice not much above a whisper. "There is something wrong here and it's coming..."

He never finished the thought as Clint slammed on the brakes again. Standing in the middle of the road, not more than fifty feet in front of them, was the tall black-robed figure from the parking garage. It was directly under a flickering street light, and swirling dust and smoke wreathed it in a ghostly shroud. They stared at it in shock as the figure reached up and slowly pulled the cowl back from its face, revealing itself to the four young men.

It was a dark face, a face that might have once been youthful, but with eyes that burned red and looked as if they had seen ages come and go. It was a face they all knew.

They had found Gideon Sumbawanga.

"No," Owen whispered in horror. "It can't be."

"Gideon?" Clint managed to say, reaching for the door handle.

Owen reached over out of instinct and grabbed his shoulder. "No, Clint," he warned, his mind rapidly trying to sort things out.

"But it's Gideon," Clint objected, pulling free and opening the door. He stepped out and stood staring at their tall friend. Fifty feet separated them, but it might as well have been the entire expanse of space.

Owen was out the other side in a moment. "No, Clint," he repeated as unspeakable dread began to smother him. "That's not Gideon. He's the one who attacked Luke. We all saw it."

"No," Clint objected, his voice beginning to oddly slur as he stared back at Gideon. "He wouldn't. He couldn't." He began walking toward Gideon, almost as if he was drawn to him.

At that point, Gideon did something to fully convince Owen of the danger they were in. He smiled. It wasn't the trademark toothy grin that had made Gideon endearing to those who loved him. No. This smile was one of absolute malice, pure pain, and certain death. This was not Gideon before them. This was something else entirely. Something deadly evil. There was no denying it now in Owen's mind— if they stayed, they would die. "Clint! Run!" he shouted with all his energy.

It was enough to cause Clint to pause and look at his friend. The connection with the creature before them now broken, Clint shook his head as if suddenly becoming aware of something. "What?" he asked, but Owen yelled again.

"Get in the car!"

Clint hesitated for a moment and turned back to Gideon. Gideon was now walking toward him with long purposeful strides. He would be on them in seconds. Clint, realizing the danger he was in, finally broke for the safety of the car. Moments later, he was back in the driver's seat, slammed it into gear, and hit the gas. The car shot toward Gideon—the young man who had once been their friend, the young man who had done the unspeakable to Luke, the young man who now stood defiantly before them, the look on his face daring them to run him down.

"This is for Luke," Clint growled, bracing for the impact. But it never came. Just before the car should have hit him, Gideon jumped straight into the air and the car shot harmlessly under him. As they flew past, all three of them turned to look in amazement. Gideon was standing there in the middle of the road, having turned to face them, his cold eyes boring into their souls. A moment later, Clint whipped the car around a corner and the specter was lost from sight. He floored the car down a straight stretch of street and right through the large wooden wall separating the RV park from the road leading out of Circus Circus.

Clint swung around onto the Strip and turned left, heading north. As they proceeded slowly through the debris and amongst the multitude of cars all trying to get out of the city, they were struck by the nightmarish remains of the riot. The clock in the car told them it was only a few hours past dark, but in those hours they had slept, Las Vegas had been largely destroyed. The night sky was black, the stars blotted out with smoke. The enormous light displays and theatrical attractions of the city were dead. Fires burned in many locations and chaos reigned. Where the soldiers had not locked down areas, people filled the streets, running in every direction, some wandering aimlessly, others standing paralyzed by shock.

Clint muttered something under his breath as he weaved between the traffic heading out of town. He hated driving in general and, after the experiences of the night, he wanted nothing more than to get out of the car as soon as possible. He turned left onto Sahara and then, after what seemed like an eternity, they merged onto I-15 and headed north. At the edge of the city they were stopped by an army checkpoint. They could see on the other side of the highway coming into town that the interstate had been completely shut down and cars filled the road for as far as any of them could see.

The soldier in charge took a look at the wrecked car and stepped toward Clint, rifle pointed away but at the ready. "Stick to the highway and be careful where you stop," was all he said, his voice strained and tired. He pointed on down the road.

"What's happening?" Clint asked helplessly.

The soldier shrugged. "You know as much as I do," he replied. "But Vegas isn't the only place this is happening. It's everywhere."

"We're from Salt Lake City," Owen said, leaning over to speak with the man. "Have you heard any news from there?"

The soldier's face darkened. "Salt Lake got hit, too," he said. "Bad. That's all I know. Godspeed." With that, he straightened and hardened his face again, then motioned them on.

Stunned, Clint eased the car onto the highway and picked up speed. They drove in silence, each of them lost in their own thoughts, each of them dealing with their own private dread about what they might find upon returning home.

"We need to get back," Owen said quietly, his mind on his family and Alexis. He turned to look in the back seat where Chad sat next to their injured friend. "But we have to take care of Luke first. We're an hour from Mesquite. Let's see if we can get him to a hospital there."

Clint and Chad nodded mutely and they drove on, each of them praying silently Luke could hold out for another hour.

None of them thought he would.

EPILOGUE

AP News Wire, Samantha Anderson Reporting – "There is panic in the streets of London today after a nuclear device was detonated within city limits. Reports from witnesses are beginning to come in, and the picture being painted is straight out of the ninth level of Dante's *Inferno*. The damage to the western half of the city is almost complete. The ground blast sent a shockwave through London, toppling buildings, blocking roads, uprooting waterlines, and starting fires that continue to spread. Satellite images are already showing the hypocenter of the explosion, a giant crater over one hundred-fifty meters wide located where Wembley Stadium once stood. There is no word yet if the bomb was a fusion or fission-based explosive, but the damage done indicates a size of at least one hundred kilotons. Officials have also confirmed that the bomb was set off at ground level. No one has taken credit for the blast yet, but the British Secret Intelligence Service is focusing its attention on known terrorist organizations. It's also not ruling out the possibility that this is the work of some new group with an as-yet undetermined agenda for causing such devastation.

"Everything within a three-mile radius of the blast is in flames, wiping out most of the territory between the M25 Orbital Highway and the city center. City officials are scrambling to contain the damage caused by the blast, and are hoping to salvage much of the eastern part of the city. Prime Minister LynnAnne Campbell, presently on a trade mission in Seoul, has ordered the evacuation of all non-essential personnel from the city. If the dust and debris flows along presently calculated wind patterns, fallout could spread as far as Paris and perhaps Amsterdam. Eurocontrol, the European Union's organization for air navigation security and safety, has closed off all flights in and out of England. As the radioactive cloud spreads, it's assumed that additional flights across Europe will be cancelled as well.

"The Greater London Urban Area is home to over eight million people, with as many as three million of them undocumented immigrants, so it will be difficult to know how many have died in this initial explosion, but numbers are clearly in the hundreds of thousands. Coupled with the large number of casualties that are sure to emerge from radiation poisoning, it may be months, if not years, before a complete number is known, but it will most certainly be in the millions.

"Antonio Malvado-Jinete, the recently elected General Secretary of the United Nations, has vowed to send aid to the people of London as soon as it can be done safely. Speaking at a previously scheduled press conference at Gutiérrez Children's Hospital in his native Buenos Aires, Malvado-Jinete quoted Winston Churchill, saying that despite all the problems the world is going through at the present moment, we will "never, never, never, never give up." He also called on nations to send all available materials for cleaning up the disaster as well as a call for engineers, scientists and volunteers the world over to help where they can.

"President Albert Abrea of the United States has pledged support, and leaders from Japan, Russia, Brazil, and India have agreed to send aid as well, but with airspace shut down and years of work ahead just to clean up the area before England can even begin to rebuild, London will be a dead zone for the foreseeable future.

"The devastation is incredible, the loss of life catastrophic, and as England looks to begin picking up the pieces, the rest of the world sits and waits for what will come next. For this reporter, it seems clear that we have stepped into a new and frightfully dark future and I am left with only one thought.

God help us all…"

RISEN

THE SECOND SEAL OF THE KRYPTEIA CONSPIRACY

The second seal has been broken…

…and the world continues to spiral out of control. Hade's gambit has completely engulfed the planet, his army of reanimated corpses has taken over most of the world's largest cities, and the unlikely band of heroes is on the run.

Alexis Kennedy, Petr Zhugravinsky, Michael Dalacourt and Owen DiConte aren't just trying to survive in a world gone mad; they are struggling to save their very souls. Clinging to long-lost scriptures revealed to them by an ancient Native American known only as John, they will struggle against each other, battle to survive, and question everything they have ever believed in - all the while knowing that good is no longer certain to overcome evil, and no one is safe from the raging storm.

Pursuing them relentlessly is Hade, the architect behind the supernatural onslaught that has brought the world to its knees. He has singled them out and will push them to their very limits and beyond. Who will be Hade's king, and who won't survive to see his kingdom rise up among the ashes of a broken world?

Dark days have arrived. Darker days are ahead.

www.ingramcontent.com/pod-product-compliance
Lightning Source LLC
Chambersburg PA
CBHW061615210726
48287CB00001B/143